Ruth

MW00618235

a way home II

---

r e s o l u t i o n

Best Wishes !
Enjoy the Story

Robert C. Vogel   7/23/09

a way home II

resolution

Robert C. Vogel

TATE PUBLISHING & *Enterprises*

Published by Tate Publishing & Enterprises, LLC
127 E. Trade Center Terrace | Mustang, Oklahoma 73064 USA
1.888.361.9473 | www.tatepublishing.com

Tate Publishing is committed to excellence in the publishing industry. The company reflects the philosophy established by the founders, based on Psalm 68:11,
"The Lord gave the word and great was the company of those who published it."

Book design copyright © 2009 by Tate Publishing, LLC. All rights reserved.
Cover design by Kellie Southerland
Interior design by Stefanie Rooney

Published in the United States of America

ISBN: 978-1-60696-422-4
1. Fiction, Christian, Suspense
2. Fiction, Mystery & Detective, General
09.02.16

For
The Children and Grandchildren in my Life

Lisa   Susan   Karen

Lauren   Gabriella   Brianna   Breelle

Rob   Jarred   Neal   Michael

and

Judy

God ... Family ... Love

Together Always

Acknowledgments

Everything good or worthwhile in this world is accomplished with the grace of our loving God. In praying to the Holy Spirit for inspiration each day, I involve the Father, Son, and Holy Spirit in my writing. I give all thanks and glory to the Lord for his help in composing and completing the second book of the *A Way Home* series.

A Way Home II–Resolution came to me shortly after the first book was finished. I wrote at all hours of the day and night, and completed the novel in six weeks. I thank my loving wife for her patience and understanding during that time.

My daughters and granddaughters also urged me to continue the series, and they were instrumental in encouraging me to continue writing. In truth, sometimes I think I am writing only for them.

I do not believe inspirational fiction should be overly religious. Instead they are stories about everyday people, people like you and me. Real people face difficulties and heartbreak each day, and my intention is to tell stories that touch the reader's heart, lift the reader's soul, and inspire the reader's mind. Since we have all fallen short of the glory of God and share our lot as sinners, telling stories of redemption that mix with the worldly trials of life may, at least for a short time, take the reader on a journey of hope and joy.

Rev. Robert F. Berger, my pastor at Mary, Gate of Heaven Roman Catholic Church in Myerstown, Pennsylvania, is not only a friend, but a mentor as well. He gives his congregation inspiration that comes from outstanding personal integrity, a thorough understanding of the Gospel, and the skill to gently guide and teach the Word of Jesus Christ. I am grateful for his encouragement to continue writing the *A Way Home* stories.

I want to thank my brother John and his wife, Linda, and my sister Mary, and her husband, Ed Braun, for their support and encouragement in writing this book.

I also acknowledge the team at Tate Publishing & Enterprises for their continuing assistance. They are a joy to work with and their staff is extremely talented. I pray that God will continue to bless them in every way.

Prologue

Four companions made their way through Washington National Airport. It was going on ten o'clock and many travelers were heading home after a hectic Thanksgiving weekend. To the casual observer, it appeared there were as many people rushing to departing gates as the number of individuals arriving who claimed the District of Columbia as their home. They were all coming and going; however, none matched the urgency of the four travelers rushing to Walter Reed Hospital in Washington.

They were newfound friends, strangers who unexpectedly found themselves on the same flight east from San Francisco. Nick and Colleen O'Connell met Harry Booth, a physician, and Angela Carson, a flight attendant, while flying from San Francisco to Washington, DC.

Two days earlier Nick had traveled to the west coast to find his sister, who dropped out of sight from the rest of her family while trying to become the next Hollywood starlet. Unknown to Nick, Colleen was seriously ill and, to make matters worse, she was pregnant. Colleen did not have the money to see a doctor and had guessed that she was about seven months pregnant Nick tracked her down through a friend to St. Agnes Hospital in San Francisco. Hoping to take her back to his home in DC, Nick met with her doctor and secured his approval to release

Colleen to Nick's care on the provision that she be admitted immediately to Walter Reed Hospital once they landed in Washington.

Nick secured two seats in first class on United Airways flight 3348–San Francisco to St. Louis. There they would transfer to United flight 1535 flying from St. Louis to Washington, DC.

Nick met Dr. Harry Booth on the flight out of San Francisco when Colleen suddenly had difficulty breathing, and the doctor offered his assistance. The flight attendant in first class was Angela Carson, who befriended Nick, Colleen, and Harry Booth. Both the doctor and Angela made arrangements to travel with Nick and Colleen all the way to Washington National Airport just in case Colleen faced another medical crisis. Being Christians, both Dr. Booth and Miss Carson saw this as an opportunity to be Good Samaritans. The light passenger load in first class enabled Angela to spend time getting to know Colleen and her brother.

While dealing with his sister's crisis, Nick faced another serious situation at Walter Reed. His wife, Maura, was eight months pregnant and had gone into premature labor. Her brother, a Catholic priest, was visiting for Thanksgiving and stayed with Maura while Nick traveled to California.

After landing in DC, Nick, Harry, Colleen, and Angela headed toward the United Airlines baggage claim area and passenger pick-up where an ambulance was scheduled to meet Colleen and Nick and take them to the hospital. Harry Booth was guiding Colleen on a wheelchair through the terminal while Angela picked up the luggage. He and Angela agreed to accompany Nick and Colleen to the hospital.

The four travelers made their way to the exit doors of the terminal and walked to the curb, searching for the ambulance. Suddenly, a hotel courtesy bus mounted the curb and sped directly toward Colleen, Nick, and Harry Booth. Standing up off the wheelchair, Colleen used all her strength and shoved the chair backwards, pushing Doctor Booth back into the doorway.

Turning to her brother, she placed both hands on his chest and pushed him backwards into the exit doors. Colleen then turned to her right and tried to avoid the bus, but it hit her full force and slammed her against a cement wall.

Angela witnessed the horror before her and tried to make her way out the doors, which were now blocked by Harry and Nick. Everything just seemed to stand still—time was frozen for those few, brief, terrible moments.

Just then, the pre-arranged ambulance pulled up to the accident scene, and the paramedics sprang into motion. Nick and Harry Booth jumped to their feet, saw the mangled bus, and ran over to Colleen. She was leaning against the wall and bleeding profusely. Nick cried out to his sister, "Colleen, are you okay?"

The medics moved efficiently yet carefully as they prepared Colleen to be moved onto a stretcher and then quickly to the hospital.

Harry Booth climbed into the bus to see if its driver needed assistance, but it was empty, and the rear door stood open. He called out, "Anybody need help in here?" He immediately wondered what happened to the driver. Stepping out of the bus, Harry Booth went back to Nick, who was standing in shocked silence.

Moments later, Nick and Harry Booth were in the ambulance with Colleen racing through the streets of DC on the way to the hospital. Flight Attendant Angela Carson followed in a cab.

In the Walter Reed hospital maternity ward, Nick's wife, Maura, met with her doctor, who had expressed concern about her going into premature labor. Discussing her case with a specialist, they concurred that the safest course of action would be to deliver her baby via C-section within the next few hours. Maura agreed to the procedure, although she wished Nick was there to help her make that decision. Her brother, Father Christopher Sullivan, was there, but Maura really needed her husband. The C-section was scheduled for ten o'clock that night.

Arriving at the hospital, Colleen's ambulance pulled into the emergency entrance where doctors were waiting. Barely conscious, she was wheeled through the doors, where she saw her cousin Father Christopher Sullivan. He was prepared to anoint Colleen with the holy oils of the Sacrament of the Sick. The "Last Rites" of the Catholic Church included the forgiveness and remission of all sins. Colleen was anointed and received her last Holy Communion, known as Viaticum.

Father Chris then told Nick about his wife's condition and her decision to have a C-section. Maura was in the operating room at the same time Nick and Colleen arrived at the hospital.

After being apart for so long, Maura and Colleen would end up in operating rooms at the same hospital. Colleen's condition was poor, and the chances of her survival were slim.

The doctors examining Colleen told Nick that his sister had to get into surgery at once. Her condition was grave, and there was no time to delay in treating her.

Arriving upstairs at the surgery suites, Nick dressed in the required medical garb to see his wife. The C-section began at ten o'clock, and her baby was delivered ten minutes later. Nick was stunned momentarily when he saw Maura holding their baby. It was a beautiful little girl. The doctor told Maura that the baby would need some additional attention since she was about a month premature. Maura's pain was tolerable, and she was anxious to hear about Colleen.

Nick broke the news about the terrible accident at the airport. She gasped and quickly asked, "Nick, is Colleen going to make it? Will she live?"

"I don't know, Maura. Father Chris gave her the Last Rites. The surgeon told me he could save her baby."

"A baby? What are you saying? Is Colleen pregnant?" Maura was stunned by the news.

"Yes, she is expecting a baby. The doctor is delivering the baby now. The doctor doesn't think she will live through the night."

"Dear God," Maura said. "I have to see her. I have to be with her. Find out if I can see her, okay? Are you all right?"

"I am fine, Maura, and somewhat overwhelmed by all that has happened. Being here with you makes everything better. I am a dad! Our baby is healthy, and you are okay, so those prayers have been answered. Now we need to pray for Colleen. I will find out when we can see her. Is it okay if I go back over to the waiting room?"

"Go back to your sister, Nick," Maura instructed. "I'll try to be there soon."

Nick made his way back to Harry, Angela, and Father Chris. They were sitting together praying for Colleen. Nick joined them and shared the news of his infant daughter. Moments later, the door of the operating room opened, and the lead surgeon, Dr. Jonas Holly, approached Nick.

"Nick, we did what we could. The baby, a little boy, looks like he will make it, but Colleen, well, it is just a matter of time, very little time, I am afraid."

"Can we see her? Can we be with her?"

"Yes, certainly, follow me. I am so sorry, Nick, but the injuries are quite severe. Her chest was crushed, and she had severe damage to her vital organs. All her ribs were broken and her lungs were crushed. It is a miracle that her baby survived."

Nick walked into the surgical suite and saw Colleen on a table holding a tiny baby. A moment later Maura (in a wheelchair), Chris, Harry, and Angela entered the room. Nick put his arm around his sister and told her how much he loved her. Maura held one hand, Harry the other. Chris and Nick leaned in close to Colleen, while Angela stood at the base of the bed.

"Nick, I love you. Thank you for saving me," Colleen said lovingly.

"Maura, will you take care of my little boy?" Please, please say yes," Colleen pleaded as tears filled the eyes of everyone in the room.

"Yes, Colleen. Nick and I will raise your little boy. We promise he will know you through us. I love you, Colleen. I love you," Maura said through her tears.

Colleen passed away surrounded by friends who were truly angels. At the end, she was blessed to be with those who loved her deeply. It was so tragic, and yet, it was also holy. Colleen crossed from this world into the next. She was too young to die. But God, in his mercy, blessed her with the willpower and strength to save two people before being hit by the bus. She saved her brother and a friend who had come to her aid. She laid down her life for others. She had received the sacraments of her church and died in the arms of those who loved her.

Death and life crisscrossed that night. Two tiny children entered life, and one young woman passed into eternity.

chapter 1

November 26, 1982

Nick's phone rang at 7:30 a.m. the day after Colleen's funeral. It was the Washington Metro Police.

"Mr. O'Connell, this is Detective John Baker. I want to express my condolences on the death of your sister. I know this is a difficult time for you, but I need to ask you about what happened at the airport. I was able to reach Dr. Booth, and we scheduled a meeting here at the precinct for one o'clock this afternoon. I would be happy to send a car and pick you up. Can you make it in today?" the young detective said with compassion and sincerity.

Nick barely had the time to think about the accident since it happened. He had to worry about Maura and the two babies that had suddenly become his family. Maura was well enough and was released by her doctor to attend Colleen's wake and funeral. The babies, only a week old, were still in the hospital neo-natal unit at Walter Reed. Dr. Elizabeth Roberts, Maura's doctor, was confident the newborns would be fine, but they would have to remain in the hospital for perhaps a month. Nick knew there were questions about the accident, but he had not thought much about it during the seven days leading up to the funeral. It was the most difficult week of his life.

"Yes, detective, I can make this afternoon. I appreciate you sending a car for me. By the way, do you have any ideas about the bus driver? Harry Booth and I talked a little about the accident, but we never finished that conversation."

Replying in a calm and concerned voice the detective replied, "We will investigate that as well as everything else about the accident."

Nick was glad that some of the mystery about the accident would be looked into and hopefully explained.

"Thank you, Nick. I will have a car there about 12:30. I look forward to meeting you," the policeman answered politely. "I'll bring you up to speed on the investigation."

About 1:00 p.m., Nick walked into Metro PD Precinct 44 on Avenue D in southeast DC. Harry Booth and Angela Carson were already there. Nick was escorted into a small conference room and sadly hugged at his friends who had shared the tragedy of Colleen's death.

"Nick," Harry said as he stood up. "Nice to see you, even if it is under these circumstances." They embraced tenderly, still feeling the pain of Colleen's passing.

"Hello, Nick," said Angela. "How are Maura and the babies?" She hugged Nick briefly as he sat down next to her.

"Everyone is doing well, thank you. The little ones probably won't get home much before Christmas, but they are going to make it."

"Have you met Detective Baker?" Nick asked.

"Not yet," replied Harry and Angela simultaneously.

At that moment, the door opened, and John Baker walked in holding a manila envelope. He was young, probably twenty-six or twenty-seven, and stood six feet tall. He was obviously fit, and he made an imposing figure. His suit was pressed neatly, and his tie hung straight from neck to belt. His dark hair was short, and his handshake was firm.

"Thank you all for coming on such short notice," the detective said after all the introductions were made. John Baker sat down at the head of the oak laminate conference table and opened the file before him. The sheet was blank except for the title line that read, "O'Connell, Colleen." He removed his Cross Pencil from his shirt pocket and twisted it open. He looked evenly at Harry, Angie, and Nick and smiled a little. Making direct eye contact, it was clear that he was in charge.

"I want to again express my condolences on the loss of your sister, Colleen," John said to Nick. "In my job we see death, unexpected death, occur so frequently, and always so tragically. I am never prepared to see a life ended before it has barely begun. So much of the work we do involves guns and drugs. I often see young lives end tragically. I speak to high school students throughout the District about the dangers of drinking, drugs, and the violence committed with guns. I deal with it, but I am never prepared for it. In your case, what seems to be a random accident may be just the result of faulty brakes or a driver who was under the influence, or perhaps, he was just sick. That is why we are all here." Baker spoke clearly and looked directly at Nick, Harry, and Angela with every word.

"We have interviewed several of the eyewitnesses at the airport, and we secured the airport security camera tapes from United. They have been very co-operative and helpful in our investigation so far." Turning the page, Detective Baker showed Nick some notes written down by the police who spoke to the eyewitnesses.

"These are helpful, and I will share whatever information I can with you, but I need to get your statements as well. I would like each of you to write down what happened, what you saw, what you heard, and any detail that may help us understand what happened there at the United Passenger Terminal. You each have your individual perspective about what occurred. While you write these, I will send for some refreshments."

Nick leaned over to Angela and Harry, while Detective Baker picked up a telephone against the far wall and whispered, "What do you think of this detective? I am impressed with him."

"I feel good about him," Angela replied.

"I do too, Nick. He seems intelligent and the type of man who will stick with it until he gets the answers he is looking for," Harry said confidently.

Each of them wrote their statements starting with when they approached the exit doors of the airport. Harry and Nick were with Colleen all the time, and Angie was away just for the few minutes when she retrieved the few bags they had checked in San Francisco. Nick knew this was painful, yet necessary. The sooner the details were out in the open, the more likelihood their memories would be accurate.

Replaying the crash in his mind was not easy for Harry. He saw a brave young woman, a woman who had surely saved his life and Nick's, too. She sacrificed her life to save them. Angela was only a moment away from being involved in the accident.

They knew these statements were important, but re-living the scene was still very painful.

The door to the conference room opened, and an officer walked in with a tray of refreshments.

Taking his seat, Detective Baker asked Angela if she would read her statement aloud. "Sure, I'll go first," she replied in a helpful tone. "I was with Colleen, Nick, and Harry walking from the plane to the exit. Harry was pushing Colleen's wheel-chair, and Nick was to his right. As we neared the exit, we saw the sign for the baggage claim area. I volunteered to pick up the luggage and told Nick I would meet them outside. I knew an ambulance had been arranged to pick Colleen up and take her to Walter Reed. The bags were already on the turnstile when I got there. I picked them up and turned to go back and meet Harry and Nick. As I approached the exit door I heard a loud crash and saw the headlights of a bus. I heard the crunch of metal and the sound of glass breaking. I was about ten feet from the doors. I saw Harry on the floor by the door on the left side, and Nick was down on the ground to the right side of the exit doors. I tried to push the doors open, but with Nick and Harry against them, I had to wait until they stood up to pry them open. The wheelchair was crumpled over Harry's legs. Everything seemed to freeze at that moment. It was hard for me to even move my feet. I saw Colleen and gasped. She was curled up in a ball against the wall, and there was a lot of blood," Angela said, shivering at the memory of the crash.

"The bus was stuck on the pavement, and the engine was idling loudly. After Nick got up, I was able to get out of the terminal, and I moved quickly over to Colleen, who was awake, but in much pain. The space between the bus and the wall was maybe two to three feet. Colleen was wedged in that small space up against the wall. I told her to hold on; help was on the way.

"A few people tried to get by the bus to help, but there was no room. The ambulance arrived, and the medics made their way to Colleen. Nick was right by Colleen's side and tried to brush the glass and metal off her blouse, which was now covered in blood. It was just a horrifying scene. I saw Harry make his way onto the bus, and I heard him call out, 'Anyone need help in here?' A moment later, I saw him get off the bus. I heard him tell the ambulance crew, 'There is nobody on the bus, not even the driver.' The medics moved Colleen over to the ambulance and placed the stretcher into the back. Nick and Harry got in. I told them I would grab a cab and meet them at the hospital. I arrived at Walter Reed right behind the ambulance thanks to a lead-footed cab driver."

"That sums it up as best I can recall. Is this helpful?" Angela inquired.

"Yes, it is very helpful. Thank you for being so observant," Detective Baker replied. "You would be amazed at how even the tiniest of details helps solve cases. Dr. Booth, would you read your statement now?"

"Well," Harry began. "My report is very similar to Angela's. We were walking through the terminal, heading for the passenger drop off/pick up area in the United Airlines terminal. As we neared the exit, Angela offered to retrieve our luggage, which was down the hall from the doorway leading outside. I wheeled Colleen out the doors to the waiting area where we were to meet an ambulance from Walter Reed Hospital. We moved toward the curb looking for the ambulance.

"Without warning, one of the hotel courtesy buses, I think it was a Double Tree Hotel bus, veered off the roadway, mounted the curb, and headed directly toward us. Colleen stood up off the chair quickly and shoved it and me backwards into the exit doors. I fell against the doors and saw Colleen put both her hands on Nick's chest and shove him back toward the door where I was lying. She pushed him clear out of the path of the bus. It was just as Angela said; time seemed to stand still. Colleen turned just as the bus hit her, knocking her off her feet and into the cement wall next to the exit doors," explained Dr. Booth slowly.

"The courtesy bus stopped short of ramming Colleen into the wall when the rear wheels got hung up on the high curb. I watched Colleen slam against the wall and knew she was injured severely. Within minutes, the ambulance that had been called to take Colleen to the hospital arrived. The paramedics moved swiftly and with great care. They began to work on her immediately. I looked into the bus to see if anyone was injured. When I stepped in, I called out, 'Anyone in here need help?' or something like that. My head had cleared by then, and as I looked around the bus, I was amazed because it was empty. There was no driver. The rear emergency door was flapping open, and most of the windows were broken. I wondered what happened to the driver, but my main focus was getting back to Nick and Colleen. I stepped out of the bus and walked over to Nick, who was guardedly watching Colleen and the medics. They secured her to a gurney and placed her in the ambulance. Nick and I got in with them. Angela said she would get a cab and meet us at the hospital. We arrived at Walter Reed in a matter of minutes. The emergency room doctors and nurses were waiting as the ambulance back up to the entry doors. We met Nick's brother-in-law, Father Chris, at the door. That's about it. I don't think I missed any details," Harry concluded.

"Thanks, doctor. You were very thorough. I can see that you are an observant person, also, and that is as important in your profession as in my own," Detective Baker said in a complementary way. "Nick, tell me your story."

"It is very similar to Doctor Booth's statement," Nick replied. "But there is something I did see that Harry and Angela did not mention. We moved outside, just as Harry said, and within seconds, the bus mounted the curb and headed toward us. I believe I saw a uniformed black man at the wheel. He had a beard and he wore glasses. I saw his face, but only for a few seconds. The glasses and the beard were definite features. Everything else that happened matches what Harry said in his statement.

"I thought at first that the driver may have suffered a heart attack or passed out, and his foot must have slipped off the brakes and onto the accelerator. The curb is fairly high along the drop-off/pick-up zone. The bus needed speed and momentum to mount it.

"After the collision, I focused on Colleen, and honestly, I didn't think about the driver at that point. Then the medics arrived. Angela was kneeling down next to me, and we tried to keep my sister awake as we urged her to hold on, to just hold on. We were at the accident scene for maybe five minutes before Colleen was placed on a stretcher and placed in the ambulance. It was a short, very fast drive through DC to the hospital. There were doctors waiting as we pulled up to the emergency entrance," Nick said as he finished his statement.

"Thank you, Nick," John Baker said gratefully. "We have learned a few things we didn't know before. We now have a partial description of a driver. We have a timeline of events from when you saw the bus until the collision. My partner, Detective Catherine Harding, is reviewing the security tapes down the hall. I am going to ask her to join us and share what she found on the footage from the cameras. I will be right back," Baker told Nick and his friends.

"Nick," Harry said, "do you think any of this helped? Why do you think the driver fled the scene? Unless he was under the influence of drugs or booze, which is a possibility, why would he have run away?"

Nick suddenly had a very disturbing thought: *What if this was not an accident?*

The door to the room opened, and the two detectives entered, rolling a television on a stand with them. "Detective Harding, I would like you to meet Nick O'Connell, Colleen's brother. And this is Dr. Harry Booth and Angela Carson."

Detective Catherine Harding was thirty-three, single, and about five feet eight inches tall. She was trim and fit and very professional looking. Nick guessed she could handle herself and didn't take any mouthing off from criminals. She had strawberry-blond hair that was cut short. All in all, she was more than average looking. She had a warm, inviting smile that put everyone at ease.

"Nick, I just ran through the security tapes at the airport. Most of the images are blurry, but I would like you to look at a few with me. Perhaps we can get more information on the person driving the bus as it crashed over the curb," Catherine said in a friendly tone.

"Sure," Nick replied, "let's take a look."

Detective Baker turned the television on and inserted the tape into the VCR.

"Nick, here is a grainy still photo of the bus pulling into the pick-up zone. The contrast of the dark night and the bright lights by the doors makes it difficult to see. This is definitely a Double Tree Hotel bus. Let me advance the tape a bit. Here is the best shot we have of the driver. Even though it is blurred, you can see the figure of a man wearing glasses and with a dark beard. He is a black man, and it looks like the cap and the jacket match. Everything looks normal so far. Now, here is where things pick up." Catherine stopped the tape momentarily and, looking into the eyes of Angela, Harry, and Nick, said, "This next part, while very grainy and blurred, is difficult to watch. A camera picked up some of the impact of the collision. I understand if you prefer not to watch this. It is not easy to look at it."

Angela really did not want to see the collision; nonetheless, she reluctantly agreed to watch the film along with Nick and Harry Booth.

"Okay then, I will continue. Here is the bus as it approaches the area you were standing. The bus picks up speed. It does not appear to slow down at all. The driver seems okay, and there are no signs that he blacked out. The bus continues to increase in speed. It now mounts the curb where Nick and Harry were standing behind Colleen's wheelchair. Look, here she stands up and pushes the chair backwards into Dr. Booth. Then she turns and puts both hands on Nick's chest, and it appears that she is shoving him backwards into the exit doors. The complete image is gone because the angle of the lens is nearly parallel to the entry doors. But we can hear a crash and some screaming. Here I see Dr. Booth stepping into the bus; he pauses, seems to look around, and then backs out of the bus. A little later on in the tape, you can hear an ambulance approaching. Now the ambulance pulls up and stops. The two medics get out and move quickly toward the doors." Detective Harding continued, "We can see you, Nick, standing over the medics as they are working on Colleen. Angela was kneeling next to Colleen until the paramedics arrived."

Watching the videotape was like experiencing the entire accident again. It was not easy for any of them, but they knew they had to help in any way they could. It had been painful enough to write their statements, but seeing the videotape was very painful to Nick, Harry, and Angela.

"Why don't we take a little break here, folks?" suggested Detective Baker. "It will give you a chance to use the washroom, which is just at the end of the hallway outside. Let's meet back here in ten minutes," John Baker suggested.

Angela, Harry, and Nick walked down the hallway and paused before a large window overlooking the crowded neighborhood outside. The temperature dropped below twenty degrees, and a light snow was falling. They looked out the window as if it was a movie screen. They never anticipated being here, like this, describing the tragic loss of a young woman's life to a police detective. Their mood reflected the grey skies and cold temperatures outside. Somehow they all knew this process, while painful, was nonetheless important. The questions about the bus crash and death of Colleen were a police matter, and they were questions that had to be answered. As Detective Baker said at the beginning, it might be just a freak accident, or not, and if not, who or what was responsible for what happened? The wound of losing Colleen was so fresh that it was painful just to say her name, much less talk about the details of how she was killed.

Nick and his companions walked back to the conference room and sat down with Detectives Catherine Harding and John Baker. "We want to thank you for bearing with us as we try to determine what happened to Colleen. On the one hand, it appears to be an unfortunate accident; on the other, it may be something more sinister that we have not looked into yet. The X factor is the unknown bus driver. Why he fled the scene is the key to solving this puzzle." Detective Harding was bright and obviously an experienced police officer. Dr. Booth saw her as a bright young woman who had a determination to get to the heart of whatever matter she was investigating.

"Catherine, may I call you Catherine?" Nick asked politely.

"Of course. We may conduct our business in a formal manner, but we are laid back most of the time," Catherine replied as she smiled at the three friends gathered around the table.

"Catherine," Nick began, "I can't imagine anyone wanted to harm Colleen or me. After high school, she enlisted in the navy for two years. Then she moved out to California. The last four or five years, she had little contact with our family. I tried to keep in touch with her. We grew up in the coal region of Pennsylvania. My wife and I worked for the army for several years before settling in on our present professions. It just doesn't make sense that we would be targeted by people who wanted to harm or kill us." Nick spoke with clarity, and his logic was sound.

"I understand, Nick, I understand," said John Baker. "But we need to look at every possible scenario since we have not found the driver of that bus."

There was a knock on the door to the conference room, and a uniformed officer asked to see Detectives Harding and Baker. They excused themselves and walked out of the room, curious about the interruption.

In the hallway, Officer Tim Oliver told the detectives they had searched the entire scene surrounding the passenger drop-off area at the airport. One of the officers found a bag in a trash can. Oliver opened a paper bag that contained a matching jacket and hat that were part of the Double Tree Hotel uniform. There was a wig, a moustache, a goatee, and eyeglasses in the bag as well. Baker and Harding looked at each other.

"Take these to the lab and see what they can find," said Catherine. Turning to John she said, "This puts a different spin on things. We have to try to find out who dressed up as an employee of the hotel. This really muddies the water. What do we tell Nick and his friends?" Detective Baker said to his partner.

"I think we keep them in the loop for now. This could be turning into a homicide investigation. We could be looking at the wrong victim. Perhaps Nick, Dr. Booth, or Angela was the intended target. Why would anyone want to harm these people?" John said almost rhetorically to Catherine.

"I agree. Let's tell them what we know and see what their reaction is," Catherine replied to John Baker.

"I'm sorry we had to step away for a moment," said Catherine, as they reentered the conference room. "Something came to our attention that we want to share with you."

Catherine and John told Nick and his companions about the wig, glasses, and uniform the police found in a trash container. Nothing made sense to Nick or Harry. Why would anyone want to hurt Colleen or any of them? Dr. Booth was traveling to see his daughter, who lived in nearby Virginia, and Angela was not scheduled to be in DC. It was hard to believe they could be targets.

Detective Baker offered an idea, "Why don't we back up a little bit and look at where you were in the days leading up to the crash?"

"We often follow this type of police procedure," Catherine added. "Let's look at where you were, what you were doing, what you may have observed, or who interacted with you in the time leading up to your return to Washington. We may learn something about what or who may have been involved."

"Harry," Nick said, "What do you think, Angela? Could Colleen have been the target of someone who wanted her dead?"

"I don't know, Nick," Harry replied. "But I think we need to look at that possibility. Heck, maybe one of us was the target! We have got to stick with these detectives and find out what we can. Strange as it sounds, we could still be in danger. Just saying that out loud seems ludicrous, but there are questions here that need answers."

"I agree with you, Harry," Angela replied. "Maybe Colleen saw something she was not supposed to see. She told me a little about her life in Los Angeles. She was mixed up with some people who might have had connections with drug pushers and pornography. Her life in LA was not a happy time. The frustrations of not getting into legitimate movies, coupled with the pressure of having no money, led her to the wrong type of people." Angela didn't mean to speak ill of the deceased, but the life Colleen had lived in Los Angeles could contain clues as to what led to her death in Washington. "I am so happy Colleen and I had the chance to talk during the flight. My duties were light, and spending time with her was the right thing to do."

Nick, Harry, and Angie agreed with the detectives to delve deeper into their activities in the time leading up to arriving at Washington National Airport.

chapter 2

"Catherine and John," Nick began. "One thing right from the beginning puzzles me. We did not have return tickets from California. I flew into Los Angeles, and then I traveled up to San Francisco where I found Colleen at St. Agnes Hospital. From there, we went directly to the airport. I secured first class tickets on a flight to St. Louis. Once there, we had to change planes in order to get into Washington around nine thirty p.m. I had no idea about when we would be flying home. I don't see how anyone could have foreseen our itinerary when we didn't know about it ourselves." Nick's comments made sense. How could someone have planned to harm Colleen when not even her brother knew what day or time they would be returning to Washington, much less what airline they would use flying home?

"Nick," Harry inquired. "Was there anyone in San Francisco who knew you would be returning to DC that day?"

"Good question, Harry," Catherine said. "Was anyone aware of your plans to get home the same day you found Colleen at St. Agnes hospital?"

"Her doctor, John Walters, approved Colleen's release from the hospital on the condition that she be admitted to Walter Reed hospital when she arrived in Washington. The nurse in the Infectious Disease wing, Maryanne Logan, said Colleen was being treated for a rare disease and that was the reason for her isolation." Nick had the gift of almost instant recall. He never forgot a name or a face. "I can't see how either of these people would be involved in anything that would harm Colleen. She was only in the hospital for two days. Dr. Walters told me her condition was life threatening. No, I don't see how they would be involved in anything criminal. And they didn't know which airline we would use." Nick truly doubted the physician could intentionally cause the death of an innocent woman.

"That is okay, Nick," Catherine replied. "But let's put them on the list anyway. Remember we are just compiling a log of people, places, and events that crossed your paths over the last few days leading up to Colleen's death."

"Harry," Catherine inquired. "What about you? Was there anything unusual in your activities the last few weeks?"

"I don't think so, Catherine. My plans were intact for several weeks. My destination was Alexandria, Virginia. My daughter, Cynthia, lives there, and I had been planning this trip for a while. My flight originated in Portland, Oregon. There was a stopover in San Francisco en route to St. Louis where I was to transfer planes and fly on into BWI Airport where my daughter was to pick me up. When I met Nick and Colleen on the flight to St. Louis, I changed my plans. Colleen was pretty sick, and I was concerned that she might need additional medical care. Angela was the flight attendant, and she helped change my tickets. Instead of landing in Baltimore, I would be flying with Nick and Colleen to Washington National. Only the people Angela spoke to about changing my ticket and the people in the first class section could have possibly been aware of my travel plans. Everything was so last minute. It seems impossible that anyone could have tracked our movements so closely to plan a way to harm Colleen, Nick, Angela, or me." Harry made a compelling argument for the random accident theory.

Detective Harding turned to Angela and asked, "What about

you? Is there anything or anybody that now, looking back, could have been aware of your schedule? Even the most insignificant detail may give us a clue or a lead on where to look next."

Angela responded, "My schedule is posted about ten days in advance on an inter-company memo. We have a telephone/fax set-up that allows us to access the schedule right up to an hour prior to our scheduled flight. We have an internal 800 number that is supposed to be confidential. I suspect it is not the best-kept company secret. During holidays there is a lot of opportunity for overtime. I was able to switch flights in St. Louis because of my seniority, and I told a lie about Colleen being a family member who was seriously ill and on the way to Walter Reed hospital. The woman at the airline I contacted about the change in Dr. Booth's ticket has worked for United for years. I believe her name is Mary Brown. I met her one time about ten years ago. I can give you her direct line. She is a sweetheart to all her flight attendants. Anyway, in the two weeks leading up to Colleen's death, I worked about fifty to sixty hours a week covering the Denver, San Diego, Los Angeles, San Francisco, Portland, and Seattle routes. It was a pretty grueling schedule that left little time for me to do anything but eat, sleep, and fly. Since my dad passed away earlier this year, I have been focusing on work. I cannot think of anyone in my life who could possibly have anticipated the moves I made the day Colleen was killed."

"Thank you, Angela. We appreciate your input," Detective Harding kindly replied to Angela.

"Let's see what we have got so far," Detective Baker suggested. He pulled an easel from the front of the room closer to the table. "Let's play a game of elimination:

"Nick's contacts that day in California include the nurse, Maryanne Logan, and the doctor, John Walters. Did you speak to anyone else?"

"Yes, John, I did. There was a young man I met at a house in San Francisco based on a tip from a friend of Colleen's who told me she was in the hospital. I met a friend of Colleen's the night before in Los Angeles, Gretchen Sanders. She gave me the address and phone number at the house in San Francisco where I met Paul Martin. I also talked with Joey Bean, the guy Colleen was involved with for a time in Los Angeles, the day before I headed to San Francisco. I just realized a possible connection for us to look into. Harry and Angela, I have not mentioned this to you previously. I was not hiding anything from you, so please understand that I was not trying to deceive you." Nick felt a little embarrassed about the information he was going to share with his friends and the police.

chapter 3

The conference room door opened slightly, and a uniformed officer told the detectives there was a phone call for Mr. O'Connell.
Nick excused himself and followed the officer to the phone.

"Nick, hello, it's Shaun. I heard from Maura that you were
meeting with the police to talk about the accident." Shaun,
Nick's brother, was a captain in the New Jersey State Police with
fourteen years service. He was near to completing his graduate degree in criminal justice. He had the rare combination of
hands-on experience coupled with an intellect that enabled him
to take facts, summarize, draw truth from a variety of sources,
and arrive at conclusions that usually delivered a guilty verdict
for the perpetrator. Shaun continued, "Nick, I don't want to
intrude, but I would like to help find the truth about Colleen's
death. I am only about five or ten minutes from the police station. Would you mind if I joined you?"

"That would be fine, Shaun. I will tell Detective Baker you
are coming. Thank you!" Nick replied. He returned to the conference room and told Catherine and John about his brother.
Catherine replied, "I look forward to meeting him, and we welcome any assistance he can offer."

Ten minutes later, Shaun and Father Chris joined Nick in the
conference room.

"I hope you don't mind me being here," said Father Chris. "I was running around with Shaun today, and when I heard he wanted to meet you here, I was anxious to join him."

"We are glad you are here," said John Baker. "We are looking for any clues, insight, or random ideas on who and why someone would harm Nick's sister. We have been working on this for two hours. Although you were not involved, I recognize your love of Colleen and understand why you want to help."

"Do you suspect this was intentional?" Shaun inquired. "I thought it was just a tragic accident."

"Yes, Shaun, that is one scenario we are looking at," answered Catherine.

"Nick, you were about to tell us something about Colleen. Please continue," said Catherine.

"Acting on a tip from Joey Bean I went to the bars along the strip not far from the airport. Joey told me Colleen's friends sometimes worked that area when they were desperate for money. By worked, I mean they were involved in prostitution. There I met a friend of Colleen's at an airport bar who was working the strip. Her name is Gretchen Sanders. I paid her the going rate and explained that I only wanted some information about my sister. She objected at first, thinking I was a cop or an evangelist intent on saving her soul. After I showed her Colleen's picture, she broke down a little and told me what she knew and pointed me in the direction of San Francisco, where I found Colleen. I encouraged Gretchen to call home and make an effort to get out of the life she was immersed in. I was pleased when I saw her at Colleen's viewing and funeral. She had really changed her appearance. She had turned a corner in her life and felt more than a little embarrassed about the poor choices she had made in California. I honored her request and kept her identity a secret. I was impressed with her determination to change her life." Nick finished his remarks and saw the near astonishment in the eyes of his brother and his friends.

"Well, that broadens the list," Catherine Harding remarked.

"We will add Gretchen to the circle of people who knew Colleen. She may not have known Colleen was flying home, but her involvement in prostitution could have put her in contact with criminals. We should put Paul Martin on the list, too. Neither Gretchen nor Paul knew Colleen was flying home that day, but they knew her. They are not suspects, but they might be able to help us nonetheless."

Detective Baker turned to Shaun and said, "Any thoughts on our process, Shaun? We are trying to compile a list of anyone who had knowledge of Colleen flying home that day or in the days preceding it. We want to find out if this was just a very strange accident or a premeditated act. And we need to find out why someone may have wanted to harm Colleen."

"John and Catherine, I just want to observe for now and offer any help if the need arises. Being a member of the family could prejudice my opinions. However, having spent a good part of my police career in solving homicides may enable me to draw conclusions we might otherwise miss." Shaun was a true professional. He wasn't about to tell the Metro Police how to run an investigation. He would observe, comment, and suggest, but he would not interfere or tell them how to solve the case.

"Okay," Detective Baker began again, "our list now includes the following:

Dr. John Walters	Paul Martin
Nurse Maryanne Logan	Mary Brown of United Airlines
Joey Bean	Gretchen Sanders

"Are there any other obvious additions to our list?" Catherine said aloud to everyone in the conference room. "Who are we missing that could and should be listed here? What about pimps? Did Gretchen and Colleen have someone setting up their appointments and collecting money? Did Colleen owe anyone money? Who else could have wanted to harm Colleen?"

Nick spoke up, "The doctor at St. Agnes Hospital, John Walters, gave me the names of two doctors at Walter Reed Hospital. I jotted their names down on a slip of paper." He opened his wallet and unfolded a small note. "Here it is. The names are Dr. Mark Preston and Dr. Jim Nelson. The doctor at St. Agnes told me they were aware of the contagious disease Colleen had contracted. What I recall is that it was a disease that attacked the immune system in the body. The individual systems–kidneys, liver, intestines for example–would shut down, pneumonia would set in, and death could follow as early as three days or as long as a week or so. The doctors just are not sure what causes this sickness or how to cure it. By the grace of God, Colleen's child did not have any symptoms of the disease. The one common element in diagnosing the disease was that gay men and drug addicts who shared needles were the overwhelming victims of the disease. In San Francisco, they were calling it 'the plague.'

Colleen assured me she did not take drugs through needles, and she was not gay."

"Okay," Catherine replied. "Let's add Dr. Preston and Dr. Nelson's names to our list. On the surface, I would not think these doctors are not involved, but we want to check out every person who may have interacted with Colleen over the last days of her life. We may contact the LA police and ask them to look into the people who knew Colleen."

"It sounds like good strategy," remarked Shaun. "But I think we need to look a little closer into the airline connection."

"What are you thinking, Shaun?" asked Catherine.

"Well, you all were traveling first class. Angela told us that the front cabin was not overly crowded on either of the flights. Could someone have recognized Colleen? Could her presence there have been a threat to someone in California or Washington?"

"I think I know where you are going with this, Shaun. If Colleen had 'dated' a public official, it could be very scandalous and career-threatening to someone who is very ambitious and hoping for a future in politics," said Detective John Baker. "We have not considered that possibility, but, believe me, here in Washington we see this all the time. This may be a random theory, but we cannot dismiss it."

Shaun was thinking the same thing. If Colleen had been with one of these philandering politicians, it stood to reason they would want to avoid any negative publicity. Could knowing Colleen pose a threat to someone's reputation that would lead him or her to commit murder? And if they were married, it could also create problems for the so-called family man who was cheating on the side. This was an ugly side of the elected men and women who govern this country. Nevertheless, most individuals living this way rarely think or care little about all the harm that cheating causes their spouses and children. Committing murder to cover up a scandal had been tried before in Washington.

"Angela, is there any way you could get your hands on the passenger lists for the flight into St. Louis and for the second flight that landed at Washington National? We could get this with a search warrant, which could take a while. If you have a contact that could help us, we might be able to keep this investigation moving."

"I notified my supervisor yesterday that I was taking some vacation time, but I think I can get those lists for you, Detective," Angela replied. "I will need a fax number here at the precinct."

Catherine stood up and said, "Angela, come with me. I will get you set up with a telephone and a fax machine."

The two women walked out of the conference room and headed down a hallway to Catherine's office. It was a small room, but neatly arranged. "Angela, I want to thank you for helping us today. I know it must have been difficult re-living the horror of Colleen's injuries and subsequent death. You seem to be close to both Nick and Harry."

"Yes, Catherine, I am. Although we've known one another only a few weeks, I consider them close friends. We experienced a lot traveling together, and we got to know one another. I believe what defines friendship is trust. What Harry, Nick, Colleen, and I shared in those hours were events that people rarely experience and perhaps never do in a lifetime. I witnessed love, faith, sacrifice, heartbreak, devastation, forgiveness, and hope. I saw the miracle of birth, the penetrating sorrow of death, and the joyful hope of personal salvation offered by Christ to believers who accept him and repent as Colleen did when she received the Sacrament of the Sick from Father Chris. We experienced so much during our time together. These became the defining moments of my own life. We question what our purpose is in life and if we are living in accordance with that purpose. I saw with great clarity that I was living a very selfish life. I recognized that I was not fulfilling my purpose or my destiny. To fully understand our purpose, we need to pray and put our trust in God. I finally got it. It is not about me, it is about others. It is about all the people who need God's love, our friendship, and our trust. Harry, Nick, and Father Chris are remarkable people. When life served up its worst, they were at their best."

"Wow, Angela, I've never heard such a powerful message. I believe you are right. I have been living in the 'me—here and now' mode also. I've gotten a lot tougher since I have been in the detective squad. When I am, now all I think about are my wants and needs. Now that's being selfish! I know I have to get right with God. I have not prayed in a long time, and I am embarrassed to tell you the last time I was inside a church. I make excuses every week for not going. I know I have to make changes in my life, but I am not sure where to start, who to talk to, or even what to say."

Catherine was surprised that she shared such a personal insight with someone she had met only a few hours earlier.

"Catherine," Angela said softly, "the first person you talk to is the Lord. Speak to him with your heart. He knows what you are struggling with in your life. Then, if you want to talk to someone, I would recommend Father Chris. I spoke with him, and

I am not a Catholic. We talked for a while, and then we prayed for a while, together, just the two of us. I felt the Lord come into my heart, my soul, and my very being. Knowing that God loves us so much made me feel a little unworthy. God's love even overcame that! If you would like to pray with me sometime, I would be honored. Just remember that Jesus knows you, loves you, and will be with you as long as you want him with you. He won't run away from you even if you stumble or fall into sin. He will wait for you and will always be there for you. That is what love is really all about—being there with you in the good days and especially in the bad ones, too."

"Angela, we better get moving. I want to talk more about this. For now, go ahead and use my office and fax machine. Dial eight for an outside line. I will meet you back in the conference room," Catherine said in a warm, friendly tone.

Angela called her contact at the United Airways Operations Center. In a matter of ten minutes, she had both passenger lists in her hand and was walking back up the hallway to the conference room.

"Angela, were you able to get the lists?" John Baker asked.

"Yes, John, here they are. My friend at the United Op Center really came through for us. I hope this helps us find some answers," Angela said.

John suggested they split into two groups so they could run through the passenger lists more efficiently. Catherine, Angela, and Father Chris took the list of passengers flying from San Francisco to St. Louis. Detective Baker, Nick, and Shaun looked over the list of people who were on the flight from St. Louis to Washington National.

"Let's concentrate on the first-class passengers," Catherine instructed. "They would be the people who had the time to recognize Colleen. It is possible that someone in coach saw Colleen as they passed her seat in the front cabin. Let's look through the lists and see if anything jumps out at us."

"I am not sure how much help I might be," said Father Chris.

"I live up in Pennsylvania and really don't know very many people in the DC area."

"Neither do I, Father," Shaun said. "It is still important for us to look at the names. Many times insignificant things can lead to profiles which then move toward identifying people, places, and things."

The two groups began scanning their lists. There were a total of 132 passengers on the flight from San Francisco to St. Louis. The first class section had twelve available seats, and seven were taken. John Baker's group looked over the passenger list from St. Louis to Washington National. Ten of the twelve first class seats were taken, and there were 118 occupied seats in coach.

"Nick, do any names look familiar?" asked Catherine.

"One does. The third name down, Scott Farmer; he is an army veteran. I met him at a Pentagon function about six years ago. He moved into the private sector about two years before I completed my enlistment. I have not seen or spoken to him in several years. I heard he landed a job as an aide to Senator Stephen Walley from Ohio."

"What kind of personal life did Farmer have? Was he married? Divorced? Kids? Do you know where he lives?" Detective Baker fired questions at Nick.

"I'm sorry, I don't know any of his personal information," Nick replied. "Do we add his name to the list just because he might be an aide to a United States senator?

"Yes, I think we should. At this point we are gathering every possible connection to the people who traveled on the flights that brought you home to Washington." Baker said in reply to Nick's question.

"John," Catherine said calmly. "It is going on five o'clock. We have been here all afternoon and we are all tired. Why don't we call it a day and pick up tomorrow morning?"

"Would you all be able to be here tomorrow morning before ten o'clock?" Catherine asked to all in the room.

"Can we all make it tomorrow? Shaun? Chris?" Nick asked.

"Yes, I will be here," Father Chris replied.

"I'm in," Shaun answered.

"Dr. Booth, can you and Angela return tomorrow?" John Baker inquired.

"Yes, we will be here," replied Harry, as Angela nodded in agreement.

"Thank you all for your help. I look forward to making more progress tomorrow. If any of you think of anything, either call me here or at home, any time of the day or night. I am serious when I tell you it is okay to call me anytime. We will do what we can on our end. Have a good night," concluded the detective.

Nick, Father Chris, and Shaun left the police station together, walking out just ahead of Harry and Angela. It had been a long afternoon. The three men never expected to be involved in a police investigation about Colleen's death.

chapter 4

Nick was anxious to check in with his wife who had left for the hospital to see the babies. Maura was breast-feeding both infants and had to use the breast pump several times a day to ensure sufficient amounts of her milk was on hand for both children. The neo-natal unit had placed a tiny shunt in the arm of Colleen's baby Christopher, so he had continuous nutrition. Maura's doctor, had instructed the hospital pediatricians to keep a close watch over the two pre-mature infants. She knew they were very special babies who came into this world in unique circumstances.

"Well, Shaun," Father Chris began. "What do you think about the possibility of Colleen's death being intentional?"

"I'm not sure it wasn't just an accident. If the driver of the bus was under the influence, he may have panicked and ran away. And it is possible that he was stone cold sober and just panicked after the wreck. He may have been very tired, nodded off momentarily, and his foot slipped from the brake to the accelerator. He could have been so frightened that he panicked and fled. This explanation would erase some of the conspiracy theories the police would not consider anyway. If the bus driver could be found and questioned, a whole lot of work could be avoided. But, and this may be a serious 'but,' why did the driver wear a disguise? If he was not an employee of Double Tree, who was he, and why was he behind the wheel of the bus? This is where the random accident theory is left in the dust. Why would someone disguise himself, steal a hotel courtesy bus and intentionally try to kill Colleen, Nick, Harry or Angela?" Shaun explained to Father Chris, while asking himself, *accident or intentional?*

"Do we even know if Colleen was the intended target of this unknown bus driver?" Father Chris asked. "For all we know, Nick, you could have been the target. You know a lot of people in DC. Could you have made enemies over the years who would want you dead?"

"I don't think so," Nick replied. "I have been at the CIA for three years and have kept a fairly low profile there. My division is logistics, not spying. We do some pretty mundane things in my office. We track vehicle use and contracts for planes, cars, and the like. I really don't work with any materials that are related to army contracts, weapons, and secretive activities. We work with a large budget which the senate oversight committee reviews each year. We have not had a budget rejected in my division in ten years. I just don't think I could have been a target from anything related to my work," Nick concluded.

"Yes, but you do award contracts, right?" asked Shaun.

"Sure, and some very large contracts are awarded every year. We work primarily with firms that have long been partners with the CIA. We open the bidding to all vendors who successfully meet the pre-bid criteria. The standards we set are fairly high, and it is tough for a new company to pass the qualifications we have in place to secure that the specific bid requirements, product specifications, and warranties are in place. It can take two or three years for a vendor to meet and pass the qualifications. Once they do it is a lot easier to stay on the approved vendor list. If they win an award for a product, the contract is often in the millions of dollars. All that effort to meet our criteria, once met, does pay off for the vendor," Nick explained to Chris and Shaun.

"What would happen," Father Chris asked, "If a vendor on the approved bidder list lost the contract to a newly approved vendor? Are they kicked back down to the bottom of the ladder?

"No, Chris, they may not be the low bidder for the current contract, but they can still provide us with a lot of product if they agree in writing to hold the price of the product to the levels at which they won the previous year's bid. They might lose a little profit, but they are still on the approved vendor list. What happens is that the new company who won the award has to work twice as hard to get the business because the previous firm had all the contacts that buy their particular product," Nick explained.

"I would have to look at this year's contract awards to see if we changed a vendor who might have lost so much business that their livelihood was in jeopardy. That type of individual could become desperate enough to seek revenge; although, that seems to be a real stretch if you ask me," Nick concluded.

"I guess you are right," Chris replied. "But, like John Baker said, we need to look at all possibilities in order to figure out exactly what happened and why."

"Chris is right, Nick," Shaun added. "If we are to get to the bottom of this, we need to consider everything and everyone with connections to Colleen, Harry, Angela, and you."

"I don't want to scare Maura," Nick said. "Let's not worry her with needless speculation at this time."

"I agree with you, Nick," said Shaun. "We are just beginning to investigate what happened at the airport. The first question is: why did the bus driver flee the scene? The second is the discovery of the clothing he wore to disguise himself as an employee of Double Tree Hotel. If the police can focus on these things, we may eventually find out that there was something more to the accident that meets the eye. These are the issues that have to be clarified, and quickly," Shaun said, as he pulled into the driveway at Nick's house. It was 5:45, and darkness had already crept into the western sky.

"Hello, you three," Maura said as they walked into the kitchen. "How did it go at the police station? Any further ideas on what caused the bus to crash at the airport?"

"Hi, sweetheart," Nick said as he gently hugged and kissed his wife. "We had a good meeting this afternoon. Unfortunately, we have to meet again tomorrow. We ran out of time today. Harry and Angela send you their regards. I hope you don't mind, but I invited them for dinner tonight. They will be here around 7:00. Is there anything I can do to help out in the kitchen?"

"No. We have plenty of food, and we enjoy their company. I was at the hospital most of the day with the children. Our little girl was awake for several hours and is feeding well. Christopher slept most of the time. The doctors and nurses are very attentive and helpful with the little ones. I thought about going back tonight, but there is enough milk there for them until noon tomorrow. I will make some more tonight and take it along tomorrow when we visit them. Any chance you can stop sometime tomorrow to see the children?"

"I sure will. We have to be at the precinct about 10:00 a.m. We will leave early and stop at the hospital before going in to see John Baker and Catherine Harding." Nick was only too happy to stop and see his little babies.

The phone rang in the hallway. "Nick, can you get the phone?" asked Maura.

"Hello?" Nick inquired.

"Nick, this is Detective Baker."

"Yes, John. What can I do for you?"

"We found the bus driver."

"That is good news. Maybe we can get some answers now."

"No, we can't," said Detective Baker.

"Why?"

"The man was killed. We found his body in a dumpster

behind the Double Tree Hotel. We identified him from the fingerprints on the glasses we found in the trash at the airport. Nick, he was murdered, shot in the back of the head. His name was Thomas Roy Clockman. He had a record. He spent twelve years in prison on a previous homicide. We sent the body to the Coroner. I am not sure of the time of death, but the body was still in good condition. I estimate he may have been shot in the last twenty-four to thirty-six hours. We got a partial print in the bus that matches Clockman's. We are certain he was the driver." Baker paused a moment after sharing this news with Nick. "This puts a different spin on everything."

"Yes, yes it does, John. We have more of a mystery now than we did earlier."

"I ordered a complete sweep of the airport hotel area. There may be clues out there that we need to examine. Catherine contacted the Double Tree to find out if any of their employees quit recently or may be missing. Clockman got that uniform from someone at the Double Tree. He wasn't an employee there; we checked. Would you share this with Shaun and Father Chris? I think we should all stay in the information loop until we get some answers," Baker said in an authoritative tone.

"I agree," Nick said. "I will tell everyone what has happened. Thanks for calling me with the news. It is quite disturbing to know he has been killed. We must be involved with people who have a lot of power and access to information. We will see you tomorrow morning, John, and thanks again for the call."

"What happened?" Father Chris said immediately after Nick hung up.

"They found the bus driver in a dumpster behind the Double Tree Hotel. He had been shot in the head," Nick said as he shook his head sadly.

Shaun stepped into the hallway with Chris and Nick. "That is not good. If the police would have had a chance to interview him, we might have gotten some answers. Now there are more questions and fewer people to answer them," Shaun stated with obvious concern in his voice.

Nick spotted Harry and Angela walking onto the porch just as Shaun was speaking. He opened the front door and said, "Welcome, Angela, and you too, Harry. You are just in time for dinner."

"Thank you, Nick. Hello, Chris and you too, Shaun," Angela replied.

"Hi, Maura, how are you feeling?" Harry said to Nick's wife. "I am glad to see you. Thank you for the dinner invitation. I hope we didn't put you to any trouble."

"Not at all," Maura replied. "We were happy to hear you were coming. I think you met Kathleen at Colleen's funeral."

"Yes. It is nice to see you again," replied Angela.

"Hey, gentlemen, your timing is perfect," Kathleen said. "Dinner is on the table."

The four men sat down at the table along with Kathleen, Angela, and Maura. The meal consisted of a salad, roast beef, corn, peas, and mashed potatoes. Kathleen had made homemade bread earlier in the day, and the aroma of the bread and beef roast gave the house the feel of an old-fashioned kitchen. Kathleen took over in the kitchen while Maura was recovering, and had prepared a delicious meal. Nick asked Father Chris if he would say the blessing.

"Lord, we thank you for this food; we thank you for our family and friends gathered around this table. We praise you, Lord, and ask that you pour your love and mercy on each of us. Strengthen our resolve to do your will at all times and in all places. Bless our tiny babies in the hospital, and help them grow strong. And bless this meal we are about to receive from thy bounty through Christ our Lord, Amen."

"Maura, tell us about Megan and Christopher. How are the babies?" Harry inquired."

"Thanks for asking, Harry. They are doing well. Christopher is sleeping a lot. They are keeping an eye on his weight. Megan is awake much more than Christopher. She is on the small size, which the doctor tells me is normal since she was a 'premie.'" Maura was animated when she spoke of the children.

"You should have seen Megan holding on to my pinky finger," Kathleen added. "She has a good grip for a little girl. She has Maura's smile. I held her and little Christopher for a while this afternoon. It is like holding two tiny angels in your arms."

"I believe they are not only a gift from God, but also a great blessing for your family and for us, too. Colleen was a very unique person, and we were fortunate to know her, even if it was for so short a time," Harry said respectfully.

"Yes, she was special," Angela added. "The time we spent talking meant a lot to me, and I think it did for her, too." Tears suddenly filled Angela's eyes. "I am sorry, I don't mean to cry," she stammered. "Being with her at the end—" Angela excused herself and walked out of the room.

Harry got up and walked over to her, and placed her in his arms as she cried. He gently put her face in his hands and used his thumbs to wipe the tears from her eyes. They stood holding one another for several minutes.

Returning to the table, Angela apologized again. "I didn't mean to do that. I hope I haven't upset anyone."

Kathleen held her hand and said, "Angela, we have been doing that about every other hour. Whoever is next to us gets the job of helping us hold on to each other as we make our way through the sea of grief we are in. We start crying and end up laughing at ourselves. Our sorrow is real, but it is eased by the presence of family, friends, and the children."

"Yes, thank God for our friends," Father Chris said. "We are blessed to have both a loving family and friends, especially our new friends," he said, gesturing to Harry and Angela.

"Nick," Maura said, as he walked into the room, "who was on the telephone?"

"It was the police. Detective Baker called to let us know they found the man who was driving the bus that crashed at the airport. Unfortunately, he was killed."

"That's terrible. It was wrong for him to run away from the crash."

"Yes, it was. But he did not deserve to be killed," Nick said compassionately. "The police are looking into every aspect of the man's past. I hope they are successful in finding who was responsible for his death."

"This could complicate things even more," Shaun added. "He was the key to solving the mystery of Colleen's death. Without him, we are going to have to work even harder to find out what he was doing driving that bus, and why he may have used it as a weapon against Colleen."

"Let's talk about something else at the dinner table," Nick suggested. "I don't mean to be rude, but we do have a lot of things to be happy about, even at this point in time."

"I agree," Harry chimed in. "We should focus on the good things in our lives, things like two beautiful little babies."

"Well said, Harry," Chris added. "It is so nice to have Shaun and Kathleen here. We haven't had the chance to just sit down and share small talk with them in a long time. Let's keep the conversation light and fun tonight."

Everyone agreed. Dinner continued, and they enjoyed a good meal as friends, sharing intimate stories of raising their children and the joys and stress of working in a world that demands so much of a person's time.

After the meal, Nick, Chris, and Shaun volunteered to do the dishes and clean up in the kitchen. Harry offered to keep the women company in the living room.

"Nick, what do you think about the death of the bus driver?" Shaun inquired. "I have to tell you, the more I think about it the more I am led to consider some type of conspiracy. There is something going on here that doesn't add up. What about you, Chris? What do you think?"

Chris answered slowly. "I thought this was just a case of

somebody being drunk, driving a bus up onto a curb, and then panicking. I thought he ran away because he was afraid to go to jail. I thought it was a random act of thoughtless disregard for the welfare of others. The 'others' in this case were Colleen, Nick, Angela, and Harry. It was tragic, but I thought it was an accident. Now I don't know. I just don't know."

"I agree," Nick said. "This has moved from a random act of violence to something more complex, perhaps more sinister. It seems a lot less likely to have been an accident. What about you, Shaun, what do you think?"

"Let's try to be objective about this. Here is what we know: the uniform that the driver wore was genuine; it belonged to Double Tree. The bus, again, belonged to the hotel. Sometime Sunday night, a black man, wearing the hotel uniform, stole the bus from Double Tree. He drove the bus up over the curb and smashed into Colleen. When the bus came to a stop, the driver ran out the back door through a crowd of people. He got rid of his disguise. Then we learned that he had been killed. Did I miss anything?"

"Hearing it told like that makes it sound more like a series of random events rather than a pre-planned attempt to harm or possibly kill someone," Chris replied.

"But objectivity usually leads to truth, Chris," Nick said. "I think we need more information before we can label this a deliberate attempt on our lives. We have to remember that as Colleen and I were making our way home from San Francisco, we were at the mercy of available flights. When we arrived at the airport, we had no idea what flight we would be on. If someone really wanted to harm us, they would have to have access to a lot of secure airline information. We booked our seats on the flight out of San Francisco less than an hour before it lifted off. That was enough time for people who really wanted that information to get it.

"If Maura had not gone into premature labor, I would not have left the hospital in San Francisco to fly home that day. It was only the people at the hospital who knew I would be trying to fly back to DC that same day. Besides Dr. Walters and Nurse Maryanne Logan, only the cab driver knew we had even gone to the airport. I just do not see a criminal connection there. I think we were on the ground in St. Louis for about an hour. If someone was tracking us, it would have to have been through the airline computers. Harry doesn't even seem to fit in this picture. He was already on the plane. The flight originated in Portland early that morning. It was sheer coincidence that he got involved with Colleen and me. No one could have anticipated that," Nick concluded.

"You are right, Nick," Shaun replied. "We could sit here and postulate a hundred scenarios that would lead us right back to your main point. If someone was tracking you, they got the information from the airline. Nick, I had planned to return to New Jersey on Friday. Is it is okay if we stay awhile longer? I want to work with Detectives Baker and Harding to find out more about this dead man who was driving the bus. I think when we go in tomorrow, we should re-examine the complete passenger lists on both of the flights you and Colleen flew east on. We need to check on everyone that was on the plane, and maybe the flight crews as well. If we are going to really dig into this, let's dig deep."

"I agree completely," Harry said as he walked into the kitchen after entertaining Maura, Angela, and Kathleen in the living room. "I heard the tail end of your remarks, Shaun, and I think that is what we need to do."

"What are you men plotting back here in the kitchen?" Kathleen asked as she entered the kitchen. "If you are done, come back in the living room so we can all visit together."

"Okay, boss," Shaun said to his wife. "We will be there in a minute."

"Let's not go into all this with the girls just yet," Shaun remarked. "There will be plenty of time later to fill in some more blanks. Okay?"

"Yes, of course, you are right," agreed Chris. "Let's join the ladies."

"Are you going back to you daughter's home tonight Harry?" inquired Maura. "I know you said you would be back at the police station tomorrow morning. You are welcome to stay with us tonight. We have an empty bedroom, and you are welcome to use it."

"I may take you up on that offer. It has been a long day. If I can use your telephone, I will call my daughter, Cynthia, and tell her my change of plans," Harry said gratefully.

Nick and Harry walked back into the hallway to the telephone. "Harry, would you like a beer?"

"That sounds good to me. Thanks."

Nick walked back to the kitchen to retrieve some drinks for his guests. He was glad that Harry and Angela were staying over for the night. They were good company, and Maura had struck up a good friendship with Angela.

"Harry, did you get through to your daughter?" asked Nick as he headed back into the living room.

"No, which is odd because I thought she told me she would be home tonight. And the unanswered phone did not activate the automatic answering machine. It usually kicks in by the third or fifth ring. I'll try back in a few minutes," Harry replied to Nick, with a concerned tone in his voice.

The conversation in the living room had turned to small talk about children and careers. Shaun shared some of his adventures prior to going to work for the New Jersey State Police and marrying Kathleen. After high school, he entered the seminary to study for the priesthood. He dropped out after one year and decided to travel around the United States. He spent time in New York City and then moved on to Chicago for about six months. After one winter in the windy city, he headed west to Las Vegas. At every stop, he was able to secure employment that paid for his room and groceries. He always sent one hundred dollars a month home to his mother. Shaun also sent postcards and short notes to his dad. Eventually he settled in New Jersey, and there he joined the State Police. He met Kathleen, and a year later, married her. Shaun was 6'2" tall and had black wavy hair. He was as fit as any officer in his command. He earned his degree mostly at night, and was completing his graduate degree in criminal justice. He was at the top of his class.

Nick and Maura were enjoying getting re-acquainted with Kathleen and Shaun. There was a period of time when most of the O'Connell children drifted apart. These were the empty years that Nick and Father Chris spoke about at Colleen's funeral. The time now with Shaun and his wife was special. Nick thought it was good for Maura to get close to her sister-in-law. They lived only a few hours apart, and both now had small children. It is a lot easier to maintain friendships with people who are sharing the same life struggles and experiences. Nick really liked his brother. There were re-igniting a friendship that began when they were just boys.

Harry excused himself and walked to the phone in the hallway. He tried to call his daughter, and again the phone went unanswered, and the answering machine did not engage. Harry was getting worried. It was getting late and even if Cynthia had gone out, she would have returned by now. He walked back into the living room, and his concern was obvious to everyone in the room.

"Harry," Maura asked. "What's wrong?"

"I can't get through to my daughter. That is strange because she did not have plans for tonight other than to visit with Angela and me. I don't have her cell phone number with me. Maybe I should just drive over there and see if everything is okay."

"Wait a minute, Harry," Shaun said. "I can get you her number even if it is unlisted. And I can call the Alexandria Police and ask them to drive by your daughter's home to see if everything is okay."

"Let's try to get her cell number and call her first," Harry said gratefully.

Shaun walked over to the phone and dialed an operator. He gave them his police identification, and within minutes he had the unlisted number. He motioned Harry to the telephone and gave him the number.

Harry dialed the number. After two rings, it automatically transferred him to the answering machine. He left a brief message and gave her Nick's number with the request for her to call as soon as possible. He hung up, waited a few minutes, and redialed the number. Again it quickly took him to the answering machine. He hung up without leaving a message. He retreated back into the living room with his friends. It was apparent that he had not gotten through to his daughter.

"Shaun, can you call the Alexandria police and see if they can check on my daughter?"

Shaun excused himself and went to the telephone in the kitchen. There he called the Alexandria Police. He spoke to the desk sergeant and detailed his position with the New Jersey State Police and explained the situation and concern they had about Harry's daughter Cynthia. The Sergeant asked Shaun to hold and radioed his men who were patrolling the area. Within minutes a squad car stopped outside Cynthia's home.

The officer walked up to the door and rang the bell. There was no reply. He noticed a light coming from the back of the house. After ringing the bell a second time, the officer knocked hard on the front door. There was still no response. The officer proceeded to move around to the back of the house. The light he saw came from a light in the screened-in porch. The officer used his flashlight and noticed some loose wires hanging from the second story of the back of the house. He was pretty sure it was the telephone line. He radioed in to his sergeant that he was suspicious about the light and had no response from either the front or back door. As he spoke, he saw a rip in the screen on the right side of the porch. He told his sergeant he was going in and to send backup.

The policeman forced open the rear door on the screened

porch and moved in towards the inner door at the back of the house. He forced that door open and immediately detected a strong odor of gas. The stove had been turned on, and the house was filling with the deadly fumes. The officer immediately radioed his sergeant again and told him to call the fire and rescue units to the house. He warned them not to do anything to create a spark that could blow up and kill everyone in the house. Moving slowly toward the stove, he gently turned the burners off.

He carefully made his way into the house and headed toward the stairway up to the second floor. Once there, he shined his flashlight into the bedrooms. He called out several times, "Hello, is anyone here? This is the police. I am here to help you." In the second bedroom he entered, he saw a woman lying on a bed, lifeless. He quickly felt for her pulse and detected a very faint one. He picked her up and hurried down the steps and out the front door. He gently laid her on the front lawn and was thrilled to hear the young woman cough.

"Wake up, Miss. Please wake up!" He nearly shouted to her. He patted her hard on the back, and she coughed again, this time harder. She weakly opened her eyes and looked at the policeman. "Are you okay, Miss? Come on, please breathe for me. Try to take a deep breath. Can you hear me? My name is Frank. I am a policeman."

Cynthia slowly opened her eyes and continued to cough. Her breathing was deep and uneven.

"Miss, is there anyone else in the house?" Officer Frank Byrd asked.

"No, no, only my dog. Is he okay? Did you see my dog?"

"Miss, I can't tell. I am sure he will be okay. Keep trying to breathe, Miss."

"He is a golden retriever and his name is Sam."

"You are sounding a little better, Miss. Keep breathing. Help is on the way. I will call your dog and see if he comes."

"Sam, Sam, come here, boy. Here, Sam," the policeman said,

before whistling for the dog. "Here, Sam!" the officer called out again.

A moment later, the dog walked weakly over to Cynthia and sat down next to her. He licked her hand as she reached out to the dog. Tears filled her eyes.

The emergency personnel arrived and immediately attended to Cynthia. They had an oxygen mask on her in seconds and were preparing to place an IV in her arm.

The Sergeant related these events to Shaun who remained on the telephone while all this was happening. Shaun was appreciative for this police courtesy.

"Sergeant, thank you. I will tell her father what has happened. What hospital will they take the woman to? We can meet her there," Shaun inquired.

"St. Mary's in Alexandria."

Shaun hung up and walked back into the living room. "Harry, we need to get to St. Mary's Hospital in Alexandria. There has been an accident, and Cynthia is in an ambulance headed there as we speak."

"Dear Lord!" Harry said as he and Angela nearly jumped out of their chairs. "Is she okay? What is wrong?"

"I can drive. Let's get over to the hospital fast," Shaun said as he pulled on his jacket and grabbed his keys.

Shaun sped away from the house with Harry, Angela, and Nick. The streets were pretty much deserted and once Shaun got on the beltway, he was going over eighty mph. The ride to the hospital took less than twenty minutes.

Angela and Harry rushed into the emergency room and asked for Cynthia Parker.

"She is in treatment room nine, straight down the hall."

A police officer was standing outside the treatment room.

Harry walked in and saw Cynthia sitting up in a hospital bed. She was on oxygen, and had an IV in her arm. She smiled at once when her father walked into the room.

"Dad, I am so glad you are here." Cynthia said gratefully, as Harry picked up her hand and kissed it gently.

At that moment, Bill Parker, Cynthia's husband, walked into the treatment room.

"Bill, oh, Bill, thank God you are here," Cynthia cried, as they embraced. "I am not sure what happed at home, but thank God this police officer arrived and carried me out of the house. I had passed out and was barely breathing."

"Are you feeling okay? I mean, are you going to be all right?" Bill asked again as he held her hand and stroked her arm.

A doctor walked into the room and was surprised to see so many people in the treatment room. "Are one of you a husband or a relative?" He inquired.

"Yes, Doctor, I am her husband. My name is Bill Parker. How is she?"

"We got to her in time. The gas could have killed her. If an alarm had gone off in the house, it could have created sufficient spark to blow it. You are very fortunate. God was watching over you tonight, Cynthia," the doctor stated. "We should give her some rest and privacy. She will be staying overnight, and we will monitor her. If everything looks fine, we will send her home tomorrow."

Nick said that he and Shaun would head home. Harry and Angela planned to stay at the hospital with his daughter for the night. They all agreed to call in the morning and see how Cynthia was doing.

As Shaun walked past the officer at the door, he identified himself as a State Trooper, and then asked if he knew what had happened to Mrs. Parker.

Officer Frank Byrd explained, "I was the first one on the scene. I had to break in through the back door. Once inside, I smelled the gas and saw the stove was on. The house was full of fumes. I rushed upstairs and found Mrs. Parker. I was able to carry her outside to safety."

"Can you tell me anything about the crime scene?" Shaun inquired.

"I didn't know it was a crime scene. I didn't know if the young lady was suicidal or just so tired she forgot to turn off the stove."

Shaun and Nick telephoned Maura before they left St. Mary's Hospital and related the news to them to assure her that everything was all right.

Nick and Shaun were pretty quiet on the drive back to the house. It was obvious that they were concerned about what had happened to Cynthia. A great tragedy had been averted thanks to the bravery and determination of a young police officer. Harry had nearly lost his daughter.

"I don't want to be a conspiracy nut," Nick said to Shaun. "But could this have anything to do with Colleen's death and the attempt on our lives at the airport?"

"I am not sure," Shaun replied. "There are a lot of questions to be answered before we can tie these events together. The police have to do a very thorough search of Cynthia's home. The big question is: Did Cynthia turn the gas on and forget about it? Did she intentionally try to kill herself? Did someone try to kill her? These things take some time, but these questions must all be answered before we speculate about motives or outlandish theories."

"You are right, Shaun. We can't jump to any conclusions until we get the facts. I know Harry was pretty shook up. Cynthia was lucky the police officer arrived when he did. You played a part in that by getting a hold of the Alexandria Police."

"That was a stroke of good fortune," Shaun replied. "The important thing is that Harry's daughter is okay. We need to thank God for that blessing."

It was going on 2:00 a.m. when Nick pulled into the driveway and turned off the car engine. Chris, Maura, and Kathleen came out of the house and immediately inquired about Harry and his daughter. Shaun and Nick quickly assured them that she was all right, and everything was going to be fine. Walking back into the house, Nick filled them in on everything they knew up to that point.

"My word," Maura said. "I wonder if Cynthia just forgot about the gas. It can happen, but it seems so unlikely that anyone would leave a burner on."

Shaun interjected. "It wasn't just one burner; all four burners were on and the setting was on high heat according to the police officer who rescued Cynthia."

"That is very suspicious," Kathleen replied. "A woman, or a man, would know immediately they were on. That is not something anyone would ignore."

"Let's not start making up things to worry about," Shaun said. "The police will investigate and let Harry know what happened. We need to get some sleep. We have a big day tomorrow. Nick, if we get up by six thirty, will that give us enough time to stop and see the babies before we go in to the police station?"

"Yes, Shaun. Let's do that. It has been another hectic day," Nick replied as he stifled a yawn.

————

Maura and Nick climbed into bed and kissed each other goodnight. She slid her fingers into his hand and said to her husband, "Nick, these events are frightening me. Maybe someone was trying to kill Harry at the airport. If someone was trying to kill him tonight, it would have been the second attempt on his life."

"I know you are scared, but I don't think the two incidents are connected at all," Nick replied softly. "Everything will be okay. Let's get some sleep."

chapter 5

The alarm woke both Nick and Shaun out of a deep sleep. After washing up and dressing, they went downstairs for coffee and a bite to eat. After that repast, they felt alive and ready to take on the day. Father Chris joined them for breakfast.

"Here is the plan for today," Nick explained. "We will stop and see Megan and Baby Christopher for a while and then get to the police precinct before ten. Hopefully we won't be tied up with Detective Baker all day."

Arriving at Walter Reed, the visitors put on the scrubs as directed for everyone in the neo-natal unit. Green hats, latex gloves, masks, surgical smocks and trousers, and plastic booties for their shoes completed the ensemble. The look probably frightened the babies. A nurse gently handed Baby Christopher to Nick and placed Megan in Father Chris' arms. Rocking chairs were furnished for visitors to help rock the babies. She handed both men small bottles with tiny nipples and encouraged Nick and Chris to feed the children. Megan took to the bottle at once. Father Chris saw Nick struggling with the tiny baby boy and took the occasion to tease Nick about his fathering skills.

"Remember Nick, I've been a 'Father' a lot longer than you," said the Priest.

The gentle humor infected all three men. It took their minds off the events of the preceding evening. And just holding the tiny babies seemed to put things into perspective. They spent about forty minutes with the infants and then headed into DC to meet with Detectives Harding and Baker.

"Good morning, gentlemen," smiled Catherine as they stepped into the conference room.

"Hello, Catherine," Shaun asked. "How are you today?"

"I am fine and ready to go! I hope we make a lot of progress today. I know you are anxious to get on to other things," Catherine replied in a pleasant tone.

The door opened again, and Detective Baker entered. He handed each of them a sheet of paper with names on each line:

San Francisco to St. Louis	*St. Louis to Washington National*
George T. Fielder	Scott M. Farmer
Victor L. Fishman	Theodore F. Houseman
Carla A. Goodman	Frederick R. Kaiser
Jeffrey J. Johnson	Marie C. Miller
Louis P. Peters	Rev. Daniel W. Pullman
Ronald R. Thompson	Michael P. Smith
	Helen B. Williams
Dr. F. Harry Booth	Dr. F. Harry Booth
Patrick N. O'Connell	Patrick N. O'Connell
Colleen E. O'Connell	Colleen E. O'Connell

"I am glad you made it today," Detective Baker began. "What you are looking at are the names of the passengers in first class on the flight from San Francisco to St. Louis and from St. Louis to Washington. This is where we are going to focus our energy this morning. Do you have any questions?"

"John, are you aware of what happened last night?" Shaun inquired. "There was an attack on Dr. Booth's daughter. Shaun believes it may be related to Colleen's death.

"I read a report on the incident this morning," the Detective replied. "I thought it might be an oversight on the homeowner or a possible suicide attempt."

"I don't think so," said Father Chris. "She is pregnant with her first child. She is happily married, and she and her husband have well-paying jobs. They both have a lot to look forward to. She was thrilled that her dad decided to move east and planned to practice medicine for the first time since his wife died three years ago. No, I would bet against it being an attempted suicide."

"John," Shaun asked. "Can you contact the Alexandria police and see if they found anything suspicious at the house."

"Yes, of course. I will do it right now. Would you folks go over the names on those lists until I return?" John asked politely.

Detective Harding sat down with Nick, Chris, and Shaun and began to scan the two lists of first class passengers. "I know we talked about Scott Farmer yesterday and that he worked as an Aide to the Senator from Ohio. We met with our Captain late yesterday, and he agreed that we needed to investigate any questionable people on the list. One of our detectives is looking into Mr. Farmer.

"What have you learned about the bus driver's death?" asked Chris. "Other than his name and criminal background, what do you know about Thomas Clockman?"

"He was released from prison sixteen months ago. His probation officer helped secure him a job at a manufacturing plant near Baltimore. Apparently he gave the impression that he had turned a corner in his life. But, he had his wages attached to pay support for three children from three different women. After taxes and child support, he was left with little money. Apparently his parents were alcoholics and used drugs. He had a rough time as a kid. He was also involved in gambling. He was a magnet for trouble."

Detective Baker walked into the conference room with a file in his hands. "I spoke with the Alexandria police. They are now convinced there was a break-in. The telephone line was definitely cut. Someone entered the house through the torn screen door. The police are dusting for prints. This was definitely not a suicide attempt. It was attempted murder."

"Who would want to kill Harry's daughter?" asked Chris.

"Chris," Detective Baker asked, "what makes you think Cynthia was the intended victim? Maybe someone intended to kill Harry, and his family was just collateral damage. Something is going on here, and we have to get to the bottom of this before someone else is killed." John Baker now believed that Harry, Nick, and Angela were in mortal danger. "This changes the program. We need to broaden our investigation and find out who is responsible for these attacks. I know you are not going to like this, but we have to restrict your movements and Harry's, too. It will help us protect you both. Maybe we can get you to a safe house," Baker concluded.

"What about our wives?" Nick asked. "If we are in danger, I want Maura moved to a safe house, same with Shaun's wife, Kathleen."

"I was going to suggest they return to New Jersey until we arrest who is behind these attacks," replied Baker. "I think we should call Harry now and fill him in on what we have learned."

"Wait a second," Shaun interjected. "I would not want to hear this over the phone. We should go over to St. Mary's Hospital and talk to him in person. I am sure he will want to protect his daughter and son-in-law."

Detective Baker secured an eight passenger police van, and they departed to St. Mary's Hospital.

It was a quiet drive to Alexandria. The detectives' thoughts were on what steps they should take to not only protect the people whom they believed were targeted for death, but on how to identify, apprehend, and arrest the criminals.

The police van pulled into St. Mary's Hospital. Shaun, Nick, and Father Chris stepped out of rear doors and were joined by

Detectives Harding and Baker walking into the front doors of the Medical Center. They made their way through the hallways back into the emergency treatment area. There they met Harry Booth and his son-in-law, Bill.

They quickly exchanged greetings and inquiries as to the health of Cynthia.

"Cynthia is feeling fine, thank God, and is being released shortly. Thank you for caring," Bill said.

"I am very happy to hear your wife is recovering. We need to speak to you and Harry somewhere private," Detective Baker said in a very serious tone.

The doctor and nurse that had been in the treatment room exited and told them they could go back in to Cynthia. Nick and the others returned to the room and closed the door.

"Hello, Cynthia," Nick started. "This is John Baker and Catherine Harding of the Washington Metro Police. We need to share some important information with you and your father."

"What is wrong?" Cindy inquired as she reached for her husband's hand.

"There was a break-in at your house last night. The gas was turned on deliberately in an attempt to blow up your house and everyone inside."

"What? Someone was trying to kill us? Who would do that?"

"Are you sure about this?" Bill asked. "We don't have any enemies, certainly no one we know would want try to kill us!"

"You are not the target. We believe that Harry and Angela are the probable targets," Catherine said in a calm voice.

"Harry, we need to get you and Angela to a safe house," stated John Baker. "Cynthia, do you and Bill have any place you could stay for a while?"

Bill answered quickly, "We could stay with my folks. They live about an hour south of here."

"That sounds good," Baker replied. "Don't tell anyone where you are or why you are going away. It is imperative for your safety that no one knows where you are. If someone finds you, they will use you to get to Harry or Angela. And if they find you, they will likely kill you. I don't want to frighten you, but I believe you are in danger."

"Cindy, listen to what they are saying," Harry chimed in. "I am not sure what we have stumbled into or who we are up against. All I care about is your safety and Bill's. I am concerned for all of us. We have to do what the police tell us."

"I will, Dad," Cynthia replied. "Bill and I will leave right away for his parent's home. I'll pick up a few things at home, and then we will head south."

"No, Miss, I can't let you go back to your house and risk the chance that someone is watching. We will provide transportation to your parents in an unmarked car."

"What about my dog?" Cynthia asked.

"The Alexandria Police told me this morning that an officer took the dog to a vet last night. I will contact them and tell them to board the dog until further notice," explained John Baker. "I will have a car here for you within an hour. Be ready, and remember not to tell anyone where you are."

After saying goodbye and exchanging hugs and handshakes, Detective Baker led the group to the van and headed back to DC. Catherine tried to keep the conversation off the danger the passengers faced. Pulling into the precinct parking lot, John Baker searched for an open space to park the vehicle. The lot was full. Shaun volunteered to move his car, so the van would be on the police lot.

"Give me the keys," asked Detective Baker. "I will have an officer move your car and then park the van in your space. You can park your car behind the van until you are ready to go."

Baker got out of the van and was walking to Shaun's car when two officers walked by. "Officer, would you move this car and park the van there?" Detective Baker asked.

"Yes, sir, Detective. Give me the keys and I will do it at once."

Shaun, Nick, Harry, and Angela got out of the van and walked toward the side door of the precinct. Catherine and John were immediately behind them. As they walked into the old stone archway entrance of the precinct, they were suddenly rocked by a huge explosion! As the officer turned the key in the ignition of Shaun's car, a blast erupted under the vehicle. The bomb immediately incinerated the second policeman standing near the car; the officer driving Shaun's car was simply vaporized.

The blast shook the foundation of the three-story building. Fires started inside and outside the old precinct. Several additional explosions occurred when some cars and trucks exploded in the parking lot. When the explosions finally stopped, the parking lot looked like a war zone. The blast below Shaun's car dug a cavity eight to ten feet deep. Every car window in the parking lot was blown out. There was glass, metal, burning tires, and debris everywhere. The private residence adjacent to the precinct parking lot had every window blown out, and the vinyl siding was melting from the heat of the blast.

The injuries to the police personnel on the first floor of the precinct were severe. Many people had lacerations from the glass and metal that was propelled through the building. The people closest to center of the blast were in shock and experienced hearing loss. Several people had broken bones and extensive cuts on their faces and arms. One officer had his uniform blown completely off and was lying unconscious up against a metal filing cabinet. The second and third floor injuries were mostly cuts and bruises from flying glass. People were dazed and unsure of what to do or where to go.

Nick, Harry, and the others in his group were blown off the stairs that led into the side entrance of the precinct. The stone block wall supporting a canopy at the entrance saved all their lives. The blast rolled over the thick stone oval shaped entrance. Shaun stood up first and looked at his friends. They were all covered in glass and dust. Angela and Catherine sat up and then helped each other to stand. Chris helped Detective Baker stand up. They were dazed, and it took a few minutes for everyone to get their bearings.

The small group stared at the damage in horror. It was a battlefield. Shaun and Nick tried to enter the building, but the door was jammed tight. Angela and Catherine were clearly stunned and needed help just to stand. They suffered damage to their ears and could not hear because of the blast.

The officers who were standing near Shaun's car were killed instantly with only their badge and belt buckle remaining. The explosion pushed the building slightly off its foundation, and parts of the stone and brick facade fell and blocked the entryways. Everyone was in shock, and no one could get in or out of the building. Maneuvering through the parking lot was nearly impossible. Emergency and Fire and Rescue Units were speeding to the precinct. Their screaming sirens frightened the people in the surrounding neighborhoods.

Detective Baker pulled Catherine Harding aside. "Get Angela, Nick, and everyone over by that fire truck on the street!" he yelled, pointing to the rescue vehicle.

Catherine gathered up everyone as Baker ordered. They crawled through the rubble and made their way out of the chaos in the parking lot. They were practically unrecognizable because of the dirt and debris. The grey cloud of dust emanating from the center of the blast covered everyone at the blast site.

"What are we doing, Catherine? We should be helping these people!" Harry said loudly.

"Detective Baker said to get out of here immediately. That was a direct order," said Harding.

The attempt on the lives of Nick, Harry and Angela failed. The degree of the destruction and the severity of the explosion defined the extreme lengths their enemy was willing to take. The stakes had been raised. There were no doubts about the intentions of the people who wanted to murder Nick O'Connell, Dr. Harry Booth, and Angela Carson.

chapter 6

John Baker gathered everyone together at the rear of a fire emergency truck.

He grabbed a clipboard and pencil and began to write:

I am sorry to pull you out of there, but we have a one-time opportunity to disappear. We have a chance to convince our attackers that they succeeded in their assassination attempt. We can let them think that we were all incinerated in the blast.

Everyone shook their heads and looked at one another. Nick's shirt was nearly torn off his back, and his wounds, while superficial, still bled heavily. Catherine had several deep cuts on her face and arms. They barely heard what Baker was saying because they all had damage to their ears from the deafening blast.

Father Chris reached for the clipboard and wrote:

Is everybody okay?

No one said anything; they just nodded their heads in approval. Chris reached inside the emergency truck and picked up a second clipboard with a pen attached and began to write:

Does anyone need to go to the hospital?

They looked at each other and shook their heads in the negative.

Detective Baker wrote again:

We need to leave here quickly and quietly. Whoever did this wanted us dead. Let's let them think they killed all of us.

Shaun reached for the pen and paper:

You are right, John. If whoever did this believes we are dead, the attacks on us would stop. It will give us time to look into who is responsible for this attempt on our lives.

Baker nodded his head in agreement. The detective walked to the unlocked cab of the truck and climbed in. He motioned for Chris, Nick, and the rest to get into the rear of the truck. As the back door was pulled shut, Baker slowly pulled away from the precinct, turned off the siren and lights, and drove the emergency vehicle away from the bombsite.

Baker understood that a perpetrator who would blow up a police precinct would take whatever steps necessary to eliminate a handful of potential witnesses to a crime and would stop only if the targets were dead.

As the policeman drove the stolen emergency vehicle from the police station, Father Chris asked Nick, Harry, Angie, Catherine, and Shaun to pray with him. "Dear Lord, thank you for sparing our lives today. Please look with mercy and kindness on those innocent people who died today. Heal the wounded and sick. Bless our families and keep them safe. In Jesus' name we pray, Amen."

"Amen," echoed through the truck by the grateful survivors of the murder attempt.

Catherine shouted up to John Baker, "Any idea where we are going?"

The detective slowed the truck down and pulled into a mall

parking lot and climbed into the back. The temporary hearing loss had improved to the point where they all could hear each other without shouting. "Any ideas?" asked Baker.

"Do you think our families are safe?" Nick asked

"I think so, especially if we 'died' in the blast," replied Catherine. We cannot take any more risks by assuming that we are safe or anyone attached to us. We have to let our attackers believe we were killed in the blast. And we have to secure the safety of our families and loved ones. If you call Maura, you have to tell her of our plan to go undercover. I believe we have got to protect them too."

"I have friends at the Benedictine Monastery in Silver Springs, Maryland. It would be safe there, and our families would be welcome too," suggested Father Chris.

"What about Maura and the babies?" Nick asked. "The infants can't survive outside the hospital yet. We have to ensure the safety of Maura and the children."

"Nick," Catherine began, "if we could get her doctor to admit Maura to the hospital, she could stay at Walter Reed and take care of the children and be safe herself. My uncle, Brian Taylor, is the head of the Pediatric Unit there. I will stay with Maura at the hospital to provide protection for her. I do not think that John Baker or I are the targets of the people trying to harm you. I think what is more important is that the killer thinks you are dead. They won't be going after anyone else if they think Harry, Angela, and you died in the blast at the precinct."

"I agree with Catherine," Shaun added. "Maura is not the target here, neither is Kathleen or me. The perpetrator of these crimes doesn't care who he kills or injures in the process of trying to take you three out. I concur with the detectives that once the killer thinks you are dead, these other attacks will stop."

"We have got to contact the Commissioner and have him sign off on our plan," Catherine explained. "We need to get out of this stolen fire emergency truck and find other transportation. This may be the best way for us to safely discover who is behind these murders. Every police officer in the District from the rookies on up to the Commissioner will be on this case. These people killed a lot of police officers today, and that will change this city into a combat zone. Every officer will be on high alert, and any suspicious activity will result in arrests. We have never seen this kind of attack in Washington, DC. Amidst all this mayhem and confusion we may be able to operate under everyone's radar. It may be our best chance to ensure our safety."

Nick borrowed John Baker's cell phone and called Maura.

"Nick," Maura said anxiously, "are you okay? The news on the radio and television reported an explosion at the police station in Southeast DC. Is everyone all right?"

"We are fine, all of us. God was watching over us today. We were at the precinct at the time of the explosion. The detectives believe that Harry, Angela, and I are the targets of the killer. We don't know exactly why, but we will find out, and the police will arrest these criminals. We have a plan to ensure your safety and Kathleen's. What you have to do now is pack and get ready to go to Walter Reed Hospital. You will be admitted there in the maternity section. You and the babies will be safe there. You cannot let anyone know we are alive. You and Kathleen will have to play the grieving widows.

"The police are going to report that several civilians, including a clergyman, were killed in the explosion. They will announce that among the dead were two women, Angela Carson and Detective Catherine Harding. The police will also announce that Detective John Baker also lost his life in the attack. This is part of the plan to apprehend the guilty parties responsible for these terrible crimes. The papers will report our death. It is vitally important that you and Kathleen play along. I don't have all the details yet, but this is what we are planning to do."

"All I care about is your safety," Maura replied. "I will do my part. You can count on me. And I will pray that the police can quickly and safely end this threat on your lives."

"We will be safe. I must say goodbye for now. I will find a way to contact you at the hospital. Please tell Kathleen that Shaun is safe and well, and that he will call her soon," Nick said as he shut off the telephone.

The next thirty minutes were a blur of activity. Baker reached the Commissioner, and he signed off on the plan to announce their deaths. An unmarked van was delivered to the mall parking lot where they exchanged it for the emergency rescue van. Catherine contacted her uncle at Walter Reed, and arrangements were made to admit Maura and Kathleen to the maternity ward. An undercover female officer would be assigned as their nurse. Father Chris contacted the Monastery and secured their assistance in protecting Harry, Nick, Shaun, and John Baker.

For the first time since Colleen's death, Nick felt they were on the offensive. With the killers believing they were all dead, they finally had an advantage.

chapter 7

Father Francis X. Murphy warmly greeted Chris, Nick, Shaun, Harry, Angela, and Detectives Baker and Harding. "Welcome to our Abbey and Retreat House. We ask God to bless and protect you while you are with us. We also ask that you honor some of our rules regarding silence during prayer times. I will do everything I can to make your time with us comfortable and safe. You are all welcome to attend our daily Mass and Benediction service. I have made one of our automobiles available for your use. We lock our front gate at ten o'clock p.m., so if you are out later than that you will need a gate pass to get back in to the Monastery. Let me show you to your rooms. And one last thing, please call me Frank."

Frank was pleasant and a natural leader. He took the men down several hallways to an adjacent building where the guests live while attending a retreat. The rooms were furnished with a single bed, a desk with a wooden chair, a private bath with a plastic shower stall with matching sink and hopper, and a closet that was no more than twenty-four inches wide and twelve inches deep. The accessories included an oak crucifix, a magazine rack, a small oval mirror, and a small holy water font hung on the wall next to the door. There was a window with plastic blinds and lime-colored curtains. The room was plain, to be sure, but not altogether unpleasant.

The main dining room was across from the residence halls, and an open courtyard and several small water fountains and an abundance of green plants filled the space between the buildings. There were floodlights in the floor, which gave the entire space light and warmth.

Harry suggested they wash up and meet in an hour to discuss their plan of action. It had been a harrowing day, and the stress of understanding just how close they came to their own death slowly crept in to the forefront of all their minds. Their reactions at the bombsite were normal for such an extreme situation. They were numb and stunned at the effects of the explosions. None of their own injuries were serious, which was amazing and perhaps a miracle.

Father Murphy supplied fresh clothing and toiletries for his guests and took care of their laundry as well. The monks at the Benedictine Monastery were told they had some temporary guests that required anonymity and would be treated as fellow travelers on the road of life. The monks obeyed that order and would make no inquiries of their guests other than how could they serve them.

Chris knocked on the doors of his companions, and together they walked over to the dining room. The monks prepared and served a meal of fresh fruit, salad, broiled chicken, and brown rice, then quickly retreated from the dining room, giving the guests privacy. Father Chris led the group in prayer, "Lord, we thank you for this safe haven and for the food our friends here at the Monastery share with us. Watch over all your children who were killed and injured at the police station this morning. Send your healing grace to the families of the dead and injured. Keep all our families safe and bless this food we are about to eat. Amen."

After finishing the meal, they cleared the table and took the dishes and utensils to the kitchen. Shaun and Harry washed and dried the dishes. It is funny how performing such a mundane task brings everything back into focus. There are things in life that need to be done regardless of the traumatic circumstances one may be in. It grounds a person back to the reality of life, of the need to go on, to keep on breathing, to continue to try to overcome, no matter how great the obstacle. Courage is rekindled, fatigue is overcome, and the determination to prevail, in spite of the odds, comes back strong.

John Baker borrowed some pens and paper from the monks and shared them with his companions. Harry and Shaun came out of the kitchen and sat down. Father Chris began the conversation. "I want to thank each of you for your courageous actions this morning. How we survived the blast is beyond me."

"You are right, Chris," Shaun added. "Nick, can you find out if Maura and Kathleen arrived at Walter Reed Hospital? Are they safe?"

"Yes, Nick," Baker answered. "I called the hospital, and they are safe. The police sent an unmarked car to pick up Kathleen and Maura, and they arrived safely at the hospital. Catherine's uncle, Dr. Brian Taylor, took care of getting both Maura and Kathleen admitted as maternity patients. One of the doctors there, Liz Roberts, knows Maura, and she has volunteered to help in any way she can. There are also two female officers assigned to work undercover there in Maternity as nurses' aides. She is confident that her situation is secure. I think Walter Reed has a fair security system. I know people are free and welcome to visit, but I wish they would set up a security card system that would restrict visitors to those who have been pre-approved."

"I will have the Commissioner contact the appropriate military people at Walter Reed and make that request," John answered. "It sounds reasonable, especially in light of the attack on the Precinct. They could announce it as an added security feature for the safety of the patients.

"The next job is a little tougher. Where do we begin to look for clues on the attacks on the police station?" John asked. "I think we were getting close to someone that was on the first-class passenger list. I have a copy of that list in my pocket."

One of the monks knocked on the dining room door and gently opened it a few inches. "Excuse me, there is a telephone call for a Mr. Baker on line two. You may use the telephone on the side table." The monk quietly backed out of the room and closed the door.

John picked up the telephone. "Baker, this is Commissioner John Dillon. I have some information regarding your case. Another body was found at the Double Tree Hotel at Washington National Airport. The deceased was employed as a bus driver. His name is Alan Carter. His body was found in an ice machine. He has probably been dead for a week or more. Whoever did this emptied the machine, put the body in, and covered it in ice. There was a single bullet wound in the side of his head. We checked with Double Tree. He has been an employee there for five years. Before that, he was in the navy for ten years and received an honorable discharge. He was married and had two children. It looks like this man was the first victim in this series of murders."

"Thanks for the update, Commissioner," replied Baker. "We have reached our destination and are just now sitting down to plan our next course of action."

"Whatever you do, Baker, try to keep those innocent people out of harm's way. We do not want another casualty in their family."

"Yes, sir. I understand. We are going to need some additional information on that list of first class passengers. I believe there is a connection between someone on those flights and the reason Colleen O'Connell was killed. Commissioner, it is vital that no one knows where we are. I know how to reach you. I don't think you should call us unless it is absolutely necessary. I think it best that everyone thinks we died at the Precinct. We might flush out the people behind these crimes. Do you agree with that, Commissioner?"

"Yes, I do," the Commissioner said as he hung up.

Baker put the phone down and returned to the table. "A body

was found in an ice machine at the Double Tree Hotel. He was identified as the employee courtesy bus driver for the hotel. The commissioner believes he was killed by the man found in the dumpster."

"I worked in homicide for two years," said Shaun. "In my experience, every murder has its own signature. Every killer has a motive unique to his or her circumstances.

"Shaun is absolutely right," added Detective Baker.

"What are we supposed to do in the meantime," Angela asked. "Are we supposed to wait here until … until when?"

"No," Chris said. "We do not have to stay locked up here. But I think we need to give the police a couple of days to run down the names on the passenger list. While we are here, we should take a second look at everything that has happened and everyone that we have talked about. We need to start from the beginning and re-think this. I know this may seem redundant, but it is important. Most situations are resolved when even the smallest details are securitized, sometimes over and over again. This may require us to be patient for a few days."

"I understand. I am sorry if it sounded like I was complaining. It is just that we were nearly killed this morning. Harry nearly lost his daughter yesterday. And Nick has already buried his sister. Dear God, what has happened to us?" Angela said angrily.

For a moment, the room was silent. Everyone there was feeling the tension that resided in the minds of each individual who had nearly lost their life. Shaun O'Connell and John Baker had faced the wrong end of a gun in their law enforcement careers. It creates a fear that never leaves you. Surviving meant you dodged a bullet that day. It doesn't mean you will do the same tomorrow.

The meeting ended about seven o'clock. Everyone was tired. Everyone was talked out. They agreed to meet for breakfast at seven-thirty the following morning.

"Mass is tomorrow morning at seven o'clock in the chapel.

You are all invited to come and pray with me," offered Father Chris.

"Thanks, Chris," Nick replied. "I'll be there."

"Me, too," said John Baker.

"Count us in," Harry and Angela said in tandem.

"Thank you all," Father Chris said. "See you in the morning. Goodnight."

chapter 8

John Baker walked down the hall to Father Murphy's office. "Frank, do you have a minute?"

"I just wanted to say thanks for opening your doors to us. When Father Chris told me this was our destination, I was pleased. We are only about thirty minutes outside of DC, yet we seem a world away. We all needed a safe haven, and you have provided that for us. I really appreciate your kindness."

"You are welcome, John. It is, after all, the business we are in. Providing for the needy and homeless is a task assigned to all of us regardless of where we are on our journey of life. I am sure you have thrown a life jacket to a drowning soul in their time of need as well," responded Fr. Murphy. "Won't you stay for a few minutes? I have the evening news on, and I am sure they will do a report on the horror that visited your police station earlier today."

"Thanks, Frank. I will," Baker said.

The commercial break ended, and the lead story on the news was the bombing at the police precinct. The still pictures showed the extent of the blast on the one side of the building. TV cameras arrived after the fire and rescue vehicles. "The tangled mass of metal and bricks was identified as Shaun O'Connell's car, in which six people perished," said the reporter. "The bomb was identified by the experts as a C 4 explosive. It incinerated everyone inside the car and several people nearby. The death toll was not yet finalized. What was left of the building would have to be torn down." The story ended with a report on vandals who stole one of the emergency vehicles while at the scene. The vehicle was recovered twenty miles away undamaged in a parking lot outside the Arlington Mall. The news then cut away again to commercials. John and Frank made small talk until the news came back on. The broadcaster did another feature story out of Washington DC–a report on a rash of car jackings that had ended in murder. Three separate incidents resulted in the death of each driver. Mrs. Helen Williams was shot outside of her Georgetown duplex backing her BMW out of her garage; Scott Farmer was shot in the head at close range pulling out of a parking garage in his Cadillac; and Rev. Daniel Pullman was pulled out of his Lexus SUV and shot in the head at American University where he was director of adult education services.

"Three needless killings," said Frank Murphy. Why don't these thugs just take the car and leave the people unharmed?"

"Frank," asked John Baker quickly. "Did you catch any of those names?"

"I think one was Farmer and one other one was a Rev. Pullman. Why?"

Baker took a sheet of paper from his pocket. "Was the other name Williams?"

"I am not sure; it could have been."

"Father, do you have a computer?"

"It's in the study," Father Murphy replied, as they walked into the room.

John got on the computer and within a minute had accessed NBC Nightly News reports. "May I print out this report?"

"Yes, of course."

The printer whirred into action, spitting out the sheet in a few seconds.

"Thanks, Father. I've got to talk to my friends. Good night."

Baker ran to the residence hall and knocked hard on the doors of his companions. "Nick, are you there? I have to talk to you," he said excitedly.

Everyone gathered in Baker's room. "John, what's wrong?" asked Harry.

"Look at this news story. Check the names; look at the names!" he said excitedly.

"Look at this!" Chris gasped. "Are these the names on the passenger lists?"

"Yes they are, Father," Baker answered. "Can you believe this? Farmer, Pullman—every name that was on the first class list! Someone is killing the people in first class on the flight that landed at Washington National! They killed Colleen; they think they killed Harry and Nick, and now they are killing the other first class passengers! This is incredible!" I have got to call Commissioner Dillon and let him know what is happening."

"I'll go with you to Murphy's room," offered Father Chris.

"Shaun, this is incredible. Who could arrange something like this? Who has access to information like this?" Nick asked. "Who has the power to do these things?"

"I am not sure, but there is one thing I want to do … no, make that one thing I *have* to do," Shaun said.

"What is that?"

"Contact the police in St Louis."

"Why?"

"I want to see if there have been any random murders in the last few days. I want to find out how far this arm of power and influence reaches," Shaun explained.

"Shaun, do you think that any random murders in St. Louis could be the work of the people who ordered these killings here?" Nick asked.

"Exactly," Nick replied.

John Baker called Commissioner Dillon and related the news. "Who else is on that passenger list?" John Dillon asked.

"The last people on the list, excluding Harry, Nick, and

Angela, are Theodore F. Houseman, Frederick R. Kaiser, Marie C. Miller, and Louis P. Peters."

Dillon scribbled the names on to a sheet of paper. "I will have some officers deploy and get these people some protection. Good work, John. You may have saved a life or two here. These people may not even be aware that their lives are in danger."

————————

Nick and Shaun were waiting for Father Chris and John as they walked through the Courtyard. Baker related what he had told the Commissioner and the steps he would take to protect those people from first class who might now be in danger.

"There are people's lives at risk here. We must find out and warn the passengers who were on Nick and Colleen's flight into St. Louis," Shaun said.

Chris, Shaun, and John Baker walked back to Father Murphy's room. Shaun was online with the St. Louis Police Department in seconds. He clicked the "Contact us" prompt, and instantly their telephone numbers were displayed. John wrote them down on a sheet of paper. Shaun glanced through their home page and searched for "daily crime statistics." He could not find any gunshot victims listed under death by shooting.

"I will call them tomorrow morning," Shaun told John Baker. "I think we are dealing with someone in the Washington DC area. At least, I hope so."

"Don't you think we should call the police tonight?" asked Frank Murphy. "It is possible that the daily log was not updated yet. John, I believe you should call them."

Detective John Baker picked up the telephone and called the St. Louis Police.

It took several minutes to reach anyone in the Police Chief's Office in St. Louis. It was going on eight forty-five p.m. central time when the phone was finally answered by a desk sergeant in the Third Ward.

"Hello, this is Sergeant Joseph Borden. How may I help you?"

"Hello, this is Detective Michael Foster calling from Washington, DC. I am trying to reach Chief William Greene. Is he available?" John Baker decided not to use his real name in identifying himself. Instead, he used the name of another detective in the DC Metro Police.

"No, sir," replied Sgt. Borden. "He is gone for the day. Is there something I can do for you?"

"Perhaps," replied Baker. "I am working on several homicides in the DC area. We got a lead that it might be gang-related, and there may be ties to groups in the St. Louis area. Have you had a spike in gang-related homicides in the last few days?"

"We average two or three homicides a week. Most are drug and gang related. Some are disgruntled husbands or boyfriends who are after their ex. However, we did have three nasty killings over these past few days. One was a middle-aged, well-to-do woman who was Chairwoman of the local library. On Saturday, she attended an event at the library–it was a sophisticated event for big donors—she was killed with a gunshot to the back of the head as she walked to her car. She was not robbed; her purse was on her arm, and it contained several hundred dollars and credit cards. Her name was Mrs. Carla Goodman.

The second homicide was unusual as well. A senior citizen was gunned down as he left his car and was walking into a local diner. Seems he ate at the same place every day, at the same time, with the same friends. There was no provocation, no fender bender setting someone off on a rant. The shooter walked right by him, stopped, pulled out his gun, and fired. One shot to the back of the head. The victim's name was Victor Fishman.

The third homicide happened this morning. The victim's name was George Fielder. He was shot walking to his church for six-thirty Mass. He went to the morning service every day. Again, there is no apparent motive. The only thing about these three killings is that the victims were shot at places they frequented. From what we can tell, they are totally unrelated. We have nothing to tie them together. How does this compare with your shootings, Detective?"

"They are somewhat different. We have two homicides that might be related. Like you, we are in the early stages of our investigation."

"Detective, I heard a news report of a car bomb at one of your Precincts. Sorry to hear about the deaths of your brother officers there. It is a horrible crime and tragic loss. I extend my condolences to you and all the DC police."

John Baker hung up the telephone and sat down. Father Chris and Shaun were anxious to hear what John learned in his call to St. Louis.

"It is not good. They had three random homicides. All three victims were passengers in first class on the flight from San Francisco to St. Louis. We have to alert the police in Saint Louis. Jeffrey Johnson, Louis Peters, and Ronald Thompson are in grave danger. We have a powerful enemy who has the resources to eliminate people anywhere in the country. I must call Commissioner Dillon and let him know the threat to those innocent people in St. Louis."

Baker finished the call to the Commissioner and hung up. Walking confidently toward Chris, Nick, and Shaun, he stopped and said, "Follow me." Angela and Catherine were sitting on a windowsill by their rooms and saw the men walking toward John Baker's room. Baker motioned for them to come with him. The small band of courageous souls gathered to continue their strategy of how to stay safe and alive.

Back in Baker's room, they sat down on the bed as John paced back and forth. "The only reason you are alive right now is because the person responsible for all these murders thinks you are already dead. It is a matter of life or death that this secret is kept. If anyone leaks this out, the party responsible for all these murders will use your wives, your children, your parents, anything to get to you. No one will be safe. Our lives are in the hands of a few people who have sworn to keep this secret. If any one of them leaks this information, more innocent lives will be lost. This monastery, Walter Reed Hospital—*nowhere* will be safe. You saw what the blast did to the precinct building. We cannot afford to underestimate our enemy."

"We need to schedule a memorial service for ourselves," Father Chris said with a smile.

"What do you mean, Chris?" asked Shaun.

"The killer thinks we were incinerated in the car. Our families should hold a memorial service for us. There are no remains to be buried, but a memorial service will help sell the idea of our death even more. It might end any surveillance the killers may have put on our families just in case we may have survived."

"I agree, Chris. Our families could hold a joint memorial service. The police would have the Honor Guard there to commemorate Officers Harding and Baker. It would be a large, public event. There might be a way for us to reverse things on the killers and get them under surveillance—if we only knew who they are," Shaun said with annoyance.

"That would help, to be sure," John Baker added. "But it is worth it to be safe. Whatever we can do to ensure your families are safe interests me. Anyone else agree?"

"Yes, I think we all agree," said Nick. "But how can we get information to Maura and the others?"

"I have an idea. Nick, you told me you had a sister who is a nun. Does she wear the habit that nuns sometimes wear?" Detective Baker inquired.

"Yes, Sister Sharon does wear the traditional habit. Why?" asked Nick.

"If Angela would be willing to wear a habit, she could pose as your sister and safely get word to Maura, Kathleen, and even Harry's daughter, Cynthia. I will not trust anyone outside of this inner circle to get word to your wives," said Baker. "So far only Commissioner Dillon and Father Murphy know where we are and that we are still alive.

"I am willing to pose as Sister Sharon. It would make sense that she would come for the memorial service. I think this is a good idea," offered Angela. "At the very least, I could ease some of Maura and Kathleen's worries about our safety."

Detective Baker sighed and thought more about the risk they would take if Angela's ruse was discovered. "There is a risk but a reward, too," he said. "I will leave it up to you to decide. I personally think it would be good for you and your families to know you are okay. And look at it this way, how many people get to watch their own funeral and memorial service?"

"Why don't we sleep on this tonight and decide after Mass tomorrow morning?" Father Chris suggested. "We can pray on it as well."

"Okay, that sounds good. Everyone in agreement?" asked the detective.

"Agreed," everyone said as they nodded their heads and then said goodnight.

Shaun paused and asked Nick if they could talk for a few minutes. "Sure, come in," he motioned to his brother as he opened the door to his room.

"What do you have in mind, Shaun?" Nick asked as he shut the door.

"I've done a lot of thinking about this situation, and I want to run some ideas by you," he replied. "Let's look at the situation again," he began. "First, we are not aware of any random murders prior to you leaving the hospital in San Francisco. The only people who knew you were flying home that day were the nurse, Maryanne Logan, and the doctor, John Walters. You didn't tell anyone else in San Francisco, right?"

"Yes, that's correct, Shaun," Nick said as he listened closely to his brother. "The guy who gave me the information that Colleen was in St. Agnes Hospital–his name is Paul Martin–I told him I was going to try to take Colleen home that day. But he didn't know whether she could be released from the hospital. His roommate works at St. Agnes. He would have had access to the information that Colleen had left the hospital. However, we don't know anything about the roommate, not even his name. Could he be the one who provided the information to the person that is responsible for all the killings? If so, everything that has happened had its origin in San Francisco."

"Yes, it does," Shaun said. "Someone found out that you and Colleen were flying home that day. That person's actions resulted in the death of many innocent people. But why would they care about you and our sister who was very ill and probably would be dead soon anyway? What threat did you or Colleen pose to the person or persons on the plane in the first class cabin? Who would have perceived you or our sister as a threat? What did you know? What did you see? What did you hear that was so damaging that someone would be willing to commit murder?"

"Here is another angle, Shaun," Nick replied. "Maybe Colleen and I are not the reason for the murders. Could we be innocent bystanders caught up in a situation where someone else in first class is the killer or the targeted victim? One of the first class passengers could be responsible for the murders. There could be only one intended victim, and all the other passengers became expendable because they could possibly identify the murderer," Nick concluded.

"Interesting idea, Nick," Shaun replied. "But the list of passengers in first class did not match any names from the flight into St. Louis with the people on the plane that landed in DC. That leads me to think that you and Colleen were the primary targets."

"Shaun," Nick asked. "Have we looked over the list of names in coach to see if any match the names on either flight?"

"No. We should check them out," Shaun answered. "Let's go through the names and see if any names jump out at us.

Nick and Shaun spread the passenger lists out on the bed and read down through the list of names on Flight 3348, San Francisco to St. Louis. One name matched–Johnson. Jeffrey J.

Johnson was in first class and Joseph J. Johnson sat in back in coach—row 6, seat C.

"Johnson is a common name," Nick said. "But what caught my eye were their first and middle name initials—J. J."

"Now," said Shaun. "We need to look at the passenger list on Flight 1535—St. Louis to Washington National Airport. I did not see the name 'Johnson' on the first class passenger list. Let's take a careful look at the names of the passengers in coach."

Suddenly, Nick pointed and said, "Shaun, look at this! I think we found them! Row 26, seat B—Johnson, Joseph J. Row 26, seat C—Johnson, Jeffrey J.!"

"Good work, Nick," said Shaun. "Now we know of at least two people who made the same connections that you did. We can get John Baker's detectives to look into them. It may be nothing more than a coincidence, but we need to know more about Jeffrey Johnson and Joseph Johnson.

"I don't know about you, Nick, but I am beat. Why don't we start up on this again tomorrow after Mass and breakfast?" Shaun said as he tried unsuccessfully to stifle a yawn.

"Good idea," Nick replied. "Have a good night. Thanks for your help today."

"Goodnight, Nick."

"Goodnight, Shaun," Nick replied as he closed the door.

chapter 9

Nick, Shaun, Angela, Harry, John Baker, and Catherine Harding arrived in the chapel at 6:55 a.m. The group knelt together in the first pew in the small church. It was a simple place of worship. The altar was a wooden table with a triangular-shaped pedestal base. It was stained in red mahogany and it matched the twelve or so pews in the twenty by forty foot room. A medium-size Crucifix hung on the wall behind the altar. The Holy Family was honored by wood carved statues of Mary, Jesus, and Joseph on the front right side wall of the altar, and a statue of Saint Benedict was on the opposite wall. There were seven stained glass windows on each side of the small chapel. Each window represented one scene from the Stations of the Cross. The arched ceiling was about twelve feet high on the sides and eighteen feet high in the center. The intimacy of the chapel easily lent itself to personal prayer and small group worship.

Each person in their pew offered very personal prayers to the Lord in the quiet moments leading up to the beginning of Mass. The safety of their loved ones was the paramount prayer of these believers. John Baker and Catherine Harding prayed for the souls of the police officers who lost their life in the bombing at the precinct. Harry was consumed in prayer for his daughter and her unborn grandchild.

The first reading was 1 Corinthians 13: 1–13, "If I have all faith so as to move mountains but do not have love, I am nothing. If I give away everything I own, and if I hand my body over so that I may boast, but do not have love, I gain nothing" (St. Joseph Edition New American Bible). The conclusion of the lesson read: "So faith, hope, love remain, these three, but the greatest of these is love."

After the Gospel reading, Father Chris offered these few thoughts to his family and friends. "I prayed over which reading to use at Mass this morning. The events of the past few days would lead us, any of us, to question love, and even wonder about God. Now we have felt that deep pain of loss very personally. Family, friends, fellow police officers, and innocent bystanders lost their lives within a few feet of where we stood only a second before. I cannot begin to answer the 'Why' question. All I can do is turn to the source of all love and life. I am confident that even in this direst of circumstances that love continues to exist, to grow, and will soothe the intense pain that we all feel. What will last after all this evil is over? Love. What will keep you going even in the worst of times? Love.

"That love comes from the very heart of Jesus Christ. Hang on to it, my friends. When you are sure you cannot go on another day, hang on even tighter to the love of Christ. I am convinced that his love will keep us alive now, even when evil men are plotting against us for a reason we don't even understand. Love may be the last emotion we want to feel right now, but it is the only thing that will keep us focused on doing what is right. We will be challenged in the days ahead to do what is right and that may very difficult. Without the love of God, it would surely be impossible. Keep love in your heart as these events play out. Remember that you are not alone. We are together and one in the Lord Jesus."

A breakfast of eggs, fresh fruit, toast, and fresh cinnamon buns was waiting on the table as the group walked into the dining room after Mass. The coffee was hot and the orange juice was fresh and cold. Father Frank Murphy entered the room and addressed the group.

"Good morning all. I hope you had a good night of rest. I trust that breakfast is satisfactory. If there is anything I can do for you today, please ask. Your confidentiality is secure. Have a good day ladies and gentlemen," said Frank Murphy, as he walked out of the dining room.

Angela and Catherine made small talk throughout breakfast. Detective Baker thanked Chris for the encouraging words he shared with them in prayer. "I have not heard a sermon on that particular Scripture passage," he said. "I hate to admit it, Chris, but I have not had much time for religion in my life these last few years. If I knew that I could get encouragement like you gave us today, I might get to church a little more often. I bet you hear that a lot. So many times I have the intention to attend church, but at the last minute, I opt out. I will make a resolution to try harder to get there."

"That would be nice, John. I like to remind people that some-times you have to give a little to get a little. I don't mean giving to the collection basket, I mean giving something of yourself, like your time or your attention. That is what the Lord is ask-ing. When you stop to think about it, we all have so much to be grateful for. Give the Lord something of yourself. I have found that when I do that, he usually gives me something that I least expected but sorely needed. Just be open, John, and something good will come to you," Chris concluded.

"Shaun and I made a discovery last night that may be a clue as to who is responsible for the murders," Nick said. "We were going to wake you, John, but it was getting late."

"What did you learn?" John Baker asked. "What is this clue you found?"

"We compared the passenger lists on both the San Francisco to St. Louis flight and the St. Louis to Washington flight. We discovered a name that appeared in the first class cabin in San Francisco and in the coach section of the second flight. We believe that there is a brother or son traveling with that person. The second person flew coach on both flights."

"What were their names?" asked Detective Harding.

"Their names are Jeffrey J. Johnson and Joseph J. Johnson. That is a fairly common name, so it could be possible that there is absolutely no connection between the two. But their initials would indicate they are related," Shaun replied.

"Nick, do you remember what this Johnson guy looked like?" asked Catherine. "Is there any way you could identify this man?"

"I am sorry, but no. I was so involved with my sister that I did not focus on anyone else during the flight to St. Louis."

"How about you, Angela? Do you remember this name at all?" asked John Baker.

"I really wish I could help you, but I cannot honestly say I remember him. According to this passenger list, Johnson was seated two rows behind Harry. Like Nick, when Colleen started having breathing problems, I paid more attention to her. I spent time talking to Harry and Nick, and I just don't remember anything off the top of my head about this passenger," Angela said sadly.

"Try not thinking about him," offered Father Chris. "Sometimes when I stop trying to remember something, the image comes back."

"There may be another way to identify this man," said Angela. "Have the police confiscate one of the security tapes from San Francisco's airport. I think I would recognize him if I saw a picture. We should also get the tapes from St. Louis and Washington National. If these two men walked out together, we will definitely know who they are, and then you can arrest them," said Angela.

"Good thinking, Angela," said Catherine. "John, you can explain to Commissioner Dillon what we are doing. I think this is a big step, and we should get on it this morning."

"We also talked about sending Angela undercover as a nun.

We want to get word to Harry's daughter and Nick and Shaun's wives that they are okay. We thought that we would plan our memorial services, which Nick's sister, Sister Sharon Marie, would naturally attend. Angela, dressed in a nun's habit, would visit with all the families of the 'deceased' and not draw any suspicion. We need to stay 'dead' for a while yet. Are we all in agreement with this plan?" asked Nick.

"Yes," said Harry, "if I can be so bold as to speak for the rest of us."

"That's okay, Harry," said Detective Baker, "We all think it will work." My biggest concern is for our safety and the safety of our families. Only Commissioner Dillon knows we are alive, but he does not know where we are. Our secret and our lives are in the hands of Father Frank Murphy. "Chris, can we trust this man with our lives?"

"Yes, John, I believe we can," answered Chris. "But I don't think we should share any of our information or strategy with him. The less he knows about what we are doing, the better for us and the safer for him."

"The first thing I will do this morning will be to call Commissioner Dillon and have him start gathering some information on the two Johnson men and request the security tapes from San Francisco International and the St. Louis airport. I will also get the ball rolling on the memorial service. We need to secure a religious habit for Angela.

Does anyone have ideas on how to get a habit?"

"I can make a habit," Angela replied. "We need to get some material to make a skirt and a veil. Catherine and I can pick up what we need at a nearby mall. If there is a religious store in the area, I will purchase a crucifix and rosary. I am confident I can conceal myself well enough to fool anyone."

"That sounds like a plan. Ask Frank Murphy for the car and directions to find the stores you need. I suggest you be as indiscreet as possible. We don't want to draw any attention to ourselves," John Baker instructed.

"I agree," said Catherine Harding, "We do not want to be recognized by anyone," she said as Angela opened the door.

"Does anyone else have any ideas on our next move?" asked Baker. "No? Then we will get together again later this afternoon to see our new 'Sister Angela' and to discuss what we get back on the Johnsons. I'll see you all later today."

chapter 10

A dark limousine turned into the private drive and made the long sweep up the 'U' shaped lane that led up to the house. The driver stopped by the main door, got out, walked over to the passenger side rear door, and opened it. A tall man in an Armani suit got out and walked quickly up the steps of the large Tudor style mansion. His wing-tip shoes reflected the lights flooding into the gardens surrounding the large home. The house was grand in an almost European way. The stones used in construction were cut large and heavy. While only eight years old, it looked ninety. Ivy clung to the walls and crept up to the roof ninety feet off the ground. A neatly dressed woman wearing a dark dress with a white apron greeted the guest.

"Good evening, Colonel."

"Good evening, Nancy," he replied. "Any messages or phone calls this afternoon?" he asked curtly.

"Yes, sir," the woman answered. "Your messages are on your desk. Your private line did receive one telephone call about an hour ago. As per your standing instructions, I did not answer it."

"I am expecting a guest for dinner this evening. I want everything prepared and served by seven o'clock," the man said.

"Yes, sir."

He walked through the main hallway of the large house. The entry had marbled floors and the main stairway to the second floor was also marble. The foyer ceiling rose to a height of thirty feet. It was an impressive and daunting entrance. Making his way to the study, the six foot tall master of the estate opened the door, walked in, and locked the door behind him. The desk in the study was a masterpiece Romweber original. The edge of the top was hand-carved, as were the panels on the front and sidewalls of the massive seventy-eight inch by forty-two inch piece of art. It resembled the President's desk in the Oval office, which was also a Romweber. The chair behind it was an original Charles Eames design covered in leather. The back credenza matched the desk It was a custom piece that contained a safe, a computer platform, and an electronic drawer that held a telephone, a fax/scanner machine, and the connections for all the tools in the unit. Behind the credenza was a large curtain behind which one would assume was a window. Below the main desk center drawer was a control box. The Lord of the Manor pushed the top button, and the curtain opened to a reveal a wall of monitors. There was a separate control box for the monitors in the credenza. Once turned on, each monitor showed a different section of the interior and exterior view of the estate. The box enabled the user to move the hidden cameras in whatever direction the user chose. There was also access to a tape of what each monitor recorded during the last twenty-four hours. The security of the house was controlled from this unit. The gates, doors, and windows could be opened, closed, locked, and unlocked at the controls in the credenza.

Opening the large top left drawer in the desk, the owner of the property lifted a telephone out and placed it on top. There was a small red light blinking on the face of the phone. He picked up the receiver and pushed the red button. The message began to play immediately:

"We need to talk. Call me tonight on my private line."

Pushing the delete button on the private telephone, the man

dialed the number that was known only to a handful of people in Washington. The phone was answered on the second ring.

"I received your message. Why did you call?" The words were spoken almost rudely.

"Our people thought you went a little overboard today. The explosion at the police station may threaten our security. You know it is vital that we remain invisible to everyone. Blowing up a police precinct could lead to our discovery. That is not acceptable. What do you plan to do about this, Colonel?"

"My agent had very little time to place the explosives. It was, after all, a police parking lot. I agree he may have used excessive force. However, he did eliminate several of the targets we identified. It is always unfortunate when there is collateral damage. But sometimes that cannot be helped. I can assure you the police investigation will be controlled. I am working on that now. As for our agent, he needs to be erased. It is a shame because he is quite capable, although overzealous. However, I have additional agents ready to step into his shoes. We are quite safe, I can assure you. The security of our organization is my primary concern. You may tell our people that this situation is under control."

"Our cost overruns are quite high this month. We must increase our available funds. We are holding several million dollars aside for an upcoming project. We want you to find a way to deposit another ten million into our bank. I am hoping this can be done in the next ninety days. We are counting on you and Jones. We do not want anything like the police station fiasco ever again. Do you understand?"

"Yes, of course, and I am certain we can meet your budget request."

He hung up the phone and immediately began thinking about the next assignment. There was one leftover task from the police precinct incident. He picked up the telephone and dialed a number.

"I have a security assignment for you," the Colonel said to the man who answered the phone. "It is a task that must be done as soon as possible. Our agent, Raphael, has betrayed us. We must take whatever steps necessary to correct this situation. When are you available?"

"I am ready now, sir. I can make the plan and execute it tonight. We must deal harshly with those who would betray us. I am prepared for this assignment."

"Advise me when you have completed your task."

He hung up the phone then closed the monitor curtain and locked the desk and credenza. He left the office and locked the door behind him.

Nancy quietly approached the Colonel and asked if he wanted a glass of wine before dinner.

"No, thank you. I will be in my room. Please let me know when my guest arrives," he replied as he walked up the long, curved marble stairway to his bedroom.

chapter 11

A dark green sedan pulled up outside a modest two story home in the suburbs of Washington DC. The driver approached and rang the doorbell. A man answered.

"Yes, may I help you?" greeted the owner of the home.

"Hello, my name is Tom Newton. I belong to the neighborhood association, and we were hoping you would join us in the Neighborhood Watch Program that works in conjunction with the police in an effort to patrol our neighborhood. May I come in for a minute? I have some literature for you about the program."

"Well, I don't have much time, but okay, come in for a minute."

Tom Newton stepped in the house. The host turned to close the front door and never felt the bullet ripping into the back of his brain. He was dead before he hit the floor. The silencer on the 45 automatic muffled the sound of the gunshot. The visitor went to his car and retrieved a vinyl body bag and a small suitcase of cleaning materials. Returning to the house, he placed the body in the bag and zipped it shut. He put on latex gloves and hospital scrubs over his clothing and shoes. He had all the cleaning materials needed to erase a crime scene. In a matter of fifteen minutes, there was no evidence of the murder he just committed. He placed all the cleaning materials in the body bag and carried it out to the trunk of his car. He never left a fingerprint, a hair, or anything else that could be discovered by the police forensic experts. The car pulled quietly away from the house. There were no tire tracks left on the street. It was as if he was never there. Agents never met each other since they were selected and trained individually. Their allegiance was to the cause of the organization because they never met the leaders of the agency. Their assignments came from two men–the Colonel and Jones. Agents knew when either man called they had to be ready on a moments notice to carry out orders.

Twenty minutes later, the sedan pulled into a secluded rear parking lot at Bayside Mortuary. The agent reversed up to a door in the back and turned off the engine. Opening the trunk, he carried his package into the preparation room of the funeral home. He walked over to the crematory and turned on the ovens. It took about fifteen minutes to reach the 1,600 to 1,800 degree temperature required to reduce bone to ash. The remains were placed on the roller table and slowly moved into the oven. The door closed automatically. It took about two hours to complete the grisly task. The oven cooled, and the platform receded back into the cold, soulless room. There were a few pieces of bone left on the tray. He placed these through a processor, and soon there was nothing but miniscule fragments and ashes. These he placed in a paper bag before antiseptically cleaning the burn room and turning off the lights and locking up the mortuary. He drove away without anyone knowing he had ever been there. The next step was to dispose of the ashes and the automobile. After a short drive the ashes were emptied into the Potomac River. He was careful to burn the paper bag after its contents were scattered into the water. He drove the car a half hour north of DC to a metal recycling center. After cleaning the car thoroughly and wiping all possible prints from the car, he drove it to the magnet next to the crusher. The magnet was activated, and it lifted the sedan into the air and moved it into position inside the crusher. The last sound he heard as he walked out of the salvage yard was the crusher destroying the automobile.

Such was the manner this organization utilized to erase mistakes and cover-up their own crimes. It was a brand of justice without mercy.

chapter 12

Door chimes rang out through the grand entry to the mansion. The maid, Nancy, opened the door and welcomed the guest.

"Good Evening, Mr. Jones. We are delighted you could come for dinner this evening. May I hang up your coat?"

"Please. Is the Colonel in the dining room?"

"No, sir, he asked me to inform him when you arrived. Let me take you to the bar and get you something to drink. I will then alert him as to your arrival."

"That will be fine. I will have my usual," Mr. Jones said.

"Crown Royal and ice, chipped," the maid said aloud.

"You are correct, Nancy. I am flattered that you remember."

The server poured the drink and then walked up the stairs and knocked on the door. "Sir, your dinner guest has arrived," she said politely.

"Thank you, Nancy. I will be right down."

A few minutes later, both gentlemen stood by the bar, shook hands coldly, and took several small sips of their drinks. Minutes later, the maid entered to announce that dinner was served. The two men proceeded into the dining room and sat down together at the end of a well-appointed table.

"Nancy, we would like not to be disturbed during dinner. If I need anything, I will buzz you on the intercom."

"Very good, sir," replied the maid, as she left the room.

Turning to Jones the Colonel began, "We have a request for additional funds. In the past you, have been successful in raising significant sums for the organization. The ante has been raised a little, and I want to give you some time to plan your strategy in meeting this significant request. Our organization has grown significantly. We have members in every city in the nation. We recognize your contributions to this growth and we will continue to support you as well. Your work has been vital to our success. Neither the government nor the police are even aware of our existence. This is one of your greatest strengths. It is men like you who understand the necessity of confidentiality in certain matters. Our work in one part of the nation is unknown to our members in other locations. Secrecy is our coat of arms, and silence is the weapon displayed upon that shield. Our goal in this new campaign is ten million dollars. Do you consider this goal within reach?"

"It is going to be more of a challenge than previous campaigns. I may need a week or two to develop the plan and secure several additional donors to make pledges. But, to answer your question, yes, I believe it is within reach. May I have several weeks to put a program together?" Jones inquired.

"Two weeks would be fine. I would like to advise the chief that the funds will be available within ninety days. As you develop your game plan, keep that ninety-day target in mind. I am confident that you can meet your goal within the time frame. Your fund-raising skills are unmatched."

"Thank you, sir. I do what I can. Is there anything else?"

"Yes. As you know, we had to take some extra measures to close the recent deal with the package from San Francisco. It was a challenging project due to the last minute maneuvering with the airlines. It appears that the matter has come to a successful conclusion with the activity at the police precinct early today. Unfortunately, there is no way to absolutely confirm that the targets were erased. We would like to keep your security team on the peripherals for another few weeks. If they report anything unusual, it would be a concern to us and further action might be required. May I count on you to take care of that as well, Mr. Jones?"

"I will personally advise our security team on the matter. Put your mind at rest."

"Thank you, Jones. I knew I could count on you."

With that the Colonel rose from the table, deposited his napkin on the seat of the dining chair, and walked out of the room. Jones finished his dinner and had one additional Crown Royal and ice.

"Shall I get your coat, sir?"

"Yes, Nancy, and thank you for your kindness," Mr. Jones replied.

"Your car is right outside. Good night, sir."

Standing outside the mansion for a moment Jones chuckled. He wondered if the Colonel even knew his first name. Multiple layers of security insured that the leaders remained untouchable. His position was high in the corporate structure, but the top men running the organization were unknown to Jones. He looked at the window in the Colonel's second floor suite for a moment and then quickly turned his thoughts to the task ahead of him—secure ten million dollars within ninety days that could not be traced.

Upstairs, the Colonel turned on his television in time to catch a breaking news story on CNN. A tape had been delivered to the Washington news division. On that tape were three hooded gunmen with AK 47's in their hands. An Arabic spokesman claimed they were part of the terrorist's arm of the Islamic Jihad. They claimed credit for the bombing at the police precinct that morning. They claimed additional targets had been selected throughout the United States and further attacks were possible.

The Colonel smiled as he listened to the news report. A moment later, the private red telephone in the bedroom rang.

"Excellent work, Colonel, goodnight."

Moments later, the telephone on the table next to Jones' bed rang.

"My compliments, Jones, well done. The Chief was pleased with your work."

"Thank you, Colonel," Jones replied.

chapter 13

Angela and Catherine prepared for their shopping trip. The plain dresses given to them at the monastery were just right to wear in public. Store security cameras could pick them up, so the less recognizable they could be, the safer they would be. They wore parkas borrowed from the Monks coat closet, sunglasses, and headscarves. The weather was damp and cold, so they did not look out of place. In Kohl's department store, Angela selected several mid-length black skirts, several nondescript white blouses, two pairs of black vests, two pairs of plain, flat black rubber-soled shoes, and two yards of flat black linen which would become her religious veils.

Upon their return to the monastery, they returned the parkas to Father Murphy along with their gratitude for his kindness. He offered Angela a number of necklaces with crosses and religious pins to finish off her nun's habit. Catherine helped Angela with the trimming and sewing on the veils. She posed in front of a mirror and was convinced her habit was authentic. It concealed her hair and, along with the modest outfit, gave her the authentic look of a Catholic Sister. Angela was confident she could pass as Nick's sister, Sharon.

""Good afternoon, Sister, may I say, you look very nice. Is that an acceptable compliment for a religious person?" asked Harry.

"Harry, you may kneel if you like, or you may kiss my ring," Angela replied laughing.

"Seriously, you look exactly like most of the nuns I've ever seen," Harry replied.

"And just how many nuns are you seeing?" Angela said with a smile.

"That is not fair. After all, I am a doctor," Harry said with feigned haughtiness.

"What are you two talking about?" asked Nick, as he and Shaun walked down the hall by their rooms.

"What do you think? Will I pass for a nun?"

"You certainly will. I am impressed. You did a great job with the habit," said Nick. "Do you have any questions about how to conduct yourself?"

"I don't think so. Even though I am not a Catholic, I've seen nuns in public. I am not worried. Besides, I will be with Maura and Kathleen."

"That sounds like a good plan. You will become our contact on the outside until this mystery is solved. I know you will be okay," said Nick.

———

Later that afternoon, John Baker stopped by Frank Murphy's office. "Frank, are you in?" He asked.

"Yes, John, come in. What can I do for you?" Murphy replied smiling.

"I was hoping to catch the early news today. I am curious about the updated reports on the bombing at the precinct," John answered.

"That's why we keep one television in the monastery. We can catch the local news on channel twenty-four," Frank replied as he walked across the room.

The television came on, and a newscaster welcomed watchers

to the five o'clock news. "Leading off tonight's news is this tape supplied to channel twenty-four through courtesy of CNN."

The tape of the Islamic Jihad bombers came on. Both Murphy and Baker watched the clip in silence. "Can you believe this?" asked Father Murphy. "These people are out of their minds. How do we let them get in the country?" he asked in frustration.

"I don't know, Father. I just don't know," Baker replied. "I am going to give the guys the news. Perhaps we will come back later. Would that be okay?"

"Certainly, please, come back with the others," Father Murphy answered.

John Baker hurried back to the dormitory and called everyone together. "You are not going to believe what I just saw. The Islamic Jihad claimed credit for the bombing at the precinct. We all know that is a lie. Why would they do this?"

"The more important question, is why someone would make a fake tape claiming responsibility for the bombing? And, who would do it?" Shaun said quizzically.

"Could it be possible that the people who have been trying to kill us are also responsible for making the false report about the bombing?" Harry asked.

"Not only possible, they *must* be the same people. Think about it. The attempt on your lives at the airport was their first murder attempt. And remember this had to be arranged while you were on the flight home. The people behind this attempt had to have individuals ready to eliminate the poor soul who drove the bus for Double Tree. These types of crimes are well thought out ahead of time. Then the people who were in first class with you flying into both St. Louis and on the flight into DC have been systematically murdered. A week later, someone following us expected us to be in Shaun's car and but for the grace of God, someone else got in the car and was killed in our place. We have got to start figuring this puzzle out, or we will not be safe anywhere," Shaun said in frustration.

"Nick," Shaun asked. "Can you think of anything that happened while you were in California that could have possibly led us to where we are now, hiding in a monastery with our lives in jeopardy?"

"Shaun, I have gone over and over everything that happened, the people I met, the hospital in San Francisco where I found Colleen and the flight back east. I just cannot think of anything I may have seen nor done that would make us a target."

"What about the girl you met at the hotel bar? What was her name?" Shaun asked.

"It was Gretchen Sanders," Nick replied. "She was a friend of Colleen's and worked both the hotel trade and in the adult movie business as well."

"Could she be involved somehow? I am not saying she is behind all this, but she may know things that could provide answers to some of the questions we are looking at now," Shaun questioned.

"I am positive she is not involved in these crimes. However, she may have information that she doesn't know is relevant to this predicament. I have a telephone number where I can reach Gretchen. Should we call her?" Nick asked.

"People oftentimes are not aware of what they might know or exactly what they saw. Certain situations may look like one thing, but may actually be another. This gives fits to prosecutors who question eyewitnesses to crimes. Three people may see a crime committed and you will get three different descriptions of what happened. People see what their mind wants them to see," Shaun explained.

"There is another thing we started to look into, the possibility of a cover-up from someone in Washington who had purchased the services of Colleen when she worked the hotel bars along the strip in Los Angeles. Just because Scott Farmer, the aide to Senator Walley, is dead now doesn't mean he wasn't in the middle of some type of cover-up," Nick said recalling the man they discussed previously.

"But what connection would he have had to the innocent people in St. Louis who were murdered?" Harry chimed in. "If all the people in first class on both flights were targeted for elimination one would think there was some type of connection between those people in St. Louis and the people who flew into Washington National."

"That is a good point Harry," Nick answered. "Some of those people in first class boarded in Portland, just as you did."

"Harry, could there be a connection in Portland?" Shaun inquired. Could you or someone on the first leg of the flight have been targeted by someone in Portland? Do we have the names of first class passengers that boarded the plane in Portland?"

"I don't think so," replied Angela. "I could get it, but that would mean one more person knows we are still alive, and I thought we wanted to limit that information."

"Good point, Angela. Do you or Harry recall if there were any first class people on the initial flight out of Portland that continued on to the flight to St. Louis?" Nick asked.

"I am pretty sure that everyone who boarded in Portland got off in San Francisco, except Harry, of course," answered Angela.

"I don't think the answer is in Portland," John Baker said. "No one knew you and Colleen were boarding that flight until forty-five to fifty minutes before it landed in San Francisco. Unless Harry is the primary target, I don't believe this all started in Oregon."

"I cannot think of anyone who would want me dead," Harry said. "I've been out of practice there since my wife died three years ago. There are just no connections I am aware of that would place me in jeopardy. My only affiliations are with the Lions Club, the local Chapter of the U.S. Medical Assn., the Red Cross and the Chamber of Commerce. I can't think of anyone who would want to harm me."

"You are probably right Harry," said Nick. "I agree with

Shaun that this mess started in San Francisco. I think you were going to be an unfortunate and expendable party in this. I truly believe Colleen and I were the targets. Your good deed of flying with us to DC has turned into a nightmare. I don't think you or Angela were anything more than people who were at the wrong place at the wrong time."

"You may be right about that Nick," answered Angela. "But we are in it all the way now. And I don't regret it. Believe me, I don't want to die, but if I can help you in any way I will. I just wish I could remember more about that Johnson fellow in first class. If we could get a picture of him we would at least have a start in finding out who is responsible for these horrible killings."

"Nick, I think you should contact Gretchen," suggested Chris.

"I will call her today."

"I think we should go to California," Shaun suggested. "I will need to travel under a false name with false credit cards and photos. We cannot take the chance of our names showing up on a passenger list. It would not be safe for me, or for any of you."

"You are not going alone," Nick said. "I will go. I've met some of these people and I know my way around. Maybe we can assume the identities of two monks here. I doubt they have credit cards, but I am betting Frank Murphy does. If we can work with him I am sure we can become monks and fly safely out to California."

"Now that sounds like a plan," said Harry. "What can I do to help?"

"Thanks," Nick said. "You are a good man, and you would make a pretty good police officer, but I think we should leave this trip in the hands of the younger guys."

Harry thought about it for a second, and then nodded in agreement.

"We should meet later and go over as many details as possible before leaving for California. And, we want to hear from Gretchen Sanders before we leave," said Shaun.

———————

Later that day Nick walked over to the courtyard and strolled around the well-manicured garden. The thought of going back to Los Angeles and San Francisco worried him. He agreed with his brother that they should go and try to unravel the mysterious and dangerous circumstances they found themselves in. The ability of their enemy to put an assassin in place seemingly within hours was troubling. His unconscious walk through the courtyard led him to the door of the Chapel. Entering he touched the holy water fount then walked up to the front of the Sanctuary, and walked over to the carved wood statues of Jesus, Mary and Joseph. He knelt down and blessed himself again. He looked into the eyes of Joseph and prayed:

Lord, you chose Joseph as the guardian of Mary, and the protector of Jesus when he was born and while he grew up. I need your help, guidance, and strength. We have a daughter, Megan, and Maura and I are going to raise Colleen's son, Christopher. I will be their protector. We are in danger now, not unlike the danger Joseph faced when Herod ordered the death of all the infant boys in Bethlehem. We are facing an enemy we have not seen. This enemy is powerful. Help me, Lord. Show me what to do. Give us the wisdom not to let our pride place us in greater danger than we now face. Please, Lord, above all, protect Maura and baby Megan and baby Christopher. Jesus, I ask this in your blessed name. Amen."

Nick rose, blessed himself and turned to leave. There in the back of the Chapel was Shaun, Chris, Harry, Angela, Catherine and John Baker kneeling in prayer. He quietly walked past them and slipped out the door. They all recognized the danger they were facing. They all turned to God for guidance, help and protection. Nick smiled as he realized again that they all had the gift of faith, and it was a wonderful thing to behold.

Father Chris took his rosary out of his pocket and quietly asked if anyone wanted to join in the prayer. Catherine said, "I don't know the words to the Catholic prayers."

"No problem," Father Chris said. "Join in when we say the Lord's Prayer. What matters is that you are in the spirit of prayer."

"I believe in God," Father Chris began.

chapter 14

Angela arrived at Walter Reed Hospital that afternoon by cab. In the event anyone was watching Maura and Kathleen she had Father Murphy drop her off a block from the Hospital. Arriving in a taxi with a suitcase gave the appearance that she had traveled as the real Sister Sharon would have arrived in Washington.

Maura and Angela (Sister Sharon) embraced when she walked into her room. Kathleen also welcomed her to their temporary quarters. Angela knew that the primary reasons Maura was in the hospital was to ensure the newborn babies would have sufficient mother's milk for nutrition, and for her own safety. When Nick insisted that she stay somewhere safe she insisted on being with the babies. The danger to Kathleen and Maura decreased after the explosion at the police precinct. With the apparent death of Nick, Harry, and Angela, the killers had seemingly eliminated their targets.

Angela brought Maura and Kathleen up to speed with Nick and Shaun's plan to go to California to search for answers to the identity of their enemy. Neither Maura nor Kathleen was comfortable with the idea of their husbands going to California, but they also knew there would be no way to stop them. Angela also shared with Maura the plan to hold a memorial service for the "deceased." Maura felt uneasy about deceiving people, but believed it necessary to in order to discover who was behind all the killings. The Memorial service would also allow Maura and Kathleen to move about in public.

Maura contacted the pastor of her church, Monsignor Jim Wilson, who assisted her family only a few weeks earlier at Colleen's funeral. They scheduled a meeting for the following Tuesday to go over the details of the memorial service. It was very difficult for Maura to accept Msgr. Wilson's condolences on the loss of her husband, family and friends. It was a necessary deception for the safety and security of Nick, Shaun and their heroic friends who were determined to put an end to the senseless killing of innocent men and women. Angela's role in the grand plan was to play the role of Sister Sharon. Nick had called Sharon who was living in South Dakota and working as a secondary education teacher on an American Indian Reservation. He explained the situation to her and secured her confidentiality. Having Angela pose as Sharon gave them one additional set of eyes and ears to listen and convey back to Shaun and Nick any questionable actions of the people who would attend the memorial service, not to mention the additional moral support she would be for his wife and sister-in-law.

Maura and Kathleen felt it was safe to return to Maura's home, but the health of the premature infants was a concern. Their health improved daily and Dr. Elizabeth Roberts felt that another few weeks in the pediatric intensive care ward would provide both babies with the nutrition and care they needed. Maura hoped they could come home in another week, but the doctor insisted that the decision when to allow the babies to go home would be made on the basis of their growth, weight gain and overall health. Both infants had weak immune systems and that left them susceptible to colds, pneumonia and other illnesses. Maura would not put the babies at risk, even though she was anxious to have them home. Maura and Kathleen had visited the hospital chapel every morning to pray for their health and the safety of their babies, their husbands, their family, and their friends. Her daily prayer was simple, humble, and sincere: "Lord Jesus, you once were a tiny baby, like Megan and Christopher. Watch over my little ones and help them grow strong and healthy each day. Please protect my husband as he endeavors to provide safety for our family. Give me the patience I need to accept your will in all things. Bless Kathleen and her husband. Keep all of us safe under the mantle of your love. Amen."

In the midst of all the chaos and danger both Maura and Nick stayed anchored in their faith. They repressed their anger with those individuals who were trying to harm them. Receiving Holy Communion nearly every day helped them remain close to the Lord. In spite of what was happening in their world they held fast to their faith, a faith that had never been tested to the degree they faced during this time of trial.

chapter 15

Harry met Nick and Shaun on the way down to dinner. Catherine and John Baker were already in the dining room. Father Chris and Father Murphy had driven Angela into the city close to Walter Reed Hospital.

"What are your plans once you get to Los Angeles?" Harry asked. "Where do you go and who do you see first to help answer the question of who is behind these crimes?"

"I have not been able to reach Gretchen yet. I thought we would meet with her first. I don't believe that Colleen and Gretchen worked independently as 'Fly Girls'. They must have worked for someone."

"A pimp," John Baker added. "You are right. That activity is fairly well organized in every city in the country. Those girls work for someone. If Gretchen can lead you to their pimp you might get some answers. I really should travel with you. I speak the language of the street, and I am more experienced in getting people to give up information than either Nick or Shaun."

"He is right about that Nick," said Harry. "You might be more successful if John went to California with you. It would give us an extra person out there."

Chris walked into the dining room and asked, "I hope I have not missed anything. We ran into traffic on the beltway coming back from Walter Reed. Can you get me up to speed with our plans?"

"We are just discussing who would go to California, Shaun or John. You did not miss much."

"The question is, should three of you go?" asked Catherine. "John knows what to do in tight situations. You don't know what you might run into out there."

"I've been a State Policeman for ten years," Shaun replied. "I am sure I can handle trouble if it arises. I have no objection however, if John wants to go."

"Shaun should stay with us. If we are discovered, our lives will be in danger. I know that John, Catherine, and Shaun have weapons with them. God forbid you would have to use them, but it could come down to that. I do not want to discount how effective Catherine would be in a dangerous situation, but if Shaun or John were here we would have double the protection."

"I think that is a reasonable concern," said Shaun. "I will stay here with Chris and Catherine in Washington. John is well equipped to handle things with Nick out in California. One of us should stay near Maura, Kathleen, and the babies. It is a better plan for all of us. However, you have one problem: you will not have any weapons with you. You are going in disguise as monks. There is no way to get a weapon on board a plane. It is too risky to tell anyone that you are traveling under cover. Perhaps Angela would know someone at United Airlines who could help with this, but that means telling someone else we are still alive. I don't think that is an option at this time."

"You're right, Shaun," added Catherine. "We have got to keep our secret. Until we know who is behind all this we won't be safe, not here in Washington, not in New Jersey. Let's stick to our plan. John and Nick will go to California. Shaun will remain here with us at the Monastery. Angela will stay with Maura and Kathleen."

"John, you and I need to meet with Frank Murphy and secure

our identities as Benedictine monks. We need a credit card, driver's license and the monk's robes. Is there anything else you can think of that we will need?"

"I wish we could take my revolver along," Baker replied.

"I will ask Gretchen how we may go about securing a firearm. She may know somebody who can help you in that regard. I know she experienced a side of life that we have not. I am glad you will be with me, John. I am sure to learn something. I also appreciate your willingness to protect my family," Nick concluded.

"My pleasure, Nick," responded Baker. "My security is now tied with the safety of your family. Believe me, I want to know who is behind the car bomb at the precinct. I lost brothers in that attempt on our lives. That brazen attack reveals the power and the desperation of the people behind the attempt on our lives."

———

Later that night after dinner, Nick tapped lightly on the open door of Father Murphy's room. "Come in, Nick. What can I do for you tonight?"

"May I use the telephone in the office? I have a friend in Los Angeles I have been trying to reach," Nick answered.

"Go right ahead."

Nick picked up the telephone and dialed Gretchen Sanders. Gretchen had told him at Colleen's funeral that she intended to move home. He hoped she had not left Los Angeles yet. On the fourth ring Gretchen picked up. "Hello," she answered cheerfully.

"Hello Gretchen. This is Nick O'Connell."

"Hello! I am happy to hear from you, and surprised too. What can I do for you?" Gretchen replied warmly.

"Gretchen we need your help, and your discretion too, Nick began. "Have you heard about the bombing at the Washington Police Precinct?"

"Yes. I saw the news reports. It was awful, all those lives lost in the explosion," Gretchen said compassionately.

"We were the people targeted by the killer," Nick explained. My brother, along with Dr. Harry Booth, Angela, and two DC Police officers left Shaun's car at the precinct while we visited Harry's daughter who had barely escaped an attack the previous night. When we returned to the precinct an officer volunteered to move the car. When he turned the key the car exploded. We escaped by the narrowest of margins."

"Oh my gosh! That is terrible. But how can I help you?" asked Gretchen.

"First and foremost, you must tell no one you spoke with me. I mean absolutely no one! What we have learned about the people behind this is they are powerful and have access to information around the country in a matter of seconds. Our very lives are in the hands of a small number of people we have confided in. Can you do this?" Nick asked.

"Yes, Nick. I consider you a brother as well as a friend. We met here in LA only once but I found my faith and the courage to change my life thanks to you. I am turning my life around because of you and the message you shared with me. I would do anything for you and Colleen's family."

"Thank you, Gretchen. That means a lot to me. Here is my plan: I will be traveling to LA in another day or two with the police officer who was reported killed in the car bombing. We are going undercover as Benedictine Monks using different names and identities. I want to find the man who manages the 'fly girls'. We think he might lead us to the next person on the ladder. I want to talk to Joey Bean again too," Nick added.

"The guy who set us up as 'fly girls' was the jerk who Colleen and I hired as our agent and manager," Gretchen replied. "His name is Devon Sharpe. I don't know for sure, but I think he has ties to the organized crime. He is a real creep. I have been avoiding him and ignoring his frequent telephone calls. I have not told any of my friends here that I am going home to Texas. I am paying all my bills so when I leave no one will come after me for money. I want to make a clean break out here, and no one will know where I have gone," Gretchen said with a confidence that barely concealed her own fear.

"I want to meet with you when we get to Los Angeles. One thing we might need is a way to purchase a firearm. The police officer traveling with me cannot bring his weapon along. I am hoping there will be no occasion to use it, but I agree with my friend that we should have a gun for protection," Nick explained.

"I have a gun. It is a .25 caliber pistol. I have never used it. In fact, it scares me a little. I got it after some of my friends were robbed. I will be glad to give it to you," Gretchen offered.

"Thank you. When we get to California we need to meet away from your usual hangouts. Since we will be dressed as monks, let's meet in a public place or at a church. I will telephone you after we land and we can finalize those details. Gretchen, I promise not to put you in danger. I will understand if you don't want to get involved," Nick said earnestly.

"Thank you for thinking of me, Nick, I want to help you. This is an opportunity for me to atone for some of the mistakes I have made in my life. I am willing to help you whatever the cost. You can count on me," Gretchen said with a quiet laugh.

"Thanks Gretchen, we will count on you. I will call you soon," Nick said as he hung up the phone.

Nick walked over to Father Murphy and thanked him for the use of the phone.

Nick sat down on an easy chair. "Frank, you and your brother monks here have treated us with such kindness. I am very grateful for your hospitality. You have sheltered us from a very real danger. The security we feel here comes from the confidentiality you and your brothers have afforded us," Nick gratefully acknowledged.

"It is our duty to shelter and feed the homeless. Beyond being a duty, it is a joy for us to share with those in need. Your need is a little different than the needs of many of our guests, but it is nonetheless a real need. I can assure you that your secret will be kept in strictest confidence. My brothers and I will protect you with our lives if necessary. Do you need anything else?" asked Father Murphy.

"Actually, yes we do. John Baker and I are going to California and we need several things. To start with we need a credit card in order to purchase airline tickets and pay for our meals and hotels while we are away. We cannot risk using our credit cards or bank cards either. They are too easily traced. The enemy we are facing has access to almost instant information. We cannot risk being discovered. Our wives, children, homes, everything would be used by the enemy to get to us. Then they would kill us all. That is what we are up against Father," Nick said solemnly.

"I knew it was serious, but I guess I didn't think it was deadly serious, " said Father Murphy.

"We will also need identities as members of the Benedictines. That includes driver's licenses, secondary photo identification, a couple of robes, sandals, the works," Nick said as he listed the items they would need in order to travel safely to California.

"We can do all that, and have it ready by noon tomorrow," Father Murphy answered.

"Thank you Frank. That would be great. May God bless you," Nick replied as he stood up to leave. Stopping at the door he turned to Father Murphy and said, "I meant what I just said, I pray that God will bless you abundantly."

Back in the dormitory Catherine and John Baker were making small talk about life in a Monastery or Convent. Nick motioned Father Chris to come into John Baker's room.

"I spoke with Gretchen Sanders. She is going to help us, and she already has a pistol that she will give to you, John. We will meet her in Los Angeles. We can count on her help, and on her discretion to keep our secret safe," Nick related.

"That is a good start for us," Baker said.

"Yes it is, John. I spoke with Father Murphy and he will have our credit card, identities and monk's clothing ready by noon tomorrow," related Nick. "We will be able to make our flight arrangements early tomorrow afternoon. If possible, we will be heading west tomorrow night on a red eye flight."

"That sounds good," offered Catherine. "The quicker we get some answers, the safer we will be."

Everything came together perfectly. Nick and John Baker each got a hair cut, and it definitely gave them a different look. Their driver's license and secondary identifications were made with their photographs in the Monk's grey cassock. Nick would assume the identity of Brother Frank Murphy and John Baker would be Brother Mark Wayne. Brother Mark gave them instructions on how to tie the cincture, the rope that went around their waist, and the proper placement of the cowl that fit snuggly on their heads. The Monks gave them two pairs of black sandals with matching socks. When they were fully dressed it was very difficult to recognize either John Baker or Nick O'Connell.

Father Murphy gave Nick his American Express Card which had only his lay name on it, and twelve hundred dollars cash. Nick protested this gift and insisted it was a loan that would be repaid upon their return.

John Baker and Nick walked back to the dormitory in their disguise. Father Chris saw them and acknowledged them saying, "Good afternoon, Brother, can I help you?"

Baker burst into laughter that spread to Nick; in a few seconds Chris realized that who it was and then he started chuckling. The laughter got louder which drew the attention from the rest of the group in the dormitory. Soon everyone was laughing. Catherine just could not believe how respectful her partner looked in his "holy clothes".

"Gentlemen," Shaun said. "You look very convincing, so much so that I was not sure it was my brother! It is a little shocking to see how reverent you both look. But I am more convinced now that you will be safe in California. I doubt anyone would recognize you."

"I agree with Shaun," said Father Chris. "You should be able to move about freely in Los Angeles and San Francisco."

"I am sorry to keep giggling," said Catherine. "But John, you are the very last person in the world who I would expect to wear the clothes of a monk."

"Hey, I have a private side that even you are not aware of. If this turns out the way we hope I may just think about converting to Catholicism and joining the Monastery," Baker replied in jest.

"I would pay to see that," Catherine replied laughing.

"Okay everybody, settle down," Nick began. "We are flying out of Harrisburg International late tonight. Frank Murphy will drive us up to Pennsylvania this afternoon. We will land in Chicago about midnight and then catch another red eye flight to Los Angeles. We should get in about four-thirty or five in the morning. We will rent a car at the airport and get started tomorrow after we have met with Gretchen Sanders. We will try to call Father Murphy around seven or eight o'clock eastern time. If you could plan to be in his office at that time we will be able to give you the latest news. You can also advise us what is happening here."

"That sounds good, Nick," said Shaun. "I hope you can get some answers quickly. Use your wit, cunning and intelligence to get information from people who won't even be aware they are revealing important details to you. I am sure that you and John will be okay. You will not be recognized. That alone gives you an advantage.

We need to find out why Nick, Colleen, Angela and Harry were targeted for murder."

Frank Murphy walked into the gathering and said, "I see you have met my two latest recruits. How do they look?"

"Excellent, Frank," replied Chris. "Your brother monks did a very good job with these two."

"I think so too. Well, we better be off. It takes about three hours to get up to Harrisburg. Chris, would you like to drive along? I could use the company on the return trip."

"I will be glad to. Thanks for the invitation."

chapter 16

Angela spent part of her day at the hospital with Megan and Christopher. It gave her great joy to help feed, change, and rock them to sleep. It was such a change in how she had lived her life over the past twelve years as a flight attendant. She never gave much thought to marriage and motherhood. While she had many male friends, she never made the leap from like to love. Her work was an obstacle to steady dating. The life of the people who fly for a living seems glamorous, but it is difficult and lonely in many respects. Many of her co-workers had become intimate with a number of different men in several different cities.

Angela chose not to live that way. She had a mature Christian attitude about sex and knew that one-night stands had big risks both physical and morally. This was not always easy. Angela knew she was very desirable. She was fit and her physical attributes attracted many suitors. She had faced temptations many times but was able to overcome her physical desires and the yearning to express herself in a sexual way. However, it was not easy. Her determination coupled with frequent prayer kept her aware of her priorities. She was determined to do what was right in the sight of God. There was another thing that was new in her life, Dr. Harry Booth. They became friends during the ordeal that sadly, led to Colleen's untimely, but heroic death.

Angela did not recognize her feelings for Harry at first. She had never truly been in love before. This was new territory for her. But the admiration, the kindness, and Harry's gentle ways fit into Angela's description of her ideal man. The strange thing was that she was sure Harry had some feelings for her.

"Sister Sharon" got along very well with Maura and Kathleen. They spent a lot of time together at the hospital and their conversations covered children, families, the future, and the fear they were now facing. Both Maura and Kathleen made an effort to call Angela, "Sister Sharon," and Angela felt comfortable getting into character. While the babies napped the trio would take walks through the hospital. Angela frequently was addressed as, "Sister." After a few awkward moments of being unsure how to respond Angela overcame her uneasiness and would reply with, "May God Bless You." This role grew on her quickly and it afforded her the opportunity to go to the chapel and pray for the safety of her friends.

chapter 17

Frank Murphy and Father Chris dropped Detective Baker and Nick at Harrisburg International Airport for their flight to Chicago where they would connect with a later flight out to Los Angeles. After leaving Harrisburg they decided to stop for dinner outside of York, Pennsylvania at a roadside diner.

"Chris," Frank began. "I have tried not to intrude or pry into your business. I can see that you are all involved in something dangerous. I have been praying for you. Is there anything more I can do?"

"Frank, you have been more than a friend, you have been a brother to me and my companions. Your generosity in allowing us to stay in the monastery, and your help with the conversion of John and Nick into two of your monks is very much appreciated. I have been reluctant to tell you what we are involved in because every time we have reached out to someone it has resulted in attacks on their lives. I was trying to protect you from all this."

"I appreciate that Chris, but your presence in the monastery has put us in danger, especially if the people searching for you find you there," Frank replied.

"I've considered that," Chris answered. "To be honest, I am concerned about it. The one thing we have in our favor is that the people who have been trying to kill us believe they have already succeeded. We were the targets of the bomb explosion at the police precinct."

"You were the targets? But the news reported that Islamic terrorists placed the bomb in the car," Frank said incredulously.

"I know. That was a way to throw the police off the trail of the real people behind the bomb. We knew then that the people after us have power, money and a way to manipulate the media. Amazing, isn't it?" Chris said to Frank.

"I really thought it was a terrorists attack. With all the turmoil in the world today I just assumed it was terrorists. I accepted that news report as an accurate explanation of what happened. I think you are right about the people behind this being very powerful," Frank replied.

"I will fill you in on everything at the right time, Frank. I promise. For now, let's enjoy a good meal and talk about our classmates and old times," Chris suggested.

Both men enjoyed a home-style meal at the diner capped off with homemade apple pie a la mode, a typical dessert in Pennsylvania Dutch Country.

Resuming their drive south on Interstate 83 Frank turned on the car radio to the all news AM channel out of Baltimore. The announcer came on with a news bulletin:

This just in: Police in Washington, D.C. have announced the attempted arrest of the three Islamic terrorists who claimed responsibility for the bombing of the Southeast Police Precinct. As the police moved in for an arrest shots were fired. Police returned the gunfire and the three terrorists died in the gun battle. We do not have the names of the three men. I repeat: the three terrorists who bombed the Southeast Washington DC Police Precinct have been killed by police in a gun battle. More details to follow.

"Well Frank," Chris asked. "Does this surprise you? There never were any terrorists. Who the police killed will probably never be known. I am not saying the police murdered these people. I believe they were sent to the location in the belief that there were terrorists there. Somehow a shot was fired, and now the three men are dead. We are facing a very powerful enemy."

"Chris, if I would not have heard it from you I would not have believed it! This is more than a little unsettling. Are you sure you and your friends know what you are doing? It seems like you are messing around with the wrong people, and that is very dangerous."

Neither man said much for the rest of the ride back to the Monastery. Frank spent most of his time in prayer.

After miles of silence Frank said, "Chris, my brother Michael is an FBI Agent. He is a good man, an honest man. Would you consider talking to him? Perhaps there is something he can do to help. I know he would keep your secret safe. What do you think?"

"I don't know Frank," Chris said. "I would have to talk to Nick first. Let me think about it, okay?"

"Sure, Chris, that is what you should do. I will pray for all of you."

It was shortly after midnight when they pulled the car into the Monastery. Both men were more than a little relieved to be safely home.

chapter 18

The flight into Chicago Midway Airport was uneventful. Nick and John had seats in coach, which was only half-full. After a brief layover they boarded the flight to Los Angeles. There were many empty seats in coach, and this allowed both men to stretch out and get some much-needed sleep.

Around four in the morning the plane hit some turbulence, which was enough to wake both men from their sleep. A flight attendant walked by their row and offered to get them some coffee. They accepted gratefully.

"Nick, we may be on a wild goose chase out here. I believe a lot revolves around what we learn from Gretchen. I am convinced that her pimp may be connected to someone in power. I have been trying to make a Los Angeles or San Francisco connection to Washington. Are we looking at government officials, CIA, FBI, or is this stretch, organized crime?"

"I don't know, John," Nick replied. It would seem that their access to information, money, and the media, all points to an organized group that operates in secrecy. This is not like the KKK with local rubes acting as demigods in one county while another does the same in the next county over. I believe this organization is sophisticated and their members move about society freely, above all suspicion.

"You have described an organization that sounds like the Cosa Nostra," said John. "I am not saying that is what we are facing, but it has many of the same characteristics. People willing to kill, people willing to die; it's downright scary."

"You are right about that," replied Nick. "When you think about it we may be in a real life David versus Goliath situation. We have stumbled onto something that no one was ever supposed to stumble into. We are risking everything we have and everyone we love. But we are in it up to our necks. If it is discovered that we are still alive, our families, children, parents, will be in jeopardy. These people will use our children to get to us. There is no compassion in this organization. We must keep that in mind as we go about our business here in California."

"You have my word, Nick," said John. "I have your back. I won't let anything happen to you. I promise to get you back safely to your wife and children."

"Thanks, John," said Nick. "I have your back too."

The plane landed at LAX on schedule. John and Nick had only carry-on luggage so they were able to move rapidly through the large terminal. They picked up a car at National Auto Rental and were out of the parking lot and on their way by six-thirty in the morning. The trip over to the area known as "the strip" was barely five miles. Both men were hungry so they stopped at a nearby Denny's Restaurant.

"Nick," John asked. "Why not telephone Gretchen Sanders now? I know it is early, but I am anxious to get started on this case."

"I thought about bringing my cellular phone along, but I was unsure how safe that would be," Nick said before getting up.

"There is a chance that if we used our own phones they could be traced. We just can't take that chance," John stated bluntly.

"You are right," Nick agreed.

Nick walked over to the pay phone and dialed Gretchen's telephone number. She picked up on the first ring.

"Hello," Gretchen answered.

"Good Morning Gretchen," Nick replied.

"Nick, is that you?"

"Yes. Hello. I hope the phone did not wake you."

"No, not at all, I've been awake for about twenty minutes. I'm just puttering around my apartment. I will be moving back to Texas soon. So I am just doing some light cleaning," Gretchen explained.

"Have you had breakfast yet?" Nick inquired.

"No, not yet," she replied. "Where are you?

"At Denny's just off the strip," Nick answered.

"I am only about ten minutes away from there," Gretchen informed him.

"Would you want me to pick you up?" Nick asked.

"No, I will meet you there shortly. I am anxious to see you again," she said eagerly.

"You must promise not to laugh," Nick instructed.

"Why would I laugh?" she asked.

"My friend and I are in disguise," he answered.

"Well, how will I know recognize you?"

"We are the only two monks in the restaurant," Nick replied.

"Monks! You are dressed as monks? I have to see this."

John was glad Nick had made contact with Gretchen, and was even happier that she was joining them for breakfast. Fifteen minutes later Gretchen walked in to Denny's and scanned the booths and tables for two monks. She took a few steps toward the non-smoking area of the restaurant and spotted the two men in gray cassocks with hoods. She walked a little closer and got a better look. It didn't look like Nick O'Connell, but they were the only two monks in the place. She approached the table and got a closer look.

"Nick," she said sheepishly.

"Gretchen. Hello," Nick said. "Let me introduce my friend Detective John Baker, also known as Brother Mark Wayne."

"It is nice to meet you Brother Mark," Gretchen answered as she shook his hand.

"It is good to meet you Gretchen. Nick has told me about you and I was looking forward to meeting you. Let me say right away, thank you for volunteering to help us. It means a lot that you stepped right up to the plate when Nick told you we were coming out here," Detective Baker said admiringly.

"I wanted to help. Nick's sister, Colleen, was a friend and I felt this may be one way to help her even though she is gone now," Gretchen said with a touch of sadness in her voice. "So Brother Mark and Brother Murphy, what is the game plan for today?"

"I wanted to spend some time talking with you before we initiated any action," John replied. "We have no idea about the enemy we are up against. They are not a local group of people. Whoever is behind all this has connections here and in San Francisco, as well as Washington DC. But every organization is made up of people in various locations who represent the entire company. I was hoping you could help us is in relating any conversations you may have had or even overheard with your manager and with any of your former clients who you met while working here at the Airport Hotel area."

"Nick, did you tell John what I used to do?"

"Yes, Gretchen. I apologize if that upsets you. It is just that we need to be open about everything, even things I know you want to forget," Nick gently explained.

"It is okay Gretchen. I wouldn't judge or condemn you for your past. I respect you for your courage to turn you life around. That is never easy," John said with encouragement and admiration in his tone.

"May I suggest," Nick said. "That we have this conversation in the privacy of our hotel suite."

After breakfast, Nick drove his car while Gretchen and John followed in hers over to the Marriot Hotel where they had reserved rooms in Brother Murphy and Brother Wayne's name. In spite of the early hour their suite was prepared and ready. The hotel attendant was quite intrigued by the sight of two monks in the company of an extremely attractive young woman.

"Will your guest be staying over with you Father?" he asked politely while thinking the worst.

"No, my sister is just visiting for today," Nick lied.

"Oh, the lady is your sister. Very good sir, here is your key. Have a wonderful stay with us and thank you for selecting the Marriot," the front desk attendant said with a smile.

"This always happens to me when I travel with a beautiful woman," John said with a slight laugh.

"How many beautiful women do you travel with, John?" Gretchen asked mockingly.

"Honestly?" John said.

"Yes, honestly," Gretchen said in reply.

"You are the first."

"Excellent answer!" Gretchen said laughing out loud.

Nick opened the door to the suite. There was a small kitchen area that included a small dining table and a living room with a sofa and two side chairs along with a television and a small mahogany desk with matching chair.

"Okay," John began. "We need to focus on solving the problem at hand. Who wanted Colleen and the rest of us dead, and was that person on the plane heading east with her? Gretchen, can you tell us about the 'clients' Colleen met when she worked the strip?"

"Colleen, Hanna and I tried to stick together when we worked the hotel bars. Devon Sharpe, our manager, wanted us to work every weekend and several nights during the week. This didn't work out because we were trying to get acting roles and, we worked part time as waitresses at the Star View Restaurant. Devon would have pushed us a lot harder but he had more than thirty girls spread out over the strip. He cut us some slack only because he was busy managing his business," related Gretchen.

"Do you know who Devon might work for? Did he ever indicate that he turned over his money to someone higher up the ladder?" Detective Baker asked.

"He always complained that he had a 'tough nut to crunch', which I interpreted to mean that he had high bills or owed money to someone. I know he forwarded cash to someone, but I don't know to who, or where it went," Gretchen said.

"What about your clients; is there anyone you can think of that might have a reputation and a secret to keep quiet?" John inquired.

"Colleen told me once she had a date with a senator from somewhere back east. I just don't remember his name. Hanna told me she had a regular date with somebody high up in Government. She only knew him as, 'Joe'. I had a few dates with some lawyers, doctors, and accountants from big time firms. These were all family men who would deny they ever dated us. They had a lot to lose if their dirty little secret ever come out."

"Tell me about Hanna," John asked.

"She is a great kid and good friend. Her name is Hanna Jones. She is from North Carolina. Her dream is to make it big in the movies, just like Colleen's and mine. But it is a lot harder than any of us thought it would be. We never quite hit the big time. Hanna reluctantly took some work in a few pornographic films to pay some bills. It is incredibly expensive living out here. We talked about the three of us getting a place together, but somehow that never happened. Working at the Star View Restaurant downtown was a way we hoped to meet people in the business, and a way to pocket cash to survive.

Then Colleen started getting sick. At first we thought it was an infection but we later learned it was morning sickness. She is pretty sure that the father of her son was Joey Bean. But it would probably take a paternity test to prove it. Hanna, Colleen, and I always insisted our dates used 'protection'. Hanna and Colleen had one guy who refused to do this. Colleen told me he had agreed one time to use one, but he discretely removed it without her knowledge. Colleen didn't realize it until it was too late. He dated me once and tried to pull that stuff with me. I told him there was no way I would see him unless he followed the rules. He went back with Hanna and Colleen rather than date me.

The thing was, he was a big tipper. I mean over and above the going rate, he would tip Hanna and Colleen an extra hundred bucks. We had to turn over seventy percent of our income to Devon Sharpe. We got to keep thirty percent and tips. Most dates were one to two hundred dollars per hour. The overnight rate was a flat one thousand dollars. Devon gave us thirty percent on overnights. We had one regular who would tip us an extra hundred for that as well. Normally we were working for thirty dollars per date, and two hundred and three hundred for an overnight," Gretchen explained ruefully.

"Is there any chance we can meet Hanna? Have you seen her recently?" questioned John Baker.

"It's been a little while. I called her and let her know I was going east for Colleen's funeral. She expressed her condolences, but was unable to come with me. I called her again when I got back from Washington. All I got was her answering machine so I left a message for her to call me. I still have not heard from her, which is odd because we usually talk at least once a week," she answered.

"Why not try to call her from here?" Baker asked.

"Sure, I know her number," Gretchen replied.

Gretchen picked up the phone and dialed Hanna's telephone number. After a few unanswered rings it was apparent that she could only leave a message, which Gretchen did, asking Hanna to call her as soon as possible.

"That is unusual. She has always been home when I call in the morning. I am worried about her. Could we drive over to her place? I want to check on her," Gretchen asked.

"Sure, we can go anytime," Nick said.

"Let's talk more about the guy who would not use protection. Any chance he paid for your services with a credit card?"

"No, John," Gretchen answered. "It was always a cash transaction."

"Any chance you know his real name?"

"No."

"When was the last time Colleen, Hanna, or you dated this guy?"

"I had an overnight with him about three weeks ago. One thousand dollars cash, paid up front. He never showed a wallet. The cash came off a money clip in his right front pants pocket. It had an inscription on it. It might have been initials or some type of identification. I never thought to really look at it. It was silver and it was round like a silver dollar and about the same size. The design was something like a dollar sign. Or it could have been the letters 'SS' or 'ZZ,'" Gretchen replied.

"It is very important that we get some idea who a few of these dates were. I think there is a tie in to Colleen's death and what has happened since then. We should talk with Hanna and ask what she might know. Then I think we should go to the library to access a computer. All of the Senate and House members are listed there, along with their photographs. The Cabinet member's pictures and biographies are listed in there also. If we can get Hanna and you to recognize someone, we will have an important lead. It is not much, but it is something," John explained.

"John," Nick asked. "Do you think Joey Bean would have any information on the people Colleen may have seen while working out here? She stayed with him for a while. Colleen told me she thought he was the father of her child. I know she gave him money that he used to buy drugs. What do you think?"

"I am not sure Nick," John answered. "He seems like small potatoes in this whole scheme. He may have just been using Colleen for his own distraction and pleasure. He is a slug and most low-level grubs like him are useless. They forget more than they know because the drugs have corroded their minds and what little intelligence they have."

"You know Nick," Gretchen offered. "Bean is not his real last name. His last name is Bolton. I was at his place once and I saw a letter addressed to him as Joseph Bolton. Bean is just a goofy name he invented while he was high one night."

"Joseph Bolton. Nick we must add that name to our list," Baker advised.

"John, I have lived a life that I sincerely regret. Something went wrong here and I fell into a trap. This trap snared my good sense and my soul for a time. I made some very bad decisions. When I met Nick something snapped. I saw the love and concern he had for his sister Colleen who was in the same boat as me. I had cut myself off from my family. I had so many high hopes for myself. I expected to be a big star, somebody famous. I was going to be earning millions of dollars.

Everything revolved around my own desires. When things did not work out I had no money, no real friends, and no one I could fall back on. The agent I hired, Devon Sharpe, lied to me about getting legitimate roles. All he had were pornographic films. I was disgusted at first, but I needed to pay my rent, buy food, and pay for my car. I was desperate. I said I would do one adult film. One led to two and then three. Between the money I earned there and the money I made at the Star View I could afford to eat. It is almost a requirement here in LA that your wardrobe be up to date and very stylish. It was all a trap. There is no way to get out of this hole. So many girls end up like me. Nick gave me the courage to call my brother. What he made me realize was that everything I was doing was for me. God did not make me to be selfish. We are made us to help others. My needs were so superficial.

"I knew God didn't like what I was doing, or what I had become. I had to face that truth. I had to go to the Lord and admit what I had done with my life. I was raised a Catholic but it was years since I had been to Confession or received Holy Communion. When I told God I was sorry for what I had done, he healed me. He healed me instantly! I prayed so hard for forgiveness after seeing Nick that I cried for two days.

"I found a church and met a priest who heard my confession. I expected him to deny me absolution. You know what he said? He said, 'God loves you, Gretchen. God forgives you. Go now and do not commit this sin again. Pray every day. Ask God to show you the way. He loves you."

"Can you believe that? All my sins and he just tells me that God loves and forgives me. I thought about that a lot. God loves me with all my faults. He loves me! Oh, I am sorry to go off on a tangent like that," Gretchen apologized.

"No apology needed. Your testimony is powerful. I am somewhat stunned and don't know what to say. Thank you, Gretchen," John stammered.

"This is a good time to head over to the library and to Hanna's apartment. Leave your car here Gretchen. We will travel together," John said.

chapter 19

The Colonel was sitting in his breakfast nook reading the Tribune Morning edition. Bold black letters two inches high practically screamed out from the front page, "Terrorists Killed in Shootout with DC Police." This was some of Jones' best work. Every step he took was calculated to lead authorities away from the organization. The police had solved the murder of the six occupants of the car that blew up at the Precinct.

The rage of the entire Metro Police Department was immeasurable. They wanted the people behind these murders and they wanted them quickly. The Mayor and even the President called for an intensive investigation that would lead to the arrest of the terrorists. The residents of DC were angry and wanted vengeance. All Jones had to do was provide three agents with identities attached to Islamic Terrorists.

The Colonel knew Jones provided the leak on where the terrorists were hiding. That amused him the most. Now the Mayor and the President would go back to life as usual. The police would be happy that they got their men and would remain oblivious to the real threat. Only certain men were able and worthy to teach this to the masses. The Colonel knew that his people already had credibility and were respected in the community. These were people of sophistication, courage, and intelligence.

As for the three terrorists, it was easy getting three volunteers from the organization. They would gladly give their lives for the cause. *These loyal, devoted comrades, they are the real heroes,* thought the Colonel. Once people understood their cause and the threat of the danger, they would thank him, but the time had not yet come to inform the rest of the population. Until that time, men like the Colonel would carry on the good fight, and young men dedicated to the cause would die. The Colonel had already arranged for the families of each of the deceased to receive one million dollars in cash from anonymous donations.

The red telephone rang again. "Colonel, I must congratulate you for the excellent work. The creativity you used in solving this problem was remarkable. The police department has heroes again. They have righted the wrong. Brilliant! May I ask if you can report any progress on the ten million dollars?

"Not yet sir, but I do have a meeting scheduled next week for an update."

"I look forward to hearing from you. Congratulations again for the outstanding work. Now sit back and enjoy your morning paper."

chapter 20

The memorial service for Nick and Shaun was well attended by family and friends. Kathleen and Maura had made the arrangements with Monsignor Jim Wilson. There were no caskets or urns. The service consisted of a period of prayer for the repose of the souls of the departed.

The half hour service concluded with the singing of "God Bless America." There was no reception afterwards. Monsignor Wilson explained to visitors that the sorrow and grief from losing Colleen, and now Nick and Shaun, was just too overwhelming for the family. They asked for prayers and understanding for all the families of the deceased.

Back at Walter Reed Hospital, Angela Carson was focused on how she could help Maura with Megan and Christopher. She enjoyed the time she was alone with the little ones. She would quietly sing to them, gently rub their tiny bellies and shower them with soft kisses. She also discovered that the interesting thing about portraying Sister Sharon was that she found herself becoming a better person. She found strength in her daily prayer in the chapel. She liked the dignity she felt wearing habit of a sister. When people approached her she was comfortable praying with them. As flight attendant Angela Carson she never would have prayed with someone in public. Now, praying felt as normal as breathing. She wondered if the aura emanating from her habit was permeating her character and her soul. She had never been an outwardly religious person. She believed in God and accepted Jesus as her Savior. What she lacked before was a daily commitment to prayer. As Sister Sharon that seemed to come natural. In her heart she felt the call to a new, higher level of individual spirituality. She did not hear a call to convert to Catholicism, but she did feel a call to personal holiness as well as a call to publicly witness to the Lord.

Angela also could envision a future life with Harry Booth. Her dreams would be enhanced if she could incorporate her new spirituality with a husband who shared her desire to serve others. It might only be a dream now, but the only way dreams come true is to first envision them, then work as hard as one can to make them come true. One of the wonderful blessings of life is that people can dream, and when they dream big it is always good to include God in their hopes and visions for the future. The miracles of God sometimes come from the dreams of ordinary women and men.

————

Out in California, Nick, Gretchen, and John finished breakfast and headed to the Public Library. Their plans were to see if any of Gretchen's clients were tied to the passenger list or held political office. The Los Angeles Public Library is classified as an example of modern architecture. It is large to overflowing proportions. It is also a haven for artists, derelicts, students, and serious researchers. Its volumes are respected and referenced all over the world, and its computer base is among the most sophisticated anywhere. It was also free.

"Where do we begin?" asked Gretchen.

"I've used similar search programs in DC," said John. "We enter a general search for current federally elected officials. We can select by State, by rank in the Senate, by party membership, by length of service, or several other ways. As the data comes up it supplies photographs, official addresses, e-mail addresses, and office telephone numbers. A secondary grouping lists all aides, secretaries, campaign managers, and staff. What we want to do is bring up every senator on the east coast, starting with Maine and going down to Florida. You want to get the photographs for both senators from each state and their top aides. If you see anyone who looks familiar, press print and we will get a hard copy of the photo. Once we are done with the Senate we can do the same for the House of Representatives. Then we can pull up information on all the cabinet members and their aides. Between the three of us we should get through this in a couple of hours. Here, I will show you how to do this. It isn't hard once you get the hang of it."

John sat next to Gretchen and Nick and walked them through the search process. He was right about it being a simple process. Nick had used computers since he began working in the logistics office for the Army. The programs he used at the CIA followed a similar set of instructions so he picked up the process quickly. Gretchen was a little slower in picking it up so John sat a little longer with her demonstrating which instructions to type in. This made her feel more comfortable. Gretchen did not mind the added attention.

The trio began searching for a man who might have purchased the personal services of Gretchen or Colleen for a date. Their purpose was to determine if a public figure could be behind the murder of Colleen and the attacks on Nick, Harry, Shaun, and their friends. If a Senator thought he might be exposed for impregnating a Hollywood prostitute, his career would be over, not to mention his marriage.

Two hours went by quickly and they had not recognized any of the senators or their aides from Florida to Maine.

"Any ideas?" asked Gretchen as she leaned back and stretched in her chair.

"Why not head west a little into Ohio, Indiana, and the rest of the central states?" John suggested.

"Do you think we are wasting our time with this?" Gretchen asked Nick and John. "I don't know for sure that the men we are looking for are elected officials."

"Let's work on this a little longer before moving on to something else. We need to be patient," Nick said calmly.

About a half hour later Gretchen stopped and stared at a photograph of Senator Bruce Purcell from Illinois. In the photo were the senator, his top aide, Lois Hanson, and her husband, Joseph.

"John, Nick, I think I recognize this man," she said haltingly.

"Is it the senator?" Nick asked excitedly.

"No, it is the husband of the senator's aide."

"John," Nick said. "Look at this name, Joseph J. Hanson."

"Joseph Hanson," Nick said slowly. "I don't recall that name from the passenger list. His initials are J. J., like the Johnson guy, but Hanson was not on the list. I am sure about this."

"It is possible that his wife uses her maiden name?" suggested John Baker.

"I think I remember him." Gretchen said thinking aloud. "There was something strange. Yes, I think I remember. He wanted two girls. He didn't want both for himself. He was paying for another guy to be with another girl. It was a little weird, but I saw a lot of weird guys with many strange requests. Colleen told me about him, and I think Hanna ended up dating this guy. I don't know who went out with the other guy."

"I told you we had to be patient. Now we have something to go on. And the fact that this guy may be Johnson is important," John said.

"Can we go see Hanna now?" asked Gretchen. "It has been a few hours since we called. I will try to reach her again. She is usually home in the morning."

"That sounds like a plan. Go ahead and call her while we clean up here," replied Nick.

Hanna did not answer. This concerned Gretchen because it was just not like Hanna to be away. John suggested they drive to Hanna's apartment to see if she was home and if everything was all right.

Hanna's home was situated in an old house that was nicely converted into three apartments. She lived on the first floor of the Victorian style home.

After knocking on the door and banging on the front window Gretchen took out a key to the apartment that Hanna gave her to use in emergencies. She opened the front door and called to her friend.

"Hanna, Hanna, are you home? It is me, Gretchen. Hanna?"

Nick and John walked ahead of Gretchen into the silent apartment. Nick walked through a doorway and entered the kitchen.

"John, come here, quick," he yelled. "Gretchen, dial 911. We need medical help right away! Hurry!"

John walked around the corner into the kitchen and came to an abrupt halt.

"Gretchen, don't come in here. Stay out!" ordered John.

Gretchen ignored John's order.

"Oh my God!" Gretchen screamed. "Hanna, Hanna, oh no."

Nick stood up and put his arm around Gretchen and walked her out of the room. He dialed 911 and told the operator they needed an ambulance and police at 3348 Swann Drive. Gretchen continued sobbing and shaking as she sat down in the living room.

John saw a puddle of blood coming from a large knife still embedded in the center of Hanna's chest. He knew enough not to touch anything. He felt her for her pulse and there was none. She was also cold to the touch. The scene revealed a struggle. There were pots and pans on the floor as well as drinking glasses and broken bottles. Drawers were open and pulled off the glides. Hanna was dead.

The police and ambulance arrived within five minutes. John

introduced himself as Brother Mark Wayne and Nick as Brother Frank Murphy to the Policewoman.

Moments later the emergency team officially pronounced Hanna dead. The rescue team leader asked the police officer for permission to remove the body. Gretchen could not look as they placed the corpse into a body bag and onto the gurney. She closed her eyes and shivered as it rolled past her to the front door.

Nick, Shaun, and Gretchen were questioned by Police Officer Michele Duffy, who asked what they knew about the victim or the attack. Duffy was observing the apartment as she questioned Gretchen, John, and Nick about Hanna. The policewoman stopped at the dining room table and reached down to touch a book placed in the center of the table.

"Have any of you touched this?" the officer asked.

"No, what is it?" John inquired.

"A Bible. It is opened up to the Book of John, Chapter 6. Miss Jones must have been an ardent reader of the good book. She has highlighted passages all over these pages, and she made handwritten notations on the pages as well," answered Officer Duffy, as she continued to thumb through the book.

Gretchen looked at Nick in surprise and simply said, "I never knew Hanna read the Bible. She never told me."

"Miss, do you know the victim's full name. Were you friends with her?" asked Officer Duffy as she took out her notepad and began writing.

"Her name was Hanna Marie Jones," replied Gretchen. "We were friends for several years."

"What did she do for a living?"

"She was a waitress at the Star View Restaurant. She was also an actress."

"Brother Murphy, what is your relationship to the deceased?" asked the Officer.

"None. We are here in Los Angeles visiting my cousin,

Gretchen. She wanted to introduce us to her friend before we went sight-seeing," Nick explained.

"Did you or your friends touch anything in the kitchen?"

"No Officer. I did reach over to check for her pulse. There was none. I did not touch anything else," John answered.

"How long were you in the house before you found the deceased?"

"We were here less than five minutes."

"How did you get into the house?"

"I had a key to Hanna's apartment. She also has a key to mine. We always kept it handy in case we locked ourselves out. I used my key to let us in," Gretchen said in a wavering voice to the female police officer.

"Do you know anyone else who has a key?"

"No."

"Do you know anyone who would want to harm your friend?"

"No."

"Did she have a husband, boyfriend, or anyone else close to her that might have gotten into a fight with her that could have led to her death?"

"No. She was not married. She got along well with everybody. I am sure she was not dating anyone exclusively. We were close friends. She would have told me if she had a serious boyfriend," Gretchen explained.

"Where can we reach you? Is there a telephone number we could call?"

"Yes," Gretchen replied as she handed the policewoman a piece of paper with her name, address, and telephone number.

"Brother, where can we reach you and your companion?" asked the policewoman.

"We are staying at the Airport Marriot. We are only here for a few days, and we hoped to visit San Francisco while we were here," said Nick.

"If necessary, how would I reach you at your Monastery in Washington?"

"Here is our contact information in DC," Nick said as he wrote the address and telephone number on a sheet of paper.

"Your telephone number is 301–555–5147, correct?" she asked as she repeated the number back to Nick.

"Yes ma'am," Nick confirmed.

"Thank you for your cooperation. I am very sorry about the death of your friend," offered the Policewoman sincerely.

"One other thing Miss, do you know the deceased parents or how to reach them?"

"I met her mom once when she came for a visit last year. I believe her name is Helen. She lives about an hour south of here. Hanna had an address and telephone book. I think it is in the corner lamp table," Gretchen said as she walked over to the table. She opened a small drawer and lifted out Hanna's telephone address book. She looked up the number for Hanna's mother.

"Would you mind staying a moment while I call her mother?" asked the policewoman as she dialed the number.

"Of course," replied Gretchen.

"Hello," answered a woman's voice.

"Hello, is this Mrs. Jones, Mrs. Helen Jones?"

"Yes, this is Helen Jones. Who is calling?"

"Mrs. Jones, this is the Los Angeles Police Department calling. My name is Officer Michele Duffy. Is your daughter Hanna, Hanna Marie Jones?"

"Yes. Why? Why are you calling?" Mrs. Jones inquired.

"Mrs. Jones, I am very sorry to tell you this. Your daughter, Hanna, was murdered in an attack that took place in her apartment. We need to have you come to the Los Angeles Medical Center."

Helen Jones dropped the telephone and slid to the floor in tears. Her husband, John, ran to her and picked up the phone.

"Hello, who is this? What is going on?" he snapped.

"Is this Mr. Jones?

"Yes. What has happened?"

"My name is Officer Duffy, and I am so sorry to inform you that your daughter was killed this morning in her apartment. It is important that you come to the Los Angeles Medical Center as soon as possible."

For Nick and John, the young woman's murder erased the good feelings they gained from their discoveries in the library, and it added another unanswered question.

For Gretchen the sudden and treacherous loss of her friend was devastating.

John, Gretchen, and Nick sadly made their way back to the Marriot. It was nearly four o'clock and they were tired, hungry, and discouraged. They talked about the crime and figured the murder of Hanna Jones would fit into a numbers of different scenarios:

1: It could have been a robbery that went awry when Hanna was home. There was ample evidence in the kitchen that there had been a struggle.

2: It could be the work of an unknown serial killer. While this was a remote possibility, nevertheless it had to be considered. Several coeds from USC had been murdered over the last two years. No arrests had been made and the crimes remained unsolved.

3: It could be tied to Colleen's murder. This would indicate the people who killed Colleen were also responsible for Hanna's death. This connection would mean the conspiracy was widening. It could also mean that Nick was getting closer to whoever was behind all the murders.

4: It could be the work of a disgruntled customer seeking revenge on the women he paid to date.

Detective Baker, aka Brother Mark, knew it was very painful

for Gretchen to talk about Hanna's death, but it was important to look closely at what happened. Colleen, Hanna, and Gretchen were good friends, and now two of them were dead. Could someone have targeted all three for death? If the answer to that was yes, then Gretchen had to be protected.

"I think we have to let the police know about our concerns," John began. "If this is not just a random murder we should let the police know that we believe Gretchen needs protection. If they place you under protection and the killer tries again you won't be alone. The police will be there to arrest or take down the perpetrator."

"John, I don't think I can trust the police. You were almost killed in the parking lot of a police station! I am ready to leave Los Angeles today. I feel safer being with you," Gretchen replied nervously.

"You would have to dress modestly if you travel with us. Two monks and a beautiful young woman will attract people's attention," Nick stated clearly.

"That is not a problem," replied Gretchen. "When I made the decision to give up this life I went through my wardrobe. I had an abundance of outfits that were way too revealing. They were the type of clothes that attracted men on the prowl. I took them to the clothing box and gave them all away. I read an article that explained the types of things that reveal our character. The writer said that verbal, clothing and body communication define who we are to other people. It is not how we see ourselves, it is how we are seen and perceived by the people who look at and judge us. I thought about that a lot. Regardless of how innocent or provocative I may have thought my clothing was, it did not represent the *real* me–the person I have decided to become. I guess what I am trying to say is that I finally realized that I was sending mixed messages to the people I met, and those messages, in some cases, screamed, 'Look at me, I'm interested in having sex with you." What I saw in Nick was the quiet confidence that comes from doing what is right. I want that, I *really* want that! That is why I can now safely say that I will not embarrass you. Please John, I am scared and do not want to take a chance of becoming the third victim of the man who has killed my best friends."

"Okay," replied Nick. "I vote yes."

"You're in," said John. "We will go back to your apartment and pick up what you need and be on our way."

Nick and John decided to see Joey Bean because they wanted to get a better feel for the relationship Colleen had with him. Even if Bean was an alcoholic and heavy drug user, he might have had some information that could help solve the mystery of who killed Colleen.

It was after six o'clock as the newly formed trio headed into the city. The freeway was jammed and it would probably take an hour to get to Joey Bean's place.

"I don't think we will make it downtown for another hour or two. Anyone interested in stopping for dinner and getting our hotel for the night?" Nick said as the car inched along in traffic.

After John and Gretchen agreed, Nick pulled off the expressway at the first off ramp he spotted. About one mile off the expressway Nick pulled into a Comfort Inn. They parked near the main entrance and secured two rooms, side-by-side

"Let's meet here in fifteen minutes. There is a Italian restaurant next to the hotel," Nick suggested. "Is that satisfactory, Brother Mark?"

"Absolutely, Brother Murphy," John replied with a small grin.

"That sounds good to me too," Gretchen agreed.

Their rooms were adjacent on the second floor of the Inn. Nick and John stretched out on the queen-sized beds and relaxed, thinking about the events of the day.

"I think it is a good idea to have Gretchen travel with us. At least we know she will be safe," Nick stated confidently.

"I'm glad she will be with us. She is a bright young woman, and very attractive," John replied.

"You do like her, don't you, John?" Nick said.

"Yes, I do, but I did not expect to like her this much. I confess I am interested in learning more about her. It's not just her looks. There is something about Gretchen that resonates with me. She is vulnerable, yet strong. She has made a world of mistakes, but she has a goodness about her that is infectious. This sounds ridiculous; I'm a cop, a confirmed bachelor. Yet, here I am interested in a woman with a past that, well, is colorful to say the least. I admit there is a physical attraction, but what I have been feeling is something deeper than that. I don't know where this will lead. I will put that in God's hands. In the meantime we have our work to do. The job got a little more complicated by adding Gretchen to our team. This gives us one more reason to make sure we find out who is behind these crimes and put a stop to them."

"Hey, are you guys ready?" Gretchen asked as she tapped gently on the hotel room door.

"Coming," Nick said as he and John walked out to meet Gretchen. "Sorry to keep you waiting. We were talking about how to proceed and prioritize our actions. We have a limited amount of time so we want to focus on the names on our list of people that we put together."

"Let's enjoy dinner tonight and start working on this tomorrow," Nick suggested.

After dinner Nick called Harry back at the monastery. While he missed Maura considerably, he did not want to take the chance to telephone her at their home for fear that the telephone may have been bugged by the people who had gone to extremes in an attempt to take their lives. While Shaun and Nick felt somewhat safe because they had been declared dead at the blast site, they still were uneasy that someone may be watching Maura for any signs that they were still alive. Having found no remains at the blast site due to the intensity of the explosion gave Nick and the others some time, but their killers could not know for certain the targets were, in fact, dead. Nick could not risk placing his loved ones in jeopardy. So, for now, all communication had to go through third parties.

"Nick," Harry said, "It is good to hear from you. How is it going out there?"

"It is troublesome, Harry. We met with Gretchen and planned to visit her friend, Hanna, who was also close to Colleen, but when we got to her apartment we found her dead."

"Nick, how did she die?"

"She was murdered, stabbed in the heart with a large knife. Gretchen was devastated. Colleen had two close friends here in California, Gretchen and Hanna. Now, Colleen and Hanna are gone. John and I decided to keep Gretchen with us. I think she is in danger. I don't want to put us in jeopardy, but we could not leave Gretchen here."

"I agree. You must assume Gretchen is a target as well. You and Detective Baker must be alert for any danger. What is your next move?"

"We will visit Joey Bean tomorrow. We found out his real last name. He is Joey Bolton. I hope he can give us some decent information. From there we are heading to San Francisco to track down Maryanne Logan and Dr. John Walters."

"Nick," Harry asked, "Joey Bean is really Joey Bolton?"

"Yes, why?"

"It could be nothing, but Joseph Bolton is the Surgeon General of the United States," Harry said.

"Well, it could be another Bolton," Nick replied.

"I don't think so. I read my recent copy of the USMA Magazine. They did a profile of Bolton and his family. He said his son, Joey, was studying at UCLA. I am sure it is the same guy. I don't know what this means in the grand scheme of things, but suppose, and I admit this is a long shot, but suppose that Joey wanted Colleen out of the way. He didn't want her to have the baby. After Colleen's funeral I recall you telling us that Joey wanted to take Colleen to an abortion clinic when she told him she was pregnant. I am sure that Joey's father would not have been pleased that his boy had impregnated his girlfriend, especially since Colleen had worked as a call girl from time-to-time. I think that this is something to think about," Harry said.

"Just so I know, the USMA is the United States Medical Association, right?" Nick inquired.

"Yes. I have belonged since I got my medical license. It is a good organization with local chapters, state chapters and a strong national presence in Washington, DC. It is a very well funded group. Every physician and surgeon in the country belongs. Their library is the best in the world and the computer system is a unique program designed by the best in the industry," Harry said admiringly.

"That is important to remember. Do you have access to the computer?" Nick asked.

"Yes, but remember, I am supposed to be dead, and if I logged on to the system, that information becomes available to anyone in the system, and that could endanger all of us."

"Harry, do you have a physician friend or relative that you could trust with your life?" Nick inquired.

"I think so Nick, but it could expose us. I would not want to add to the danger we are already facing," Harry observed.

"Of course you are right, but give this some thought," Nick suggested.

"Give me some time. I will sleep on it and let you know the next time you call. I know it is important, Nick. We just need to be very careful. Don't you agree?"

"Yes, I do. You are probably right," Nick replied. "I need to think about what we would hope to learn by getting into their system. There would be no need to risk our necks if the information we want isn't there. Let's both sleep on it, okay?" Nick ended.

"Good thinking," Harry replied lightheartedly.

"Have you talked to Angela?" Nick asked.

"Yes. She reports that Kathleen and Maura are fine and they miss you very much. We all wish this ordeal was over. Maura wants you to come home, even if it is to the Monastery. We are all worried about you and Detective Baker in California. We all pray for you at mass in the morning, and throughout the day. I think I may now know more about Catholicism than some of my Catholic friends do," Harry said laughing.

"Well, if anyone needed a dash of holiness, it was you," Nick retorted. "Seriously Harry," Nick continued. "I will talk to John about the USMA thing and we will get back to you in a day or two. I am not sure if I can call tomorrow, but I will get back to you as soon as possible. Goodbye, my friend. Give my regards to everyone."

"Goodbye, Nick, and may God to keep all of you safe."

chapter 21

Mr. Jones arrived at home at six-thirty every evening without fail. You could set Big Ben by the exactness of Jones' habits. The only variable was his suit—all were dark shades of blue, grey, and black. From ten yards away they all looked the same. His regularity was carried over from his time in the US Marines which he joined after graduating from Duke University where he earned a Bachelors and Masters Degree in Government Science. After three years in the USMC he left the service and returned to Duke University where he earned his Medical Degree. He graduated near the top of his class at Duke, and began an internship at Johns Hopkins in Baltimore. He completed his studies and graduated as a Doctor of Anesthesiology.

There were more job offers and business opportunities for Jones than he expected. One recruiter's letter stood out among all others. It contained an invitation for dinner. If Jones was interested in leading a nationwide group that impacted the lives of all Americans, and if he was interested in creating government policy without the nonsense of elections and cabinet appointments, and if he had a vision of the future that meant true freedom, he would accept the invitation and have dinner the next evening.

Jones was blessed with an intuitive sense that enabled him to know when someone was being honest or not. This dinner invitation intrigued him to the degree he had to accept it. There he met the Colonel for the first time.

Recalling that dinner now, Jones realized that he had accepted the job just by accepting the invitation. The Colonel talked about power, real power, and he talked about a future prosperity for America. He talked about providing healthcare, education, housing, food, and job opportunities to Americans who were willing to work for those blessings; he talked about how things really got done in government; and he spoke of the need for organizations that operated with great discretion. The position the Colonel had in mind for Jones was as a director of an Organization. The position would involve raising private funds to accomplish short and long-term goals; it would involve recruiting and training individuals who shared the same dreams and ideals of the Company. It would require bending the standard rules of law from time-to-time in order to ensure the ultimate success of the company. Success for the company meant success for the America the Colonel's organization visualized. If Jones was interested in a position that would utilize his education, his leadership abilities, his contacts from college, the Marines and Johns Hopkins, then this was the job for him.

The most interesting part of the proposal was the compensation package. He could name his salary and money was available to him for any personal use he desired. Should he need money to buy a home or an automobile, it was available to him. In exchange for the liberal salary plan, Jones would be called upon to make certain things happen, things that could not be traced to the organization. This level of expediency was acceptable to Jones. He learned many things in the Marines, and expediency for the greater good was acceptable to him.

Over the past few years Jones had invested wisely with a financial advisor who stayed on top of his stocks, bonds and mutual funds. In less than four years Jones' personal worth exceeded two million dollars. He had the financial security and the power he envisioned for his career. In addition he had successfully orchestrated his division's investments and took its net value from one hundred million to seven hundred million dollars in a little over three years. The accountants and investors on his staff were graduates of Wharton, Harvard, and Stanford Universities. These men were loyal to the company and worked in well-appointed and secure offices. The Colonel never asked for details. Jones reported the results to his superior and received notes of gratitude and substantial bonuses. He wisely shared bonuses with his key operatives. The individual remuneration for members of the organization was incentive-laden and the rewards for performance were substantial. It was the best paying job ever; consequently there were few turnovers in personnel. The organization recruited well, rewarded well, and secured loyalty with its employees. Even sub-contractors were paid twice the normal rate. It was not easy to be an approved sub-contractor.

Their operatives had to demonstrate the ability for complete discretion; they had to be invisible, much like the organization itself. If a subcontractor made one mistake they lost all future contracts. Mistakes were not acceptable. People disappeared if they made mistakes, or suffered sudden heart failure. Doctors and coroners served the Company in hospitals across the land. Autopsies were performed according to the Company's directions and the results were never in question. The power at Jones' disposal was greater than the CEO of General Motors, Boeing, and Microsoft. The primary goal of the organization remained the long-range commitment of bettering the lives of Americans by supporting the efforts to provide education, housing, healthcare, food and employment opportunity for Americans willing to work for the security that comes with those blessings. The Company would decide how these goals would be achieved.

This opportunity to work with an organization of professional members who were convinced that leadership was most effective outside the restriction of politics, and the law was intriguing. The Companies' leadership sat next to the highest office in the nation. Its Board of Directors sat among the most powerful cabinet seats in Washington. The men and women who sat next to the Company men didn't have a clue as to who possessed the real power in Government.

chapter 22

Dr. Harry Booth could not get Nick's request off his mind. Did he know a physician friend that he could trust his with his life and the lives of his friends? Mentally he ran through his list of undergraduate classmates at UCLA. There was no one there he could trust. He thought about his class at Portland General Hospital where he did his internship. Again, he came up empty. It didn't help that he dropped out of circulation when his wife, Alice, died three years ago. Even after praying and pacing the halls half the night he still was not sure whom he could trust. If it were only himself, Harry would choose any one of eight to ten doctors he knew and worked with over the years. But how could he possibly put the lives of his friends on the line? He decided to turn to the Lord in prayer. Although he was not a Catholic, he attended Mass that morning and prayed for insight.

———

Sitting at breakfast after Mass, Chris sat next to Harry. "I could not help but notice that your mind was wandering this morning. Is there anything wrong?" he asked.

"Nick asked me yesterday if I knew anyone I could trust our lives to. I've wracked my brain going over everyone I've known since med. school and I cannot be sure about anyone! It is so frustrating. I guess I am just too afraid to make a choice like that."

"You are not afraid, Harry. This is a dilemma none of us should ever have to face. I may be able to help. One of my class-mates was a physician before entering the seminary; his name is Father Thomas Carroll. He was ordained a Jesuit about two years after my ordination. He was assigned to a Catholic hos-pital in Bogotá, Colombia. I know he came back to the states about ten years ago. We renewed our friendship two years ago when we met at a Priest's retreat in Emmitsburg, Maryland. He was stationed at a Catholic Teaching Hospital in Boston–I think it is Saint Clare's Hospital."

"Chris, that sounds good. Let me ask you the question Nick asked me, can you trust this man with your life, and the lives of all of us?"

"I believe so," Father Chris replied.

"I don't mean to be unkind Chris, but there is a world of dif-ference between, 'I believe so' and, 'Yes, we can absolutely trust this man with our lives,'" Harry repeated.

"Yes Harry, we *can* trust this man with our lives," the priest answered solemnly.

"I've got to get word to Nick. We need to know what Tom Carroll can find out for us. I am sure that Nick and Detective Baker have something specific in mind, don't you think?" Harry replied.

Chris and Dr. Booth walked over to Shaun's room and shared the information with him.

"That is good news!" Shaun said. We have been looking for something to break in our favor and this might be it. We have to find a way to reach Nick and John and find out what infor-mation we need from the computer files of the U.S. Medical Association."

I think we need to get Frank's help with this.

"Good morning. What can I do for you?" Frank asked as Chris, Shaun, and Harry knocked on his open door.

"Frank," Harry started. "When I talked to Nick last night he talked to me about contacting someone at the USMA. Chris might have someone who can help us. He told me he would try to call us back soon. It is very important that we talk to Nick as soon as possible. Please let us know right away if he calls."

"Of course I will," Frank replied. "This sounds important. Is there anything else I can do?"

"Frank, you are truly a good friend and your reward in heaven will be great. We owe so much to you already."

"Thanks, Chris. I'm going to need help to make it up to the 'big house', so I will accept your support, gratitude, and prayers," Frank replied laughing. "I will let you know as soon as Nick or John calls."

Shaun offered to brew some fresh coffee while they discussed what they hoped would be their first bit of encouraging news since they arrived at the monastery. Shaun poured the coffee as they sat down at a table in the dining room.

"Let's talk about the Medical Association connection," he suggested. "Harry, what do you think we might learn from getting into their computer system?"

"Their program contains vast amounts of data. There is personal as well as professional information. The set-up of the Association is outlined. The organization has multiple layers. There are local chapters by city and by county that contains a list of every physician, surgeon, anesthesiologist, and medical doctor in the area. Next are the state levels, which are headed by committees and appointed leaders. Then there is the national level, which is made up of elected representatives and upper level managers who made the real decisions about who does what on each level of the Association. The overview from above is similar to our State and Federal government. The International organization is an upshot of the National group. The real power lies in the national level leadership. It is a powerful group with more connections in our government than any lobby. Only the Supreme Court of the United States has more power in

Washington than the USMA, and I would not be surprised if many of their decisions regarding health care issues are dictated by the Medical Association," Harry explained.

"Harry, I would bet that ninety nine percent of American citizens have no clue or idea about this whatsoever!" Shaun said in astonishment.

"You are absolutely right," replied Harry. "That is why we must talk to Nick as soon as possible. We need a way to access their system. Just getting some basic information could point us in the right direction. We need to log into their system without being discovered. Maintaining our security is critical. Any slip-ups on our part could cost us our lives. We must talk to Nick and let him know we have a trustworthy source to access the Medical Association computer."

chapter 23

Gretchen awoke at sunrise the next morning. She started the coffee maker in her room and stepped into the shower. Afterward she dressed in jeans and a modest top. She poured her coffee and stepped out on to the balcony to enjoy the early morning sun. Sitting quietly she began to study the few people in the parking lot. Two men dressed in business suits, a young couple perhaps hurrying home after an all night tryst, and a single guy still a little hung over after a night of serious drinking. Fortunately the drinker had the good sense to get a room instead of driving home. There was a black sedan with two men sitting in the front seat. They had binoculars and looked to be searching the east wall of the hotel. The man with the binoculars seemed to be gazing at each balcony on the hotel. Gretchen quickly, but smoothly rose from the chair and re-entered her room and closed the drapes.

She opened the hallway door and peered to the left and right, searching for anything out of order. The hall was empty. Gretchen quickly moved to Nick's door and knocked quietly. John rose, walked to the door, peeked out the privacy lens and quickly opened the door for Gretchen.

"John," Gretchen quickly spit out. "I think we are being watched. Look out your window. Look for the black sedan in the fourth row, the third car in. There are two men in the front seat. The guy in the passenger seat has binoculars. He was scanning the balconies on the hotel. I am not sure, but I don't think they saw me. Can you see them?"

"Yes, I see them. Nick, wake up," he ordered.

"What is it John?" he asked.

"Get dressed. We have to leave, now!" the detective replied.

Nick immediately dressed in the monk's Cassock, Cincture and sandals. John kept checking the black sedan in the parking lot. The two men remained there, scanning the hotel and anyone leaving the building.

"Nick, I have a plan. Gretchen put this habit on. Pull your hair back tight. Put it right over your clothes. Let me see how it looks," John fired the orders at her.

"Okay, pull it up a little, slide the excess under the rope, like this," he said as she adjusted the length to fit her height.

"Here is our plan. I will walk out the front door in my civilian clothes five minutes before you. Nick, you and Gretchen will then walk out to the car. Gretchen you stay on Nick's left. Walk out to the car slowly and look normal as you go to the car. I will walk over to the right side of the building and make my way through the parking lot. I will have their car covered. If they make a move, I will drop them. Pull out of the lot and turn right. There is a McDonalds a half a block up. Pull in there and I will meet you. Do you understand?"

"Yes, John," Nick answered.

John Baker opened the hotel room door and made his way down to the lobby by the fire escape on the north side of the building, taking him to the far side of the parking lot above the black sedan.

Gretchen took one more look in the mirror and seemed satisfied with her disguise. If she kept her head down she would pass for a Benedictine monk. Nick touched her hand and smiled.

"You can do this. Do not be afraid. John is going to be sure we are safe. Are you ready?" Nick asked.

"I am. Let's go," Gretchen replied.

Nick and Gretchen walked out of the room, down the hall to the stairwell and then over to the lobby. They walked at a normal pace, side-by-side, out to the parking lot and to the car. To any observer they were two religious men on their way to morning Mass. Nick pulled out of the driveway, turned right and drove up the block as John Baker instructed. They sat in the car for a few minutes wondering what had transpired at the hotel. The rear door opened and John stepped inside.

"How do you do that?" Nick asked.

"What?" Baker asked.

"Just appear out of nowhere, that's what!" Nick answered.

"So, what happened?" Gretchen inquired.

"I was able to make my way close to their car. I kept a clear line of sight in case I had to shoot. They looked over at you then glanced down at something on their lap. I am guessing it was a photograph. They were not looking for two monks. After you pulled out they continued to scan the balconies on the hotel. I slipped away unnoticed and walked quickly up to the car. I also got the license plate on their car."

"Thank you John, I don't know if they were looking for me or not, but it sure did scare me when I saw them," Gretchen said gratefully.

"You may have saved us, Gretchen. It was good you spotted them before they saw you. We need to be alert and careful. If someone is looking for us we need to be extra careful. I am concerned that we are very easy to spot. I believe someone is searching for Gretchen and we have to protect her. Colleen is dead, Hanna is dead, and if we don't protect her, Gretchen could die too. That is a cold way to state the case; I apologize for being blunt," Baker said as Nick drove out onto the freeway.

"John, I have an idea. I want to call Frank Murphy. There has got to be a Benedictine Monastery or Convent in Los Angeles. We could disguise Gretchen as a nun, dressed in the complete

Nun's Habit. You would have to cut your hair, and perhaps even dye it a different color. What do you think, John?" Nick asked.

"I would cut my hair, and do whatever would be needed," Gretchen replied.

"It is a good idea, Nick," John replied. "We will call Murphy from a safe telephone when we stop for breakfast. I don't know about you, but I am starving!"

"Gretchen," John said softly. "Forgive me for speaking so bluntly. I don't mean to frighten you, but I want to keep you alive. I very much want to keep you alive."

"I understand, John, I want to live. I am angry now, very angry. My best friends are gone. Someone thought they could take me out too. Well, I will not go down without a fight. I will do everything I can to stay alive. I don't mind disguising myself, but if it comes down to hand-to-hand combat, I will fight like a wildcat."

"Well, if we are smart, we will avoid all that. We just have to be smarter than our enemies. I promise I will do everything I can to protect you," John stated firmly.

"Thank you, John. I trust you with my life," Gretchen replied gratefully.

Nick pulled over at a Pancake House and found a separate parking spot where Gretchen could return John's gray cassock and cincture so he could resume his role as Brother Mark. They walked into the restaurant and were seated promptly. After ordering they focused again on the events of the morning and their plan to protect Gretchen and the others back in DC.

"There is a pay phone by the door. We should call Frank Murphy and see if he can help us with a contact person here in Los Angeles. The men in the car this morning were not looking for Benedictine monks, they were looking for a young woman. We were smart to separate. They have not connected us to Gretchen, and that works in our favor. Gretchen, if we can disguise you we might buy a few days of safety for all three of us. We would be foolish, to believe that our pursuers will give up and go away."

"I agree," Nick added. "We must use our time out here in California judiciously. We cannot get Joey Bean to speak to us as monks. Can we pass ourselves off as police or the DEA?"

"That might work," agreed John. "We could fool him into believing we are with the DEA and that might scare him into talking with us."

"How do we turn the conversation around to Colleen and what he might know about her death? Will I be able to control my temper? I feel so much animosity toward this man. Will he remember that we met less than one month ago when I came out here searching for Colleen? Now that we are so close to him I find myself angry all over again," Nick said as his voice rose revealing his bitterness and inner hostility toward the man responsible for using and abusing his sister.

"Nick," John began. "I share your anger. We all have lost loved ones and friends in the last few days. It would be best if I did the talking when we get to him. We want to find out if he knew about Colleen's death. I am concerned that this guy may be so far into drugs that he may not even remember what he did yesterday. If his brain is really fried there is no way he could have planned the details of all that has happened since Colleen died. I doubt he is a player in the big leagues. I'm hoping he is careless enough to think he is smart and will start talking to us."

"Harry said he might be the son of Joseph Bolton, the Surgeon General of the United States. His father would be very displeased that his son was sleeping with a call girl, much less getting her pregnant. Let's say he is right about all that. Certainly Joseph Bolton would have the smarts to hire someone to make sure Colleen was taken out of the picture."

"Yes, he would," John agreed.

"You agreed with me too quickly," Nick asked. "What are you thinking?"

"I am thinking if that is true, we may be in way over our

heads, and that alarms me. Just think about what happened at the precinct."

"You are right. We must be careful. Lives are at risk," Nick added somberly.

It took another thirty minutes to get into downtown Los Angeles. Nick recalled the directions to Joey Bean's apartment and pulled over near his home. Detective Baker and Nick took off their monk's garments. With their recent haircuts, it was unlikely anyone, let alone a heavy drug user, would recognize Nick. As they approached the door, the detective reminded Nick to let him do the talking.

"Yeah, coming, hold your horses man, I'm coming," Joey Bean said as he stumbled to the door where John Baker and Nick stood knocking.

Baker had his wallet in his hand and the gun Gretchen gave him tucked into his jeans, but plainly visible. He rang the bell once, waited ten seconds, and then used his fist to pound on the door. As the annoyed Joey opened the door the detective flipped his wallet open and shut quickly, which was just enough time to see a badge, but not enough time to read it.

"LAPD, we are here to see Joseph Bolton. Is he here?"

"Yeah man, that's me," said Bolton, "but everyone calls me Joey Bean. Why are you here? What do you want?"

"We need to talk with you," ordered Baker. Looking quickly inside the squalid apartment the detective suggested they sit down at a round table in the kitchen.

"So what is your name?" asked Joey. "What do you want from me?"

"My name is Cooke, and this is my partner, Smith. We have some questions about a woman who is reported to be your girl-friend," Baker said slowly to Joey.

"I have lots of girlfriends," stammered Joey, who was obviously high.

"We are looking for a girl named Colleen. You know any girls by that name?"

"Yeah, I know Colleen. So what?"

"Have you seen her in the last few weeks?"

"No man, she split on me. She said she was moving back east to be with her family," Joey replied. "Something was wrong with her. She had a sickness we called the 'gay plague.'"

"And why is that?"

"Because gay people get it. They get it from the perverted way they make it with each other. It is just sick, man, real sick," Joey explained shaking his head.

"So Colleen has this sickness?" inquired Baker.

"Yeah, no, well, maybe, that is what I heard anyway. We were close, Colleen and me, real close. I might have the disease myself for all I know. I'm lucky I know a doctor in San Fran who keeps me straight," Joey revealed.

"What is this doctor's name in San Francisco?" Nick asked.

"Walters, I think his first name is John. He and a couple of guys specialize in this plague. He sees a lot of 'those' kinds of men, the homosexuals. Funny thing, he tells me none of the sick gay guys live very long. I wonder if he is lying to me. You know, trying to scare me from living life the way I want. I just want to be free man," Joey slurred.

"How did you hook up with a doctor in San Francisco?"

"I had a little problem a while back. You guys already know about my arrest, and so you know those charges were dropped. I hated to do it, but I went to my old man and told him I needed some cash. Well, anyway I picked up a bad case of the clap at the same time. I told my father I needed some help with the arrest, and with my personal problem. The old man was really ticked off. He made a few telephone calls and, presto, my arrest went away.

"He told me about this Doctor Walters and ordered me to go see him right away. The doc gave me some penicillin and some ointment to clear it up. Then he takes me to the hospital ward where he works and shows me a couple guys sick with this 'gay-plague' thing. He told me flat out that these guys would be dead in a day or two. I asked him how he could be so sure about that, and he told me he sees it all the time. He went off on a rant telling me that perverts like these men don't deserve to live. He replied that they pass this virus on just by, 'incidental contact'. I asked him what he meant by that. He replied that a healthy person can get this curse from any gay man or woman who is infected by shaking their hand, sitting on a toilet seat they have just used, French kissing an infected person, and unprotected sexual intercourse with either a man or a woman who is infected. He told me he knows first hand people who have this, 'incidental contact' become carriers of this virus. He said carriers should not be allowed to live either.

"The doc gave me a lecture about not sleeping with sluts who pick up this virus that causes the plague, which, by the way, has no cure. I told him I was with this girl Colleen who I think gave me the dose of the VD, and who knows what else, including this virus plague thing. He told me to get Colleen up to see him right away. I hooked her up with a guy I know in Frisco. She got some cash from a relative and flew up there. After that she just disappeared. I didn't know where she went, whom she was with, or whatever. Maybe the doc took care of her like he did the men up there. My father threatened to cut me off if I don't stop sleeping around and partying all the time.

"Who were your 'regular' girlfriends?" inquired Baker.

"That is none of your business," Joey angrily replied.

"Joey, so far this conversation has been just a couple of buddies sharing stories, catching up. But we can take this downtown if you get smart with us. It is up to you. I can call the narcotic squad to pay your apartment a visit. It is up to you, pal," Baker snapped back to Joey.

"Okay, there is no need to do that. I hung out with three girls regularly: Colleen, Hanna, and Gretchen. I got lucky with these three. They are beautiful girls, man."

"Where can we reach these girls?" demanded Nick.

"Well, I told you I don't know where to find Colleen. Hanna

and Gretchen hung out at the strip along the LAX airport. I never went to their places. We always met here or at a bar out near the airport," Joey admitted.

"What about their 'pimp'? Did you know him?" Baker asked, sniffing around for more information.

"Yeah, I know him; I met him a while ago. He seemed like an upright guy. I know he was connected to someone up the ladder, or 'corporate structure' he liked to say. I tried to avoid him just because of that reason. His name is Devon Sharpe. My old man warned me about staying away from the pimps. It seemed like he knew what he was saying, and I can't afford to be caught ignoring good old dad," Joey responded.

"All right Joey, what if I said I needed to hire someone to commit a crime for me?" asked John Baker. "If I needed a guy to hurt someone for me, maybe even kill someone for me. Would you know who to call about that?"

"I think I know someone who knows someone that might be able to help you like that. " Joey said cautiously. "I don't know this for a fact, but there are a couple of guys who contract for that type of work. All I know is their initials, 'JJ.'"

"Give me your home and cell phone numbers Joey, just so I can keep in touch with you if need be," Baker told him as he and Nick stood up to leave. "Thanks for your cooperation."

"That's all I get, "thanks for your cooperation," that is the thanks I get from spilling my guts out to you?" Joey said contemptuously.

"Well Joey, it is like this. The DEA and the local drug unit had you marked down as part of a raid. I will notify them that you helped in our investigation. How is that?"

"Okay, that works for me. Thanks," Joey answered with a criminal's sarcasm.

"I can let your daddy know you were a good boy and helped us out," Baker said.

"Funny, man, real funny," Joey replied shaking his head.

Baker and Nick returned to the rented car where Gretchen

was waiting. She saw them smiling and nodding and that made her feel good. Gretchen hoped they got the information that would help them solve their mystery.

Nick got behind the wheel of the car and pulled out into heavy traffic. After settling into the center of four lanes he looked over at John Baker.

"How did we do, Detective? How good is this information?" asked Nick.

"It is very good information. When we dissect it we will learn even more. That was a good interview."

Nick drove north toward the airport and pulled into the parking lot of a Holiday Inn. There he re-dressed into his monk's Garb along with Nick. They entered the restaurant for a cup of coffee to discuss the meeting with Joey Bean.

"We learned a lot today," Baker started. "There are a number of people involved in these crimes. Of particular concern to us is who is responsible for the planning and execution of Colleen. Here is what I think happened. Joey Bean's father, Joseph Bolton, ordered the death of Colleen, Hanna, and Gretchen. I think this was a vindictive order. He believes, rightly or not, that Colleen, Hanna, or Gretchen is responsible for exposing his son to a fatal venereal disease. I don't think Joey's father knew about Colleen's pregnancy. If he had known he would have ordered her to be killed sooner. This is an evil man and we cannot afford to underestimate his power. I believe he ordered the killing of Hanna and Gretchen. He is using hired hands to commit these crimes. These are efficient, cold-blooded killers. They are good at their work, and very dangerous. My guess is that the Johnsons are the hired killers. These men have contacts throughout the States. They were able to make the connection about Colleen, Harry and Nick over the phone while you were in the air on your way home from San Francisco. They are sophisticated and very well connected. They get things done. The big question is who do they get them done for? Who is the person or persons ordering and approving the murders? I would bet my badge that the 'JJ' Joey mentioned is the same Johnson on the passenger list."

Gretchen clasped her hands together and shook her head in despair, as she finally understood the sinful extent of the poor choices she made in her life. "I never thought anyone would get hurt by the way I chose to live."

"Gretchen, the men who took Colleen's life and Hanna's life are responsible for her death, but our actions, all of them, have consequences. We have to stand up and face the truth about how our bad decisions impact the lives of all we touch."

"The first targets were Colleen, Hanna, and Gretchen," John Baker explained. "Their plan changed when Nick came to take his sister home. Harry and Angela became targets just because they were good Samaritans. The Johnson's were able to arrange a hit at Washington National in a few hours time. It had to be the Johnson's and their connections on the ground in DC."

"I think we have to be careful about who we share this information with. We don't want to run out and get people arrested. We must use this information wisely," John suggested.

"You are right about that, Nick," Detective Baker replied. "How we use this information could mean life or death for us. These people are not going anywhere. So far, they believe they have succeeded in silencing us. I realize that we can't hide out forever. We have our wives and families to think about and we have to resume our lives in some way or another, and I do not want these people chasing us forever."

"Let's re-focus on what we know. The highest power we are dealing with so far is the Surgeon General. It is possible that his motivation is a twisted cry for help to keep his wayward son out of trouble. He knows his boy is a drug user and is trying to cover his son's tracks. His son has made a lot of mistakes dating prostitutes and strippers. The weak attempts to cover his son's tracks have failed. He is getting nervous and is making mistakes. I believe he will continue to make mistakes as he tries to eliminate anyone tied to his sons' drug use and sexual escapades," John detailed.

"We should try to think big. Who would the Surgeon General trust to get someone to commit murder for him? It seems unthinkable. Whom would he turn to?" Nick asked.

"My instincts point to the Johnson's as the killers," said John Baker. "They could be the executioners for the Surgeon General. Joseph Bolton would have to remain above suspicion. He communicates his orders through someone in the group. Johnson's names are the only ones on the passenger lists of both flights from San Francisco to Washington DC. They also have political ties through his wife's connection to Scott Farmer."

"Help me think this through," Gretchen said. "How does knowing that the Surgeon General wanted to kill the girls his son slept with have anything to do with an attempt on Harry and Nick's life? The Surgeon General didn't know them or anything about them. Why would he take the chance to kill someone he didn't know?"

"You are right Gretchen, he didn't know them, but the men who he hired to kill Colleen, you, and Hanna possibly made that decision for him. That is what would make them even more dangerous. These are killers who make assumptions and act on them without the approval of the people who hired them. They have the option to kill anyone who gets involved with the primary target."

"It is like having an open contract on any victim that has been associated in any way with the primary victim, in this case, Colleen," Nick explained.

"That is frightening!" replied Gretchen. "What do we do next?"

"We have to call Harry, Chris, and Shaun," Nick said with concern. "We must reach them today!"

chapter 24

Back at the Monastery, each hour seemed to pass slower than the one before. Harry wondered how Father Chris held his patience. He seemed to be at ease in the anxiety of this day. Chris had the same uneasy feeling as Harry, he was just able to conceal it a little better.

Meanwhile, Gretchen, Nick, and John were at a crossroads on how to proceed with their findings. The primary concern was whether to travel up to San Francisco to meet with Dr. Walters who treated Colleen when she was a patient there. Walters was the only person Baker could tie to everything involved in this mystery. He was the physician treating Nick's sister in San Francisco at St. Agnes Hospital. Detective Baker was sure Doctor Walters was involved in something illegal.

"Do we risk revealing our identity to Walters, or should we head back to Washington and plan our next move together?" asked Nick.

"I'm not sure. If it was just the doctor I would agree. But, remember folks, there are people higher up on the ladder," Nick said. "We have to gather some information on Doctor Walters and, if we are clever enough, we might throw them a curveball that might keep them off our track for a little while longer."

"I agree. There might be a chance to distract them a little, and that may give us a window of opportunity we could use in the future. There is one thing we must do, and now is time for us to try to reach Chris and Shaun at the Monastery."

"They are three hours ahead of us making it five p.m. eastern. I will use the pay phone adjacent to the rest rooms," Nick informed Gretchen and John. "Keep an eye on the area and let me know if anyone acts suspicious. Gretchen, why not fold up that large red napkin and wear it over your hair. There is not a lot of blond showing with it pulled back, but let's keep it under wraps, okay? Remember, you are traveling with two monks."

The telephone in Father Murphy's office rang only once. Five sets of hands reached for the handset at the same time. Frank Murphy, Shaun, Father Chris, Detective Catherine Harding, and Harry Booth all looked at each other and laughed at the same time. Father Murphy picked it up and handed it to Shaun.

"Hello," Shaun replied.

"Shaun, it's Nick. I hope all is well back at the Monastery. Have you heard from Angela, Kathleen, or Maura?"

"It's good to hear from you Nick. We have been worried about you and John. How are you making out?"

"Okay. Does Frank Murphy have a speakerphone? If you are all there we could save some time and by not repeating things."

"Yes," Shaun said. "We have you on speaker now. Harry, Chris, Catherine, and Frank are here with me."

"Hello, everyone. I am on a public telephone at a restaurant in Los Angeles. John and Gretchen are with me. There are several things I need to share with you, so if you don't mind, I'll tell you what is going on here and what we might need."

"First off, Frank, do you have a Monastery or Convent in Los Angeles where we could get a nun's habit for Gretchen? She will be traveling with us because her life is in danger; her friend Hanna was killed by the same people who were responsible for killing Colleen. If she had a habit we would not draw any attention to us. Can you help us with that, Frank?"

"Yes. I will look up the number and name for you while you are on the telephone with us now," the priest replied.

"We are thinking of visiting Dr. John Walters in San Francisco. We met with Joey Bean out here. He *is* a slug. Harry, you were right about him being Joseph Bolton's son. Joey confirmed that his father was responsible for Colleen going to St. Agnes Hospital in San Francisco. We also think that Surgeon General Bolton was responsible for hiring the men who were on the plane Colleen, Harry, and Nick were on out of San Francisco, and on the plane from St. Louis to Washington National. Those men were able to make the necessary contacts while in the air to have men ready to commit murder when you stepped out of the airline terminal. From Joey Bean we were led to the Surgeon General, then to Doctor Walters. Every which way we turn we are running into the power of politics and medicine. We think there is a link to the United States Medical Association. When we get back we have to explore that connection. We have been reluctant to get into their files because going there may expose us. We have gone to such lengths to keep our secret safe that to blow it now would be devastating."

"Chris," Nick asked. "Have you been able to reach your friend, the priest doctor?"

"Yes, and I am certain our identity is safe with Father Tom Carroll. I spoke with Tom and explained our dilemma to him. I am certain he will do everything he can to protect us. I have his password, his social security number, and his medical license number which is what we need to access the 'insiders' data of the USMA. I agree that we should not access the files from California. That would send up a red flag because he has never been in California. We can check things here at the Monastery. If someone would randomly check his usage reports they would see routine activity."

"Nick, this is Catherine speaking. How is John holding up out there in Los Angeles?"

"He is good, Catherine. I will tell him you asked. I know it is tough for both of you right now. We don't talk too much about the bombing, but I can tell John thinks about it often, and the friends and officers you both lost," Nick said sympathetically.

"Is there anything else we can do to help you, Nick?" asked Father Chris.

"Did you get any information on the Benedictine nuns in Los Angeles?" asked Nick.

"Call Sister Martin de Pores at 716–555–1457. I know her from a retreat here about a year ago. I will call her immediately after we hang up and tell her to expect your call. She will not ask any questions. She will know what to do and how to transform Gretchen into a Benedictine nun," said Father Frank Murphy.

"Thank you. I will call her shortly. We will make our decision about going to San Francisco this afternoon. We will call you and let you know our plans and when we are coming home. Please give Maura my love," Nick said.

"Will do. Give our best to John and Gretchen. We look forward to meeting her," said Shaun. "Goodbye."

The group of friends sat silently in Frank Murphy's office replaying the telephone conversation in their heads. Clearly Nick, John, and Gretchen were skirting grave danger in California. If their assumptions were correct there were powerful people with close connections to very dangerous individuals, people unafraid to commit murder.

"I knew the day of the bombing that our lives were in jeopardy, but I did not imagine that a conspiracy possibly headed by the Surgeon General of the United States would be behind such a murderous plot," Chris said to his companions.

"You are right, Chris," Shaun agreed. "This is bigger than any of us could have guessed. It may be time to call in the FBI. I know we wanted to discuss this with Nick and John, but it may be the best of course of action now."

"Let's pray on this tonight and bring it up to John tomorrow," Father Frank suggested. "I am heading over to the chapel now. I invite you all to join me."

Everyone rose from their chairs and followed Frank Murphy.

chapter 25

Nick got the directions from Sister Martin de Pores to the Benedictine Convent at St. Ambrose College. It was about twenty-two miles north of the central downtown district of Los Angeles. Once there, Sister Martin escorted John and Nick to a waiting room equipped with comfortable sofas and chairs. Then she took Gretchen by the hand and led her out of the waiting room.

Approximately forty minutes later Sister Martin de Pores reentered the waiting room along with another Sister. She introduced John and Nick to Sister Gretchen Marie.

Before them stood a Nun in Benedictine habit, which included a light grey, full-length dress with long sleeves and a white cincture about three inches wide. She had dark grey shoes and a grey veil-like cowl that covered her head and ears. It had a white collar and a matching white forehead band—all about three inches high, matching her waistband in color and size. She wore a black rosary that hung off the cincture around her waist.

Neither man knew what to say. They were stunned at the transformation. No one would possibly recognize Gretchen. There was something very different about her besides the habit she wore. Her countenance had changed.

"Well, gentlemen. I trust I have fulfilled my task to your approval," Sister Martin humbly asked.

"Yes, Sister, you did a great job with Gretchen. I am grateful."

The three religious figures climbed into the car and pulled away from St. Ambrose College. "Would you look at us? Three wayward souls now closer to heaven than any of us thought we ever could be! I actually feel like a nun. I know I look like one, but I did not expect to feel like a real nun." Gretchen said.

"I can see a difference," said John. "You wear the habit well, and I doubt anyone can recognize you. Did the sister cut a lot of your hair off?"

"Yes," said Gretchen. "It is a page-boy cut. It is thinner than I had before and so much shorter. I like it a lot."

"I feel much better about your safety," John remarked. "I agree with Nick that it is almost impossible to tell it is you. We can move about without detection, at least for a little while."

"What is our next step, John," Gretchen inquired. "Have you thought any more about going to San Francisco?"

"Yes. We will go see Dr. John Walters and then return home. There might not be any additional witnesses here. We got a ton of information from Joey Bean. I want to get a look at Dr. John Walters up close. Hopefully he will reveal a little more about the organization. I must be careful in what I say or do. I will not jeopardize our mission, or our friends and families by having someone recognize us as anything other than three religious people traveling together."

chapter 26

Back in Washington, Thomas Jones was reviewing the month end field reports and financial statements. This was an audit of the state chairmen who reported how the "special fund" money was allocated. Each chairman had to report any fund money spent on security issues and problems. In a coded file each chairman would detail the date, time, project target, any unusual details of the project, and identification of the agent who performed the work. No one in the organization knew the password to this file, or the language of the code, which was alpha-numeric when he received it and then re-coded in a different numeric-alpha language. Neither the colonel nor his superior knew the second code existed. Access to that information was contained in Jones' head. He sent an audited file with all names deleted and with all activity described as "sales presentations", "sales pending", and "sales closed" to the colonel.

The reviews took several hours to complete and Jones did the audit in his meticulous manner: 'A' to 'Z' in even months and 'Z' to 'A' in odd numbered months. The reports were for the month of November, so they were in the 'Z' to 'A' format. The state of California didn't come up until mid-afternoon. It was a very busy month for California and the file was sizeable. Essentially the data contained the information on the work assigned to code name JJ. There were several thousand dollars in airfares to and from Washington, DC, as well as the accompanying car rentals and hotel bills. There were two subcontractors in Washington. The primary target was a young woman, Colleen O'Connell, and secondary target were those traveling with her. There was a sub-contract for a "cleaner" whose job it was to target the shooter at the airport.

Jeff Johnson also had two additional primary targets in California: Hanna Jones and Gretchen Sanders. JJ took this project himself since his father was delayed in Washington DC on a major assignment at the southeast police precinct that included secondary targets involving substantial collateral damages associated with a primary target. Several of those targets were not acquired, and removed from the "prospect" list after the successful operation at the precinct.

There were additional costs to remove a subcontractor after the police precinct incident. The last detail on that project was the very public erasure of three agents who posed as Islamic terrorists. Jones was impressed with the month's activity and costs, which at one hundred thousand per capita was in line with the costs across the country. He was ready to re-enter the data into his computer when he scanned the report a second time. A name jumped out at him, Hanna Jones.

I wonder, he said to himself as his mind raced. *Is it possible that this is Hanna, my sister Hanna? That is very unlikely. She probably was in Hickory working at Windsor Furniture. She could not have been a prostitute in Los Angeles.*

He quickly backtracked into the previous month's entry when the targets were first recommended. He didn't recall seeing Hanna Jones' name before. He ran his finger along the computer screen and saw that three targets had been named, C. O'Connell, H. M. Jones, and G. L. Sanders.

"I never put that together. More than likely "Hanna Jones" was an alias the girl in California created. There are so many people named Jones, but her initials are, H. M. Jones. My sister is Hanna Marie.

There are probably many, many women with the same initials. Still, I should investigate this.

Hurriedly he reached for the phone and called the younger Johnson in California and ordered him to do a thorough background check on Hanna Jones. He wanted all the personal and professional information on her and he wanted it in a few hours. He warned JJ that his information had to be absolutely correct and absolutely confidential.

Once he concluded that task, Jones went back to his audit. However, his mind was not on the details he retrieved and entered into his computer. His mind was on Hanna Jones and the possibility that he had approved the death of his own sister.

He relaxed in his leather chair and closed his eyes. There he saw their home in Hickory, North Carolina. It was a two and a half story white clapboard home on a half-acre of land. There was a large wooden garage at the rear of the property where his father had a 1952 Chevrolet that he worked on in his spare time. It was black and ordinary much like the ordinary life the family lived in this furniture-manufacturing town of about twenty thousand residents. His parents married when his dad, John, returned from WW II where he served in the Army. His father was part of the assault on Omaha Beach in 1944. That bloody day never left his father's memory, yet he only ever spoke one time to his son about his experiences in the war.

The story he told his son Tommy was about the day his unit landed on Omaha Beach. He was eighteen years old. The machine gun bullets were ripping through the helmets, heads, and bodies of the soldiers who were lucky enough to make it through the blood-stained water to the beach where the only protection was the body of the soldier who was shot down in front of you. John told his son that was the only time he ever felt real fear. His best buddy, PVC Thomas Mancuso, ran through the water and blood alongside John. They dove onto their bellies and tried to burrow into the sand as the bullets rained down around them. Tommy shouted to John, "C'mon Johnny, I see a clearing. C'mon buddy."

John started to stand up and run toward his close friend. In the blink of an eye Tommy was blasted into eternity. Tommy's helmet rolled toward John who had ducked back down into the sand. The helmet was smoking and Tommy was gone. Just like that. Gone! John grabbed the helmet and saw a picture and a note tucked inside. It was a photo of Tommy's girl and a letter to his mom. John stuffed these into his shirt. He was still afraid, but now he was very angry. He rose up out of the divot he had made and joined a group of soldiers charging up the beach, screaming like madmen. The fired their rifles wildly and reloaded on the run. Some men fell; others ran up from behind and filled in the line. It was an unconventional way to fight, but it worked. The anger in all those soldiers came from a wellspring of love for their country, but even more for the love of their friends who had just paid the ultimate price.

As the soldiers approached the hillside the firing grew more intense. It was so hot you could smell the gunpowder blowing by in the bullets that swarmed all around them. You could also feel the sweat, the fear, and the anger of the man running next to you. These young, brave boys continued their bloodcurdling screams up the hill. It was incomprehensible, but they continued anyway. At the top of the hill the fighting turned into hand-to-hand combat. The boys used their bayonets with a fierceness that drove their blades through the cruel hearts of the enemy and into the ground beneath them. Then they used their rifles as clubs and they fought like men possessed. The sound of a man's jaw being smashed resembled the sound of lightning striking a tree branch. The crack was loud and often fatal as the nose bone was shoved up into the enemy's brain. The soldiers really took the fight to the Krauts who only minutes earlier had the best of the battle shooting cannon fire down from a safe position above. But when the going got rough they were not so brave. Many of the Germans were boys about the same age as

Johnny and Tommy. There was no thought about that during the battle. Anger, vengeance, and outright hatred for the enemy who had killed their buddies were the greatest motivators for the majority of the men who made it to the top. The Germans were so frightened by the banshee yells of the boys who were out to avenge the murderers that had gunned down Tommy, and all the other Tommy's laying dead on the beach below. The Germans were surrendering but the boys would have none of that. They were shot dead on the spot. They had to pay for the courageous young souls they killed, and for the severed limbs and cruelly maimed and disabled boys whose only goal was to fight for Uncle Sam in defeating the Nazis, and then make it home alive.

The fight up top lasted maybe an hour. Sweat, blood, spit, urine, and tears were shed in buckets that morning. When it was finally over the men sat in groups of five to ten; they were spent, silent and victorious. Some talked, some prayed silently, and some cried. What mattered most was their sense of accomplishment in getting even with the Germans who killed so many men in the attack on the beach. And they were all thirsty. In fact, they had never been so thirsty. They emptied their canteens and then took the canteens off the dead bodies of the enemy.

John had never been so tired in his life. His taut muscles twitched. He was in the best shape of his life but the battle took everything out of him. His arms and back ached. His fingers were burned from the heat of his rifle firing over and over again. Nothing in basic training equaled the physical challenge those boys faced that morning. Most of the men in John's unit that started the attack were dead. Only eight soldiers in his company made it to the top.

God only knows what dreams the men had that day. For Johnny, he knew he was alive and that he had distinguished himself as a soldier, and as a man. The pain of losing Tommy Mancuso hurt like no other hurt in his short life. John knew it could have been him. But it wasn't. He had lived through one of the deadliest battles of the war. Only God knows why or how. But he lived, and he knew he would get home alive. He would get back to his girl and marry her. And he did.

That was the only war story Thomas ever heard. The old man only told it one time. It meant something so special to his father that he kept it to himself. His father named him after his best friend, a man his father loved and served with, a man who died at eighteen years of age on a beach in defense of freedom.

How far he had come from that day when his father shared this story with him. How could he have changed so much? When did he lose the values of courage and honesty? How did he stray so far from the faith of his family?

He remembered his mother, Helen, in the small kitchen at the rear of the house. She loved her family, and next to her faith, it defined her as a woman. Helen saw the restlessness in her son's soul even as a young boy and figured the best way to combat it was to encourage him to focus on athletics and scholarship. He grew to six feet three inches tall by his tenth year of school. He was a strong young man blessed with speed and coordination. He was the football and basketball star at West Hickory High School. Like most teenage boys, he grew apart from his mother and father and rebelled against their faith and religious practices. His academic achievements and track and field skills earned him a scholarship to Duke University.

After thirty-five years, Thomas' father earned the position of Plant Manager and he seemed satisfied with his life. He was not driven to earn more, be better off, or attain a higher status in the community. He owned his home. He had his job. He had his family.

This status quo attitude was what young Thomas couldn't accept. He swore he would never reach the point where he was happy with things just the way they were. He would earn more, do more, and manage the circumstances in his life so that he would always be in control.

After graduating from Duke University, Thomas elected to enlist in the Marine Corp. He had completed his undergraduate studies in three years and earned his Master's Degree in his fourth year at the University. He had a number of job opportunities but he saw something in the Marines that he desired. It would challenge him in both a physical and mental way that he had not faced in College. He wanted to be stronger and smarter. He also needed to learn how to lead other men. He saw so much dishonesty in the business world.

The Marines provided the arena where he would grow strong and understand what power can do and when to use it to its maximum effect. Every minute in basic was enjoyable because he knew it was enriching his life. After the marines, Thomas was still hungry for knowledge and with all the emphasis on strong, healthy bodies that the Marines preach he saw a new challenge - medicine. He returned to Duke and earned his medical degree and then did his internship at Johns Hopkins in Baltimore. He became an anesthesiologist and graduated at the top of his class. He had job offers pouring in. It was then that he met the Colonel.

Now Jones had an underling searching for the identity of a woman with the same name as his little sister. He had approved the execution of one H. M. Jones in Los Angeles, California. He was sure it was another woman with the same name as his sister. It was a common name, and chances are this Hanna Jones was anyone but his sister. But deep down in his heart he feared the worst. He was not a praying man, but he prayed that this was not his sister. He waited anxiously through the afternoon to learn the results of the search on Hanna Marie Jones.

Shortly after five o'clock Jones' telephone rang. It was Jeff Johnson with the background check on Hanna M. Jones. "Sir, would you like me to e-mail this to you in code?"

"Yes, Johnson e-mail the report to me. Thank you for the prompt response. I will contact you if I need anything more."

"Thank you, if you need anything else just call me."

Within moments Jones knew that the dead woman was indeed his very own sister.

It was true. He, in fact, authorized the death of his own sister! All his intelligence, all his military training, everything he had become suddenly meant nothing to him. He had killed his only sister. All the reasons he ran away from that ordinary life in Hickory seemed to pale as he realized the horror of his action. This strong, brave man was nothing more than a murderer. No matter how much he dressed it up with business terms, what it really amounted to, was murder. He began to rock in his chair and cry out loud. He hid his face in his once strong hands that had now become like the quivering hands of an old man. He wept hard and long. This once almost robotic leader of a nationwide organization with estimated revenues of over two hundred million dollars a year cried like a child. His evil had come home. He faced his moment of truth head on. It was that time in a man's life when he chooses between right and wrong. Such a choice will impact the rest of his life. He was horrified at what he had done and terrified at what he had to do to make things right. The task ahead overwhelmed him. At this moment he wasn't sure where or how to begin. But he knew he had to do something, and it had to be right.

His telephone rang again. It was the Colonel. "Hello Jones. I need a report on the fund raising effort. The CEO has requested an update. He wants to know if we will make the ten million by the deadline. How are you coming with the program?"

"I'm happy to report that we are on track, Colonel," Jones replied as the words nearly gagged in his throat.

"Jones, do you have a cold? You sound like you are coming down with something. Are you ill?" the Colonel inquired.

"No sir, just a little bothered by allergies. I'll take some medicine when I get home tonight," he lied.

"I thought men like you never got sick. Tell me more about the ten million dollar program."

"I've instituted a nationwide Medicare-type billing program

for our doctors and hospitals. Instead of them using their own resources and billing departments I've created regional and state billing centers. They must use our billing program; it is not optional. As members of the USMA they are required to participate. I've created incentives for the participants. When they reach certain tiers of dollars billed we rebate ten percent additional points to them. This insures their patient reporting will be increasing monthly. We control all the rebates to the physicians and hospitals. Our fees for the service are substantial. In the first four weeks we generated over two million in revenue. Looking into the next sixty days I expect the revenue to exceed ten million. Over the course of a year we can expect in the neighborhood of twenty-five million. This revenue stream will not stop. I am certain the Chief will be pleased with the program. It is heavy on equipment costs upfront because the computers we are using require super high-speed capacity and massive memory size. The beauty of it is that it is low on people costs. After we assemble well trained people in each office we will be able to reduce personnel costs because of the technology and equipment we are putting in place," explained Jones.

"That is excellent work! On another matter, it appears that things are calming down in Washington with the elimination of the terrorists. You handled that quite well. This can be messy business, but the overall goal of the organization requires us to make difficult decisions from time-to-time," the Colonel remarked matter-of-factly.

"I am going to take some time off Colonel," Jones said coldly.

"I don't blame you. You deserve some time off after handling everything so well these last few months," the Colonel said in appreciation. "How long will you be away?"

"One week, maybe two."

"Will I be able to reach you while you are away?"

"Yes, Colonel. I will check my e-mail regularly and will have my phone with me most of the time."

"I'm sure nothing critical will come up while you are away, and I will try not to bother you. Enjoy yourself and come back refreshed."

"Thank you, Colonel."

"You're welcome Jones. Have a good vacation."

"Colonel."

"Yes."

"Do you know my first name?"

"I don't know, I guess I do not. I have it on your resume and employment papers.

Why?"

"My name is Thomas."

"Of course, now I remember. "

"Thank you Colonel, goodbye."

Thomas buzzed his secretary and had her contact the company manager of the corporate jet. He wanted to fly to Los Angeles as soon as possible, and no later than the next morning. If the company plane was not available he asked her to make flight arrangements for the earliest flight out of one of the three Washington area airports.

He copied Johnson's report to his laptop computer and coded it into his secret file at the office.

Sung Li, his secretary, buzzed his telephone and advised him the corporate jet would be available that evening to fly him to Los Angeles. He arranged to leave about eight o'clock that evening. Sung Li inquired if he wanted her to make his hotel or car rental details. Thomas gratefully accepted her offer.

He left the office a few minutes later and went home to pack for the trip. He had his parent's telephone number but decided not to call them yet. He also called the mortuary to inquire of the day and time of Hanna's final services and learned that they had not been finalized. He quickly packed and prepared to fly out to Los Angeles. He arrived at the airport and went directly to the hangar housing the two leer jets owned by the company. Within minutes the plane was airborne. There would be a stop in Kansas City to refuel. He would arrive in Los Angeles early the following morning.

The jet was well designed and could comfortably sit ten to twelve passengers. The crew consisted of the pilot, the co-pilot and one attendant who prepared and served meals and drinks. Thomas knew the pilots, Captain Steve Burton and Captain George Newton, well, having flown with them over a hundred times. Cornelia Banks had worked with American Airlines for ten years before coming on board with the company. She was an attractive black woman that Thomas guessed was about forty years old. She was pleasant and schooled in current events and professional football. She was an avid Pittsburgh Steeler fan and overall somewhat opinionated, but still tactful. She possessed a charm that put her passengers at ease.

"How are you, Mr. Jones?" Cornelia said after the plane reached comfortable altitude and flight speed.

"I am fine, Cornelia. And you?"

"Couldn't be better, sir."

"Cornelia, my name is Thomas. I am starting a vacation tonight so I would like to lose 'Mr. Jones' starting now. Please call me Thomas, or Thom, whatever you would like."

"Well, I am very glad to know you are taking a vacation. Behind your back many of us think you don't eat or sleep. We thought you might be a robot. No offense, sir."

Thomas laughed. "None taken. I can assure you I am human. Maybe not human enough, but I hope to change that. How is your family?"

"My son will graduate high school this year. He is carrying an A minus average on all his subjects and he is playing tennis again this year. He is quite something to see on the tennis court. Anthony is a good boy, and we are proud of him. He was accepted at the University of Pittsburgh, which makes me quite happy, and proud."

"I recall you also have a girl, Regina."

"Yes, Reggie is a freshman in high school and is struggling

with academics. We are working with a tutor to get her grades up a little. She averages a B minus, but she is in two honors courses and they are difficult. I swear I don't know what the math books are teaching. We never had things like that. But Reggie is trying and I'm confident she will be okay. She is in the band and can play the flute like an angel. Thank you for asking about my youngsters. That was very nice of you."

"Did you mean, very human of you?"

"Yes, that too," Cornelia said laughing. "You are going to be all right, Thomas."

"Yes, I think I am going to be fine."

The trip to Los Angeles was routine and almost on time. There was a backup at LAX and they had to circle the airport for about fifteen minutes. Once on the ground Thomas picked up his rental car and headed west toward Santa Monica and the Marriot Hotel. The Cadillac he rented was oversized and powerful, and he maneuvered through the traffic on the freeway easily.

Jones checked into the Marriot and settled into his suite. He turned on the financial news, poured himself a bourbon and ice, and opened his laptop computer to retrieve the file Johnson e-mailed him. There was a reference to an older brother, Thomas, but no data existed on him. Jones did not concern himself about the possibility of JJ connecting him to Hanna Jones. No one in the field knew his name, and most people thought Jones was not his real name. He read over the information on his parents and was surprised that they moved from Hickory to Santa Monica. His dad retired and would now be about sixty-eight or sixty-nine. If he was in good health, and really wanted to be closer to Hanna, the move to California made sense. His father always enjoyed the outdoors and Santa Monica is very close to Topanga State Park and the Santa Monica Mountains National Recreation area. He could camp, fish and enjoy the outdoors to his hearts content.

All these thoughts were concealing the true reason he kept

reading the report. He had to face his parents and decide if he should tell them the truth about his life. They would be devastated over losing Hanna and if he told them he was responsible for her death it could push them over the edge. He also was avoiding how he would face the consequences of his actions. He knew he had to make things right, but he was unsure how far he should go. He would face this question over and over in the days ahead. He was a man who was moving from a world of expedience that focused on the bottom line, to a world of ethics and morals that focused on the divine.

chapter 27

Nick, John, and Gretchen decided to drive to San Francisco. The long drive would give them an opportunity to absorb again what they had learned from Joey Bean and create a plan on how to approach Dr. John Walters. They planned to take Rt. 170; get on I. 5 North; take Rt. 580; exit at Tracy, drive west toward Fremont; then north into San Francisco.

"John, how do you think we should approach Doctor Walters? I thought we might tell the hospital we are Benedictine monks who work with the terminal patients. We might offer a hospice service to the patients at the hospital. That way we would have to meet with Walters. What do you think?" Nick asked.

"That is not a bad plan, Nick. I have to think that over and compare it to my plan to go in as a Private Investigator hired by Mrs. O'Connell to learn about the treatment and diagnosis he made on Colleen. He has the option to refuse to answer any questions based on doctor/patient confidentiality. My plan has holes. I am not sure it is the way to go. Gretchen, do you have any ideas?"

"I might. Nick, you told us that when you found Colleen you got information from a guy in San Francisco. He told you his roommate worked at St. Agnes Hospital. Could we get him to give us a name of a patient in Dr. Walters ward? If we had a name of an active patient we could pose as relatives and visit them. You or John could request a meeting with the doctor. What do you think?"

"That is a good idea, Gretchen. Let's think about it and consider if there would be any danger to our alternate identities which could then endanger our families and friends," remarked Nick.

"Nick, you might be at risk. What is the man's name that told you about Colleen being in the hospital? John asked.

"Paul Martin. His roommate worked at the hospital. Paul seemed like a good guy. I was with him for maybe fifteen minutes. He could recognize me but I don't know if he would tell someone, however, I am not certain about that," Nick replied.

"That is a chance I don't think we should take," Gretchen said. "I have heard you talk about the size and power of the organization that tried to kill you back in Washington. We should not underestimate them even if they think we are dead." Gretchen definitely grasped the danger they were in and understood their vulnerability.

"Let's keep looking at ideas and see if we come up with a plan," answered John.

They drove about two hundred and fifty miles over the next several hours thinking about a plan that would get them to see Dr. Walters. They decided to pull off the freeway and drove into a Comfort Suites hotel. After washing up they met for dinner at the Austin Steakhouse Restaurant that was in the hotel. The drive from Los Angeles takes about six hours and they covered four of those hours before stopping. The nice weather and some beautiful scenery made the trip tolerable.

"Well, my friends," began Detective Baker. "What brilliant plan have we decided on for our meeting with Dr. Walters?"

"I had a thought about calling Father Murphy and asking him to call the Director of St. Agnes Hospital and ask if some of his order could visit the hospital, especially the hospice ward where the terminally ill are treated. The purpose for this visit would be to gather information so that the Benedictines could offer similar services to other hospitals. We could all visit and ask to interview the physicians and nurses. Even though it was short notice, we could ask to visit tomorrow afternoon. What do you think of this plan?" asked Nick.

"I think it would work," Gretchen said nodding in agreement. "What do you think, John?"

"I admit it is better than anything else we have proposed. The only risk we would have is if anyone at St. Agnes would recognize Nick. It has only been a few weeks since you were there. They might remember you," John said thoughtfully.

"My appearance is vastly different. However," John proposed. "For the security of all of us I would limit my conversation with Dr. Walters. I believe we should come up with a set of questions about in-hospital hospice care and ask these questions and let them do most of the talking. Gretchen and I could take notes, walk around and get the feel of the place."

"I agree. This is a good plan. I think this would get us close to Walters but it would not endanger our false identities, or our family and friends," Gretchen said eagerly.

Nick walked over to a pay phone by the check-in desk and called Father Murphy. He picked up on the third ring.

"Hello, Father Murphy speaking, how may I help you?"

"Father Chris, it's Nick."

"Nick! Good to hear from you. How are things going? Did Sister Martin de Pores take care of Gretchen?"

"Yes, and we were very pleased with her help. Father, I have another request for you."

Nick explained their plan to visit St. Agnes Hospital and how crucial it would be to the plan to meet Dr. Walters. After explaining everything Father Murphy understood his role and agreed to help them.

"Nick, after I speak to the Administrator at St. Agnes where can I reach you to confirm that everything is set up for your visit?" Murphy asked.

"We are still concerned about our enemies finding out where we are. Suppose I call you about noon your time, nine a.m. pacific time? Tell them we are in San Francisco and would like to visit tomorrow afternoon or the following morning. Okay?" Nick asked.

"Yes, I will take care of it."

"Thank you Frank," Nick said gratefully. "You have been a big help to us. We hope to fly back home in another day or two."

"I will tell the others of your plans. We are all praying for you. Take care and we will see you soon. Go with God, Nick," blessed Father Murphy.

Nick returned to the table and shared the news with his traveling companions. It was a relief to finalize their plans to visit St. Agnes hospital. It was important that they relax and get a good night's sleep. They enjoyed their meal and the light conversation that accompanied it.

"So, what do you men think of my religious conversion into a nun?" Gretchen asked playfully.

"I imagine you never expected to become 'Sister Gretchen,' did you young lady?"

John Baker replied.

"No, I never thought I would look like this. I must admit it is quite a remarkable transformation. It is like the habit contains magic or a power that changes both the exterior appearance and the interior predisposition. Does that make sense?" asked Gretchen.

"I think it does," Nick said. "The change in both the internal and external appearance is evident to John and me. You have a pure, uncomplicated look about you."

"Pure! I never thought I would appear pure again. After the way I have lived my life these last five years I just figured I looked like a girl out for a good time. I never wanted that life, or enjoyed doing it. We needed the money to live, and I guess we all compromised our morality," Gretchen said.

"I think we all have put on something far more that a just a cassock or a habit. We know that these garments do not have spiritual powers that will miraculously change the person wearing it, but if the person wearing it is open to the possibility and expectation of the grace that can change the heart and soul, then the power of God may be at work," Nick said solemnly.

"I think I get what you are saying Nick," John interjected, "If a person changes their heart away from the material things of this world to the spiritual things that are eternal, then they will change. What these garments do for us is give us a sense of what it might be like to be considered holy, to be out of the ordinary, and to be a believer who is not afraid to display their belief in God."

"That is true," Gretchen added. "We see people looking at us and many of them nod or say hello. Some just look away, but for the ones who look at us I think we make a one second difference in their day. For just that moment or two they think about God. I know from experience, I never stopped to think about God. But now, wearing this habit, I am thinking about God almost all the time. I am not praying, but I just have this awareness of his presence. I cannot believe it is me saying these things. But I am telling you the truth."

"I think one thing we should remember right now is that our words and actions should reflect our commitment to the faith that the real wearers of these habits exhibit every day. We must do them honor by displaying respect for God and everyone we meet," John said profoundly.

"I am very impressed with your comprehension and expression of your Christian faith, John," Nick said in admiration. "I could learn a lot from you, my friend."

"And I, from you, Nick," John replied.

"I see our dinner is on the way. Let's enjoy our meal and meet in our suite later and figure some questions about hospice," Nick said to his friends.

chapter 28

Thomas Jones rose at six a.m. after arriving in Los Angeles from Washington. He wondered if his parents, John and Helen Jones, had made Hanna's funeral arrangements yet. All through his shower, shave, and dressing he debated whether to just show up at the front door of his parent's home, or to telephone them first. He called room service and ordered breakfast and continued to debate the question for another hour. He finally decided to call them and inform them he was in Santa Monica, and if they would allow it, he would go to their home and visit with them. He understood that they might hang up and tell him to get lost. He had cut himself off from his family and had not made any effort to contact them in years. He did not deserve to be a part of their lives. But he had to reach out to them. The phone was answered on the second ring.

"Hello," Helen said hesitantly.

"Hello, Mom. It's me, Thomas."

"Thomas? Is it really you?"

"Yes, Mom. I am so sorry to hear about Hanna."

"John! John, come here. It's Tommy on the telephone," Helen said to her husband as she handed him the phone.

"Hello, is it you, son?"

"Yes, Dad. I heard about Hanna and had to come. I am calling you from the Marriot in Santa Monica," Thomas said soberly. "Dad, can I come over and see you and mom?"

"I guess so. It has been a long time since we heard from you. I have to tell you son, you really hurt your mother. It hurt me too. If you have come back just to say goodbye to Hanna and then disappear out of our lives again, then do not bother coming," John sternly said to his son.

"No, Dad, I promise. I won't disappear again, ever."

"Well, then come on over. You know how to get here?"

"Yes. I'll be there shortly," Thomas said as he hung up the telephone.

Feeling relieved Thomas flossed and brushed his teeth, finished dressing, and headed for his parents home. He knew this was not going to be easy, but it was the first step in turning his life around. He arrived within fifteen minutes, parked on the driveway, and walked onto the porch of a modest ranch home that looked about the same as every other home in the neighborhood. The front door opened before he could knock. His mother flew into her son's arms. She held on to him with a mother's grip of love, and she didn't let go until she nearly lost her breath through her tears and sobs.

"Tommy, my son, I can't believe it is you. Oh my how you have grown and become a man! If only Hanna could be here to see you," she said melting into tears again just over the thought of her little girl lying dead at the funeral home.

"Dad," Thomas said shaking his father's hand. "It is good to see you. How are you holding up with everything?"

"It is rough, son, very hard. We moved here three years ago after I retired to be closer to Hanna, and now she is gone, killed by an intruder. Your mother's heart is broken. It is a good thing you called and asked to come home. She needs more than me right now. Losing Hanna is harder than not knowing what happened to you. But this," he paused so he could compose himself, "this is just rotten."

"I am so sorry for disappearing out of your lives. I went

through a time where I thought I knew everything and didn't need family or friends. I busied myself with my career and rose quickly to lead a national corporation worth millions of dollars. When I learned of Hanna's death my world crashed inside me and I realized how wrong I have been. I flew out here from Washington DC last night after hearing about Hanna. I did not know if you would welcome me or not, but I had to come here. I hoped you would let me mourn with you. Is there anything I can do to help?" Thomas asked.

"God bless you son," Helen said, still clinging to her boy's hand.

"We are due at the funeral home at eleven o'clock this morning. We have not seen Hanna since I identified her at the morgue in Los Angeles. We have to select her burial clothing, the casket, and everything that goes with her passing."

"I would like to join you. May I?" Thomas asked his dad.

"Yes, of course, son."

John and Helen Jones, along with their son, drove to Cronin's Funeral Home in Santa Monica. They were greeted by Joseph Cronin, the proprietor of the business. He escorted them to a conference room where they met with Mary Cronin, the secretary of the funeral home, and assistant to her husband.

"Let me say how sorry we are about losing your daughter, Hanna," Mary Cronin offered in sincerity. "This must be a terrible time for you and your family. We hope we can ease some of your burden by being as helpful as possible. Please ask any questions or stop me if I go too fast or say something that doesn't make sense."

"Thank you, Mrs. Cronin," Helen said to the kind woman.

"Call me Mary, please," Mrs. Cronin insisted.

"Do you have a burial plot?" Mary began.

"Yes. We have four plots at Gate of Heaven Cemetery," John answered.

"Good. We have a good relationship with Mr. Daniels, the Manager there."

"We met him when we purchased the plots two years ago," said John.

"Do you have any of Hanna's clothing? Have you selected anything for her to wear at burial?"

"No, we hoped you could provide a gown or something," Helen said sniffling.

"Yes, we do. I will show you some things when we are done here. Have you any thoughts as to what type of casket you would like?"

"Red was her favorite color, then blue," Helen answered.

"I thought we might do something in wood rather than metal," John chimed in.

"We have some very lovely wood caskets. I will show you both our wood and metal caskets and that might make your decision easier. Another choice is the vault. There are three that we offer. All are good and are guaranteed not to leak. The choice is in color and if you would like a brass façade over the concrete."

"The plain one will be fine," John decided.

"Very good," Mary said as she wrote the details on the invoice sheet. "There are several selections of casket interiors. All are lovely, but we offer a deluxe interior made of satin and lace."

"The basic one will be fine," John stepped in and said again.

"Good, there are only a few other questions on the casket. Would you like a nameplate and a crucifix on the exterior?"

"Yes, we would," Thomas said.

"We need to put together an obituary notice. I have samples here that could help you in filling this out," Mary said as she slid the samples across the table.

"Will you be having a viewing for the deceased?" We offer the use of the funeral home for an evening and a morning viewing."

"We thought about having a morning funeral service. Rev. Michael Powers from our Baptist Church called us when he heard of Hanna's death. He is our pastor. He offered to hold the service at the funeral home and at the cemetery," John explained to Mary Cronin.

"Good. I will take care of contacting Rev. Powers and give him all the information about the day, the time, etc.

"Will you be accepting flowers for the funeral?"

"No, we thought that instead of flowers we would ask people to remember Hanna by contributing to the children's ward of Santa Monica Hospital."

"That is a beautiful way to remember your daughter. I will make sure that is stated clearly in the obituary notice in the newspaper. Would you like prayer cards with Hanna's name, birth date, and date of her passing on the back? We have a selection of beautiful cards."

"Yes, let's look at them now," Helen quietly said to Mary. It was obvious that this was very difficult for both Helen and her husband. It was heartbreaking for Thomas as well.

Helen selected a card with a Guardian Angel on the front and a simple prayer message on the back.

"Would you like a Guest Registry? This is a book that people sign as they come to the visitation. Would you prefer to bring something from home?"

"Yes, we will bring something from home," John pronounced.

"Dad, let them provide the Guest Book. Okay?" Thomas suggested.

"I have a difficult question," said Mary Cronin uneasily. "Will you be having Hanna embalmed? The choice is to keep the body refrigerated until the day of the service or to have her embalmed once she arrives here at the funeral home."

"Does it cost a lot to be embalmed?" Hanna's father asked.

"It is expensive; however, most of our clients select this option." Mary wrote a number on a piece of paper and slid it across the table.

"What?" John said loudly. "We buried my mother back in

Hickory for less money than this. How can embalming cost this much?"

"I understand, Mr. Jones," Mary said. "Things do cost more here in California. I have a price list that we register with the state—this is required by the State Funeral Board—and I will be glad to show this to you."

"No thanks. I have a weak heart as it is. I might keel over if I read your price sheet!" John said.

"Mom, if it is all right with you, may Dad and I select the casket and vault while you and Mrs. Cronin select the clothing for Hanna?" Thomas suggested.

"Well, okay. Is that okay with you John?" Helen asked her husband.

"Yes, dear, Mr. Cronin can show Tom and me the box while you and Mrs. Cronin select something nice for Hanna to wear," John said to his wife.

As the men walked to the conference room Thomas whispered to Joseph Cronin to go ahead and have Hanna embalmed. Joseph nodded and did not say anything. Thomas and his father then selected a lovely rose-colored coffin with red highlights. The vault was chosen and the nameplate and crucifix were selected to match the finish of the coffin. Mrs. Cronin and Helen selected a lovely white gown with a red sash. Helen, John, and Thomas sat down together and composed a moving obituary for Hanna. Joseph Cronin then sat down with John and Thomas and went over the invoice line by line to ensure everything was covered.

Thomas took the invoice from his dad and stepped aside with Joseph Cronin.

"I will be paying for Hanna's funeral. What is the total for everything?"

"Ten thousand seven hundred dollars," he replied. "That includes all the cemetery costs as well."

Thomas wrote a check for the full amount.

"Are you satisfied?" asked Mary Cronin.

"Yes, we are. Thank you for helping us through this," Helen said shaking Mary's hand and not letting go of it.

"We will call you later today with the details. We will try to schedule everything for the day after tomorrow. And we will call your pastor today and let him know the schedule. Thank you for selecting our funeral home," Mary said sincerely.

Thomas, Helen, and John walked out of the funeral home feeling fatigued and emotionally spent. This most difficult of tasks was completed and now the only thing facing them was the final service and farewell to Hanna. They would have a day or so to prepare for that last goodbye.

———

Later that day Rev. Michael Powers telephoned. He told John he had spoken with Mr. Cronin at the funeral home and that the service was scheduled as planned on Wednesday. He asked if he could stop by that evening and find out some additional information on Hanna for the memorial service. He agreed to come by at seven thirty.

Thomas and his dad spent the next few hours going over the details of how John had restored his old 1952 Chevy. It was a beautiful restoration. The interior looked as if it had never been out of the showroom. The car had wide side whitewall tires and a chrome exhaust. It was obvious how proud John was of the car. The only thing Thomas thought about was all the time he missed working on it with his dad. He was busy making his own world bigger, better, richer, and more powerful. After the car discussion they sat down on the deck and had a beer together. Helen came out and joined them with an iced tea.

"Now don't you too drink too much, remember Rev. Powers is coming over soon," Helen scolded.

"Don't worry, Mom," Thomas said, "I will keep an eye on Dad."

This type of dialogue, so simple and yet so loving, was what

Thomas lost in his world of power and money. He was beginning to understand the value of something that has no price. A mother's love, a father's respect, these things are priceless. Yet he had walked away from this thinking he didn't need it in his life. He saw now how wrong he had been.

Rev. Powers arrived on time and sat down at the kitchen table with Helen, John and Thomas. He seemed quite pleasant and compassionate. He knew John and Helen well and was very comforting and supportive in his words and demeanor.

"Helen, John, you know how sad we are over the death of your daughter, Hanna. I am sure she was a good woman. With parents like you, she must have had strong faith. It is difficult for young people today. I believe a child like Hanna, had a faith that she just didn't show to anyone. Another sad thing about today's younger people; they just don't understand that God loves them so much. I believe that Hanna is in a place where God has shown her how much he loves her."

"Thank you, Pastor. You are so kind. We invited Hanna to go to church with us often, but she never showed up on a Sunday morning until close to noon. I'm sorry we didn't do better," Helen said remorsefully.

"Helen, you and John did more than your share to raise Hanna right. Sometimes young people don't understand the need for God's love and forgiveness until they face a crisis in life, or when they finally just say 'yes' to Jesus' call. I believe Hanna had a chance to say 'yes' and there is nothing to prove she didn't. Only the Lord knows what is in our hearts, our minds and our souls. The Lord's arms are extended wide up on the cross because he died for everyone, and wants all his children to come home to him. I understand that the police found a bible in her apartment."

"Yes, Pastor. They are returning it to us after they check it for fingerprints. It is comforting to know that Hanna read the Word," Helen said as her last few words trailed away in tears.

The next hour was spent going over stories of Hanna's life

as a child and teenager. Pastor Michael was a charming, holy person with a heart that was open and kind. He was sincere when he spoke of God's love and forgiveness. By the end of the hour Rev. Powers had enough information for his prayers and eulogy for Hanna. He asked Thomas, Helen and John to pray with him for the happy repose of Hanna's soul.

"Lord, we know that Hanna is with you today. You have shown her mercy that we cannot understand. Bless us here as we suffer through losing her so unexpectedly. Help us to accept that it was your will to call her home to you at this time. Please give Helen and John and Thomas the special graces they need right now. We pray this in the name of Jesus Christ, your son, our Lord. Amen."

Thomas walked Rev. Powers out to his car and thanked him for his friendship with his parents. "I may need to speak with you sometime after the funeral. I have been away from the Lord a very long time. I may need someone to show me the way back."

chapter 29

Gretchen, John and Nick met for breakfast at six-thirty a.m. They still had several hours of driving ahead of them and Nick intended to arrive in San Francisco before noon. They ate, washed up, and were ready to go by seven-thirty. Nick took the wheel and headed out of the parking lot of the Comfort Suites and turned right onto the ramp of Rt. 580. Nick noticed John, who was in the back seat, had his head bowed.

"Hey John, are you going to fall asleep back there?" Nick inquired.

"No, I was just thinking about what we would do today."

"If I were to dare a guess, I would guess that you were praying," observed Nick.

"I was praying," answered Detective Baker.

"I did not mean to intrude, I'm sorry."

"It is okay. I usually don't pray out loud, but if you would like, I will."

Gretchen chimed in, "John, please, I need help to pray. If you don't mind, please pray for us."

"Lord," John prayed, "Please bless us on our journey today. Keep us safe on the highway. I thank you for this day and praise you for all you have made. Help us forgive those who want to hurt us. Give your healing grace and peace to all the families who lost loved ones at our precinct house. Guide us in our quest to find those responsible for that terrible attack. Jesus, I believe you are the Son of God. I place my life in your hands. Amen."

———————

After a long discussion the trio decided that it would be best to just be natural, nosy, and non-threatening about what was happening at St. Agnes hospital.

"What I would like to do," John Baker said. "Is speak with a nurse without the doctor standing right there. If Joey Bean was telling us the truth about Doctor Walters, I believe we are dealing with a guy who may be responsible for the deaths of his hospice patients who have this disease that attacks the immune system, the 'gay plague' as Joey Bean called it."

"I believe if we can get some idea about Doctor Walters, get a handle on him, so to speak, he may lead us to the organization that carried out the killings and attempted murders. Remember that this all started with Colleen. She was directed here by Joey Bean who is the son of the Surgeon General, Joseph Bolton. I believe that if I had not taken her away, she would have died here! I did take her from here but she was killed several hours later by an assailant that may have ties to Doctor Walters. We have come back here because everything started here," Nick said in detail.

"I feel terrible about the things that have happened. The people who killed Colleen were also willing to kill Dr. Harry Booth, Angela Carson, and me. The only reason I can fathom is that we all had contact with Colleen before she died. This doctor apparently thinks that anyone who has had contact with someone with this disease should die. This is the starting point for the crimes committed by a group of people who think the same way that this doctor does. I want this visit today to be the start of the end for these people."

"You are right Nick, absolutely right! It is critical that we confirm our suspicions here. Everything we do from here on will be determined by what we learn at St. Agnes Hospital. We must be sharp, observant, and careful. We do not want to endanger our family and friends back east by revealing our identities here. Nick, please keep that in mind as you move among the people you met before."

"I will, John," Nick said. "I will be very careful."

"I think I am the safest one in our group," Gretchen added. "I have never been here and I have never met any of the people who work here. At least I am unaware of having met anyone here."

"You are right, Gretchen," John said. "You may have an advantage we don't. If we get separated just keep asking questions and listening to the best of your ability."

"That I can do," Gretchen replied laughing.

The rest of the ride up to San Francisco was uneventful. They arrived just past eleven thirty a.m. Nick pulled into a Gas n' Go Station. John took care of filling the gas tank while Nick went to a pay phone and called Frank Murphy

The telephone was answered on the first ring. "Hello, this is the Retreat House, Father Murphy speaking."

"Hello, Frank. This is Nick."

"Good to hear from you. I spoke with the Administrator of St. Agnes Hospital, Jason Young. It turns out he has a cousin who is a Benedictine Priest who is currently stationed in San Salvador. We had a nice talk. I explained that you three were studying in-hospital hospice care and that you would like to stop in and speak with the physicians and Nurses involved in the St. Agnes program. He said he would welcome you personally. The doctor who is the Director of the hospice program, John Walters, would be in meetings most of today, but would clear time for you tomorrow morning. I asked Jason if you could snoop around this afternoon. He said that would be fine."

"That is great Frank, thank you for clearing the way for us. Once again you have come through for the team. I am going to owe you big time when we get back," Nick said in appreciation.

"I am just glad to be able to help. You and your family and friends were truly in need. That is why God puts us in places and circumstances where the good we do can have some positive effects on those that cross our paths," Father Murphy said. "Just think how rewarding it is knowing that what you do is a blessing to someone in need!"

"Well stated, Frank," Nick replied. "We will get over to St. Agnes this afternoon and will try to call you tonight if it doesn't get too late. We will definitely contact you and let you know our plans to travel home."

"Listen Nick, we wanted to run an idea by you. My brother is an FBI agent her in DC. Maybe it is time for us to bring them in to help us. Please run this idea by John and Gretchen and let us know what you think. We could use all the help we can get. Let me know what you decide."

Nick rejoined John and Gretchen and shared the news he received from Father Murphy.

"Okay, here is our plan for today," Nick announced. "We will get a hotel near St. Agnes and make our way over there this afternoon. Since Walters will be in meetings we have sort of free range to observe and ask the nurses questions. I suggest we keep a low profile and not upset anyone over there."

"I agree," John said. "If we make a good impression this afternoon we may get a little further with Dr. Walters tomorrow."

Nick drove to St. Agnes Hospital and began looking for a hotel nearby. About two blocks away Gretchen spotted a Hilton Hotel. They registered and settled in their adjoining rooms. John suggested they have lunch before walking over to the hospital. There was a seafood restaurant in the hotel.

Detective Baker, Gretchen, and Nick walked into St. Agnes Hospital at three o'clock and proceeded to the information desk to ask for Mr. Jason Young. They were directed to the second floor of the original building. They found the Administrator's office and knocked on the door. The secretary, Mrs. Lucy Dallas, invited them into her office and asked them to have a seat. John made the introductions and Mrs. Dallas expressed her delight that they had chosen to visit St. Agnes Hospital. The door to the rear of Mrs. Dallas' desk opened and Jason Young stepped out.

"Welcome to St. Agnes. I spoke with Father Murphy this morning and he told me about the work you have begun on studying in-hospital hospice care. Our program began about a year and a half ago. We are pleased with the program, but, unfortunately, as you know, the best efforts of our program still result in a patient losing his or her life. We try to make the process of dying tolerable for the patient and especially for the family. It is the most difficult time in a family's life. We don't have all the answers, but we are constantly reviewing the process and hope to improve with each case."

"I am sorry; I didn't even allow Mrs. Dallas to introduce us. You are Brother Murphy?"

"Yes, same name, but no relation to the Abbot of the Monastery you spoke to this morning. It is a delight to meet you, Mr. Young."

"Call me Jason."

"This is Sister Gretchen Marie and I am Brother Mark Wayne," John said as he shook Jason's hand.

"Why don't I let you to your work and I will return to mine?" Jason proposed. Mrs. Dallas, please tell our guests how to get to Eight West. "Brothers, Sister, have a good afternoon," Young said as he returned to his office.

"Mrs. Dallas," Nick said. "We can find our way to the ward. There is no need for you to trouble yourself."

"Well, let me just tell you that once you get off on the eighth floor elevator follow the new signs that say, 'Family Care Center.' We are experimenting with the name of the center. We've taken all signs down that formerly read, 'Hospice.'"

"Thank you for the information. We will be fine. Sister

Gretchen would never forgive us if we got lost," said John light-heartedly.

Upon reaching the hospice ward Nick saw the same signs that first alarmed him several weeks ago when he came for Colleen: "All Visitors must wear Hospital Gown–See Nurse for Details." They stopped at the nursing station and Maryanne Logan smiled at the three religious strangers and welcomed them to the center. She told them that Mrs. Dallas had called to let her know that the two Benedictine Monks and one nun would be there shortly.

"Thank you for visiting St. Agnes Hospital. Our Life Center here was formerly known as the Hospice Care Center. We do require that you wear these hospital surgical gowns over your clothing, and we ask that you put these booties over your shoes. We also insist that you wear the surgical masks as well. We recommend that you have no physical contact with our patients. We are trying to control the environment as much as possible. Even a small cold can hasten the death of one of our patients. Do you have any questions?"

"Yes," said Gretchen as she placed the hospital wear over her gray Habit, "Do the patients receive any physical contact? Can their parents or brothers and sisters hug them and kiss them?"

"We strongly discourage all physical interaction. It does happen, but we have seen so many people get sick after touching their loved one. We have even had one case where the mother of a young man whose condition was fatal returned to us as a patient within nine months!"

"Are all of your current patients being treated for this new disease, this thing they call the plague?" asked John.

"Right now, yes. It is very unfortunate that these young men have chosen a lifestyle than leads to this, a difficult death, painful and many times alone."

"May I ask a question?" Gretchen asked politely. "Can you please explain this 'lifestyle' thing to me?"

"Certainly dear, these men commit sodomy with each other.

The Bible is very clear on this sin. It says it is an abomination before God. In a way, they deserve what they are getting for being indecent and immoral."

"Do you have any religious people visiting them and bringing spiritual relief?"

"We have the clergy visit once a week. Unfortunately many of these men die very quickly. Their choice seems pretty clear to me. Do what God says and live. Doing these terrible things with other men is insulting to God and he will deal with them at the judgment table."

"I must say, Mrs. Logan," Gretchen continued. "You seem to have an ability to compartmentalize your feelings about these poor souls. One minute you are compassionate and the next you seem so cold when you talk about the patients. I am curious about that. Is this attitude something that just developed or have you always been like this?"

"Well, that seems like a very rude question," the nurse replied.

"Please, forgive me. I guess what I meant was do the nurses here, including you, get any counseling to deal with the issue of handling death on a daily basis. This has to be very difficult job," Gretchen said kindly?

"We meet with Dr. Walters every week to talk about how to make the Care Center even better than the previous week. He reminds us that we should save our compassion for the poor souls who come in here with cancer or some other fatal disease. These men and their friends don't deserve to be treated after the way they behaved to contract this disease, which, by the way, has spread across the country and around the world. Dr. Walters and his team are setting up centers throughout our country and training physicians how to act and react around these people with what we call the 'gay plague'.

"Mrs. Logan," John said, entering the conversation. "We have heard about this sickness. It attacks immune systems, I believe."

"That is correct," the nurse replied. "Dr Walters has given the disease a name based on what it does to the patient."

"What is the name he uses?" asked Nick.

"AIDS; the patient has developed an *A*cquired *I*mmune *D*eficiency *S*ystem.

"I see, and the primary way patients come down with AIDS is through sexual contact with another person?"

"Yes," Nurse Logan answered. "We have seen this disease growing in alarming numbers here in San Francisco. The number of these patients is increasing each week in our hospital. Dr. Walters is in contact with other hospitals nearby and they are experiencing the same increase. He has tried many different medicinal therapies, but to no avail. Personally, I think God is punishing them for the illicit behavior they have engaged in. We don't know the level of contagion this disease has for the general population. Suppose this spread to innocent children through childbirth? Dr. Walters and the two men he works with from Washington, DC are in contact with the Surgeon General and are trying to come up with ways to protect the population from a massive breakout of the disease. They are working with other doctors around the country on vaccines, but nothing looks promising. I don't mean to frighten you, but this is what we are facing. My innocent children could possibly be infected by drinking from a glass that an infected person used but was not washed properly. It scares me and makes me very angry. This is one disease that should never, ever have come into existence. The sinful action of men being intimate with other men is unnatural and that is why this disease is here today. You are religious people, trained in the Bible, surely you know what the good book states about this type of behavior."

"Yes," John answered. "I understand your fear and anger. If this would spread throughout the general population we would have a death rate that could equal the Black Plague. It is comforting to hear that Dr. Walters has a team working on this. Could you tell me the names of the doctors he works with in the Washington, DC area? I am stationed in Silver Springs, Maryland, which is not far from the Capital."

"Dr. James Nelson and Dr. Mark Preston are the two men on his team studying this problem. They work at Walter Reed Hospital," Mrs. Logan answered. "He also works with some people from the Center for Disease Control in Atlanta. I have not met those people. Dr. Nelson and Dr. Preston are here today in meetings with Dr. Walters. I don't know what their schedules are, but if they are here tomorrow you might be able to meet with them."

"Nurse Logan," Gretchen said kindly. "I believe I was unkind to you earlier. Now that you have explained the threat of this disease I understand your anger and your frustration. Please forgive me if I sounded judgmental. I did not understand the disease and its potential for great harm to the general population. I guess I am concerned about the impact on your life as you deal with this on a daily basis. That must be difficult."

"Sister," Nancy Logan replied. "Forgive me too if I seemed to snap back at you. I do get upset from time-to-time, and I guess it comes with the territory. I know that you want to learn about Hospice Care here at St. Agnes. Unfortunately about ninety eight percent of our patients here have been men with this disease. Dr. Walters has recommended we send other terminally ill patients to other hospitals so that we can focus on treating these men. Perhaps we can learn something about how to prevent it from spreading. It does get overwhelming."

"May we speak to the patients?" Nick asked.

"I would ask that you do not disturb or upset the patients. Perhaps you could pray with them. I would avoid talking about their care," Nurse Logan instructed. "Please be sure to keep your face mask and gloves on."

"Thank you. I can assure you we will do nothing to upset them," Nick replied.

Nick suggested that they split up at this point and visit only with patients who are awake. "If someone seems like they don't want company, just leave quietly."

"Gretchen, can you do this? You can stay with either John or me if you are uncomfortable," Nick quietly asked.

"No, I think I will be all right," she replied.

Nick walked into room 825 and said hello to a young man in his twenties. "Good afternoon, my name is Brother Murphy. May I ask you name, and how are you doing?"

"My name is Phillip Morgan. I am not very well. I am not a Catholic, so why are you here?"

"Phillip, I am a Benedictine monk and we are studying hospital wards like this all over the country. If I am intruding, I will leave."

"No, Brother, please stay, at least for a minute," Phillip pleaded.

"Sure, I am happy to stay. Are you getting good care here?"

"Yeah, if you want to call being drowned in medication good care. I am asleep most of the time. But that is better than being awake. Usually I am throwing up or spewing my guts out. I know I will be dead soon and all this will end. The one thing about coming to St. Agnes is that I knew it would be over quick."

"Phillip, why do say that?" Nick asked.

"No one lasts more than ten days here. It is a fact. I have had friends here who lasted eight, six, nine days. I bet if you saw the patient records you would see I am right."

"How long have you been here, Phillip?" Nick asked.

"Six days."

"Would you like me to pray with you before I leave?" Nick offered.

"Could you just give me a blessing? I have accepted my fate and made peace with God," Phillip replied.

"May God's love and mercy be with you Phillip, and fill your days with hope. Remember Phillip, the thief on the cross next to Jesus attained his salvation that very day by his proclamation of faith. May you too be with Christ in paradise when he calls you home," Nick prayed.

"Thank you, Brother," Phillip said as his eyes filled with tears.

"You are welcome, Phillip," Nick said softly, go with God, son." Nick reached out his hand and gently brushed Phillips hair. "Goodbye, my friend."

———————

Down the corridor, Gretchen walked into room 828 and quietly walked over to the patient who had his back turned to her.

"Hello, are you awake?" she asked.

"Yes, who is there?" The patient answered.

"My name is Sister Gretchen," she said making her way around the far side of the hospital bed.

"What do you want?" he demanded.

"I am just here visiting. I didn't want to leave without saying hello to you," Gretchen explained.

"Oh, you are a Sister?"

"Yes, I am. What is your name?"

"Bruce Palmer."

"Well, it is nice to meet you, Bruce Palmer. How are you today?"

"How the hell do you think I am? I am dying!"

"I know, Bruce, and I am so sorry about that. I don't mean to upset you. Would you rather I left?" Gretchen spoke so softly that Bruce had to strain his ears to hear.

"Well, no. Please, won't you stay a little while?"

"Yes, I am happy to stay."

"I am sorry about swearing. I just am so angry."

"I can imagine."

"Sister, I am twenty six years old. Twenty six! I was supposed to live until I reached eighty or so. Now, I am days from my death. My God, I am a dead man," Bruce said crying.

Gretchen placed her one hand over his and with her other

she wiped away his tears and sweat. "Bruce, you may die, but you will never be alone. God is with you always, even here, even now."

"God gave up on me a long time ago."

"No, I can assure you, God does not give up on any of us," Gretchen said speaking from experience.

"Yeah, well you are a nun. You are going to heaven."

"I was not always a nun. I lived a life that I finally grew ashamed of and changed. I was sure God didn't want me," Gretchen added.

"I don't think God wants men like me in heaven."

"Bruce, did your father ever get mad at you when you were a boy when you disobeyed him? I bet that happened. Didn't your own father forgive you? Sure he did. Your dad is just a human being and he forgave you. God made you, and he knows everything about you. If your human father can forgive, certainly your heavenly Father will forgive you too. You will be surprised at how much he loves you. All you need to do is tell him you are sorry for whatever sins you committed. And if you have forgotten some sins, tell him you are sorry for those too. You can just say you are sorry for everything, and that you want him to be with you."

"You make it sound so easy."

"It is, especially if you are sincere. God doesn't like liars."

"Will you pray with me?"

"Yes, Bruce. I would like to pray with you."

Gretchen held Bruce's hand. "Lord, Bruce and I are here in your presence. Please send us your grace. We don't know what lies ahead for either of us, Lord. Please forgive any sins we have committed. Bruce is frightened right now. Let him know you are with him. Bless him and keep him near you, today and always."

Gretchen was so moved and so touched to be able to pray with this dying man that she nearly lost her composure. She swallowed hard two or three times but made it through. Bruce reached up and hugged her when they were finished. As he lay back down on the bed he seem relieved and at peace.

"Thank you Sister. I forgot to ask you, does it count if I am not a Catholic?"

"Yes, Bruce, it counts for you, and for all believers."

"Sister, this is my eighth day in this ward. I will be dead in another day or two. You came to see me at just the right time. Thank you so much."

"You are welcome. But why do you say you will be dead in two days? Only the Lord knows when we will die."

"You don't know the history of this place?"

"No. Tell me."

"Nobody lasts longer than ten days. Nobody."

"How do you know this?"

"There have been at least twenty guys I know who ended up here and every one of them died within ten days. I visited a couple of them and even if they seemed okay, sure enough, by the tenth day they were dead," Phillip stated. "Please don't tell the evil head nurse I said anything."

"Mrs. Logan seems very nice. Why do you call her evil?"

"She follows Doc Walters around and says the worst things to us. If we soil ourselves and she has to clean up it is awful. She tells us we are going to hell and we deserve our fate."

"Will you come back and see me tomorrow?" Phillip asked.

"Yes, we will be here one more day. I will stop in to see you. God bless you Bruce," Gretchen said as she made the sign of the cross on his forehead before leaving his room.

———

At the same time that Nick and Gretchen entered rooms 825 and 828, Detective Baker walked into room 830 and quietly asked, "Hello, may I come in?"

"Yes, who is it?"

"I am a friend. My name is Brother Mark. I am a Benedictine monk visiting the hospital. May I come in for a few minutes?"

"Sure, come in. My name is Archie McAndrews. How are ya?" Archie said pleasantly as he reached out and shook John's hand.

"Hello Archie. It is nice to meet you."

"Why are you visiting the dead man's ward? The only way we leave here is toes first," Archie said laughing.

"You have a good sense of humor, Archie."

"I always said you only live once so you might as well be happy. Besides, most people don't know when they are going to die. I have them beat! I've got four days to go."

"Archie, you can't be sure of that."

"Brother Mark, you are not from here are you?

"No."

"Well let me fill you in; every patient here dies by the tenth day of their stay. Not a few, not some, but every one. Some die sooner, but nobody beats the ten day rule."

"You are all pretty sick, so it could be a coincidence, right?"

"Nope, no, no way, zero chance."

"I'm glad you are sure about that," John said.

"Look, you should not ask the head nurse about the ten day rule. She is a pawn of Doc Walters who makes sure we get the right amount of medicine to keep us sedated and then he administers the big blast that sends us into a coma and death follows within twenty four hours."

"You have seen this?"

"Yes, sir."

"You know what you are implying?"

"Yes, I know. Don't tell anyone anything. Okay?" Archie said.

"I won't."

"You know what type of life we led, right? We prefer men to women. That is not a very popular idea right now. Most people hope we all die of this 'gay plague' and disappear. We don't have anyone who cares enough about us. We are not a popular cause. It stinks, but that is the way it is."

"Is there anything I can do for you Archie?"

"Yes, there is one thing. Will you baptize me?"

"Do you want to become a Christian?"

"Yes."

"Are you sure?"

"Yes, I am certain."

"Can you tell me one reason why?"

"Yes. I read in the Bible that unless a man be baptized and accept Christ he cannot get to heaven. I have accepted Christ in my heart, but I have not had the nerve to ask anyone to baptize me. Can you do it?"

John picked up the glass of water on the bedside table and said a silent prayer. "Lord, bless this water that I am about to use to baptize your son Archie."

"Archie, just lean back against your pillow, I will pour some water over your forehead and pronounce the words of the sacrament. Are you ready?"

"Yes. Go ahead."

"Archie, *I baptize you in the name of the Father, of the Son, and of the Holy Spirit.* As he said the words of the baptism, John poured water on Archie's head and then handed him a towel.

"That's it?"

"Yes, Archie, you are now a Christian. You have already accepted Christ. I might suggest you ask God to forgive all the sins of your life so that when you see the Lord you may be pure of heart."

"What should I say?"

"Tell the Lord you are really sorry for all the wrongs of your life, and then accept that he has forgiven you."

"You are sure that's all I have to do. I don't have time to make amends to the people I have hurt."

"Make that part of your prayer. Tell God you wish you had the time to do that and that you wanted to atone for your sins.

He will work things out with you when you get to heaven," John explained.

"Thank you, Brother Mark," Archie said smiling. Would you get this letter to my folks after I die? We have not spoken in a long time. My dad and I just couldn't get along. I was not the man he expected. So we parted in anger. I'm really sorry I hurt my mom and dad. This letter is important. Please, make sure they get it. Okay?"

"I promise I'll get it to your mom and dad."

"Thanks. You better go. There are other guys who might need your help. Pray for me, please."

"I will. Goodbye Archie. Remember that God is right there with you. He won't quit on you. Hang in there."

John walked out and wondered who had really been helped in that room, Archie or himself.

Detective Baker walked over and chatted with Mrs. Logan while waiting for Nick and Gretchen who were in visiting other patients. Gretchen emerged from room 832 about ten minutes later and Nick returned from room 836 shortly after where they visited and prayed with other patients.

"Mrs. Logan," said John. "You have been most helpful. Perhaps we will see each other tomorrow."

"I am glad to have been of service to you. If you need anything more please do not hesitate to contact me."

"Goodbye Mrs. Logan, and thank you," Gretchen added.

John, Gretchen, and Nick walked out of St. Agnes Hospital in silence. They were grateful for the opportunity to have met some patients and to pray with them. On the other hand they were horrified at what they learned about the way patients were treated, and that none of them lived longer than ten days.

"Let's talk about this back at the hotel," Nick said somberly.

Gretchen just about exploded by the time they reached the hotel. As they walked into Nick's room she let out a loud guttural growl.

"You would not believe what is going on over there! These

poor sick men are treated horribly. That nurse, Maryanne Logan is evil!" said Gretchen.

"Gretchen, you have to calm down," John advised. "I think we all are stunned by our visit today."

"You don't understand," she continued. "That doctor is killing them! When they are admitted there they know they will be dead in ten days or less! That is horrible!"

"Gretchen, I spoke with two patients. Both confirmed what you just told us. How about you John? What did you learn today?"

"I heard the same thing. I spoke with one man and he shared the same story, but begged me not to tell anyone until after he has died. I went into another room but the patient was asleep. I have a question Nick. One man asked me to baptize him. I asked him if he wanted a priest or minister to do it, but he said no. I said a silent prayer and then I baptized him as reverently as I could. "

"You actually baptized the man?" asked Gretchen. "What did you use?"

"I took the water in the glass on his table and prayed that God would bless it so that it would become the blessed water of baptism."

"You are the best," Gretchen said to John as she walked over and hugged him.

"I have not been hugged by a nun before. It's not as bad as I imagined it would be," John said while laughing.

"Okay, we now know there is a definite pattern of maltreatment of the patients. How does that help us in our pursuit of the people who killed Colleen and our other friends?" Nick asked.

"First off," John began. "It is obvious that Walters and his crew are comfortable killing. When they decide to eliminate someone it happens quickly. I don't think they care if people around the target are also killed. I am sure in some cases they intend to take out multiple victims. I believe that Nick, Harry Booth, and Angela Carson were all targets at the airport. They want, first of all, anyone associated with this AIDS disease dead. That is a brutal assessment of their activity, but their crimes are truly brutal. The connection to the Surgeon General and to the US Medical Association is another critical link that should give us an idea of the extent of what Walters and his gang are up to."

"I had a terrible thought as we were walking back to the hotel," Nick said. "It is very possible that what Walters is doing here is the pilot program for hospitals across the country that have hospice care. If the Surgeon General is involved, this same program could be implemented at every Veteran's Hospital across the country! Think of the gravity of such a program. A hospital could elect to place any critically ill patient in its hospice program and decide when to terminate them. That may be taking this situation to the extreme, but it is certainly within the realm of possibility."

"It does overwhelm me," said Gretchen. "How can we do anything to stop this? We might be the only ones aware of what is going on at St. Agnes Hospital."

"Gretchen," John said calmly. "We can't think that way. We must think of what is in front of us. While I am aware of the big picture, I can only control what is in front of me. If we allow ourselves to let the size of the problem in front of us overwhelm us, we may be thrown into a state of paralysis. That won't help anyone."

"I understand, I think," Gretchen replied. "It's just that we seem outnumbered by a million."

"Numbers will not mean a thing when we break the news to the public. These people think they are operating above the law. It may take a little time, but we will triumph in the long run," said John reassuringly.

"John, what Walters and his people are doing costs money, lots of money. Where would they get that kind of cash?" asked Nick.

"Since things seem to be centered around Washington I would not be surprised if there wasn't a tie-in to one of the

Political Action Committees. Those animals raise more money in a month than many of the fortune 500 businesses raise in a year. There is very little accountability with those committees. They outsource their fund raising to anonymous companies who somehow raise huge amounts of money. If the Surgeon General is behind this he has the ability to deflect any investigation or audit of the company raising the funds. If big money is involved, you can usually count on someone in Washington having their fingers in the pot," said John.

"Knowing what we learned today, how do we proceed tomorrow?" asked Gretchen. "What do we say to Dr. Walters?"

"We ask him those questions about the in-hospital hospice care," Nick instructed. "Just as we planned. We do not say a word about what we learned today. I am sure Nurse Logan will try to find out if any of the patients told us anything she did not want us to hear. We cannot say nor do anything to jeopardize the welfare of the men we spoke with today. If Dr. Walters suspects we know anything about what is going on we may even become targets. I think we should act a little naïve and stick to our questions."

"I agree, Nick," said John nodding his head. "I have a suggestion. Let's try to forget about this for a little while. We can relax a little, have dinner, walk around town and then get good nights sleep. And, I don't know about you, but after the mess we experienced today, I have to shower."

"I agree with that," said Gretchen.

"Me too," Nick agreed.

chapter 30

Nick and his companions met at the breakfast bar in the hotel at seven a.m. the next morning. "How is everyone feeling today?" he asked.

"I feel much better than yesterday afternoon," Gretchen replied. "The walk we took last night refreshed me and I think I am in a better mental state. I am confident that I can handle things today."

"John, how are you doing?"

"I'm fine, Nick, how are you? You seem a little distant this morning," Detective Baker observed.

"I've made a decision. I cannot go back to the hospital today. I may have imagined this, but I thought that Nurse Logan was staring at me several times yesterday. I also noticed they have security cameras in all the hallways. It is possible that there are also hidden cameras in the patient rooms," Nick said. "If Logan or Walters were to really study the tapes I could be recognized. It is just too risky. Can you two handle everything today?"

"Certainly, Nick," John answered. "I agree with your decision. I will tell them you had something come up unexpectedly and cannot make it over to St. Agnes."

"Good thinking."

Detective John Baker, alias Brother Mark Wayne, and Sister

Gretchen Marie, alias Gretchen Sanders, boldly walked into St. Agnes Hospital at 9:30 a.m. pacific time.

Nick stayed at the hotel and telephoned Frank Murphy back at the Monastery. He wanted to fill Shaun in on what they learned and keep everyone up to date on their activity in San Francisco. The Abbot answered the telephone on the second ring.

"Hello, Father Murphy speaking."

"Father, it's Nick. How are you?"

"I am doing fine. Can you hold a minute? I see Chris and Shaun in the hallway. Let me tell them you are on the phone."

A minute later not only Chris and Shaun arrived in Frank Murphy's office, but also Catherine Harding and Dr. Harry Booth.

"Nick, I am going to put you on speaker phone," said Frank.

"Hello everyone, I trust you are all well," Nick said happily. "I hope to be home with you in a day or two. We have all missed you very much. Our work here in San Francisco is nearly complete. John and Gretchen are at St. Agnes now. I decided this morning that I was putting everyone in danger. I believe that Dr. Walters would have recognized me and that would jeopardize not only what we are doing here, but it could put us all in danger."

"Nick, this is Shaun. I think you made the right decision. It is better to be safe. How did you make out at the hospital yesterday?"

"You are not going to believe this. We met with five patients and four of them shared just about the same story. When they are admitted to St. Agnes they have ten days to live."

Harry rose from his chair and moved towards the phone excitedly. "What do you mean they have only ten days to live? Are they that sick?"

"No, Harry, every patient with this disease has died by the tenth day of their stay at this hospital. I believe they are systematically murdering these men."

"How are they killing them? And why wouldn't someone there notice it and go to the authorities?" Shaun inquired.

"Most of the men have been abandoned by their families. They have no health insurance. They have no support system other than some friends who probably have the disease as well. One patient told us that the head doctor, John Walters, prepares a 'cocktail' of drugs that puts them into a coma, and death follows within twenty-four hours. They do not perform an autopsy on these men at St. Agnes because they are fearful the virus will spread throughout the hospital and community," Nick explained.

"There is no doubt that Walters and his colleagues have ties to the Surgeon General and possibly someone higher up in the Government. The two doctors from Walter Reed, Jim Nelson and Mark Preston, are here in San Francisco now. They had a meeting with Dr. Walters yesterday. These are the doctors that Walters told me to contact at Walter Reed when I came home with Colleen. He seemed genuinely concerned about her when I met him here."

Harry began pacing anxiously. "Nick, this is incredible. These men are doctors! I am at a loss to understand how a doctor could be involved in crimes like this."

"These people believe that the general population is in danger of getting this disease. There is no antidote, medicine, or vaccine for it. They have taken it upon themselves to deliver the population from this plague. John and I talked about where they would get the huge amount of money it would take to make this happen. He believes that a Political Action Committee has hired a private company to raise the money they need. I suspect that the USMA is in on this plan. The Medical Association can raise funds incredibly fast. Whichever group is holding the power has cleared the way for not only killing sick people, but anyone around the infected patient as well," Nick stated forcefully.

"Nick, this is Catherine, has John any idea which private company is acting as the controlling interest in all these crimes?"

"I am not sure. We only came up with this theory yesterday. I believe we are on the right track. But make no mistake about it; we are dealing with perhaps the most powerful enemy we have faced, Catherine. They have powerful allies, they have lots of money, and they are ruthless. Their soldiers are professional executioners. Believe me, this won't be easy," Nick explained.

"Nick, Chris here, what can we do to help you? I feel so helpless here at the Monastery, as do the rest of us. There must be something we can do."

"Chris," Nick replied. "I think you have to wait until we get back. Then we can go into the USMA file that your friend gave us access to with his ID information. Then I think it might be time to get Frank Murphy's brother involved."

"Nick, I will bet my life that we can trust my brother Michael. He has been with the FBI a long time. He may be able to tell us things they are already investigating in this matter. I will defer to your opinion, but I really urge you to think about using Michael."

"Frank, you make a good case for bringing Michael in on this investigation. I know John thinks that FBI can be trusted and can help us. We are agreed then to contact the FBI upon our return," Nick said.

"I will call you later today when John and Gretchen come back to the hotel. We plan to fly home in a day or two. I cannot tell you how much we appreciate your help and prayers for us out here," Nick said gratefully. "We think about you often and pray for you daily. I am going to go see Maura when we get home. Shaun, I suggest you become one of us monks. That way when we go to my home we can go see Maura and Kathleen together. We will be simply two monks visiting Maura to offer their condolences for the loss of their husbands. I have to see Maura and I miss the babies more than I could ever have imagined."

"I am with you, Nick. I miss Kathleen too." Shaun said.

"Okay, I will say goodbye for now. Expect a phone call from me within twenty-four hours. I guess we all should be ready to act when we get back and form a plan," Nick said with hope in his voice. "Thank you again for you thoughts and prayers."

Nick slowly hung up the telephone, wishing he was back in Washington with Maura and their two babies.

The extent of the threat from Dr. Walters and his group seemed to be increasing each day. Nick knew that they had to find one person in the conspiracy that would break. They had to find one doctor who was willing to say "stop" and stand up for what was right. It might be difficult, but it was critical if this threat to human life would be overcome. There was also the matter of justice for all the innocent victims at the police precinct.

Nick was suddenly overcome with the need to get on his knees and pray. He responded at once and knelt down by the hotel bed. "Lord, I feel your call to pray. Please watch over John and Gretchen. I sense they are in danger. You have been with us all through our journey and I am thankful for your support. Heavenly Father, be with us today and every day of our lives. Bring John and Gretchen safely back to me, and protect our families. Amen."

chapter 31

Gretchen and John made their way back to the Family Care Center and were met by Nurse Logan. Her mood was decidedly less pleasant than the previous day.

"Where is the other monk?" she rudely inquired.

"Brother Murphy had an emergency and will not be joining us today," John answered.

"That is too bad. Dr. Walters was looking forward to meeting him," said the unhappy nurse. "The doctor should be here in about twenty minutes."

"May we pay a short visit with some of the patients we met yesterday?" Gretchen asked politely while smiling at Nurse Logan, hoping to soften her mood.

"Unfortunately we lost a patient last night and another has fallen into a coma. We would prefer that you not visit the patients right now. Some are getting their baths and we dispense medicines shortly. For the patients' dignity we prefer visitors wait until we complete rounds. I am sure you understand," Mrs. Logan said coldly. "You may wait in room 800 where we have set up a lounge. There is coffee and tea on the table. Help yourself."

"May we ask which patient died last night?" Gretchen asked, again trying to be pleasant and friendly.

"That is confidential. Dr. Walters may choose to inform you. I cannot divulge doctor/patient information," the nurse said curtly.

John tugged on Gretchen's arm and started walking toward room 800. They walked in and sat down on two chairs surrounding a small table. The coffee urn was on a table up against the wall by the door. He poured a small amount into a cup and dipped one finger into it and took it to his lips. He looked at Gretchen and shook his head, then pulled out a pocket-sized notebook and a pen and began to write:

Do not say anything about the patients. I have a very bad feeling about this room and our visit today. Do not drink the coffee or tea. Follow my lead.

Gretchen nodded that she understood.

John said out loud, "Sister, please pray with me for the sick and dying patients here at St. Agnes."

"Certainly, Brother Mark," Sister Gretchen replied.

"In the name of the Father, the Son, and the Holy Spirit, Amen," John began. "Lord we ask you to bless the man who died here last night, and to look over the patient who lapsed into a coma. Bless the doctors and nurses who have dedicated their lives to serving these desperate souls. Inspire them to find a cure for this wretched illness. We ask you to bless all the patients here at this hospital. In Jesus' name we pray, Amen."

"Thank you Brother Mark, that was a beautiful prayer," Gretchen said out loud while writing on John's note pad:

What do you think is going on?

I am not sure, but I am getting a bad feeling about being here. Be very careful what you say. And no matter what, do not get separated from me. We stay together.

The door to the lounge opened and a tall man with dark curly hair wearing a white smock walked in. He was either quite elegant or very arrogant.

"Hello, I am Dr. Walters," he announced.

"It is nice to meet you, Doctor," John said, shaking his hand. "I am Brother Mark and this is Sister Gretchen."

"I understand you had a chance to meet some of our patients yesterday. What did you think?" asked the doctor.

"We were impressed with the care they receive. This must be a very trying ward to spend all your time in. Nurse Logan is an angel. All the patients spoke of her care. The only thing I wondered about was the abbreviated clergy schedule," John said almost haltingly.

"Brother Mark, we tried to have an open clergy policy. Unfortunately we found that very few clergymen were willing to visit. We do tell our patients that they may request a clergyman anytime and we try to accommodate them. Tell me, what did Brother Murphy have to say about our Care Center?"

"He too, was impressed with the care level and attentiveness of the staff and doctors," John replied without making eye contact with Dr. Walters.

"You visited with Archie yesterday didn't you, Brother?" asked Walters, his mood turning sharply.

"Yes, Doctor," John replied.

"You prayed with him?"

"Yes."

"Anything else?"

"No."

"You baptized him, didn't you?" Dr. Walters said angrily. "He didn't deserve to be baptized."

"What?"

"You know how these men were infected. This disease is a result of immoral behavior. This behavior has the possibility of infecting the general population."

"That is frightening thought, Doctor."

"You are darn right it is frightening. Innocent lives are at stake here. Your family, my son, your nieces and nephews, all are at risk!"

"Forgive me Brother for losing my temper. When I see the potential damage this disease poses to not just every American, but every citizen of the world, I get upset. I have compassion for the suffering of these patients, but I have no compassion for the activity that causes the disease. What I am doing here at St. Agnes is trying to find a way to contain it and then find a cure. As a doctor I have an obligation to the health of society and when a disease as deadly and contagious as this one stares me in the face, I have to act aggressively and swiftly. Do you understand?" Walters demanded.

"Oh yes," said Gretchen. "Bless you for your work. I will pray for you."

"I am glad we understand each other."

"This has been truly enlightening for me," John said shaking Walters's hand. "I am sorry if I did anything to upset you. Please forgive me."

"Done. Won't you have some coffee? We make a decent blend up here. Much better than you would get in the cafeteria," Walters said as he readied to pour a cup for Gretchen and John.

"Thank you, Doctor,"

"You are welcome. I have to make a call. Make yourself comfortable. I will be back shortly," the doctor said as he walked out the door.

John heard the distinctive sound of the click of a dead bolt being engaged from the outside the door.

"Do not drink that coffee!" John whispered to Gretchen as he picked it up and smelled the aroma in the cup. "I don't recognize the odor, but I bet it is poison. We need to get out of here."

"How are we going to get out?" asked Gretchen nervously.

"Let me try the door." John walked over to the door and turned the handle. The handle engaged, but the dead bolt was locked solid. He reached into his pocket under his cassock and pulled out a tool that looked like a wide-barreled pen. He unscrewed the pen and took out something that appeared to be a long thin metal spike. John took a second, thinner spike from the barrel of the pen and inserted them at the same time into the narrow opening of the key slot of the dead lock. He fiddled a bit, moving each spike simultaneously until he heard the sound of a click.

"Gretchen, hold onto me, do not let go," John said.

"What are we going to do?"

"Do you have your jeans and a shirt on under your habit?"

"Yes."

"Take your habit off," John instructed, as he removed his cassock.

"Can you run in your shoes?" John asked.

"I think so."

"If you can't, kick them off and run barefoot. Are you ready?"

"Yes."

"Let's go!"

John opened the door carefully and peered both ways down the hall. He held on to Gretchen's hand and they walked out of the room quickly. Without their religious clothing they did not draw any attention. Rather than take the elevator, they took the stairs to the street level. Once outside they sprinted to the hotel and up to their rooms.

"Nick, we have to go, now!" John commanded.

"What is going on?" Nick said as he gathered up his clothing.

"Walters knows who we are. I can explain after we are out of here. Check out by telephone and tell the front desk to have our car brought down."

Nick understood the dire urgency of the situation. He dressed in street clothing and was ready to go in less than five minutes.

They took the elevator down to the street level where the car would be delivered. As they waited anxiously for the car, they heard the sound of screeching brakes and metal bending. Suddenly, from around the final curve of the parking garage, Nick's car came barreling down the ramp and slammed into the wall at the base of the ramp three feet from where they stood. The driver slumped over the wheel.

They hurried out of the garage and hailed a cab. "Take us to the airport, fast," John shouted at the driver.

The cab sped away from the hotel zigzagging through traffic. John and Nick looked out the rear window in time to see hospital security personnel running down the street from the hospital toward the Hilton.

"What happened?" Nick asked John.

"They were onto us. Walters was very disappointed you were not with us. I believe he intended to poison us. We probably would have been killed and listed among the AIDS patients."

"What is our next move?" asked Gretchen.

"We get a plane and leave the area," John said plainly.

"Do we head back—?"

Before Nick could finish his sentence, John reached across the seat and covered Nick's mouth as he shook his head back and forth.

Nick understood that John did not want them to reveal their plans or destination to anyone who could share that information with anyone who wanted to track them down.

The cab driver dropped them off in front of the American Airlines terminal. They picked up their bags and walked into the building. John suggested they sit down and talk about their situation.

"Gretchen, are you and Nick okay?" John asked.

"Yes, I'm okay," answered Gretchen.

"I'm good," said Nick. "We got out of there in the nick of time. How did you know that Walters knew who we are?"

"I don't think he knew Gretchen or me, but he was sure about you," John explained matter-of-factly. "We were escorted to a patient room that had been converted into a guest lounge. On the way into the room I noticed the door had a dead bolt lock mounted on the outside. Walters came in and offered us coffee.

I sensed he was insincere. When the lock snapped on the door, I knew we had to get out of the hospital."

"What do you suppose happened at the hotel parking garage?" asked Gretchen.

"My guess," Nick replied, "Someone cut the brake lining. When the valet started down that circular ramp there was no way to stop the car."

"What is our next step? Should we head back east? We have got to put a plan together. I want to get as far away from Dr. Walters and San Francisco as possible," Gretchen said anxiously. "Can't we just catch the first plane out of here?"

"They will be expecting us to do that. We need to put some distance between them and us. They will think we got on a plane and headed east. I want to throw them some kind of a curve," John said as his mind was already examining alternate plans.

"Let's rent a car here and drive to Las Vegas. It is a two-day drive and it should throw them off our tracks for a little while. We can fly back to DC from there. I am anxious to get home, but if one day can buy us some time, I would be willing to sacrifice it," Nick said.

"That is not a bad plan. Even if they track us here to the airport and find out we did rent a car I doubt they would think we would be driving east. They might think we drove back to Los Angeles or over to Sacramento. It is unlikely they would think we would drive to Vegas."

"We have another issue that we must take care of here before we leave," Nick said seriously.

"What is that?" Gretchen inquired.

"I must notify Shaun. He has got to get Maura, Kathleen, and the babies to safety. If they recognized me our family and friends are in jeopardy. They will put two and two together and figure out where Catherine, Harry and everyone else are out at the Monastery. These people are desperate and have no fear of killing. Look at what they did at the precinct building."

"Nick, you are right. We have to call them, and we have to call them now!" said John Baker with deep concern in his voice.

Nick walked over to a pay telephone and called Father Murphy. "Hello, Frank, this is Nick. Is Shaun anywhere near the phone? If not, could you send for him?"

"Nick, Shaun is not in my office. I will ask someone to get him."

"Thank you, Frank."

Frank Murphy put the phone down and asked a monk to round up the visitors, especially Shaun.

"He will be here in a minute. What is wrong, Nick? I can hear it in your voice, my friend," Frank said with sincere concern.

"I will tell you in a minute after Shaun is on the line."

"Okay, Nick. I see them coming now. Hold on, I will put you on speaker."

"Shaun, I need your help. Dr. Walters recognized me somehow. John and Gretchen went to St. Agnes this morning and met with him. He tried to kill them. They escaped from the hospital thanks to John's wits and training. They cut the brakes on my car and it crashed at the parking garage. We grabbed a taxi and headed to the airport where we are right now. You are all in danger. Worse than that, Kathleen, Maura, and the babies may be in even greater danger. You have got to get Maura and Kathleen, and Angela away from the house. And you have to get the babies out of Walter Reed. I am not exaggerating these people will kill everyone. I don't think anyone is safe at the monastery either. Can you take care of this?"

"Yes," Nick. "I will take action immediately. What are you going to do and where will you be?"

"I don't know yet. We thought about renting a car and driving to Las Vegas and flying home from there. We are trying to trip them up by driving east."

"You know they will find out you rented a car and they can easily get the State Troopers to look out for your car. I am not sure that is the best plan. Why don't you drive over towards

Sacramento and ditch the car you rent at the airport somewhere and get a local car rental place that accepts cash?"

"That sounds like a good idea. Shaun, I am scared for the family. I know I can count on you to protect them."

"Nick, I will do it. I am worried about your safety. You and John need to come up with a plan to get you east without being detected by Walters' group. Be smart and watch your back at all times. I mean it," Shaun concluded. "Be careful."

"I will Shaun. Thanks."

"Can I get my brother to help us Nick?" asked Frank Murphy. "I think it's time."

"Yes; the sooner the better."

"Nick," it's Chris. "We are all in this together. We knew that from the beginning. We need to band together and accomplish several things. First we need to make sure Maura, Kathleen, Angela, and your children are safe. Then we need to ensure the safety of all of us here at the Monastery. And finally, we need to find a way to stop these people. I am sick of hiding and I am ready for a confrontation."

"Nick, this is Harry. I have a suggestion that could keep your whereabouts safe for a little while longer. I have a retired friend in Portland who owns a plane. He had a nice business for many years then sold it for a fortune and took up flying. He could fly down to Sacramento and meet you and fly you to an alternate airport. All it would take would be a telephone call from me and I am willing to bet he would say yes. He was always looking for reasons to fly. I have flown with him and he is a safe pilot. What do you think?"

"This is a great idea," said Shaun. "If Harry can make this happen you will be able to fly into any airport without filing a flight plan. These smaller aircraft have the run of the skies at the lower altitudes."

"Harry, call this man as soon as we hang up and I will call you right back," Nick said excitedly.

"Stay on the line, Nick, I will use the office phone here at the

Monastery," Harry replied as he walked over to the telephone in the adjacent office.

"Nick, this is Catherine, is John nearby? I would like to talk to him if I could?"

"Yes, I can wave him over. Here he is now."

"John, hello, this is Catherine. Are you okay? Things took a turn for the worse out there. Are you three going to be safe?"

"Catherine, it is good to hear your voice. I have missed you, partner. We are doing as well as can be expected. You know that old sixth sense I tell you I have, well today it came in very handy. We escaped from a locked room and got out of San Francisco just as the they were closing in on us. But we made it. We are all right. Nick told you what we are up against. You are going to have to work with Shaun and get those people to safety. Be careful. I want to see you in one piece when I get back."

"I will, John. I will. You take care," Catherine said.

"John, this is Harry. Tell Nick I have his answer."

"Here, I will put him on the phone."

"Nick, I spoke with Harold Tilden, my friend with the plane. He is ready and willing to help out. He said he could be in Sacramento in about two hours. He agreed to fly you anywhere as long as you pay for the gas. Can you write his name and his planes tail letters down?"

Harry proceeded to give Nick Harold Tilden's information and phone number. The arrangements were made to meet him in Sacramento at the private plane hangar. Nick thanked Harry for this important contribution toward their safety.

"God be with you, my friends," Nick said as hung up the telephone

"So, Nick, what is the plan?" John inquired.

"We are going to Sacramento."

chapter 32

John and Helen Jones left their home at eight thirty a.m. and drove to Cronin's Funeral Home for the final services and burial of their daughter Hanna. Thomas insisted on driving them to the Mortuary. Rev. Michael Powers, their Pastor and friend, greeted John and Helen at the door and walked with them into the viewing room where Hanna's open casket sat in the front center of the small room that could seat about twenty-five mourners. Pastor Powers held Helen's left hand while her husband held her right hand as they approached the Hanna's coffin. As Hanna's face came into view Helen began to shake and seemed unable to walk any further. Thomas was immediately behind his mother and would have caught her if she fell. Helen regained her balance and took a few more steps toward her beautiful, young daughter. Her eyes filled with tears and she tried to pull away from John and her Pastor. They held on a little tighter.

Helen freed her hand from her husband and tenderly touched Hanna's cheek and hair. Pastor Powers released her left hand and she balanced herself by leaning on the side of the casket. She bent down and kissed Hanna's forehead and touched her daughter's hands ever so lovingly.

"Help me to a chair," she asked, just as she began to collapse under the mountain of grief that overwhelmed her.

John and the Pastor helped Helen to a chair placed near the coffin. Thomas then approached his sister and stood there staring down at the little girl who used to follow him everywhere and mimic his every movement. He was stunned at how beautiful his sister had become. She looked almost angelic in her eternal sleep. He bent down close to Hanna's face and whispered, "I am so sorry, Hanna. This was my fault. Please forgive me." He kissed her on the cheek and placed a red rose in her hands. "I promise to make this right, Hanna," he whispered again. Then he turned and sat down next to his mother.

Hanna's father was filled with grief. He could not understand how anyone would harm his beautiful little girl. All the memories of her growing years flooded over him like a wave that nearly knocked him off his feet. Her first steps, her first puppy, her first day at kindergarten, her first day in high school, her high school basketball team winning the city championship, her graduation, the angry outburst that led to her decision to move to California, and now, here, dead. He bent down close to her and said, "I love you, Hanna." He straightened up and walked over to his wife and tenderly held her hand.

A few friends from the Star View Restaurant came to pay their respects, and a few neighbors of John and Helen. Some of the Parishioners from their church also came to offer their condolences.

"In the name of the Father, the Son, and the Holy Spirit, Amen" the pastor began. He proceeded to read and pray several psalms from first the Old Testament. Then he read selected passages from the New Testament. Several times he walked to the casket and blessed Hanna's remains. He offered special prayers of intercession for Hanna's soul and for the family left behind. Then he offered a eulogy that outlined Hanna's life from the time she was a little girl until the time of her passing.

Thomas stood up, cleared his throat and began to speak: "I am Hanna's brother. I am ashamed that this is the first time I have seen her in many years. I gave up my family in the pursuit of wealth and power. I realize now that was wrong. What really matters is family and love. I tried to reject the principles and morals that my parents instilled in Hanna and me. But nothing could ever replace the love and acceptance that my parents had for my sister and me. How sad it is that it took Hanna's passing for me to see that. If I would have been involved with her life I may have made that slight difference that would have enabled her to be alive today. One or two very small decisions in our lives can make all the difference. I loved my sister as a little girl, I only wish I would have known her as a grown woman because I am sure I would have loved her even more."

It was a short ride from the church to the cemetery. When the casket was in position, Pastor Michael resumed the funeral prayers. "Hanna is now with the Lord. Unknown to us, she was studying the Bible. John and Helen have her Bible and it is filled with her side notes and highlights. I think she was searching for the same answers we seek. We believe that she is in a far better place now. Our hope lies in the resurrection of Jesus Christ that one day we will see Hanna again in heaven. Hold onto that hope each day and your mourning will turn into dancing at the Lord's appointed time."

John drove his parents back home. It was a very somber drive home from the cemetery.

"I have a question Thomas," John asked, "What did you mean when you said you were responsible for Hanna's death?"

"I meant that if I would have stayed in touch with her, stayed close to her, I might have been able to influence her decisions, decisions that eventually led to her dying."

"What are you going to do to, as you said, make it right?"

"I have the resources to conduct a more thorough investigation than the police. I know I can find out who did this."

"You are not going to hurt someone are you?" Helen asked.

"No, Mom, but I will be able to affect the outcome of what happens to the man who committed this crime."

"Be careful, Thomas. You can get into a lot of trouble when

you do things like that," his father advised. "Do not seek to avenge Hanna's death. Leave that to God."

"Trust me, Dad. I won't get into trouble."

When they arrived back at his parent's home Thomas checked his messages; there were two from the Colonel. He excused himself and used the telephone in the bedroom to return the Colonel's call.

"Hello Colonel. I got the message to call you."

"I called yesterday, why the delay in getting back to me?"

"Sorry about that. I skipped checking messages for one day.

"Okay. Forget it. We have an emergency. Where are you?

"I'm on the west coast."

"Good. We need you to fly up to San Francisco and meet with a few people about a crisis that came up yesterday."

"I can catch a plane this afternoon," Thomas said.

"Good. You are to meet Dr. John Walters at St. Agnes Hospital at ten o'clock tonight. Two of our associates will also be there. You may have to come up with a creative way to solve a security issue."

"I will meet them at St. Agnes hospital tonight, Colonel," Jones replied.

"Thank you, Jones. I knew I could count on you," the Colonel said, as he hung up the telephone.

"Problems at work, son?" John asked Thomas as he walked into the living room.

"Yes, something I have to take care of today. I hate to leave, but I must fly up to San Francisco for a meeting tonight. I will fly back down tomorrow and be back with you for several more days. I hope you understand. I will be back, I promise." Thomas said to his parents earnestly.

"I understand Thomas. Take care of your business, but please come back tomorrow. We need you right now, both of us," John said with a ring of sadness in his voice.

"I will. I promise to come back tomorrow. I will leave my things here. All I need to take along is a change of underwear and a clean shirt."

Thomas telephoned Air West and secured a ticket for a two o'clock flight direct to San Francisco.

Thomas grabbed a few things, kissed his mother goodbye, and headed out the door. He turned and walked back in and gave his father a sincere hug. "Thanks, Dad. I love you," he said hurrying to his car.

Thomas arrived at the airport at twelve fifty p.m., and checked in at the Air West terminal. The plane was on the ground and he was at the car rental desk within two hours. He drove into San Francisco and registered at the Hilton Hotel near St. Agnes Hospital where a package was awaiting him.

Inside were pictures of Dr. Harry Booth, Nick O'Connell, Shaun O'Connell, Angela Carson, Detective John Baker, Detective Catherine Harding, and Father Christopher Sullivan. There was a newspaper picture of the destroyed police precinct in Washington along with a story of how the people in the photograph were all killed by the blast. The date of the newspaper story was highlighted, nine days previous. Another photograph showed two men in grey cassocks with hoods and a woman in a nun's habit walking into St. Agnes Hospital. Someone had drawn a circle around the faces of the two men. Under the face of the men was written in white ink, "Nick O." and "John B." The photograph was dated the previous day.

I guess the people in the photograph of the precinct were not killed after all, Jones thought to himself. *That will get everyone in an uproar. I promised Hanna I would do what is right. Now I have to follow through on that promise.* Thomas smiled to himself and began to formulate plans to implement the beginning of the end of this murderous company and all its associates. *The time has come,* Thomas said out loud looking at his reflection in the mirror.

chapter 33

Jones arrived at the hospital at nine forty five p.m. and walked over to the hospital directory to find Doctor Walters' office number. As he examined the board, a security guard approached him.

"Excuse me sir, are you Mr. Jones?" he asked politely.

"Yes, I am."

"Welcome to St. Agnes. Please follow me."

Thomas followed him into a new wing of the hospital where many of the physician's offices and conference rooms were located. The security guard stopped at room A 308 and knocked gently on the door.

"Enter," the voice inside instructed.

Jones walked into the room and was greeted by Dr. John Walters. He introduced him to Dr. Mark Preston and Dr. James Nelson. Walters turned to Mr. Jones and said, "I believe you know Joseph Johnson and his son, Jeffrey."

"I know who they are but we have never met in person. Hello, Joseph," Jones said shaking hands. "Hello, Jeffrey." As he shook Jeff's hand he could not have guessed he was shaking hands with the man who had knifed and murdered his sister Hanna.

"Did you receive you packet of information I sent over to the Hilton Mr. Jones?"

"Yes."

"Very good. Did you have a chance to examine its contents?

"Yes."

"What are your thoughts?" Walters questioned.

"It is apparent that at least two of the men we thought were eliminated in Washington are quite alive. I did not recognize the woman."

"Exactly. I had our security people review the tapes of the lobby, the elevator, and the Family Care Center where most of our work is performed. They questioned my nurse about the man, but she could not positively identify him as Nick O'Connell. He was here a few weeks ago and removed his sister from the hospital. He was taking her home to Washington, DC. We arranged an accident, but unfortunately only the sister lost her life. I had Nelson and Preston standing by if she made it alive to Walter Reed Hospital.

According to our friends, the Johnsons, O'Connell befriended some people on the plane who provided some type of medical care to his sister. We could not risk her revealing our hospice protocol, so we made a decision to eliminate her and the people who helped her—Dr. Harry Booth and Flight Attendant Angela Carson. JJ and his son had some agents standing by ready to respond and eliminate the problem. Unfortunately three of the girl's companions escaped harm. That laid the foundation for our plans to eliminate all of them at one time at the precinct. We thought we had succeeded, but to our dismay, we did not. This poses a grave threat to our organization and our plans."

"What are your primary concerns right now, at this minute? What do you expect JJ and his son to do?" asked Mr. Jones.

"O'Connell and his friends must be stopped! We have to find them and stop them from going to the police, or worse, to the newspapers back in Washington. I don't know exactly what they know about our operation, but no one has ever been this close. I don't like it at all, not one bit. I would rather overreact that sit back and hope for the best," Walters explained.

"I would say you know how to overreact quite well, after the fiasco at the police precinct. No one in the hierarchy of the company wanted that. To make that go away required a lot of money and several innocent lives," Mr. Jones said in a scolding voice.

"Better to be more zealous now than later when we might become targets ourselves," John Walters said in a voice heavy with bitter sarcasm.

"Remember whom you are talking to Doctor," Jones said reminding the doctor that he was the President of the company.

"My apologies," offered Walters.

"Accepted. Now what have you done so far?"

JJ leaned forward on the table. "We thought we had them at the Hilton. Jeff cut the brake lining to their car and it crashed, but only the valet was killed. The three targets ran out of the hotel garage and hailed a cab that took them to the airport. We suspect they are going to fly back east, but we have not had any hits from the credit card they are using. They are out of sight at this minute. I have men at the airport searching for them."

"Do you think they slipped away under other names?" Thomas inquired.

"No. I believe they will surface at one of the airlines heading east. The cabbie told me he dropped them off at American. Our search is centered there," JJ answered.

"I want to send Jeff back to Washington to confirm that O'Connell and Baker survived. If they are alive, perhaps more your targets at the precinct survived as well."

"What will Jeff do?" Thomas asked.

Jeff pulled closer to the table. "If I have to I will take his children. They are in Walter Reed Hospital. Preston and Nelson could help me get the infants out of the hospital. I would trade the babies for whatever I need from O'Connell."

"I don't like kidnapping. It attracts the FBI. Taking premature infants from a hospital will arouse the public as much as the destruction at the precinct. What will you do if those babies get sick?"

"Nothing," said JJ, smiling.

"That is cruel," Jones said bitterly.

"Life is cruel."

"I do not like this at all," Jones said. "Can't we do something else?"

"Mr. Jones, if you had a kid and someone took it, you would do anything to get them back. Am I right?" asked the senior Johnson.

"Yes, but I am not going to approve this action. You cannot go ahead with this plan. The two government agencies we cannot engage are the FBI and IRS. You kidnap someone; the FBI will be breathing down our necks. I will not sanction this. I want you to focus on finding O'Connell and Baker here in California. Inform me immediately when they are found. Keep them under surveillance until you notify me."

"I agree we need to find those two men, but I think we should be prepared to move against his family," argued Dr. Walters. "However, I will obey your orders."

"Here is what I want from you as we move forward: first, clear every move and I mean *every* move with me ahead of time. No winging it anymore! Do you understand? I do not want any more innocent victims. If you track these people down I want to know about it before you take *any* action. You are not to act independently on this. Is that clear? I will give you my private phone number and you may call me any time, night or day. I don't want to have to explain to my two superiors why something is going wrong. Do you get it Dr. Walters? Another thing; stop with the poisoning of the patients. End you ten-day program. I want to hear that people are surviving longer than ten days in your hospital. If any of you decide not to follow this warning, there will be serious consequences for all of you. I want to know the minute you find out what Nick O'Connell and his two companions are up to and I want that information fast. In fact, I want a copy of your portfolio on O'Connell before I leave here tonight. I will be involved first hand on how we handle O'Connell and his friends. I have the resources to deal with him in a far more effective way. Your job is to find them and let me know *before* you take any action. Is that crystal clear to everyone in this room?"

"Yes, Mr. Jones. It is quite clear," muttered Walters.

JJ cleared his throat and raised his hand as if he were in elementary school. "I have a question, Mr. Jones."

"Yes."

"What about the other survivors at the precinct?"

"What about them?"

"We traced the credit card they are using to a priest who lives at the St. Ambrose Monastery and Retreat House. I have men watching the place. We believe the other priest, Father Christopher Sullivan, and Detective Harding are hiding out there. How should we proceed there?

"This is good information. It gives me an opportunity to plan a positive action against them that will not incite public opinion against the company. Give me a day or two and I will call you. Tell your man to lay low, and be patient. We will deal with these people."

Jones stood up. "I read the report on the murder of a young woman here in Los Angeles. Miss Hanna Jones. Apparently she was a companion of Colleen O'Connell. Who ordered this action?"

"I did," Walters said proudly. "She was one of three women who dated Mr. Bolton's son. He thought one of them infected him with a venereal disease. Mr. Bolton was livid when he learned about this and ordered me to take severe action to punish the people his son was sleeping with. I treated the son, who is a drugged out bum. He has been with so many women he could not even guess who he got the clap from. But the old man wanted to send a message. I asked Jeff to handle this job himself and he did quite well. The crime scene looked like a typical burglary gone wrong. He used a large kitchen knife and struck the pig over and over again."

Jones lowered his head and bit his lip. Every instinct in his body cried out to avenge his sister then and there. If he had a weapon he would have killed JJ and Walters on the spot. Somehow he managed to regain control of his emotions. He never felt such hatred before. He now knew what he suspected and he was sick about it, but he had to maintain a calm demeanor. "Thank you for the information," he said with ice in his eyes and vengeance in his heart.

The meeting concluded shortly thereafter. Walters secured a copy of the file they had put together on Nick and his family. Jones gave everyone his private line number and reminded them again of the order not to touch the infants or Nick and his traveling companions.

The meeting ended and Thomas Jones said a curt "good night" to criminals seated around the conference table. He was anxious to wash off the scent of deceit that permeated everyone in Dr. John Walters' office.

Walking back to his hotel, Jones felt satisfied that he had indeed taken the first step in his life to turn things around and to keep his promise to Hanna. His heart ached thinking about what Jeff Johnson said about killing his sister. His anger turned to the Surgeon General who he always suspected was a manipulative criminal that justified his actions almost as well as Dr. John Walters.

Returning to his hotel room, Jones opened the dossier on Nick and examined it thoroughly. He read about Colleen's death. The report outlined Nick's actions from the time he arrived in California. It was clear he was searching for his sister's killer. It was clear he was a man to be reckoned with, and a man of character. Jones admired him even though they never met. He made a decision to contact him as soon as it was safe.

chapter 34

Thomas rose early the next day and took a morning flight back to Los Angeles. He was anxious to get back to his parents, as he had promised. He arrived at their home before noon.

"Dad, I'm home," he called out as he walked through the door.

"Hello, son," Helen said from the kitchen. "I am making lunch. Your dad is on the deck."

Thomas walked past his mother and gave her a quick kiss. He then walked out the back door and sat down on a deck chair next to his father.

"Did you have a good trip, son?"

"Disturbing."

"Bad news?"

"You would not believe."

"Anything I can do to help?"

"Thanks for the offer, but no, I have to handle this myself."

"Tommy, tell me what is going on."

"You will hate me, and I don't want that to happen."

"Nothing could make me hate you, Tommy."

"I found out who killed Hanna."

"How?"

"I told you I am the president of a very large company. We

have divisions that are made up of people who carry out orders. Sometimes those orders come across my desk after things are done and it is too late."

"I don't follow, son"

"Someone in my company committed the murder."

"What?" Jones' father said angrily. "Why would anyone in your company murder Hanna? This just doesn't make sense. What are you saying?"

"It doesn't make sense, Dad, but what I learned last night was very disturbing, yet true."

John slammed his first on a nearby table. "You had someone kill Hanna?"

"I did not do this intentionally," Thomas explained. "One of my operatives acted on orders from one of the directors in our company and I signed off on the order not knowing Hanna was on the list of people this person wanted killed."

"For what possible reason?" Jones' father said as she shook his son's shoulders.

"One of our directors has a son that Hanna was intimate with. This director thought Hanna may have given his son a venereal disease. Without proof the director went ahead and ordered the death of three young women. I saw the report on this after it was done. But it is my company. That makes it my responsibility."

"How could you order the death of anyone? How could you do this, son?" Jones' father sat down slowly. "I don't know what to say or think right now."

"Dad, looking back now, I honestly don't know how I could have done these things. I rationalized so much and I crossed the line of doing what was right. I set morality aside in the quest for power and money. I am so sorry, Dad. Please forgive me. Had I known it was Hanna I would have protected her."

"I don't know what kind of company you run, but if you are the leader, it is your obligation to make this right. That may be the toughest thing you will ever face in your life. But you have to try, no matter what the consequences."

"I know, Dad. I started that process last night. I didn't want to tell you this, but I had to. I understand if you hate me. I promise you that I will do what is right no matter how hard that may be."

"I don't hate you, Thomas. You better do what is right. You could lose everything you have, but you will gain your soul. I will stand by you. I am angry and struggling with everything you've told me. But I love you, and somehow I will forgive you. It is going to take a lot of prayer."

"I know, Dad. I don't deserve to be in your life. I will do what is right. I promise," Jones said as he embraced his father."

"We can't tell your mother this news. At least not yet," John whispered to his son.

"I understand, Dad."

"Lunch is ready," Helen called out.

Helen served a lunch of tomato bisque soup along with grilled cheese sandwiches. It was one of Jones' favorite lunches while he was growing up.

"Mom, how are you today?"

"I am still really sad, but a little less than yesterday. I've been praying a lot and the Lord seems to be sending me the grace I need right now. How are you?"

"I am still really upset about Hanna. I think if only... but I know that won't change what happened. It makes me angry too."

"Our pastor called this morning and asked how we were holding up, bless his heart."

"He is a good man."

"He asked about you too. He told me he would like to get to know our boy."

"Tell you what, Mom, I will call him back this afternoon."

"That's good, Tommy. That's good."

chapter 35

After lunch Thomas went into the guest bedroom and dialed Nick O'Connell's phone number. Maura picked it up after two rings.

"Hello, Maura O'Connell speaking."

"Mrs. O'Connell, you do not know me, but I know your husband is alive."

"What are you talking about?" Maura said, sensing alarm.

"I am a friend. Please trust me that I am telling you the truth. I have a message for you and Nick. The people who are responsible for the police precinct bombing know that Nick is alive, along with his companions. Your babies are at risk and you have to let your friends know that their enemies are aware that they survived the blast at the police station. You and your sister-in-law are also in danger. You have to get the children and get away before they know you are gone."

"Why should I trust you?"

"I know about Nick's trip to Los Angeles and San Francisco. I know about St. Agnes hospital. I know about Colleen. I know who tried to kill Harry, Angela, and Nick at the airport. I cannot tell you who I am yet, but I swear to you I am a friend. I want to do everything I can to protect you, your family, and your friends. Please, believe me. How would I know about Dr.

Booth's daughter Cynthia and her husband? They are staying with his parents. Get your children out of Walter Reed. Maybe Harry Booth can come up with a plan to get them transferred to another hospital."

"Can I trust my doctor?" Maura asked.

"What is her name?" asked Thomas.

"Elizabeth Roberts," Maura replied.

"I think so. I have not seen her name on any documents. I would say yes," Thomas answered confidently.

"I will do as you asked. Thank you for the warning. Can you tell me who you are?" Maura inquired.

"I cannot tell you yet. I will soon. Just know that I am on your side," Jones answered sincerely.

"Do you know where Nick is now? Is he safe?"

"Yes, he is safe. The people searching for him have not located Nick or his companions," Jones replied honestly.

"Thank God. Thank you for helping us."

Thomas Jones hung up the telephone feeling better than he had in months, maybe years. He knew he was on the right track and he was determined to stay there. He studied the O'Connell file that Dr. Walters gave him the night before in San Francisco further and found the telephone number for Father Francis Murphy. He picked up the telephone and dialed the number.

"Hello, St. Ambrose Monastery," Father Murphy said.

"Father Murphy I cannot reveal my identity to you, but I called to warn you and your friends at the Monastery."

"I don't know what you are talking about," Father Murphy replied. He saw Dr. Booth walking by and motioned for him to come in. He put his finger to his lips giving Harry the message not to say anything. He then put the telephone on the speaker feature.

"Could you repeat what you said," Murphy asked the unknown caller.

"I am unable to reveal my identity at this time, but I can assure you that the people responsible for the bombing at the

Police Precinct know that you are alive and hiding in the Monastery. I am calling to warn you that they are watching you. In addition, there is a danger to Nick's wife, Maura, and Shaun's wife, Kathleen. I spoke with Maura only minutes ago and told her she had to move the babies out of Walter Reed Hospital. Two doctors there are involved with these criminals. I suggested to Mrs. O'Connell that she speak with Dr. Booth and try to come up with a reason to get the infants out of that hospital."

Frank Murphy left the room and ran to get his friends to the telephone. Shaun and Catherine dashed to Murphy's room and listened to the end of the warning message Jones was giving them.

"Do you know where Nick and his friends are? Are they safe?" Shaun inquired.

"They have eluded their pursuers for now. Nick is traveling with Detective John Baker and an unknown woman. They will have to be very clever to stay alive. The people looking for them are dangerous. I cannot guarantee that they won't be hurt, or worse. I believe you are all in danger and need to take action quickly. I will try to keep in touch with you, but I cannot be sure of my own safety," Jones said to the roomful of fugitives.

"If we move out of the Monastery, how will we reach you?" asked Shaun.

"You can't. I suspect I am in danger and will have to move around quickly. Please move as soon as possible. Goodbye and God speed," Jones said, as he hung up the telephone.

After they hung up, Shaun quickly dialed Maura's telephone number and she picked up on the first ring.

"Maura, its Shaun, is Kathleen with you?"

"Yes, she is here. I have something to tell you. A man contacted me about Nick, you and the others at the Monastery. You are in danger," Maura said nervously.

"I know; he called us here. We hung up just minutes ago. We have to move you to a safe location. I don't know how much time we have, but we can't delay. May I speak with Kathleen?" Shaun asked eagerly.

"Kathleen, we all have to change our location if we want to be safe. I promised Nick I would take care of Maura and the babies. Harry and I are coming to meet you within the hour. Harry is coming up with a plan to get the babies out of Walter Reed. We will be staying with you until this mess is cleared up. Will you and Maura be ready to leave the house?" asked Shaun in his State Policeman voice.

"Maura and I want to get Angela out of the hospital as well," Kathleen said. "She has been going over with Maura every day and remaining there until Maura goes back late in the afternoon."

"I know that Harry will be thrilled to see Angela again. Her safety is very important to him. It will be good to be back together again. I am going to hang up, Kathleen, so be ready for us in about an hour. I love you, babe."

"I love you, Shaun," his wife replied affectionately.

Frank picked up his telephone after Shaun finished talking to Kathleen and called his brother Michael at the FBI. He was put on hold and after a few minutes he heard his brother's smiling voice, "Frank, hello. How is my favorite brother?"

"I'm your only brother," Frank replied.

"What drove you to call me?" Michael inquired, sensing the urgency in his brother's voice.

"I need your help. My life and the lives of some very close friends are at risk."

"What are you involved in, Frank?"

"It is a little complicated to go over everything on the phone. We need a safe house and we need it today."

"I can make that happen but I will need something to tell my supervisor."

"Tell him the people who bombed the Police Precinct have targeted me and my friends for elimination. And tell him the two detectives from the Precinct bombing are alive."

"How do you know this?"

"I am staring at Catherine Harding right now and I spoke with someone only minutes ago who guaranteed me that John Baker was alive."

"Hold on a minute, will you?" Mike said as he put his brother on hold and walked into his Supervisors office. Less than three minutes later he picked up the phone again.

"Frank, my boss is on the line with us. Frank meet Jerry Locket; Jerry, this is my brother Frank on the other end."

"Good to hear from you, Frank. Mike tells me you are staring at Detective Catherine Harding. May I speak with her?"

"Hello, this is Catherine Harding."

"How do I know you are who you claim to be?" asked Agent Locket.

"I have worked at the Precinct twelve years, the last five as a detective. I am assigned to work with John Baker. My Captain is Rodney Ebersole. My badge number is 17492."

"What do you need? How can we help?" Locket asked.

"We need a safe house, maybe two. And we need safe passage out of the Monastery. The people responsible for the precinct bombing are watching us. If you come storming in here we may all be in even greater danger. What do you think of getting an unmarked bus in here, or one with a religious banner somewhere, which references the St. Ambrose Retreat House? That way if someone sees a bus entering the grounds they will think it is a pilgrimage to the Monastery. We could all make our escape on that bus," Catherine suggested.

"I am putting that plan into motion right now. We will try to get that bus there within two hours."

"We will have everyone ready. Thank you, Agent Locket," said Catherine gratefully.

"Mike, I have another favor to ask," Father Murphy said to his brother once he was on the line again. "We told you that Nick, John, and Gretchen Sanders were alive and traveling together. They are in Sacramento and will be boarding a private plane to fly them out of the area to safety. What are the chances you could intercept them and fly them back home across the country? His wife and their two infants are in danger as well."

"Where are they?" Mike asked

"The infants are still in Walter Reed Hospital. They are both premature babies and need care and nourishment that only a hospital can provide. Nick's wife and his sister-in-law have been staying at their home, but they are in serious danger now. Shaun is driving to Nick's house to pick up Maura and his wife, Kathleen. They should be with us in the same safe house if possible."

"Shaun, I will have an agent meet you at Walter Reed. He will escort you and your party to a safe location. You may call me anytime if you run into trouble," advised Agent Locket.

"Thank you, sir," Shaun replied.

"Father Murphy, Shaun, you all heard what the FBI Agent said. Let's get ready to leave the Monastery in two hours. Thank you, Frank, I am very glad you called your brother," Catherine said gratefully.

———

FBI Agent Jerry Locket gave instructions to Mike Murphy to form a detail of Agents and brief them on the situation. They were then ordered to infiltrate the area around the Monastery to observe any unusual activity there and report it back to Murphy. Agent Locket did not want to risk any kind of attack on the Retreat House prior to evacuating the men and women to safety. He figured if someone had been brazen enough to place a bomb at a police station, it would be nothing to break into an unguarded building like a Monastery. The other matter that both Murphy and his boss understood was the need for confidentiality, even among their own men.

Shaun and Harry Booth took Frank Murphy's car and drove to Nick's house to pick up Maura and his wife Kathleen. They had an emotional reunion driven by their deep love for one another and the time they were forced to spend apart guarding the secret that they had survived the blast at the Police Precinct. Shaun hugged Maura and told her not to worry about Nick, that he was safe, and that they would soon be reunited. Harry was warmly greeted by both Maura and Kathleen, who had come to think of Harry as a dear friend and almost a member of the family.

"Are we ready to go?" asked Shaun, obviously in a hurry to get everyone to safety.

"Shaun, do you really think the babies are in danger?" Maura inquired. "I mean they are at a military hospital run by the government."

"I know Maura, but there are a couple of doctors there who we believe are tied to the criminals who blew up the Precinct building. They know about Nick and the evidence he has gathered against them. They would kidnap the babies, you, and anyone with ties to Nick. They would try to exchange the infants for Nick. These men are getting desperate now so we can't take a chance with your lives, or the babies," explained Shaun.

It took about fifteen minutes to reach Walter Reed. Angela Carson, still in her disguise as a Catholic Nun dressed in a traditional habit, greeted Shaun, Harry and the others at the entrance to the maternity ward.

Angela led the party into the hospital and up to the maternity ward. At the same time, a man in a dark suit walked into the area. Shaun walked over to him and introduced himself, "I am Shaun O'Connell. I believe you are waiting for us."

"Yes, sir, I am FBI Agent Daniel Mannion," he said as he showed Shaun his badge. "How may I assist you?"

"We need to get a doctor to sign a release form for two premature babies. It is not safe for them here. I may need you to convince either a doctor or nurse that we need to move the infants," Shaun explained.

At that moment Dr. Elizabeth Roberts walked into the ward.

Maura spotted her and waved to get her attention. Dr. Roberts walked over to speak with her.

"Dr. Roberts," Maura asked. "Is there a room where we can talk?"

"Yes, around the corner. Is something wrong?"

"I will explain in a minute," Maura said as she took Dr. Roberts by the hand and walked around the corner in the hallway along with her family and friends.

"What is going on?" Dr. Roberts asked. "Is that you, Dr. Booth? I thought you were killed in the police bombing."

"I assure you, Dr. Roberts, I am very much alive."

"Doctor, we have to move the babies out of here, and we must do it now! There are people who want to hurt our children," Maura pleaded. "We need your help to sign them out of the hospital."

"Maura, this is a federal military hospital. Who possibly would or could want to hurt baby Megan or baby Christopher? Surely there are no doctors here involved in such a crime?" the doctor asked.

"Yes, there are, Doctor. Both Doctors Preston and Nelson are involved. They are connected to the same people that tried to kill Nick, his brother, Shaun, who is standing right next to me, Harry, Angela and the others," Maura said as she pointed to Shaun.

"Who is this other gentleman?"

"I am FBI Agent Daniel Mannion."

"Where will you take the children?" asked Dr. Roberts.

"To a safe house," the Agent replied.

"I will call my boss and tell him I have a family emergency and need some time away. I have some vacation time I can use as well. If it is all right with you, I would like to stay with Maura and the babies. The infants are getting healthier, but they are not as well as I would like. Maura, I want to stay with you and the children. May I come with them?" asked Liz.

"Dr. Roberts, I don't know, it could be dangerous," Maura said cautiously.

"My obligation is to those two tiny babies, and to you. I am not trying to be a hero or anything, but I am determined to see those two infants survive," the doctor stated.

"Agent Mannion is that all right with you?" asked Maura.

"Yes, ma'am; it is probably a good idea to have a doctor in the house with the babies. Doctor, can you bring along some of the supplies you may need in caring for the infants? Gather what you can, sign the children out, and come with us. You cannot contact anyone or tell anyone where you are. Are you willing to accept that order? Mannion asked seriously.

"Yes, I am," the doctor said. "Willingly."

For the next fifteen minutes, Dr. Roberts, Kathleen, and Maura scrambled around the maternity ward for all the materials they might need in the care of Maura's three-week old son and daughter. Angela and Harry helped with that chore while Shaun and Agent Mannion observed every person coming and going in the Maternity Ward. Shaun took two infant safety seats out to the car and installed them in the third seat of the van.

Just as he finished, a small parade of people left the hospital and walked toward the vehicle. Maura, Dr. Roberts, and Angela rode in the back of the van while Agent Mannion drove with Shaun in the front seat and Kathleen and Shaun sat in the second row of seats. The infants were secured in the third row, just in front of Maura and Liz and Angela. The Agent drove them to a safe house just outside Falls Church, Virginia, to a secure building that once was a convent for retired nuns from the Sisters of Mercy Order. It was a gated home made of large stones and concrete, with eighteen bedrooms, seven bathrooms and a large kitchen equipped with modern appliances large enough to feed twenty to thirty people. The windows had ornate bars, and access to the home was limited to the double doors off the courtyard inside the gates that were remotely controlled.

The next few hours were busy with the activity of moving the babies into their temporary home. Liz had Shaun place the two bassinettes in her room, which was right next to Maura's. The bedrooms were furnished with sheets, pillows, and bedspreads, and all the basics were supplied in the kitchen Shaun fulfilled the promise he made to his brother to get Maura and the babies to safety.

chapter 36

Nick rented a car at the San Francisco Airport and headed toward Sacramento with Gretchen Sanders and Detective John Baker. They were to meet Harry Booth's friend, Harold Tilden, who would fly them out of danger. Their narrow escape in San Francisco was clear proof they were running for their lives.

Harold Tilden, a retired businessman, had known Dr. Harry Booth for twenty years, first as his doctor, and later as his good friend. He had built a small manufacturing company into a viable competitor to other major manufacturers in tool making. A large competitor offered to buy his company at an amount Harold happily accepted. Harold's avocation was flying, and selling his company enabled him to invest in a larger plane than the one he previously owned. He was now flying a Hawker 700 A–GNS–XLS jet that could seat ten to twelve passengers comfortably. Harold equipped the jet aircraft with two televisions, a video recorder, and a modern surround sound system. He particularly liked his forward galley warming oven and the full size lavatory. He could cruise at twenty to twenty five thousand feet at speeds up to three hundred miles per hour. Harold regularly flew to Las Vegas, Helena, Los Angeles and Phoenix, and was more than happy to help his old friend Doc Booth when the doctor called and asked for a favor.

Nick took Interstate 5 out of San Francisco and headed east to Sacramento.

"We could drop this rental car off in Woodland, which looks like a small town that might have a local car rental business that would fall under the radar of Walters and his friends," John suggested, as he scanned a map.

"I agree, John," Nick answered. "We can also check back in with Harry and Father Murphy to ensure everyone is safe and that everything back home is okay."

Nick pulled into Woodland and slowly searched the main streets for a car rental business. Just outside of town they passed a small used car dealer that offered daily rentals at low costs. "John," Nick said, "Look over there at 'Champ's Used Cars.'"

Nick pulled over to the curb next to the used car lot and parked. He left the keys in the ignition and his window open about five or six inches, just enough room for someone with sufficient temptation to steal the car. John had gotten out and was engaged in a lively discussion with the proprietor of Champ's, when Gretchen pointed out that there was a pay phone next to the office of the used car lot.

Nick walked over to the phone and called Frank Murphy. "Nick, it is good to hear your voice. We are getting ready to leave the Monastery. Shaun has left to meet with Maura and Kathleen to take them to Walter Reed to get your children and Angela to safety. Where are you?"

"We are just outside of Sacramento. Has Harry confirmed our trip with his friend?"

"Harold Tilden spoke with Harry and advised him to have you meet at Mather's Airport on the east side of Sacramento. It is a small airport and leaving from there will give you additional time to get away from your pursuers."

"I saw Mather's on one of our maps. That is not a problem. How will I be able to reach you if you move to a safe house?"

"I called my brother at the FBI. Mike has provided us with not only a safe house, but he is bringing a bus to evacuate all of us at one time. I will give you my brother's number. He has indicated that he will fly you and your companions east on an FBI plane. All you have to do is give him the location."

"Thank you, Frank. That is a relief. I look forward to being back with all of you very soon. Goodbye my friend."

"Goodbye Nick. God be with you."

By the time Nick finished his phone call, John Baker had already successfully negotiated a cash transaction for a 1974 Buick station wagon. The odometer was not working so they had no idea how many miles the old car had on it, but it did hum along fine and in a short time they arrived at the small airport. Nick parked the car in the visitor's lot outside the service hangar for private planes. They were escorted into a lounge area where they awaited Pilot Harold Tilden in his Hawker 700 jet aircraft. Fifteen minutes later the private jet landed and taxied over to the hangar where Nick, Gretchen, and John Baker were waiting.

The lounge door opened and a short, older man outfitted in a captain's uniform walked in.

"You must be Harold Tilden," Nick said.

"That's Captain Tilden, young man. How do you do?" he said shaking his hand. "Any friend of Doc Booth is a friend of mine."

"Thank you Harold. I would like to introduce you to my companions. This is Miss Gretchen Sanders, and this is Detective John Baker of the Washington DC Metro Police," said Nick as both Gretchen and John stepped up and shook Captain Linden's hand.

"Got your gear ready?" Tilden asked.

"Yes, sir, we are ready to roll," John answered.

"Let's get moving. I only fly in daylight," Harold said, smiling.

The party boarded the plane and Tilden took it over to be fueled. Nick then sat down in the co-pilot's seat across from Harold and asked if he had any destination preferences.

"Well, we can decide that together. From what I gather you three are trying to elude pursuit from someone trying to take your lives. That is one reason why I told Harry to have you meet me here at Mather's. I can get in and out of here without question. I suggest we look for a destination with a small airport somewhere east of California. I can stay in the air for about five to six hours. I am seventy-four now and I do get tired, so that is about my maximum time in the air. What do you think of flying over to Helena, Montana?"

"Any reason you recommend Helena?" Nick asked.

"The flight there goes over part of the Rockies and I just love the scenery. Helena Regional airport is a great airfield, and the most important reason is that my son lives in that area and I have not seen him in a couple of months. He has twin daughters that are three years old. They are pistols. I just love them so darn much I can't help but go over every month or two to see them. It is only about a four hour flight"

"I believe Helena would be a fantastic destination. Shall we take off now?" Nick said, smiling as he admired Harold for his love of family.

"Step back into the cabin with me please," asked the pilot.

"I never take off before praying with my passengers. Will you all pray with me?"

"Yes, Harold, we would be honored to pray with you," replied Gretchen.

"Lord," Harold Tilden began, "we are about to take off and fly to Helena. Fly with us today, Lord. Protect us in the air. Please keep our engines working properly and help us reach our destination in safety. Lord, watch over each of us and give us your grace to always be good to others and to carry out your will. We make this prayer in Jesus' name. Amen."

"Amen," they all repeated aloud.

Harold turned and walked quickly back into the cockpit and said, "C'mon, Nick, you are my co-pilot on this flight."

Nick saluted the white-haired pilot. "Aye Aye, Captain,"

Minutes later they were speeding down runway three and lifting into the air. Nick was very impressed with Harold's skill. He handled the plane with confidence.

"This baby darn near flies itself," said Harold through the aviation headset. "She is equipped with auto pilot and the manual says it could land on its own in an emergency. I hope I never have to find out if that works. It is a great plane. I am blessed to own it. I am hooked up with the Make a Wish Foundation. I fly sick kids and their families to Disney Land and over to the Grand Canyon. Last year I flew medical supplies down to Mexico after the earthquake. I took some doctors and nurses down another time. It is a guilty pleasure. I think I get more out of doing those things than the people who benefit from the use of the plane. God has blessed me more than I deserve so I feel like I have a duty to use my good fortune in praise of the Lord and in service to others. I've met some real nice folks in the Pilots organization too. They do a lot of good. I am humbled to know them and to be part of something that is much bigger than me."

"Harold, I admire you, and congratulate you on being one of the few people in the world who have their priorities straight. I can see why you and Dr. Booth are such good friends."

"Thank you, Nick. Always remember you must give more than you think you can. It will come back to you many times over," said the wise man.

"Do I have the ability to call someone from the cockpit?" Nick asked.

"Can do. Turn you radio to channel 13 and press and hold your speaker button. An operator will come on the line and ask for the number you are calling. That's all there is to it," instructed Harold.

In seconds Nick was connected to Michael Murphy's telephone at the FBI office in Washington, D.C. "Hello, may I speak with Michael Murphy?"

"Who is calling?"

"Nick O'Connell."

"One moment, please."

"Hello, this is Agent Jerry Locket speaking. Is this Nick?"

"Yes, Agent, it is. I am calling for Michael Murphy."

"Nick, I am Agent Murphy's Supervisor. He is on the way to the monastery to evacuate his brother, your friends, and the other monks. We are working together on your case. I have some good news for you. Your brother has taken Maura, Kathleen, Angela, and your two infants to our safe house. A doctor insisted on traveling with the babies so we have one extra body at the house. Your wife and children are safe."

"That is great news! Thank you," Nick said in a relieved voice.

"I can tell you are in the air. What is your flight destination?"

"We are flying into Helena, Montana with an expected arrival time of three hours forty-five minutes. Are you able to get a plane there for us?" Nick inquired.

"Yes. I can have a plane there by six p.m. mountain time. We can fly you back to Washington and have you in the safe house early tomorrow morning," Locket said.

"We can work with that schedule," Nick said as Harold gave him a thumb's up, indicating they would land by six o'clock.

"I look forward to meeting you, Nick. Have a safe flight," Agent Locket said, as he hung up the telephone.

"Thank you, Harold, for allowing me to make that call. I want to tell Gretchen and John the news. Do you have an intercom?"

"Affirmative. Just press and hold the second button on the right side of the mike," instructed Harold.

"Ladies and Gentlemen, this is your co-pilot speaking. May I have your attention?

I have received word that the FBI has moved my wife and children to safety, and that the other members of our team are being evacuated from the Monastery to a safe house. We are flying into Helena, Montana and expect to land before six p.m. mountain time. We will fly east on an FBI plane and be in Washington early tomorrow morning," Nick announced.

"Why don't you go back there and get a group hug?" Harold suggested.

"Great idea, Harold," Nick said as he left the co-pilots seat and stepped into the cabin. "What do you think of the news?"

Gretchen stood up and hugged him. "That is great, Nick. I feel relieved, and safe for the first time in a while."

"We will never be completely safe until we expose these people to the public and stop their murderous attempts to silence anyone who comes close to knowing what they are really doing," John said. "I do not want to discourage either you or Nick, but there is important and dangerous work still ahead of us. Having the FBI watching our back is more than a small comfort. They should also be helpful in tracking down these murderers."

"I know John, I really do understand. But ever since I saw Hanna dead in her kitchen, all I could think about was getting as far away from Los Angeles as possible," Gretchen explained. "Now that we are in the air I feel a little safer."

"I know Gretchen, I know," Baker said.

Nick returned to the cockpit and took the co-pilots seat. They were approaching the west side of the Rocky Mountains and the scenery was indeed beautiful. They had a clear afternoon and the visibility was extraordinary. Eagles and hawks glided smoothly a thousand feet beneath the plane, which Captain Tilden had taken down to two thousand one hundred feet. Snow was visible on the rugged peaks of the Rockies. It was a fantastic day to fly. Nick, John and Gretchen had a chance to see some of God's best work in the western landscape.

Their reverie was broken by the crackle on the radio from the air controllers at Helena Airport. They were forty minutes outside the airport and had begun to slow down. Minutes later they were on final approach and in a few moments they were on the ground. Harold steered the plane safely to the private plane hangar and parked the plane as directed by the ground crew. Gretchen, John, Nick, and Harold walked away from the hangar into the lounge area.

"Harold, we can't thank you enough for getting us here. I know I speak for all of us when I say you will remain in our thoughts and prayers," Nick said while shaking his hand.

"You just tell old Doc Booth that I am a captain now, okay?"

Gretchen walked over to Harold and placed a kiss on his cheek while she hugged him in gratitude for his contribution to their trip home. John Baker shook Harold's hand generously and thanked him for being a friend.

The FBI plane landed twenty minutes later. It taxied over to the refueling pad and then over to the private plane hanger. Nick and his companions boarded and the plane was in the air moments later. All three passengers were asleep within ten minutes. They landed in Grand Rapids, Michigan to switch pilots, and then resumed the trip to Washington National Airport. They arrived at three a.m. eastern time. An FBI van picked them up and took them to the safe house in Falls Church, Virginia.

As the weary trio walked slowly into the darkened house the lights suddenly came on and Maura jumped into her husband's arms. Shaun and Kathleen kissed and hugged Nick and welcomed him home. Father Chris was shaking hands and hugging John, Gretchen, and Nick. He smiled and told him how good it was to see him. He hugged Nick a second time before giving him back to Maura. Catherine Harding ran over and hugged her partner, John Baker. Everyone gathered around for introductions to Gretchen and the explanation of her friendship with Colleen. It was a moving reunion of people who had been thrown into a life-threatening situation. Harry grabbed Nick's hand, shook it, and then said, "What the heck, c'mere son," and hugged him and kissed him on the cheek. Even Dr. Roberts welcomed Nick home with a hug.

Slowly they all returned to bed; it was obvious that Nick,

John, and Gretchen needed to rest. Nick peeked in on his children, Megan and Christopher, who were sleeping in Dr. Roberts' room.

Nick and Maura hugged again in the privacy of their room. Maura closed the door and took Nick by the hand to the side of their bed. She knelt down and he followed her lead. Holding hands they bowed their heads in prayer.

"Lord," Maura prayed. "Thank you for bringing Nick safely home to me. I praise you and thank you for the grace of his safe return. Please keep my family and friends safe in the coming days. Help us to overcome those who have threatened our lives and have chosen evil over good. We make this prayer in Jesus' name, Amen."

"Maura, I love you," Nick whispered to his wife.

"I love you so much. Never, ever leave me."

"I won't, Maura, I promise," Nick said, as he tenderly kissed his wife.

He was asleep as soon as his head hit the pillow.

chapter 37

Thomas woke up early and went for a run in the quiet neighborhood of retirement homes where his parents lived. He was worried about the previous meeting he held at St. Agnes Hospital in San Francisco. More than ever he believed the both Joseph Johnson and his son Jeffrey were loose cannons. They were the soldiers that the company used on security issues. Both were skilled in the art of killing. Thomas suspected that Jeff was also schizophrenic. Jeff enjoyed killing. Jones learned that Jeff had independently decided to eliminate every passenger in the first class flights that Nick and his sister Colleen had taken on their way back to Washington. Jeff was the kind of man who would disobey a direct order. If he decided that someone was a threat, they would be killed. Jeff had murdered Hanna, and there would be a day he would pay for that crime; first Jones had to formulate a plan to expose everyone in the top echelon of the company, in the Federal Government, and in the United States Medical Association.

The five-mile run did little to ease his concerns. He decided to make an appointment to visit with the pastor of his parent's church, Michael Powers. He made a decision to try to make peace with God. He had lived his life so dispassionately and so immorally that he was able to justify almost any action. He had reached the brink of destruction, peered over the precipice, and made a decision to reverse direction. It would not be easy, but from now on he was determined to do what was right.

Thomas returned to the house, showered, and joined his mother for breakfast. His dad had left on a few errands and would return later in the morning.

"Mom, I called Michael Powers a few minutes ago. I am going over to see him shortly. I hope you don't mind me leaving for a while," Thomas told his Mother.

"Mind? Not at all. You will be happy you talked to Pastor Michael," she replied.

"I want to come back to Christ and his church. I may not do it today, but I know I need to make a new start."

"I promise not to nag you, Tommy, just remember that Jesus loves you no matter what. Okay?"

"Yes, Mom, I know," her son said, smiling in love at his mother.

Thomas finished breakfast, washed up, and dressed for his visit to Pastor Michael Powers. He walked over to his mother and embraced her and kissed her. "I love you, Mom," he called out as he left the house.

"I love you too son!" she shouted back.

The drive to the Pastor's home was less than eight minutes. Michael greeted him warmly at the door and invited him to enter his house. "Why don't we sit on the deck, Thomas?" he suggested.

They settled in two comfortable deck chairs and began a conversation of what each other's lives were like. It was a gentle way of probing Thomas Jones' background without him feeling like he was being interrogated. Slowly the conversation got around to religion.

"Thomas, do you consider yourself a Christian?" the pastor asked.

"Yes, I think so. At least that is the way my parents raised me.

I was baptized and confirmed. I attended church for many years with mom and dad."

"So, you drifted away from church when you were in college?"

"No, I think I had drifted away a few years earlier. I was in church, but my mind was not there."

"After college you joined the marines, right?"

"Yes."

"Why?"

"I wanted to be a leader. The marines teach leadership better than anyone. I loved my time in the marines."

"And then?"

"I returned to Duke University and attended Medical School."

"And after that?"

"Johns Hopkins."

"When did you begin your present job?"

"After graduating from Johns Hopkins."

"You did not pursue medicine at that time?"

"No."

"Why?"

"I had a better offer."

"With your current employer?"

"Yes."

The dialog went on like this for quite some time. Michael wanted to dig deeper into Jones' work, but Thomas was reluctant to reveal any details about what he had done for the company.

"Thomas, we need to talk more, but I have another appointment. I am giving you a Bible and a Bible Study book. I recommend that you read the book of Psalms in the Old Testament and the Acts of the Apostles in the New Testament. Follow the Bible study book's suggestions as you read these two books. These will give you a jump start on renewing your Christianity. I strongly urge you to contact a Pastor near your home. I believe you have to crawl before you walk back to Christ. What is important is that you have taken the first step. I will pray for you. God Bless you, Thomas," Michael said sincerely.

Thomas gratefully accepted the two books, shook the pastor's hand, and said goodbye. He was not sure what he had accomplished, but he knew he had taken the first few steps of a very long journey. And he knew the destination was the right one.

He pulled into parent's driveway and saw that his dad had not yet returned. There was a dark sedan parked near the driveway. Jones walked into the house and called for his mother.

He saw her standing by the entry to the kitchen. "Are you okay, Mom?"

Suddenly she was shoved forward with a large butcher's knife impaled in the center of her back. Her lifeless body fell to the floor.

"Mom!" Thomas shouted as her moved toward her.

Standing in the entryway was Jeff Johnson with his gun drawn and a second large knife in his left hand. He lifted the gun to fire. "Hey, Jones, come and see your Mommy. Come here and hold your Mommy. Your Mommy wants you, Jones." His voice was raised in excitement. "You thought you could tell me what to do. Nobody tells me what to do."

Jeff squeezed the trigger of the .25 caliber pistol and fired. Thomas dove for the floor. Jeff fired again through the sofa where Jones had taken cover.

"You pansy. You are nothing but a weak suit and tie," Jeff shouted as he walked closer to the sofa and fired three more times. The noise of the gun firing seemed to get louder with each shot. "This is poetic, sheer poetry if you ask me," Johnson rambled on.

"First I killed your sister, now your mother, and you are next. After you're dead I will wait here and kill your dad."

Jones reached for a small lamp table and flung it in the direction of the crazed murderer. Johnson lost control of his gun momentarily when the table hit his arm. Thomas thought of charging at him but that was too risky.

"I knew you were a coward. Why don't you stand up and take it like a man? Even your sister put up a fight. Man, she was fine!" Jeff screamed at Jones. He lifted his gun to fire again, this time even closer to Jones than he was a moment ago.

A shot rang out. The killer's hands went limp as the gun and knife dropped to the floor. Thomas jumped over the sofa and grabbed the gun. Jeff Johnson tried to turn around but could not move. John Jones walked into the living room with his gun in his hand. Johnson went to his knees. He was trying to talk but only gurgling sounds emanated from his mouth. Thomas Jones' father fired his gun a second time into the stomach of the murderer.

"He is finished now, son."

John walked over to his wife's body. He cradled her in his arms and quietly cried.

Thomas walked over to his father and sat down next his dead mother. He put his arm around his dad and they both wept. All Thomas could say was, "I am sorry, Dad, so sorry," as he glanced over at the murderer.

Thomas kept watch over Jeff Johnson whose life force was oozing out of his body. Jeff Johnson's eyes were burned with hatred as he lay dying on the floor and he was unable to move. The pain was excruciating.

"You stinking murderer!" Thomas said bitterly to the man dying on the floor of his parent's home. "You deserve to burn in hell. You betrayed the honor of your service to this country. You betrayed humanity. You betrayed God."

"Help me," the younger Johnson mouthed to Jones.

"I will. In a few minutes when all the blood in your body is gone and you are on your last breath, then I will call for help.

Five minutes later, Thomas Jones stood up, looked at Johnson, and then dialed 911.

The paramedics arrived shortly and began their work. After

confirming that both Mrs. Jones and Jeff Johnson were dead they prepared to move the bodies.

Johnson's portable telephone suddenly rang. Thomas fished it out of the murderer's jacket. Thomas pressed the green, "answer" button. A voice on the other end anxiously said, "Jeff, it's Pop. Did you accomplish your mission? Is Jones dead?"

"Johnson," Thomas said in a rage, "his mission is *not* accomplished. Your son, Jeff, is dead!"

"Jones, did you kill my boy?"

"Yes, he is dead, and soon you will join him," Jones said menacingly.

"You are a dead man, Jones. I am coming for you!" the elder Johnson screamed into the telephone.

"Come. I can't wait to face you!" Suddenly, Thomas heard the sound of screeching brakes and metal crunching metal. The phone went dead.

The police officer that arrived earlier heard the tail end of the telephone conversation. "Who was that man, Mr. Jones?" he asked.

"He is this man's father."

"He threatened to kill you?"

"Yes, in fact he promised, but I will kill him."

"I would not do that," the police officer said.

"This man killed my sister and my mother."

"Why would he do that?"

"I don't know."

As Jones hung up the phone, another police officer walked into the room. "Mr. Jones, I want to detain you for questioning, please do not leave," said the officer.

"Thom, come over here a minute," his father said.

"Look, son, this may be your chance to get out of the business you are in. Do the right thing."

"That is a good idea, Dad."

"Officer, may I speak with you out on the porch?" Jones asked.

"Yes, Mr. Jones," he replied as they stepped out onto the front porch.

"I am involved with a number of major crime issues at the highest level of the Government. I should be talking to the FBI. What happened here was pretty cut and dry. Jeff Johnson killed my mother and would have killed me if my dad had not shot him. It was self-defense. I can give you and the FBI a list of the people this man has killed in the last month. Not only that, but he was directly involved with the bombing of the police precinct in Washington, D.C. I can give you and the FBI information on the crimes this man and his father have committed over the last ten years. Call your captain and tell him what I have told you. Ask him to get an FBI agent here as soon as possible," Thomas instructed.

"Sir, I will call my Captain. But please don't think about leaving here," the officer said.

"I will not leave, you have my word."

The paramedics removed Jeff Johnson's body. A second ambulance was called to remove Helen's body. Her husband sorrowfully watched as the medics respectfully lifted her body off the floor and onto a stretcher. He wanted to go in the ambulance with Helen, but the medics explained that was not possible. The police also wanted to finalize his statement on the shooting.

Losing Helen was more than his father could bear. Thomas saw the hurt in his dad's eyes and it broke his heart to see his father in such pain.

"Dad, why don't you go in and lay down for a while?" his son suggested.

"I think I will, son. Help me get up."

Thomas helped his father into his bedroom. Everywhere there were pictures of Helen and John and their children. John sat on the side of the bed and kicked off his shoes. He lay down on the bed and closed his eyes.

"Dad," Thomas asked, "where did you get the gun?"

"I had it in the old Chevy. When I saw the dark car there I

got suspicious. I looked in the back window and saw him holding up your mother. I got the gun and came in firing. I had to protect you, son. I love you, boy."

"Thanks, Dad. I love you too. You saved my life," Thomas said, as he kissed his father on the forehead.

He closed the door and walked out to the kitchen where the police were waiting for an FBI Agent to arrive.

Pastor Michael Powers, driving by the Jones house, stopped when he saw the ambulance and police. He came to door where a police officer stopped him and inquired who he was and why he was there. After getting the police approval Michael walked into the house and embraced Thomas as he voiced his condolences over the tragic events of the day. Jones introduced him to the police officer and invited him to sit down. He explained in detail what had happened that morning. He explained the horror that began when he walked in the door fifteen minutes before noon.

"May I speak with John?" Pastor Michael inquired.

"Sure, Dad is in the bedroom. He might be asleep. I am sure he will be glad to see you.

Michael Powers opened the door to the bedroom quietly, hoping not to disturb John if he was asleep. He walked over to the bed and looked down at his friend.

Two minutes later Pastor Mike shouted, "Thomas! Thomas, come here."

Thomas and the police officer ran to the bedroom and saw Pastor Michael on his knees next to the bed. John Jones lay on his bed with an angelic smile on his face. He had died only minutes before his Pastor walked in to visit and pray with him.

Thomas reached over and felt for a pulse on his father's neck. There was none. He looked down at his dad and fell to the floor in tears. The pastor and the policeman helped him up to a chair. Thomas could not control his sobbing. He walked over to the bed and knelt beside his father's body and picked up his hand and kissed it.

"Dad, I love you. I love you so much," he repeated over and over. His grief was overpowering. He shook and his tears flowed as never before. He rocked back and forth on the bed beside his dad. Michael Powers sat down and embraced him. He consoled Thomas with his quiet prayers and comforting words. Finally Thomas regained his composure. He stood up and looked at his father's face intently.

"Michael, he is smiling, and he looks completely at peace," Thomas said through his grief.

"Yes, he does," Michael agreed. "I believe he did not want to be separated from Helen. His heart was broken. I think he died so he could be with her as they go into heaven together. I don't recall ever seeing anyone who looked so happy in death. He knew you were going to be all right and it was okay to leave now. He was at peace and ready to meet the Lord."

"I lost all those years and opportunities to be a part of my family. Now, in the space of two weeks, I have lost Hanna, my mother, and now my father. That sounds so selfish. Did I bring death to my family?"

"No, Thomas. You did not bring death here. You brought hope here, and happiness. The joy of your mom and dad over reconciling with you was a blessing that God gave to them before he called them home. Remember only the joy of your mother as she saw you for the first time after all those years. She ran into your arms. All the hurt, worry, and disappointment dissolved in your arms. Remember the happiness of your father as he welcomed you home. Jesus himself told us of the joy of one sinner who repents. There was joy in this home and you delivered it in abundance. For as long as you live hold onto that memory," the pastor advised him.

"Thank you, Michael. I will remember that. You are a friend and a good man. I thank God you came here today. I know I will need your help in the days ahead. I believe mom and dad are together. Please keep them in your prayers," Thomas asked sincerely.

"I promise I will, Thomas. Call me anytime, day or night. I will be there for you," Michael replied. "I must leave now, but call me, please, even if it is just to talk."

"I will, Michael. Thanks," Thomas replied.

chapter 38

An FBI Agent arrived a few minutes after the Pastor departed. "Hello Mr. Jones, I am Agent Stephen Green," he said as he showed him his badge. "I am sorry for your loss. I was briefed on my way here of the shooting and the assault on your life. Your father is a very brave man."

"Mr. Jones, as I understand it you have information on the bombing of the Police Precinct in D.C. We believed that case was solved."

"Agent, I called the tip in to the police where the so-called terrorists were hiding. I set those men up in that hotel room with instructions to protect the building against a phony attack. I instructed them to dress as guerilla fighters and to shoot first if approached. My company financed the entire thing. The two men who were directly responsible for the bomb at the Precinct were Jeff Johnson and his father, Joseph," Thomas confessed to the Agent.

"Joseph Johnson?" Green asked.

"Yes, Joseph Johnson," Jones said.

"Turn on your television a minute, will you?" asked Agent Green.

Thomas turned on the television and turned to a Los Angeles all-news channel. They were broadcasting a story of an automobile accident on Interstate 10 near Santa Monica. A driver in a pick-up truck was killed when a truck hauling lumber in front of the pick-up suddenly braked for an accident. The load of lumber shifted and 2"x 4" boards loosened and flew backwards into the pick-up truck striking the driver who was impaled by the wood that crashed through the window. The driver's eyes were severely damaged by the spikes and shards of glass and lumber that shattered the window and penetrated his torso. The driver had his left arm amputated and three boards penetrated his torso. The crash forced the engine of the pick-up truck into the passenger compartment setting the driver on fire. The driver also suffered two broken legs and a broken pelvis. The driver of the pick-up, a fifty six year old man lived approximately fifteen minutes prior to succumbing to the massive injuries and burns sustained in the crash. Police and paramedics tried to remove the driver from the burning truck but were unable to do so before he died. Police report that the man had a loaded rifle and two pistols on the front seat of the pick-up truck. They have identified the driver as one Joseph Johnson. He had no known local address. The Police and News Channel stated that it was the most grizzly accident scene ever reported in the greater Los Angeles area.

"Was that the same Joseph Johnson you were talking about?" asked Green in his deliberate manner.

"I believe so. He swore he was coming here to kill me," Thomas replied. "He and his son committed murder not only here in California, but throughout the nation."

"Mr. Jones, tell me something. You seem prepared to confess to any number of crimes. People don't usually do that. Why should I believe anything you tell me?" the Agent inquired.

"Agent Green, let me just tell you that I have seen the light. I have lost my family as a result of some of the actions of my company. There are plans in the works by people in the Government and in the Healthcare business that, if left unchecked, could have the most devastating effect on American society ever. I should be talking to people in Washington, no offense to you, sir," Thomas explained.

"Give me one thing that my supervisor can tell Washington that could connect you to any of what you say," asked Green.

"Tell him to look at the death rate at St. Agnes Hospital in San Francisco. Tell him Dr. John Walters is behind all those deaths. That should get their attention. Look, I want to help, but I cannot help here. You need to get me to Washington. I have files, notes, coded information that will give you all the information you need to investigate and make arrests," said Jones.

"Okay. Let me call my people. You sit right here," Green ordered.

Green called his Supervisor and gave him the information. The Supervisor contacted Washington and after two transfers was finally connected to Agent Jerry Locket. He gave Locket the information and asked what he knew about all this.

"Agent Green I do not know Thomas Jones, but I do know about St. Agnes and Dr. John Walters. I have people here who have had direct contact with Walters. Is this Jones willing to help us in the investigation?" Locket asked.

"Yes, sir, he is," Green said.

"Bring him to Washington. We know this man is connected to people who have committed some major crimes here and around the country. If he is willing to work with us we might be able to save a lot of lives and close this case," replied Locket.

"Yes sir. I will have him in Washington tomorrow afternoon. Thank you Agent Locket," Green said, as he hung up the telephone.

"Well Mr. Jones, we will be in Washington tomorrow. What am I going to do with you? You are not under arrest, but I cannot take the chance that you will run. I have a little problem here."

"Stay with me. I have to make funeral arrangements for my parents. I may not be here for their burial, but I still must take care of them. Go with me to the funeral home and then if you want to incarcerate me you can take me to the nearest Precinct. You can handcuff me if you are more comfortable with that," Jones offered.

"I think I will stay here with you. I'm not going to worry about cuffing you. But know this, if you make any move to run I will shoot you," Green said menacingly.

"I believe you would, Agent. I will keep my word," Jones promised.

Agent Green escorted Thomas to Cronin's Funeral Home where Thomas made arrangements for both his father and mother. He selected matching caskets and vaults. Pastor Powers agreed to hold the service for his parents. He even offered to host the viewing if Thomas was unable to return for the service. Thomas wrote a check to cover the costs of his parent's funerals. They returned to his parent' home after finalizing the funeral plans. He packed a bag for the flight to DC, sat down, and opened the bible Mike Powers gave him earlier that morning.

Agent Green made arrangements to have a plane fly them to Washington along with another Agent who would meet them in the morning. Green called his wife and asked her to bring him some shirts and slacks, and the necessary overnight items he would need for the next few days since he was staying over-night with a suspect on a major case.

Thomas watched the news footage of Joseph Johnson's death again and thought of how swift and sure justice can be at times. He felt somewhat guilty about being happy they were dead, but he also realized his responsibility in the crimes they commit-ted.

Agent Green and Thomas Jones arrived at Los Angeles International airport at seven thirty a.m. where they met FBI Agent Rosemary Beckett, who accompanied them on the flight to Washington National airport. The flight plan included stops in Des Moines, Iowa where they picked up FBI Special Agent Eugene Martin who had investigated the bombing of the Precinct. They made a second stop in Youngstown, Ohio to refuel. The plane touched down in Washington at four thirty p.m. Thomas and the Agents went directly to FBI headquarters in downtown DC.

Agent Locket greeted Thomas Jones, Agent Rosemary Beckett, and Special Agents Martin and Green. Locket suggested they wash up a bit and then go downstairs to the commissary for dinner. Jones asked Locket for permission to check his messages. When he did he had four calls from the Colonel, the last three were panic calls ordering Jones to return his calls immediately.

Thomas explained to the Agents who the Colonel was and that it may be interesting for them to hear this telephone call. Locket agreed and set up a phone with a tap so that they could pinpoint the location of the Colonel. Thomas suggested they use a telephone that could not be tapped since the Colonel may have the same technology and it would not be good for him to know that Jones was working with the FBI.

They set up the safe telephone and Jones made the call.

"Why haven't you called me sooner?" the Colonel yelled into the phone. "Where are you?" Do you know what has happened in Los Angeles?"

"Colonel, I have been traveling all day. What are you referring to?" Jones asked innocently.

"Our man Johnson was killed today. You didn't hear about it?"

"I told you I was traveling all day. Which Johnson was killed and how did he die?" Jones asked facetiously.

"It was Joseph, the father. He was killed in a horrible automobile accident. I spoke to him only minutes before he died. He was very upset and ranting about getting revenge. Apparently he couldn't stop for an accident ahead of him. He died horribly."

"I am sorry to hear that," Jones said casually.

"Do you have any idea why he was ranting and raving? You

saw him in San Francisco. Was he all right when you saw him?" inquired the Colonel.

"Yes, he seemed fine," Jones replied.

"Do you know where his son is?"

"No, but they usually aren't too far apart," Thomas said, smiling at the irony.

"I want you to find him, Jones. Do you hear me? I want to know where he is and I want to know now!" the Colonel ordered.

"I will do my best, sir," Thomas answered.

"Where are you Jones? Did you leave the west coast?"

"Not yet. I am still on vacation, Colonel."

"Well, I want you back in Washington today! That is not negotiable Jones. I mean it. Get back here."

"Yes, Colonel."

"Listen Jones, what did you learn at your meeting with Walters?"

"He and his pals are pushing the edge. He believes he can implement the Ten Day Program at hospitals throughout the country in a matter of weeks. I think he is rushing it a little, Colonel."

"Jones, you have to understand, the sooner we get this program in place, the safer society will be. I have made sure that not a single pharmaceutical company in the United States is working on effective medication to stop this plague. The way to stop this is to kill off everyone who has it, and possibly everyone who is close to them. Sure these are drastic measures, but just think of the lives we will save in the long run. You would understand if you had a son who nearly was infected by the disease. Just imagine how you would feel if a normal son of yours was infected with this disease by a woman who was foolish enough to be intimate with a man who had been intimate with another man and contracted this disease! You would be ready to take whatever measures necessary to protect your son in that case.

And you would want the people responsible to suffer. Trust me, I know."

"Yes, Colonel, I understand how angry I would be, but Walters and the Johnsons take everything too far. They put us at risk, especially with the O'Connell affair."

"Jones, that was necessary. You were a marine. You know when certain targets are eliminated that other people can get hurt. It's called collateral damage."

"Colonel, you were targeting people who had nothing to do with your war on the plague. Dr. Booth and the flight attendant were innocent bystanders, along with Nick O'Connell."

"Mr. Jones, are you questioning me? Do I detect disloyalty?"

"I would never question you. I am concerned about the fallout from negative press and the need to cover up so many of the Johnson's messes."

"You have been superb to date of handling what I call sensitive issues, Mr. Jones."

"Thank you, Colonel. But I would rather not spend other minute fixing their mistakes. I am fearful that Walters, Nelson, and Preston will implement their program before we are ready to roll out the positive aspects of it to the general population. I believe the program will be a disaster if it is not presented properly, and that is what Walters will do." "If he bungles the introduction of the program I will see that he is distanced far from us. Look, Jones, we have in excess of fifteen million dollars on hand to roll out the program across the country. We have the USMA behind us. We have the votes in the Senate to back us. That is what fifteen million can buy us, Jones. You know that."

"I know money buys votes, Colonel. But if this is botched we will face a nation of very unhappy citizens who will never trust their doctor or their government again."

"You make me laugh, Jones. Do you really think anyone trusts their government now? Strong men throughout history have made difficult decisions for the good of society. It may take a while for the citizenry to come around to our way of thinking, but eventually they will see things our way. Once this plague is contained we will be hailed as heroes."

"That is what the Nazis told the German population Colonel. It is not that different than the holocaust. Can't you see that?"

"Jones, it is completely different. We are eliminating immoral people who have violated the laws of the Old and New Testaments. Jews, Christians, and Muslims see this sexual behavior as abhorrent. It is not like the holocaust at all. We are not burning bodies and abusing corpses like Hitler and his crew did. I do not see the comparison at all. You just don't understand how devastating it would be to have a son of yours infected by this killer disease."

"Colonel, do you have a son infected with this disease?"

"I did not say that, Jones. No, of course not, no! I've had enough of this argument. Just get back here, Jones. That is an order! Goodbye."

Agents Locket and Beckett took their headphones off as Thomas hung up the telephone. "I cannot believe what I just heard," Locket said out loud. "Is this 'ten day plan' a formalized idea to eliminate every person infected with this plague within ten days of being admitted to a hospital?"

"Exactly, Agent. I saw the plan first hand. Walters has been using the drugs for over six months. He has every Forensic Pathologist in northern California convinced that autopsies are too dangerous due to the fear of infection," Thomas explained. "Dr. Nelson and Dr. Preston over at Walter Reed Hospital have tested the drug and they swear it is undetectable. And they all believe that Congress will support their efforts in eliminating the disease through this program."

"What is your role in the scheme, Thomas?" Agent Rosemary Beckett asked.

"I was the fund raiser. I have put together programs over the last five years that have defrauded the Government of millions of dollars. In addition, I have used the USMA to collect fees from every physician in the country. I am talking about enormous sums of money that are being used in the development of the ten-day drug. I have used my influence with many Pharmaceutical Companies convincing them not to focus on the development of any drug that could affect these plans. We have one company working with us. They know if doctors support this drug it will sell. I have made it clear that no one will support drugs that curtail the spread of this self-inflected disease. People want to feel safe. Doctors make people feel safe. Doctors then will do whatever they can to keep those safe-feeling people coming back to see them regularly. The doctors recommend drugs that people want. The people want to feel safe from this disease called the gay plague. The doctors will do their part in making the people feel safe from this disease. That means the ten-day program will succeed beyond our wildest expectations."

"Jones, who came up with this idea?" Locket asked.

"I understand Dr. Walters developed the concept at St. Agnes Hospital," Thomas replied. "It has gotten way out of control. The entire incident with Nick O'Connell and his family is a good example. Once the Johnson's got involved they just escalated the killing of anyone who could possibly link them to the murder of Colleen O'Connell. Jeff Johnson murdered everyone who flew first class with the O'Connell's when Nick brought his sister Colleen home from St. Agnes. They were unsure if Colleen had been infected. Walters pronounced her infected, but people at the hospital were not sure he was right with his diagnosis. However, he used the fear of infection to keep everyone from getting too close."

"What brought this whole mess out into the open?" asked Agent Beckett.

"I think Detective John Baker and Nick O'Connell followed their instincts after they successfully fooled everyone, including the Johnson's, into believing that they were killed in the bomb blast at the Police Station. I certainly thought they had died there. They flew to California and started snooping around after Detective Baker suspected that Colleen O'Connell had not died accidentally, but at the hands of an unknown predator.

Somehow O'Connell and Baker were able to hide their six or seven companions who everyone thought were dead. They hid from their wives and families. We thought Jeff Johnson and his father had killed them. I heard Nick O'Connell showed up dressed as a Benedictine monk at St. Agnes a few days ago along with an unknown female and Detective Baker. That infuriated Dr. Walters and he ordered the Johnson's to take any actions necessary to stop O'Connell and Baker from disclosing what they learned from the patients at St. Agnes."

Agent Murphy smiled and said, "My brother Frank is a Benedictine monk and Rector of St. Ambrose Monastery and Retreat House in Silver Springs, Maryland."

"I see," said Thomas. "The victims of the bombing were hiding at the Monastery here only miles from our offices. That was nicely done, Agent Murphy, nicely done."

"I can't take credit for that. Father Christopher Sullivan, Nick O'Connell's brother-in-law, is an old classmate of my brother. They set everything up long before I was aware of what was happening."

"Why did they wait to call the FBI?" Beckett asked.

"I believe Nick and John were concerned about how deep the conspiracy went. They did not want to risk telling too many people that they had survived the bomb blast at the Precinct house," Agent Locket explained.

"Do you have any idea where Nick and Detective Baker are now?" Jones inquired.

"Yes. Here in DC at a safe house," Agent Locket said.

"They made good on their escape out of San Francisco," Jones said. "I know Walters wanted them dead. I am glad to hear they are okay. Who is the young woman traveling with them?"

"One of the three young women that Walters ordered killed. The first was Colleen O'Connell, the second was Hanna Jones, and the third was Gretchen Sanders. They were good friends who worked together in Los Angeles," Agent Murphy replied.

"Hanna Jones was my sister," Thomas said quietly.

"I am sorry, Thomas, I did not know that," Agent Beckett said regrettably. "I am sorry for your loss. You have lost your entire family to these monsters?"

"Yes, I have," Thomas answered, "But I have gained something too. My dignity and my soul have come back to me. My mother and father helped me find what I had misplaced for such a long time. It is not easy for a man with such excessive pride to bare his soul and confess to so many sins. Whatever courage I thought I had before is nothing compared to the courage it took to admit to you what has been happening. What is at stake for me is my immortal soul and that means so much more than my reputation or the money I have in the bank. I will show you my records, my monthly reports, and my coded messages to the Colonel. The one thing I cannot give you is something I don't know and that is who the Colonel reports to. As you know, the Colonel is the Surgeon General, Joseph Bolton, but he reports to someone on Capitol Hill and no one in the Company knows that person's identity. That has to be one of your targets. It won't be easy because everything has been coded and there are layers and layers of protection between the Colonel and his boss on the Hill."

"Thomas, I am grateful you have come forward like this. I cannot promise anything in the way of a deal. I have to talk to my superiors and to the Attorney General before anything like that can be considered," Locket said with some regret in his voice.

"Agent Locket, I have not asked for a deal or for immunity from prosecution. I would only ask that you be very selective whom you reveal this information to. I cannot stress enough that there are security breaches at every level. If my presence here is revealed, I guarantee I will be killed. Please be careful," Thomas pleaded. "Trust no one."

"I will be careful Thomas. It's getting late. We are going to incarcerate you in the holding cell downstairs for the night. We can continue with the interrogation tomorrow morning. Get a good night's sleep. You are safe in this building. Thank you for stepping up to the plate and taking responsibility for your actions."

Agent Beckett took Jones down to the holding cell and locked him in for the night. He had a toilet, a sink, and a concrete cot with a thin mattress to sleep on. The first thing Thomas did was to kneel down beside the cot, bow his head, and begin to pray.

chapter 39

Nick awoke at seven a.m. and took a walk around the safe house that the FBI had provided for his family and friends. He was impressed with the security of the facility. An intruder would be prevented from climbing the walls surrounding the home because of the iron spikes placed across the top of the stone wall. Even the doors were secured by an electronic entry system. He was satisfied that his wife and children would be safe here.

Father Chris was awake reading his daily prayers when he heard Nick walk by his door. Upon completing the scripture readings he walked down to the kitchen where Nick had just began brewing a pot of coffee.

"Good morning, Chris," Nick said to his brother-in-law.

"Good morning Nick, how are you?"

"Good. A little weary with jet lag, but otherwise I am fine. How are things with everybody?" Nick replied as he yawned.

"It got a little crazy yesterday when we moved out of the Monastery. There was the terrible apprehension about a possible attack from unknown enemies. We vacated the place in less than an hour. We actually had to wait on the bus that brought us here. Frank Murphy's brother in the FBI, Michael, drove a bus into the Monastery that had a plastic sign on each side of the bus that read, "St. Ambrose Monastery." We were relieved at the sight of it. The monks living at the Monastery also took the bus out. Frank was concerned about them and I know he was relieved at their safe exodus from the Retreat House. We were all praying for you. It was tough not knowing where you were or if you were in danger."

"You would be appalled at what Dr. Walters has done at St. Agnes Hospital. He has a Ten Day Program that includes a medicine regimen of drugs that are guaranteed to have the patient die by the tenth day. He has been administering this program for months. We believe all the patients have been men diagnosed with the gay plague disease. He has been working with doctors around the country including Dr. Jim Nelson and Dr. Mark Preston from Walter Reed Hospital here in Washington. From what John and Gretchen gathered at their meeting, Walters was planning to roll out this program with the assistance of a number of influential physicians around the country. John and I talked about how they would coordinate such a roll out and we believe he is using the USMA as the conduit to communicate with this organization of physicians who support this program of death."

"That is almost too hard to believe. I have seen a number of articles about this gay plague out in California. It seems to be limited to men who are intimate with other men. Most people consider this sinful. But, as Christians, we believe we can love the sinner while detesting the sin. Jesus gave us that message when he spoke to the woman accused of adultery. When no one was left to condemn her he simply said, 'Go, and do not commit this sin again.' It is unconscionable that a physician who has sworn to do no harm would intentionally poison his patients. How has he kept this quiet?"

"Chris, no one wants to touch these men. Walters has put such a scare into everyone, including pathologists, that even incidental contact with an infected person will lead to a full-blown case of the disease. This fear causes good people to make bad decisions."

"Don't we have people working on a cure for the disease?" Chris asked.

"That's where the power of the USMA and the Federal Government comes in. The Medical Association has raised millions of dollars to develop and promote this drug. They have put enormous pressure on the major pharmaceutical companies, and the Government, not to waste funds on trying to develop a drug that might help medically, but would never change human behavior. Walters way of changing human behavior is to eliminate those members of society who pursue sexual activities considered immoral and sinful," Nick explained.

"This is almost unbelievable. Could this happen in an open, free democratic society?" Chris said as he pondered the implication of the question.

"When it comes to medicine, healthcare, and fear, fear will always win. We spend millions of dollars trying to stay healthy. Doctors prescribe drugs to take care of every real or imagined illness people believe they have, or are coming down with. The combination of the fear of what this AIDS disease does to a human body, along with America's almost blind acceptance of what the doctor says or prescribes makes this situation not only possible, but almost probable," Nick replied. "None of us want to die. We all know we will die someday, but we don't want to rush that day, especially if that day involves suffering with the many facets of the disease. And remember, Chris, ninety nine and a half percent of Americans know nothing about the disease, they only know what they have heard about the disease. The sad truth right now is that the disease attacks so many of the normal body functions in such a painful way that any sane person would have a fear of contracting the disease under any circumstances. All it takes is one strong voice to convince people that we face extermination unless we destroy all the carriers of this disease. Those who are killed may even be hailed as martyrs because they choose to die rather than threaten society."

"But Nick, murder under any circumstances is wrong!" Father Chris pronounced.

"Yes, and everyone I know agrees with that, but if they or their wives and children were threatened by this plague, they would think their actions were justifiable," Nick said.

"You are right, Nick, people would think they have a right to defend their family's lives," Chris said sadly.

"That is the power that the people like John Walters understand. I think it is close to the propaganda that Hitler used in Germany," Nick said. "If all these people are killed how different would it be from the holocaust?"

"None, Nick. It would be the same," Chris replied.

"Hey, what are you two chatting about this morning?" Maura asked as she walked into the kitchen. "You look like you are trying to solve half the world's problems this morning."

"You might be right," Nick said laughing as he walked over and kissed Maura. "Did you sleep well?"

"Best night I have had since you went away. I woke up a few times just to touch you and make sure you were really here and that I wasn't dreaming," Maura said as she snuggled into her husband's arms. "What are your plans for today?"

"I need to talk with the FBI and I was hoping we could get more information on the Medical Association using Father Carroll's ID code to break into their files and find out more about its members and the Walters plan."

"Please spend some time with Megan and Christopher this morning. You have not held them since you went to California," Maura said, as she tugged at Nick's sleeve.

"I can't wait to get those little ones in my arms," Nick said smiling. "Do you think they are awake yet?"

"Here they are now," Maura said as Doctor Roberts walked into the kitchen holding a baby in each arm.

"Good morning Dr. Roberts," said Nick as he reached for baby Christopher. "Did I thank you last night for being here to help with these little angels?"

"Yes, you did. I am very happy to be here with you and Maura. The babies are getting stronger each day. I hope they will be able to get on normal infant food soon. They are doing great with their Mother's milk and nutritional supplements so far. I am so glad you are alive and safe, Nick. I really thought you were lost in the bombing incident."

"Thanks, Doctor. I am very happy to be here. Detective John Baker was smart enough to get us away from the bombsite before anyone realized we had survived. It gave us the opportunity to be safe as we tried to figure out who and why such a crime was committed. Everyone made sacrifices and contributions to getting us some answers, and getting us home safely," explained Nick.

All the residents were up by eight a.m. and revisited the joy of the early morning reunion. Father Chris planned to say Mass in the tiny Chapel at nine a.m. and invited everyone to attend. He promised to keep his remarks short. Most of the guests in the safe house attended Mass and offered thanks to the Lord for the safe return of the travelers. They also prayed for the sick men at St. Agnes who were so near to death. Chris prayed that the Lord would guide and bless their efforts to overcome the sinful plans of the evil men behind the plot to kill so many people. It was pretty much an average start to a normal day, something that none of the refugees had experienced in a while.

chapter 40

Thomas Jones woke up early in the holding cell in the basement of the FBI Building after a restless night. The thoughts of his mother and father's untimely passing overwhelmed him with grief. Several times he rolled off the cot and onto his knees to pray. Despite Pastor Mike's encouragement, he felt responsible for what happened to his sister, his mother, and his father. It was difficult to hold onto the mercy offered by a loving and forgiving God. In spite all his education and training he found the struggle to be the most difficult fight of his life. Despite his returning to the Lord, the power of evil still tried to suck him into a web of doubt and self-destruction. Thomas fought the despair with every muscle, tissue, and tendon in his being. He held onto the belief that God might still love him in spite of his many sins. He prayed his way through much of the night defeating the suicidal temptations Satan placed before him.

Now, facing the sunrise, he knew he could accept whatever disgrace he had earned. The only restitution he could offer was total compliance with the authorities. Thomas felt surprisingly calm. He felt real peace in his soul, perhaps for the first time in twenty years. Everything began to fall into place. It was complex, yet simple. It would be difficult, as all good things are, but it would never compare to the struggle for his soul that he had faced that night.

Agent Locket arrived at seven fifteen carrying coffee, orange juice and a bagel for Thomas. He opened the cell door and pulled two chairs over to a small table by the cell.

"Hungry Thomas?"

"Yes. Thank you, may I call you Jerry?"

"Yes, you may. Do you go by Thomas or Thom?" the Agent asked.

"Thomas is fine, or you may call me Thom."

"In spite of our circumstances," Agent Locket said. "I think we will end up friends, or at least I hope so."

"Yes, I think we will."

"Did you sleep well here in the cell?"

"Not really. I tossed and turned all night. I thought a lot about my parents and sister. What kept me going," Thomas said. "Was the thought that Hanna, my mom, and my dad are all behind me in making the decision to work with you in stopping the evil that these people have planned. It is the right thing to do."

"It *is* the right thing to do. It's not going to be easy, but it is right," Agent Locket said. "Now is the time to stand up and be counted."

"I agree completely and I give you my word I will share all my knowledge and information with you and your team."

They finished their coffee and Agent Locket took Jones over to a washroom so Thomas could get cleaned up. They then went back up to Agent Locket's office where Agent Rosemary Beckett and Special Agent Eugene Martin were waiting.

"Good morning Agent Becket and Agent Martin," Jones said politely.

"Where do you want to start Thomas?" asked Agent Locket.

"I have a question. Do you know if the Santa Monica Police released any information on the death of Jeff Johnson, the man my father shot while defending me?"

"I will check and verify that information," Agent Becket offered.

"Why do you ask Thomas?" Locket wondered.

"If the Colonel, Joseph Bolton, and Dr. Walters do not know he is dead, I will still have access to my office and files. If it is possible we should go there today so I can retrieve everything. You have my laptop computer and there are some coded files there, but the most damning information is in my office. If I can copy those files today you will have enough work for four or five agents for a month doing nothing but decoding my files and preparing arrest warrants for perhaps up to a hundred or more people."

Agent Beckett returned to the office to report on Jeff Johnson. "The Santa Monica Police deferred to our local FBI office regarding the release of the details of the death of Jeff Johnson. It has not been given to the press."

"Thank you Agent Beckett. As I said, that will be helpful in getting our hands on the materials that you will need to arrest these people," Jones repeated.

"How do you propose to take me into my office?" asked Jones. "If I come in with several Agents, many people will ask questions and we risk exposure."

"We can't let you walk in there alone, that is out of the question," Agent Martin said authoritatively.

"May I suggest a way that would not attract any attention?"

"Go ahead Thomas," said Locket.

"I often interview candidates for both field work and for positions at the home office. Could Agent Beckett escort me to my office? I will be in her sight at all times." Jones suggested.

"Agent Beckett, are you okay with that plan?" asked Locket.

"Yes sir, that is fine with me."

All preparations for Jones to return to his office were completed within an hour and they left the FBI building and headed for Farragut Square and the World Bank Building where TMJ, Ltd. leased three floors of office space.

Agent Rosemary Beckett and Thomas Jones stepped out of the elevator on the ninth floor and walked into the executive offices of TMJ, Ltd. The reception area was tastefully done with a display wall of Awards and Recognition Plaques from Hospital Clients, the United States Medical Association, Pharmaceutical Companies and various local organizations. The mahogany backdrop matched the custom reception desk. A small waiting area with several chairs and a table welcomed visitors.

"Good Morning, Mr. Jones," said a smiling receptionist.

"How was your vacation, sir?"

"Enlightening, Sung Li, and refreshing. And of course, way too short and over too quick," Thomas said as he started to walk away.

"Do you have a visitor today, sir?" asked the receptionist.

"Yes, I am sorry. I should have introduced you. Sung Li, this is Rosemary Brown. I made this appointment myself after I left last week. Rosemary is interviewing for a field representatives position," Thomas explained.

"It is nice to meet you Rosemary. I am Sung Li Fong, the receptionist and the person in charge of Mr. Jones appointments. Good luck today in your interview."

"Thank you," Rosemary replied smiling.

Thomas and Rosemary Beckett walked through a row of private offices on the way to Thomas Jones' corner office. He held the door for Agent Beckett then followed her into his office. He had a surprisingly modest office. Two walls were windows and the other two were decorated with detailed paintings of nature. His desk was not overpowering in size and it was clear except for a small calendar and a two-foot square leather pad on which he placed either his notepaper or his laptop computer. Behind his deep cherry stained desk was a matching custom credenza that housed his personal computer. The platform that held the monitor was concealed behind two doors that slid back out of sight, and the top center section of the credenza lifted up and smoothly slid back behind the unit. A keyboard tray slid out from under the monitor. He had three comfortable leather chairs that matched his own executive chair.

Thomas got to work immediately downloading his coded files from his PC into his laptop computer. He decided not to work on decoding the files there in his office. He would take the material back to the FBI building and give them the codes and let them begin the arduous task examining each file. The task of transferring the files would take several hours due to the sheer volume of material he had saved over the years. Agent Beckett suggested he work on the most recent files since some of the older files exceeded the statute of limitations. This cut the job in half and they completed the task in two hours.

Jones checked his voice messages and found several calls from the Colonel. There was also a message from Dr. John Walters reminding him of the USMA National Conference scheduled for the following week. Jones was to be a featured speaker. His topic was the newly rolled out TMJ Billing Initiative and the new Federal Government initiative, written by TMJ and nego-tiated with the US Attorney General. The Senate and House leaders had already agreed to pass the measure swiftly, partly because TMJ, Ltd. promised to donate significant amounts of money to re-election campaigns.

This initiative guaranteed every hospital, medical center, and physician cap protection on excessive awards in civil lawsuits. The cost saving results in this plan would save every doctor and practice in the country approximately sixty percent of their current liability insurance costs. Thirty percent of the savings would go directly to TMJ and the balance went back to the Physicians. The estimated annual contributions from these two programs alone exceeded one hundred million dollars.

A third message also came from Dr. Walters. He called to talk about the accidental death of Joseph Johnson and who his replacement would be. Walters had some additional security issues that needed to be handled prior to the USMA National Conference.

"Agent Beckett," Jones explained. "Security Issues was code for a request to have someone removed permanently. It could be a staff member or colleague who needed to be killed for any number of reasons, including imagined slights toward Walters, Nelson, or Preston."

"What role do Nelson and Preston play in this drama?"

"They are John Walters' protégés. I sometimes thought of them as his lapdogs. To their credit they are outstanding doctors and diagnosticians, a skill that Walters taught them. For the last several years their work in diagnosing this AIDS thing has consumed them. Nelson and Preston received a ton of grant money to study the problem in various sites in the east coast. Walters also received several million dollars to study and develop new and better ways to identify the disease. He and Preston spent a lot of time examining how the disease was spread. They concluded that the disease is spread most commonly between male men living the 'alternative lifestyle'. The exchange of bodily fluids has been seen as the leading cause of the disease. It is practically non-existent in sexual activity between heterosexual couples. Sexual activity between members of the same sex had seen a contagion rate of nearly ninety percent when homosexuals have random, sexual encounters with multiple partners. Walters saw this as a sign from God. Several times in the Old and New Testaments this type of activity is called an, 'abomination,' and always sinful. Walters turned from a diagnostician into an agent of destruction.

The unholy trio of Walters, Nelson, and Preston met with a Pharmaceutical Company and asked them to develop a medicinal regimen that would take a patient already in the latter stages of the disease to the final ten days of their life. The meds he helped develop are used to kill someone in the span of ten days, thus ending the possibility of that infected individual of infecting others. I have heard that one pharmaceutical house developed a pill that would delay the onset of the worst last stages of this killer disease. But his mission is not to delay those who are sick. He wants these people erased from the face of the earth."

"But Thomas," Beckett said with astonishment. "Why have doctors and hospitals gone along with such an insane idea?"

"Part of their message is the very real threat to a Physician's life. Most doctors pry and probe into parts of our bodies we ourselves don't like to touch. He has convinced them that their rate of infection is higher than that of society in general." Jones explained. "The fear of contracting a disease with the rapidity of symptoms that lead to death in such a short time is a frightening aspect of the disease. Right now we don't know whether it is spread via incidental contact, shaking hands, drinking from the same glass or bottle, or even sitting on the same bathroom seat. Can you imagine the fear the general public will have?"

"Yes, I can," Rosemary replied. "There will be an outcry in the land. And if John Walters has a solution, even if it is not the best solution, at least it will be a way to rid the populace of the carriers of this killer disease. If the disease would come anywhere near epidemic, even Congress would support such a drastic measure."

"Exactly!" Jones said to Agent Beckett. "You stated the entire program in a nutshell right there. That is the Ten Day Plan that Walters wants to roll out at the next USMA National Conference. What's more is that our Company has diverted millions of dollars into his hands over the last three or four years. There are sufficient funds right now to support this program for up to ten years. Over the next two to three years the funds will quadruple or more thus allowing the program to run for the next thirty years."

"Where does the Government help come from?" inquired Agent Beckett. "Who is backing this plan?"

"It starts with the Surgeon General, Joseph Bolton. He works for someone on the Hill, or someone in the White House. Despite all my inquiries I have not been able to pinpoint who is supporting this effort in this Administration," Jones said with obvious disappointment.

"I have to tell you," Beckett said to Jones. "I cannot picture the President supporting anything like this, even behind the scenes. He is a good man, maybe not always the best President, but an honest, decent man who could not be involved with something like this."

"I agree Rosemary," Thomas said. "President Lewis is above this."

"What to you think about the Vice President?" Agent Beckett asked.

"Lodge? Maybe. He is from California, so he is aware of the problem there. He is a retired physician so he has ties to the USMA. Vice President William Lodge is a good place to begin," Thomas mused. "He can direct legislation and he has a ton of party support. He could be our man."

"Where do Nelson and Preston get their support?" asked Rosemary. "Do they have strong ties with anyone in Washington?"

"Nothing compared to Walters. I think they may be the experts working with the drug companies. Whenever Walters schedules a visit from a Pharmaceutical Company Nelson and Preston are always present," Jones related. "I am guessing this is their specialty."

"Do your records indicate the dates and times of these meetings?" asked Agent Becket.

"Yes. The list includes all that plus a summary of their meeting notes."

Jones and Agent Beckett began to pack up the computers and hard copies of files Jones had prepared to turn over to the FBI.

Sung Li buzzed him on the intercom. "Mr. Jones, you have a call. Are you taking calls during your interview?"

"Do you know who it is?" Jones asked.

"I believe it is Dr. Walters, sir," she replied.

"Please put him through."

"Jones, is that you?" Walters asked rudely.

"Yes. How are you today?" Thomas asked, trying to act as normally as possible.

"I cannot reach Jeff Johnson. I need to take care of some important personnel issues. Have you taken care of a replacement for his father?" asked the doctor who seemed to be in a near state of panic.

"Doctor, are you sure he is not on an assignment outside of California? He must have heard of his father's accident. Perhaps he is simply not answering his phone since he would be grieving his father's death," Nick said.

"That is no excuse for him not to answer my repeated telephone calls," an enraged Walters shouted into the phone. "Can you to get a field agent in touch with me within the hour. I have pressing business that must be addressed at once."

"Doctor Walters, calm down. I will have an agent call you shortly. He or she will be available for your assignment by the end of the day. Goodbye Doctor Walters," Jones said firmly as he hung up the telephone.

"Agent Beckett, this is an opportunity for the FBI to get first hand evidence against Walters. Let's get back to your office and see if your supervisor agrees," Thomas said.

"I will call him right now and see if he is willing to work with us on this," Beckett replied.

After explaining the phone call to Agent Locket, Agent Rosemary Beckett made a suggestion to her supervisor. "Sir, we could put a local FBI Agent inside Dr. Walter's office. It is obvious that Walters wants someone killed. Our man could go under cover, wear a wire and get sufficient evidence to arrest the doctor on attempted murder charges."

"Does Jones believe Walters would just tell a stranger that he wanted someone killed? He may be too smart for that. We could be putting an Agent at severe risk, and I am not comfortable doing that," Locket replied with understandable concern.

Agent Beckett handed Thomas Jones the telephone and

asked him to explain his plan to Locket. "Agent Locket, Walters will only speak in code to the Agent. If I give your Agent the code words for what Walters wants done, he will be in and out of Walter's office in less than five minutes. The only words not in code will be the name of the intended target. I urge you to consider this action," Thomas said convincingly.

"Are you sure our Agent will be safe?"

"Agent Locket, Dr. Walters is a madman, but he is very careful about saying or doing anything that will incriminate himself. Your man will be safe. To put your mind at ease I will tell Walters that these two men are being groomed to replace the Johnson team," Jones said confidently.

"Okay. Get back here and we will contact our office in San Francisco. We will put our men undercover. I will contact the Regional office in San Francisco and set this up. I will have an Agent there call you for the code words. I am putting this man's life in your hands," Agent Lockett said somberly.

"I understand. I won't let you down. It is dangerous, but you may be saving a life," Jones replied.

chapter 41

Nick and Detective Baker asked Shaun, Detective Harding, Father Chris, Father Frank Murphy, and Dr. Harry Booth to meet with him in the dining room after breakfast. They wanted to be sure everyone was on the same page as far as security was concerned, and he wanted input from the group for their immediate plans.

"Thank you for the warm reception you gave us last night. As you know we have identified Dr. John Walters as one of the key figures in arranging Colleen's death. We know he is working with two doctors from Walter Reed. We know that Colleen was one of three young women targeted by Walters. Hanna Jones was the second, and our girl Gretchen Sanders who traveled home with us was the third. We know that Walters has deep ties to the USMA. We hope to tap into the USMA computers to find out more about this AIDS plague that Walters has focused on for the last few years. From what John Baker, Gretchen, and I learned he has been essentially executing his patients suffering from this plague using a Ten Day Program that uses an increasing dose of undetectable poisons that puts the patient into a coma on day eight or nine, and death follows on day ten. Is everyone with me so far?" Detective Baker asked.

"What is the real threat of this plague? Why would the public be afraid of it?" Frank Murphy wondered.

"The disease is always fatal, and the end is very painful," Dr. Booth answered. "I never saw this first hand, but from what I have read and what John and Nick told me, this is a pretty nasty way to go."

"No women have the disease?" asked Catherine Harding.

"We did not see any at St. Agnes. From what we learned speaking to the patients, the disease is primarily centered among homosexual males. It is possible that men who have the disease may infect women. Walters uses the bible to say that death is the appropriate end result for this sinful behavior. Somehow he is going to roll out his death program to hospitals and medical centers across the country. With the USMA backing this program there will be financial resources available to influence the Senate and the House to support a plan like Walters' Program," Nick explained. "There is the real possibility of a societal panic that would force the government and doctors to isolate the infected men and subject them to Walter's drug plan. Fear will go a long way in determining what happens."

"What will you do with the FBI?" Father Chris inquired.

"I want to thank Father Murphy for contacting his brother Michael at the FBI. I also want to apologize to all of you for suggesting that we wait to do so. When we made that decision we did not know the extent of the conspiracy that threatened our lives and the lives of our loved ones. I thought it was too dangerous to reveal our location to anyone. Thankfully, that is behind us now. My plan is to share all the information we have gathered about Walters with the FBI. Michael and his colleagues can take over and find ways to arrest the men responsible for the death of Colleen and the others. I will offer our assistance to the FBI," John Baker said. "I am going to call the FBI. You have all played crucial roles in keeping us alive and I owe you the respect of including you as we turn our safety concerns over to the care of the FBI. I also want you to hear what they have to say." Detective Baker dialed the number and asked for Agent Murphy.

Agent Michael Murphy picked up his phone. "FBI Agent Murphy speaking. Can I help you?"

"Agent Murphy, this is John Baker calling. We are prepared to go over all our statements and wondered if you wanted us to come downtown today."

"We thought you might want a few days of rest, but if you are up to it today I can have a car pick you up," Michael answered.

"That works for us. We will be ready when the car arrives," Baker concluded.

"We will see you shortly," Mike said as he hung up the phone.

A large black van pulled into the Convent property about an hour later, and Nick and his party arrived at FBI headquarters at eleven a.m. where they were greeted by Agent Murphy and Supervisor Jerry Locket.

"Welcome to the FBI," Agent Jerry said as he introduced himself to Nick, John, and the others who had taken residence in the Falls Church Convent. "We will be meeting in the fourth floor conference room.

"I have someone I would like you to meet," Agent Locket said to Nick, John Baker, and the others. "Agent Murphy, please bring Agent Beckett and her guest into the conference room."

Beckett escorted Thomas Jones into the room. "I would like you all to meet Thomas Jones. Thomas is the CEO of TMJ, Ltd., the fund raising company behind Dr. John Walters and his partners."

No one said a word. Nick's felt his fists clinch.

Locket continued, "I know you are wondering why he is here. I know you may have questions for him. I know you may be angry with him. But let me first say that Thomas had the local police in Santa Monica contact our office there because he was aware of some of the actions Walter's and his people were planning. He has volunteered to give us as much information as possible on the criminal activities his company and the USMA has been involved in over the past ten years or so.

Thomas stepped forward without any expectations of immunity or a plea bargain. He came to us because he knew it was the right thing to do. You may ask him any questions you want, but before you do I want you to know that Mr. Jones has lost his family at the hands of some very evil men in his own organization. His sister was killed a little over a week ago and his mother was slain only a few days ago; his father died shortly after his wife was killed. He is the man who called you about getting to safety. He telephoned the Monastery and also called Maura at her home."

Nick stood up and stared at Jones. "Are you responsible for the death of my sister Colleen?

"Yes," answered Thomas Jones.

The room was still. Everyone's eyes were on Nick. The tension was thick.

"I knew Walters and his pals were trying to protect the secret of his, 'Ten Day Program,' Jones began. "While I did not know he would target individuals that had been in his care, such as your sister Colleen, I knew he was willing to take serious steps to protect his plan. So, yes, I accept responsibility for the death of your sister.

The men he used to carry out this crime were very cruel people. I can tell you with certainty that both of these men are now dead. One at the hand of my father, the other was killed in a traffic accident just two days ago. I am ashamed of the actions my company helped to finance. In the end I am as responsible for Colleen's death as the man who drove the bus up onto the ramp and killed her. I pray that you may find a way to forgive me for what I have done to your family," Thomas concluded while standing perfectly still in front of his accusers with his head bowed.

"How did the bombing happen at the Police Precinct?" Detective Baker asked.

"The two men responsible for that crime were Joseph Johnson and his son, Jeff." Jones began. "Let me back up a minute. When Nick, Dr. Booth, and Angela Carson survived the attempt on their lives at the airport I believed that the Johnson father and son team had completed the mission Dr. Walters gave them, which was to kill Colleen for fear that she would reveal any of Walters' Ten Day Program to the public. I read Colleen's obituary in the paper and thought that the matter was concluded. Only later did I find that the Johnson's intended to kill Nick, Harry, and Angela.

The Johnson's apparently believed Colleen had leaked information to them on the flight back to Washington. Consequently they put a plan into motion that would involve eliminating the three of you. Joseph followed you to Washington, DC, while Jeff Johnson, the son, then went on a killing spree across the country in an attempt to murder every person in first class on both the flight from San Francisco to St. Louis, and the flight from St. Louis to Washington National. This action was done independently without the authorization from anyone in the USMA or my company.

"A few days after Colleen's funeral Johnson learned that the police were looking into her death. Their original plan was to make it look like an accident. Johnson was supposed to meet the driver after it was over. He planned to inject him with a drug that would cause a fatal heart attack. It seemed like a perfect plan. The driver instead panicked and threw away the clothing he had stolen from a Hotel Shuttle Bus employee he had killed. Jeff Johnson followed him to the hotel, shot him and hid the body in a freezer. Both Johnson's at this point knew that things had gotten way out of hand and had to plan a major operation to try to eliminate anyone connected to Colleen O'Connell.

"Joseph Johnson stole a policeman's uniform and walked into the Southeast Precinct building to snoop around and find out which detectives were working on the murder of Colleen. He was in the precinct house the day Detectives Baker and Harding interviewed Nick and Dr. Booth. He also saw Shaun and Father Christopher Sullivan in the conference room with the detectives.

He apparently then made a decision to kill everyone who had been associated with the investigation. He had an operative go to Dr. Booth's daughter's home in an attempt to kill him and his family there. Fortunately the police found her in time. The operative was instructed to be sure that all three occupants of the home were asleep before breaking into the house and setting up the explosion. When that failed Joseph Johnson believed he had no alternative but to eliminate all of you at his first opportunity.

"Dressed again in the police uniform, Johnson went to the Precinct and planted a bomb in Shaun's car. Johnson never knew you left the precinct. He believed that you were killed when the bomb exploded. Neither the Johnson's nor anyone else in the organization knew you survived the blast. Whoever made that decision saved all your lives. It was also a good idea to go to the Monastery."

"That was Detective Baker's idea," Shaun said. "And Father Chris knew the Abbot at the Monastery."

"Hiding out in the monastery was a smart move," Jones said admiringly. "The Johnson's believed you were dead and that they had effectively prevented any leaks about Walters' program. When they got back to California, Walters told them about the close friendship between Colleen, Hanna Jones, and Gretchen Sanders. Johnson took that to mean they had to kill Hanna and Gretchen. They searched in vain for Gretchen for several days because they did not know she had flown east to attend Colleen's funeral. Had she not done that it is very likely she would have been killed then.

It was easier to find my sister, Hanna. Jeff Johnson viciously and maliciously stabbed my sister over and over again until she was dead. They continued to search for Gretchen, but obviously never found her. They had a number of operatives searching for her and actually thought they had found her in a hotel in Los Angeles. Somehow she slipped through their net and escaped."

"Gretchen saw the men searching for her. We dressed her in a Monk's cassock and slipped away without being detected by Johnson's spies," John Baker explained to Thomas.

"Again, that was a very smart move, one that may have saved her life," Jones said. "Getting back to Detective Baker's question on the Police Precinct bombing, due to the many casualties, I knew we had to ensure that the USMA and my company would never be tied to such a heinous crime. Let me be clear on this, Jeff and his father Joseph Johnson acted alone in this matter. I made the decision to use people like the Johnson's, therefore I ultimately bear responsibility for their actions. It is easy to say I never wanted them to bomb the Precinct. However, I had employed them to take care of security issues, which often meant eliminating someone. I cannot claim innocence of their crimes.

"After the bombing I received instructions from the person I report to, known as the Colonel, but who, in reality is Surgeon General Joseph Bolton. He wanted the mess cleaned up fast. We leaked a fake memo to the police and news outlets that the bombing was done by Islamic terrorists, which of course was a complete lie. It was effective, however, in raising the level of fear and hatred toward a target. We leaked that other sites would be targeted. The operatives were told that the terrorists would be coming to their hotel dressed as Washington Metro Police. Their instructions were to stop the bombers. The police were notified where the terrorists were hiding.

"The operatives, outfitted in army fatigues, hid in an apartment. They were armed heavily. They knew they had to take whatever measurers necessary to stop the bombers who were dressed like policemen. The real police arrived, armed with five times the manpower, and took out the pseudo terrorists.

"Our organization was protected; the public demand for justice and revenge was sated. Please accept my apology for the attack on your lives, and for the death of the men and women in your Precinct. I would have stopped Joseph Johnson if I had known what he intended to do. I understand your anger and why you would hate me. I accept full responsibility for the crimes these men committed."

"I am guilty," Thomas said quietly as he stood before the FBI, the Metro Detectives, Nick, and his friends.

The room was silent. No one uttered a word. No one moved nor blinked.

"Thomas," Nick said ironically, "You told us that this whole mess started because Walters thought Colleen knew something about his plan. Is that right?"

"Yes."

"Colleen never said a word about what Walters was doing. She had no idea that he was killing off his patients. All the killings, the attempted murders, and the attack on the police precinct, all this was for nothing. Colleen never knew Walters even had a plan."

The room grew very quiet again. They just sat there and shook their heads.

Detective Harding ended the silence "Mr. Jones, you said you report to Joseph Bolton. Is he the head of this organization of yours?

"No, Detective Harding, he is not. I have never met the top man. We were speculating about his identity earlier today. My best guess is that Vice President Lodge may be mixed up in this. He is a Californian and he practiced medicine before he got into politics. I have turned over all my files and reports on what I have told you to the FBI. I do not believe there is any reference to him except for an occasional mention that the Colonel makes to the CEO. The bigger problem is that there are many elected officials and Cabinet Members who will support the Ten Day Program Walters has been working on for so long. The reason for that has a lot to do with money. We support campaigns with millions of dollars that are not reported. We collect money from the USMA members every month to the tune of three to five million dollars. I have just instituted a new program that will bring about four million additional dollars a month to the organization. I have top accountants and CPAs on my staff, along with brilliant financial investors. We have the best legal minds in the country on retainer. Every member of Congress owes us loyalty, as do ninety-five percent of the Senate members."

"How long have you headed this company?" Nick inquired.

"Ten years.

"And you have avoided suspicion and investigation all these years?" Baker wondered.

"Yes. I built a company that is almost untouchable. There are layers of protection deflecting responsibility from every key member of the company. As the president of the company I am an easy target, but I have enough evidence in my coded files to expose many people. Joseph Bolton thinks he is immune, but he is not. The man above him is going to be hard to get to. I am hoping that Bolton will have evidence on his superior. I think Bolton is weak. He will do anything to save his own hide. If he has something on his boss, he will sell him out, I guarantee it."

"It sounds like you are willing to do everything the FBI wants, why?" asked Dr. Booth.

"I have lost my family. I have lost my reputation. I nearly lost my soul, and I cannot let that happen. I have seen the light and I know I have to do what is right. I am not seeking clemency or immunity for what I have done. What I hope to do is stop Dr. Walters and his plan to kill everyone infected with this gay plague. His people are closely tied with many pharmaceutical companies and they are taking Walters' instruction not to develop medicines that will cure or slow down the effects of the disease. His plan is to kill those infected even faster than ten days. What he is planning is genocide. He is creating, along with the USMA, an atmosphere of fear in this country. The fear is that innocent people can be infected through incidental contact with someone who has this disease.

Somehow we have to expose him for what he is. I have no idea how many deaths have come out of his ward at St. Agnes Hospital. If he has five to six deaths every week he will kill about two hundred fifty per year. Roll that out across the nation to every hospital and the numbers are staggering. If he is successful in the United States with this program, he will certainly introduce it to the world. A staggering number of deaths would ensue."

"What is in it for USMA or the people supporting such an evil program?" asked Shaun.

"The obvious answer is money, and lots of it. Walters will reap enormous wealth from the program. I do not believe he is concerned about the impact of this disease upon the general population. He has chosen to kill, and profit greatly from it," Jones answered.

"What can we do to help?" Detective Baker asked.

"Work with the FBI in any way they ask. There really is not a lot you can do on your own to stop his plan. That work has to come from the police and FBI. It won't be easy, but he must be stopped before it is too late," Thomas replied.

Agent Locket stood up. "Thank you for listening to Thomas. We believe he is genuine in wanting to stop Walters from making his death program the rule of the land. Your anger over his involvement in the deaths of your family members and friends is understandable. I hope we can all work together in stopping Walters. I am going to split you up into small groups of two or three and assign an Agent to each of you to get detailed written statements of your activity and knowledge of what has happened so far. We will be working on decoding the files that Jones gave us. One very important thing, you may not speak of this to anyone. Even the slightest leak could jeopardize innocent lives. Your silence is absolutely necessary. Does anyone else have anything before we break up?"

"I might have something," Chris said.

"Yes, Father," Locket answered.

"I have an access code to get into the USMA data files. We had intended to use it to find out what Walter's next step would be. Do you think it might help us?"

"Absolutely, Father, will you and Nick work with Agent Beckett and Mr. Jones?" Locket asked.

Nick thought about it a second and considered saying no. Why would he want to work along side the man who was responsible for Colleen's death? He was unsure if he could contain his anger. Nick thought about the big picture and said, "Okay, we will work with Agent Beckett and Jones."

They walked over to a small conference room with four chairs, a table, and a computer desk. Agent Beckett signed in on the computer and turned it over to Father Chris who used Dr. Thomas Carroll's identity code to access the USMA computer site. There were the usual medical updates and ads for the USMA National Convention scheduled for the following week. Thomas asked Chris to go to the 'Pharmaceutical News' file. It was filled with information on new medicines that were being tested. A lot of technical jargon and incidental data on each drug filled page after page. After fifteen minutes of examining new drug information they were making no progress.

Thomas asked Chris to switch to a new file titled "New FDA Approved Drugs." There were perhaps six pages of newly approved medicines. On page three one item caught their attention: a drug called Chlordiazimbatrol. In the short test history notes it stated:

Developed by Armorialse Laboratories in conjunction with Dr. John Walters of St. Agnes Hospital, San Francisco, California. Armorialse Labs is headquartered in Paris, France and has developmental labs in the United States, India, China, Australia, and Argentina. The United States Labs are located in Wilkes-Barre, Pennsylvania, and San Francisco, California. The drug Chlordiazimbatrol is to be used with terminally ill patients to reduce pain and induce rest.

"Agent Beckett, I want to print this page out. Where will it print?" Nick asked.

"The Printer along the side wall," Beckett replied, pointing to the machine.

"Can we go back to the home page and open the file on the National Convention?" Thomas asked politely.

"Let's see if they have Walters scheduled to speak," said Thomas while Chris scrolled down the schedule and various meeting agendas offered during the convention.

"There!" Thomas said. "Stop. Click on Walters' name. The computer screen showed a picture of Dr. John Walters along with Dr. Mark Preston and Dr. James Nelson. The copy under the pictures gave a biographical sketch of each man. A little further down the topic of his talk was outlined:

Dr. Walters, in association with Armorialse Laboratories, has developed a new more effective medicinal treatment for terminally ill patients. The new drug, Chlordiazimbatrol, has minimal side effects and reduces pain, inflammation, and anxiety, while inducing rest without the side effects of many similar medicines. The new drug does not incur disorientation for the patient. Information on the studies completed at Walter Reed Hospital and St. Agnes Hospital reveal the effectiveness of the drug and the minimal numbers of patients who have been unable to tolerate Chlordiazimbatrol.

Every word of the report was a lie. It was a complete fabrication.

"Father Chris, hit the print button again," said Nick.

Agent Beckett called Locket over to the small meeting room and explained what they had found. "Thomas did your company back this drug study?" he inquired.

"My company did not contribute to the development of this killer drug. We poured a lot of money into the USMA and it is my belief that Walters and the USMA are in this together. I channeled funds into an account controlled by Joseph Bolton. I am confident the money for this drug came from there," Jones explained.

"But where does the initial money come from?" Locket asked.

"From the income my company charges for the services we provide to the members of the USMA. My investment bankers are world-class people. We have increased our holdings substantially every year for the past ten years. We are talking about millions of dollars agent. I mean millions and millions of dollars."

"And how much of this is channeled to Bolton?"

"The Colonel asked me to provide ten million dollars for a project he is working on. He needed the money in ninety days. I have the money for him now, and we are on day sixty-three. I put together a Medicare billing program, made it mandatory for all USMA doctors, and had it up and running in less than thirty days."

"I have a question Agent Locket," Detective Baker said. "How can we stop the introduction of this drug Chlordiazimbatrol? If the FDA has given its approval there is a good chance that doctors throughout the land will be dispensing a medicine that will result in the death of the patient in ten or fewer days. We have got to stop the distribution of the drug.

"Detective you are absolutely correct. We have a unit that will focus on the drug company and we are already preparing for multiple arrests. I will have a car return you to the safe house. Thank you for your help today. Have a good evening. We will talk again tomorrow," Agent Locket concluded.

"Nick," Thomas began. "May I have a word with you in private?"

Nick looked coldly at Jones and felt a shiver of hated run through his body. His first intention was to say no, but after a moment of introspection, he agreed.

"Okay, Jones," Nick answered.

"I don't know why I agreed to this meeting," Nick said leading off. "No matter how you help the FBI it doesn't lessen the pain of losing Colleen."

"I understand that now. I just wanted to tell you again how sorry I am. When I learned my sister Hanna was dead, it devastated me. I am lost in a sea of grief. I understand now the loss you are experiencing. One day I hope you can forgive me."

chapter 42

The FBI van pulled out from the basement garage for the nine-mile drive back to Falls Church. The driver took Constitution Avenue to 66 West. Traffic was already building which meant the ride back to the convent would take thirty minutes or more.

Nick looked at his companions who were all lost in their own thoughts. He paused, but then spoke to them. "I did not think the person behind Colleen's death would look like Thomas Jones. Instead he is a contrite individual, intelligent and personable.

"I saw something sincere in Jones," Father Chris said slowly. "He is a suffering soul right now with the death of his family. I believed him when he said he did not seek immunity or a plea bargain. He is a man ready to face the consequences of his actions. I am struggling to forgive him for his part in Colleen's death, but I know that it is the one thing I must do."

Frank Murphy nodded his head in agreement. "It won't be easy to forgive, but remember, Christ forgave the men who were cruci—"

FBI Agent Eugene Martin, the van driver, glanced into his rearview mirror and spotted a black Chevy Suburban make a sudden pass behind him. The car pulled up along side the FBI van traveling forty miles per hour. The passenger side windows opened and two hooded men with AK 47 automatic rifles opened fire on the car. Frank Murphy fell immediately when two bullets penetrated his skull. He died instantly.

Agent Eugene Martin was hit in the neck and immediately fell dead over the steering wheel. Shaun yelled for everyone to get down just as he was hit by a bullet that tore through his chest. The shooters rained ammo into the vehicle making a sound like miniature missiles streaking through the car. Detective Harding threw herself over John Baker and took a fatal hit in her upper torso. Father Chris was protected when Frank Murphy fell on top of him as he fell to the floor of the van. Harry Booth took a bullet in his left hip and screamed in pain. Nick took a shot across his forehead smashing him against the forward seat and he slid to the floor bleeding heavily. The inside of the car was filled with blood. The shooters continuing firing into the van as they sped away down the expressway.

The FBI van bounced hard off two cars, spun around in a circle, and rolled over twice before hitting the concrete medium and coming to a stop. John Baker crawled through a blown out window and attempted to open the sliding side door of the van. He managed to open it slightly. He crawled inside and yelled, "Is everyone okay? Does anyone need help?"

Baker reached Catherine Harding, and shook her arm. "Catherine, can you hear me? Catherine. Catherine." When there was no response he felt her carotid artery for a pulse. There was none.

Father Chris moaned and moved a little. He saw John and reached for his hand. "John, can you help me?"

"Chris, are you all right?" Nick asked.

" I am stuck between the seats," the Priest replied.

"Nick, where are you?" Baker asked.

"I'm under the middle seat."

"Hold on, Nick, I am going to get Chris out first."

Many people who witnessed the accident pulled off to the

side of Highway 66. They came running to offer help while others used their telephones to dial 911.

Shaun regained his senses and tried to move, but could not. "Help me, please," he managed to say.

Police, fire emergency vehicles, and ambulances screamed their way to the site of the shooting in less than eight minutes. Within fifteen minutes, all the victims were out of the van.

Father Chris immediately began to pray over and bless the injured and dead. He anointed his old friend and classmate, Frank Murphy, and then moved on to Agent Eugene Martin who had been driving the van. He then prayed and blessed the body of Detective Catherine Harding, who had given her life to save her partner.

An FBI car pulled up to the accident scene and Agents Locket, Beckett, and Michael Murphy jumped out and hurried over to the carnage. Murphy asked immediately for his brother. John Baker walked him to the side of the van where his body was covered in a white sheet. Michael ran to his brother's side, knelt down, and lifted the sheet off the body. He pulled Frank to his chest, tenderly hugging his fallen brother and then gently laid him on the ground and covered him with the sheet. He wiped his eyes, got up, and returned to Agent Locket.

"Are you all right, Murphy?"

"Yes sir, I am okay. Let's see if we can help the others."

Catherine Harding died immediately as did Frank Murphy and the driver. Nick had a superficial head wound. Harry was in a lot of pain but his wounds were not fatal. Shaun had been hit in the chest, but the paramedics thought the wounds were not life threatening. Harry and Shaun were transported to Georgetown University Hospital together in the same ambulance.

Nick, Chris, and John sat in the back of another ambulance and gave their statement to both the Metro police and to Agent Locket. Everything had happened so fast it was hard for them to give a cohesive statement.

Nick's wound was bandaged and, outside of being shaken by

the events, he was okay. He turned to Agent Jerry Lockett and angrily asked, "What happened here Agent? We were supposed to be safe with you!"

Agent Rosemary Beckett said calmly, "Nick, we don't have an answer yet. I know you are hurt, scared and angry. What you have to do now is get checked out at the hospital. I am going to be there with you. We are going to have an Agent assigned to each of you. Nick, I want you to know we will find out who did this and punish them. I promise you and your family will be safe. Please trust me on this. I will not let you down."

Nick relaxed a little and thanked Agent Beckett for her understanding. "Can I call Maura? I want to talk to my wife."

"Of course, use my phone."

Nick dialed the number and Gretchen answered the phone. "Gretchen, hello, this is Nick. May I speak with Maura?"

"Sure Nick, I'll get her," Gretchen replied. "Are you all right? You sound a little out of it."

"I am okay. Can you get Maura for me?" Nick said anxiously.

"Nick, its Maura. Is everything all right? There are about ten FBI Agents here at the house. What is going on?"

"We have been in an accident. Some of us are hurt badly," Nick said trying to be calm.

"Nick. Are you okay?"

"Yes, I am okay. I got banged on my head pretty hard, but I'll be all right. Harry was hurt and has been taken to the hospital along with Shaun."

"Shaun is hurt? I have to tell Kathleen. What is wrong with him?"

"Shaun was shot in the chest."

"*Shot!* Nick, you said you were in an accident. How was Shaun shot?" Maura demanded to know.

"Here is what I know. A car drove past and fired shots into our van. Shaun was hit in the chest but the medics said he would survive. Harry was shot in the hip and he will be all right too."

"What about the rest. What about Chris?" Maura asked fearfully.

"Thankfully Chris was not injured. Father Frank was hit and fell on top of him protecting him from the barrage of gunfire" Nick explained.

"Catherine Harding, Father Frank, and the driver died. The rest of us are going to make it," Nick answered quietly.

"Catherine and Frank are dead!" Maura said as her voice trailed off. "Who was the driver?"

"His name was Agent Eugene Martin. Maura, I have to go now. I just wanted to tell you I am okay and that I love you."

"I love you, Nick."

"I love you," Nick echoed as he hung up the telephone.

Highway 66 was shut down between exits 68 and 69 by the Police as they gathered evidence from the shooting. They found in excess of two hundred shell casings on the roadway. It was obvious from then number of casings that the weapons were automatic rifles. The exact number of rounds fired at the van was unknown because some of the casings bounced off the concrete highway and others were run over by cars and trapped in the grooves of their tires. The holes in the side of the van indicated that the shooters used armor-piercing bullets. Everything pointed to a well-planned execution. It was a miracle that anyone survived the assault.

Nick, Chris, and John rode together in an ambulance to Georgetown University Hospital in Washington, D.C. where Harry and Shaun were taken minutes earlier.

Locket, Beckett, and Mike Murphy met for a moment before sending them to stay with Nick O'Connell and John Baker. "I am starting an immediate investigation at the Bureau to find out who was responsible for this information leak and attack. We will be working until we find the leak."

Locket picked up his telephone and called the director of the FBI, Peter Morrison, and gave him a report of the shooting and accident scene. Morrison ordered Locket back to the

Bureau building as soon as the site was secured and the FBI crime scene team had taken charge of the investigation. Locket then returned to the bureau building and went immediately to Morrison's office as requested.

"Agent Locket, what happened there?" the Chief demanded to know.

"Sir, the attack was intended to kill all the witnesses who have stepped forward in the Thomas Jones case involving the USMA and the Surgeon General," Locket replied.

"The evidence does not indicate that this was a random shooting. The shooters used armor piercing bullets. They knew who their targets were. His or her intent was to kill everyone in the van. Of the seven passengers in the van three were killed instantly, two were injured seriously, two sustained minor injuries, and one escaped without a scratch.

"You are convinced that the leak came from inside our office?" Morrison asked, as he tapped his fingers impatiently.

"Yes sir, I do. I want to start an investigation inclusive of everyone in the garage and everyone on the fourth floor," Locket said.

"Why would you include the garage in your investigation?" Morrison demanded.

"Sir, only the people in the garage and the people on my floor knew these people were here. The others at the safe house knew they were here but the only person at the Convent not part of the group of witnesses is Doctor Roberts. She is a Pediatrician and has been with the O'Connell children since they were born. I believe she is above suspicion. We had no interaction with anyone else in the building. I suspect the attackers were waiting here for the van to come out. They most likely followed them to an open stretch of road and waited until they could get decent shots. Highway 66 opens up to a four-lane highway there. The driver pulled along side our van and opened fire. They were only a short distance from exit sixty-nine, which was the off ramp that takes them into Falls Church. Sir, I have got to believe this was an inside job."

"Locket, I want this taken care of quickly. I want you to do everything in our power to find out the responsible parties."

"Yes sir, I understand. It will be done," Locket replied as he backed out of the director's office.

Locket called together his remaining three agents and explained the facts regarding the urgency of the investigation they were about to begin. Agents Carl Edwards, Julie Summers, and Joseph Andrews stood at attention while Locket explained what they had to do and in the time frame it had to be done.

"I am asking you to investigate your fellow agents, your support staff, and the people in the parking garage. You may lose some friends and make some enemies. Remember that you are carrying the torch of your fallen brother, Eugene Martin. You are also working for the innocent victims of the attack on an FBI car."

"Sir, we understand and will do everything in our power to find the leak in our building. We will not let you down," Agent Summers answered.

"Good, get to work," Locket ordered.

chapter 43

Dr. John Walters picked up his telephone at two fifteen p.m. pacific time.

"Walters, this is the Colonel. We have to talk."

"Colonel, you are upset about something. What is wrong?"

"Our worst fears have been realized. Jones has turned on us!"

"My contact at the FBI building notified me that he saw Jones with three FBI Agents inside the building. I told him he was mistaken. I spoke to Jones yesterday and I thought he was a little argumentative about some of the actions we employed against the O'Connell family and their friends," the Colonel stated angrily.

"It is possible he called you from the FBI offices. They may have recorded your conversation. Did you saying anything that would endanger our cause? I am about to introduce the new drug to the medical community next week. Nothing can prevent me from rolling out this program. Nothing!" stated the doctor who was moving from a slow burn to a hot boil.

"I do not believe I said anything incriminating. However, we also have another problem that I think was solved only moments ago," said the Colonel nervously.

"What other problem?" inquired Dr. Walters.

"My man at the FBI building called me earlier today. He

told me he had definite proof that Nick O'Connell, Detectives Baker and Harding, the priest and the doctor are alive," said the Colonel.

"Impossible. The Johnson's swore to me they were killed in the bomb blast at the Police Precinct. What proof did your man have?" Walters said with real concern.

"He has a video of these people entering the FBI building inside their parking garage. He sent me a copy of the videotape on my computer. I saw O'Connell and his brother, the doctor, and the detectives. I made a decision to eliminate these people. I contacted several of our operatives and gave them their instructions."

Walters continued to grow more and more concerned. "Were they successful in eliminating this threat?" Walters asked.

"Our people followed their van after it left the FBI building. They then attacked the vehicle with AK 47 automatic weapons equipped with armor piercing ammunition. I am not sure if everyone was killed, but they believe that in the ensuing crash everyone in the van was either dead or seriously injured. Even if someone survived I suspect they will end this crusade they have been on to solve the mystery of Colleen O'Connell's death."

"That is good news, Colonel. I congratulate you for taking aggressive action against the people who would destroy the good work we began several years ago. I could not have made the giant strides of the last year without the financial support you provided us. If Jones has betrayed us it would be a shame. He was the most effective fundraiser and creative mind I have ever met. Is it possible that Jones was taken in for questioning? If he gave them any incriminating evidence wouldn't they have come after us? Wouldn't they at least have taken you in for questioning?" Walters wondered out loud.

"It is possible. One piece of information I had not shared with you was that Jones' sister, Hanna, is the girl you had the Johnsons kill. You instructed Jeff Johnson to eliminate the O'Connell woman, Gretchen Sanders, and Hanna Jones. That alone could have influenced him to turn against us. Jones told me he was on the west coast on vacation. I believe he was there for his sister's funeral. Our people advised me that Helen Jones, and her husband, John, both died this week. Their funerals are to be held in the next few days. I believe these were Jones' parents. If he lost all his family he certainly could be angry enough to betray us. He could be seeking revenge against you doctor. After all it is obvious that you employed the Johnson's to commit these crimes," the Colonel said with rancor.

"Listen, we are all in this together. Isn't that what you have said from the beginning? You cannot bail out on me when the going gets rough. Just today you ordered the deaths of seven people. I would not call that the work of an innocent man," replied Walters.

"Okay, I get your point. I just wanted to give you a heads up on what was happening here in DC. You better be careful. Keep you eyes open and trust no one but me. We may have to consider using your exit plan. While it is the most drastic of actions, it will eliminate all possible leaks and betrayals," the Colonel said.

"It is the ultimate end solution. I am prepared to execute it, but sincerely hope to avoid making that decision. The fifty state chairmen of the USMA will be attending our conference. Many of them have made valuable contributions to the Ten Day Program and for that reason they may have to make the ultimate sacrifice. It won't be easy, but it may have to be done," Walters said matter-of-factly.

"We don't have to make that decision today. But you and your team must be ready to put it in motion. Make sure you are prepared," the Colonel ordered.

Moments after hanging up the private phone rang again. The Colonel was reluctant to answer and let it ring four times before picking up the receiver.

"Joseph, I thought you might be avoiding me. It took you a

while to decide whether to answer the telephone. You are not trying to duck me, are you?"

"No sir. I apologize for not picking up right away. I just hung up with Dr. Walters and we were discussing some security concerns."

"You seem to have far to many security issues these days. What is the story on Jones? I know the FBI grabbed him in Santa Monica and flew him here to Washington. I have learned that your two operatives in California were killed. Apparently the elder Johnson lost his life in a horrendous automobile accident. The reports I read indicated he was burned alive after being impaled by wooden beams that flew off a truck in front of him. That must be a nasty way to die. The younger Johnson apparently was shot and killed either by Mr. Jones or his father. Johnson killed Jones' mother then the father killed Johnson. This is truly the stuff of fiction," the caller said laughing.

"Yes it is sir, however we did lose two of our best men. Men like the Johnsons are hard to find," the Colonel said proudly.

"Only if you consider homicidal maniacs good men," the caller replied sarcastically.

"Of course, you are right. The people we use in the future will be men of restraint. We are, after all, professionals," the Colonel said.

"Let's talk about Jones. Do you believe he would betray us?" the caller inquired.

"Sir, I normally would say no, however, he lost his family. He may have reacted to that loss and turned on us. I believe we must go forward assuming that he has betrayed us," the Colonel suggested.

"Jones was careful about insulating not only himself, but also us, in the event things ever went terribly wrong. He has been in custody for over twenty-four hours and the FBI has not made a move against you. I do not want you to plan any action against Jones until we determine if he betrayed us. Do you understand that Colonel?" the caller instructed in the most serious of tones.

"Yes sir, I understand," replied the Surgeon General of the United States.

"Good," said the caller.

"Sir, I found out earlier today that the people involved with the Colleen O'Connell murder are still alive. Nick O'Connell, his brother, along with the doctor and the flight attendant, the two police detectives and the priest were spotted at the FBI building late this morning," the Colonel said while nervously waiting for the caller's response.

"How could this happen, Bolton? You assured me that these people were dead. What action did you take?" the caller asked angrily.

"Two of our operatives followed their car when they left the FBI building and attacked them over on Highway 66 near Falls Church. The reports are just now coming in and it seems that three were killed and the rest were seriously injured. I believe, Sir, that even if there are survivors they will be too intimidated to pursue us any longer," explained the Colonel.

"You fool! Bolton, have you lost your mind? An attack like that in broad daylight will do nothing but bring the Feds to a boil. Do you really believe that this Nick O'Connell will give up, or his brother? You better pray that neither one of the brothers survived. These people are smart, a lot smarter than you and your operatives. Killing Colleen O'Connell caused the organization nothing but trouble. She may be the reason you and your people meet their end," the caller said, as he slammed down the receiver.

The Colonel stood there and cussed out his superior, and then said aloud, "If I go down, I am taking you with me."

Bolton walked over to his desk, opened the file drawer and lifted out a bottle of Bourbon. He poured himself a double and threw a few ice cubes in. He needed this drink after the day he was having. As he downed a long gulp his private telephone rang again.

"Hello, this is the Colonel," he said dryly.

"Colonel, this is Thomas Jones."

chapter 44

John, Nick, and Father Chris arrived at the Georgetown University Hospital a few minutes after Shaun O'Connell and Harry Booth. Shortly after their arrival the bodies of Agent Martin, Father Francis Murphy, and Detective Catherine Harding arrived at the hospital. The four injured men were in adjoining treatment areas and were able to speak to one another.

"Shaun, how are you holding up, brother?" Nick inquired.

"I am hurting pretty bad, but at least the bleeding has stopped," Shaun answered.

"How are you feeling, Harry?" asked Nick.

"It hurts like the devil. I can barely move my right leg," the doctor said painfully.

"Nick, where were you hit?" Chris asked. "I saw you go down and I feared the worst. It looked like you were shot in the head."

"I was grazed by a bullet. It caused a lot of blood, but no serious injuries, thank God," Nick said with gratitude.

At that moment Maura and Kathleen walked into the treatment area and went to their husbands and hugged them.

"Shaun, my word, your clothing is covered in blood! Are you all right?" Kathleen asked, fearing the worst.

"I am going to make it," replied her injured husband.

"Nick, I thought I was going to lose you. You have to stop chasing these men. They are too dangerous. Tell me you will stop, please. I want to have a normal life again," Maura said as she cried on her husband's chest.

"Maura, sweetheart, we will talk about this later," Nick said to his distressed wife.

Four FBI Agents entered the area and each stood nearby their assignments. Agent Rosemary Beckett stood by Nick. She walked over to Maura and introduced herself.

"Mrs. O'Connell, my name is Rosemary Beckett. I have been assigned to shadow your husband, Nick. Wherever he goes I am to accompany him. I promise you he will be safe. I will lay down my life for my assignment if necessary. We have made a commitment to protect these brave souls, and we will."

"Thank you, Agent Beckett. I appreciate your help," Maura said between the tears running down her cheeks.

"I am going to talk to Harry and see how he is doing. I will be back in a few minutes," Maura said as she walked over to check on Dr. Booth. Chris intercepted her before she spoke to Harry.

"Maura we are very close to exposing the people who were responsible for not only Colleen's death, but for many others as well. There is a very real possibility that these people are planning the death of hundreds, perhaps thousands of people. We cannot step aside just to protect our own lives. Please understand, none of us want to die, and I would never forgive myself if anything happened to Nick," Chris said sincerely. Maura looked into his eyes but did not say a word. She stepped into Harry's treatment area.

"Harry, hello dear, are you in much pain?" Maura inquired.

"No. They are giving me painkillers. Maura, did they tell you that we lost Father Frank and Catherine, and the driver of the van?" Harry asked.

"Yes, Nick called me and told me they died. The FBI said there were casualties, but they didn't know who they were. Father Frank was such a good man, and Catherine was a sweet young woman. This is terrible! May God bless their souls and welcome them into paradise," Maura said quietly.

––––––––

Across the hall in the hospital trauma center, John Baker sat impatiently on the side of a treatment table. Walking to the open door of the room, he saw the body of his partner, Catherine Harding, wheeled by. He called out to the orderly who was pushing the gurney to the morgue. "Stop! Please wait a minute."

The orderly stopped and John walked over to him. May I say goodbye to my partner," he pleaded.

"Yes sir, go right ahead," the aide said as he stepped away from the body.

John lifted the sheet off Catherine's face and gasped. There was his long-time partner. Her beautiful face and hair betrayed the fact that she was gone. Baker felt overwhelmed with grief. A thousand memories of the experiences he shared with Catherine flooded through his memory. He swallowed hard, bit his lip and tried to control his tears as he realized she was really gone. He leaned in close and whispered, "I will stop them, Catherine, I promise. " He kissed her cheek gently and lifted the shroud over her face. "You can take her now," John said to the orderly as he walked back into the treatment room wiping the tears from his eyes.

––––––––

A few feet away in another treatment room, Kathleen and Shaun were holding hands waiting for the surgeon who was reviewing the x-rays taken when Shaun arrived at the hospital. The doctor walked into the treatment area and pulled the privacy sheets around the treatment table Shaun was laying on.

"Hello, Mr. O'Connell, my name is Dr. William Sugars. I have been looking at your films and I wanted to review the situation with you and your wife."

"What have you seen in the films?" Shaun asked with concern.

"You were very fortunate. The bullet missed your major organs; however, it is lodged in a very precarious location. Can you see it on the x-ray?" the doctor asked as he held up the x-ray to the ceiling light. "It is a hair away from your spinal column. Removing it will be a very delicate procedure. It can be done, but there is a grave risk of paralysis, and of course like all surgeries, there is a risk of death. I would like to refer your case to Dr. Richard Balderman at Jefferson University Hospital in Philadelphia. He is the leading spine surgeon in the country. Jefferson also partners with Magee Hospital of Rehabilitation in Philly. If anything would go wrong in surgery, Magee is the best rehab hospital perhaps in the world. These are worst-case scenarios, not at all how I think it will go. I know Balderman personally and I can send him your x-rays and see if he will take your case. If he does you will have the choice of either riding in an ambulance or taking the helicopter to Jefferson. I understand you are a New Jersey state policeman. I believe that would qualify you for a free ride in the chopper. Talk it over and let me know what you decide," Dr. Sugars said as he began to walk out of the treatment area.

"Dr. Sugars, go ahead and contact Jefferson Hospital. I want that doctor to look at the films. How soon can we get to Philadelphia?" Shaun asked.

"I will call Balderman's office and see if he will take you. I think this is the right decision," Dr. Sugars remarked as he headed toward his office to call Jefferson University Hospital.

———————

As Shaun was being evaluated in one room Harry was visited in adjacent room by an orthopedic surgeon. He read the initial examining physicians report and looked over the x-rays of Harry's injuries.

"Dr. Booth, I am Dr. Palmer. You took a bullet to the right hip. That has to be removed. It appears from your x-rays that you need a hip replacement. The bullet damaged the bone, muscles, and tissues around the hip. I would like to get you into the operating room as soon as possible."

"How long will I be on the mend?

"About four to six weeks. You will be walking the day after surgery. You will work with our physical therapists and they will push you hard to walk, climb stairs, get into and out of the car and all the normal things you need to do in your daily life. Your stay in the hospital will be either four or five days. If all goes well you will be back at one hundred percent in about eight weeks. Do you want to sign off on surgery now? I can call and get the availability of the OR. We can definitely do the surgery tomorrow morning, or possibly tonight–the sooner the better. What do you want to do?" asked the doctor.

"Let's do this the first chance we can get. Where do I sign?" Harry inquired.

The doctor handed him the approval form and a pen. Harry signed the release form and handed it back to Dr. Palmer who walked out of the room, turned and said, "Harry, have a good night I will see you soon."

———

In an adjacent treatment room, an ER doctor cleaned Nick's wound and prescribed an antibiotic to fight off any possible infection. He was released from the hospital, along with John Baker. An FBI car took Nick, Chris, Maura, and John back to the safe house. Shaun and Kathleen remained at the hospital to await their trip to Jefferson Hospital for his spine surgery. Harry's surgery was scheduled for the following morning.

Agents Becket and Murphy traveled back to the safe house with Nick and John Baker. Their assignment was to stay with them around the clock.

chapter 45

Agent Locket returned to the bureau building to report to Director Peter Morrison. He gave all the information to Morrison and awaited his response.

"I am glad there were survivors. This was a horrible crime. You did the right thing in assigning agents to guard them. Are they secure at the safe house? Is it possible the killers knew where they were staying?" Morrison inquired

"I do not think anyone knows where they are staying. I believe the safe house is the most secure location we have in the system."

There was a knock on Morrison's door.

"Enter," he ordered.

"Sir, Agent Joe Andrews here. I have information about the leak in the Bureau that might help us find out who is responsible for this attack."

"Go ahead Agent, tell us what you found," Morrison ordered.

"Sir, I was examining the bank accounts of the people on the fourth floor and in the garage. I discovered that Fred Sellers, a ten-year employee who has always worked in the garage, has deposited two thousand dollars a month into his saving account for the last twenty four months. I checked it against his payroll earnings and there is no way he could afford to make such a deposit based on his income. His wife works as a waitress in a small diner. This kind of money is coming from somewhere, and it is not from here. I think we should bring him up for questioning," said the rookie Agent, who was proud he made this discovery.

"Good work, Andrews," Locket said.

Locket instructed Agent Joe Andrews to get two additional agents and go down to the garage and find Sellers. Within minutes the agents secured Fred Sellers and accompanied him back to the fourth floor.

"Sellers, do you have any idea why you are here?" Locket began.

"No sir, I have no idea," Sellers said defensively.

"Agent Andrews, please explain what you found in Mr. Sellers bank account," Locket instructed.

"Sellers, you have been depositing two thousand dollars a month into a bank account. I have compared your accounts for the last five years, but it is only the last two years that you have made these regular deposits. Can you explain this?" he demanded.

Nervously, Fred Sellers tried to explain his monthly deposits. "My wife has had some real good tips the last year or so, plus I have won small amounts on the lottery from time-to-time."

"I don't believe you, Fred. You know what I think? I think you are selling information to someone. I think you are taking an extra two or three grand each month by reporting to someone who we may be interrogating. You contacted someone earlier today, didn't you?" Locket demanded to know.

"No, I didn't do anything," Sellers said in denial.

"Give me your phone," ordered Andrews.

"You can't take anything from me without a warrant." Sellers yelled back at Andrews.

"Yes, I can. See you are in our custody and you are an employee.

The FBI can confiscate anything while you are in our employment," Locket exaggerated.

Reluctantly Sellers gave up his cellular phone. Agent Andrews opened the phone and pushed the code button to reveal the last twenty-five incoming and outgoing calls. One number stood out from all the rest. Andrews dialed the number. The phone rang three times.

"This is the Surgeon General speaking, who is calling?"

chapter 46

Nick, Maura, Chris, and Detective Baker returned to the safe house after being treated and released from the hospital accompanied by FBI agents Beckett and Murphy. Kathleen remained behind at the hospital with Shaun, who was soon to be transported to Jefferson University Hospital in Philadelphia for high-risk spine surgery.

As the SUV pulled into the driveway, everyone in the safe house welcomed them back to their temporary home. Everyone was concerned about the injured, and relieved that Nick, Chris, and John were safe.

Nick led everyone into the dining room and sat down to explain to everyone exactly what had happened out on the highway. Father Chris said he would conduct a special prayer service and Mass for the injured and dead at eight o'clock the following morning and invited everyone to attend.

"How much longer do we have to remain here?" Angela inquired. "Are we still in danger of being discovered?"

"I am not sure how much longer we will be here," Nick answered. "Obviously after the attack on us today we are still in danger. The FBI is aggressively investigating the people responsible for not only today's attack, but also for the death of Colleen and many of the patients at St. Agnes Hospital. I believe the end is in sight."

"Nick is right," interjected Agent Michael Murphy. "We are close to making arrests and filing charges against the leaders of the group who hope to introduce a drug that will kill not only terminally ill patients, but possibly many more. You folks have gotten mixed up in this because the enemy made a terrible mistake. They did not know that the O'Connell family and their friends would be such unrelenting adversaries. Your intelligence and determination to bring to justice those individuals who were responsible for Colleen's death was something your enemies never anticipated. Your faith and belief in doing what is right was just something they didn't plan on.

"You want to go home, back to your lives of safety. You are probably at your weakest point. Death has come and taken some of your friends. It came today and stole my brother Frank from me. I urge you to pray tonight. Pray for my brother, for Catherine, and for Agent Martin. And lastly, pray for yourselves. Pray that God will give you the vision to see what lies ahead. Pray for deliverance from the evil these people have planned for our country. Pray that our nation is not the godless society that Walters and Bolton believe it to be. Pray that you will find others just like you. They are out there, just waiting for the tiny nudge to speak up, to act out and stand up for what is right and for what is moral."

No one moved or said a word for a long time. Every person in the room heard the challenge Agent Michael Murphy described to them in perfect detail.

Maura was the first to speak. "You are right, Agent Murphy. I really want out. I am so fearful for Nick, and for our family. I see now how selfish that is. All of us have to stand together and see this through to the end. I will pray with all my heart that we will remain safe and that the FBI will arrest the wicked men and women behind the murderous plans of Dr. Walters and his compatriots. We have done our part and sacrificed so much, but we cannot quit now. If this is the test that the Lord has laid out before us, we are obligated to take it on and overcome our enemies. Agent Murphy said our adversary didn't count on just how stubborn we have been. To quit now would ensure the defeat of what is right and what is good. In this time and place we have been selected to fight and prevail over a terrible evil that would mean the death of many innocent people. Is it so different than when Herod ordered the death of the Holy Innocents? I don't think so. If someone doesn't stand up to these people, they will kill many more souls than Herod's soldiers did not long after the birth of Christ. Today we experienced the loss of several friends. We are all frightened. I have never been this scared. But we must not give up or give in to our fears."

chapter 47

Thomas Jones calmly dialed the Colonel's telephone number. It was time to demonstrate to the FBI his commitment to do what was right.

"Jones! Where are you?" Joseph Bolton roared into the telephone while pacing nervously in his office. My people reported that you were taken into the FBI for questioning. What happened? Are you under arrest?" the Colonel asked nervously.

"Colonel, calm down. I am fine. Yes, the FBI took me in for questioning. Let me explain what has happened. First off, I am not under arrest, and I have not revealed any information about our company or our contacts. I must apologize to you for not being completely candid about my trip to the west coast. My sister, Hanna Jones, was murdered. When I heard this, I was quite upset and I had to go to her funeral. While I was there, Jeff Johnson killed my mother; shortly after that my father died. The local police arrived and questioned me. They were not going to arrest me until they identified Jeff Johnson. He was a person of interest in a number of homicides in California. When they ran his prints they discovered the FBI was investigating him. They called the local office and they contacted the bureau here in DC. They wondered why Johnson had targeted my family. Most of the questions the FBI asked were what I knew about Jeff and his father. I could not tell them why he decided to kill my family. I thought at first that perhaps you had given him an order to eliminate me. But we have come so far in our work I knew you would not issue such an order," Jones explained to the Colonel.

"Jones, I would never do such a thing. We have traveled a very long way together. I could not betray you and I certainly believe you would not betray me," the Colonel stated.

"One thing is clear, Colonel, we might be a target for the FBI. You have little to worry about because I have created layers of protection for you and your superior," Jones said to a relieved Colonel.

"I would like to meet with you and talk more about our impending activities. When are you available?" asked the colonel.

"I am available at your convenience, sir," Jones answered.

"Be in my office at ten tomorrow morning," said the Colonel.

"I'll see you then. Thank you, Colonel," Jones said as he hung up the telephone.

"Well done, Jones," said Agent Locket

"Thank you, Agent," Jones answered.

"When you meet with him tomorrow try to focus on the dates they have planned to roll out Walter's new program. Try to find a way to get him to reveal the name of his superior. Get as much information as possible without jeopardizing yourself," Locket instructed.

"I will get everything I can out of him."

"We are taking a huge risk letting you leave here alone, Jones. I believe you will keep your word and return here after the meeting with Bolton," Locket advised.

"Do you have any questions about the wire you will be wearing?" inquired Locket.

"No. I am comfortable with it. You realize he will probably have me searched,' Jones related.

"I am counting on it, Jones," Locket replied. "Our Agent Summers will drive you to your home. Have a good night. We will see you tomorrow after your meeting," Locket said, as he returned to his office.

Agent Julie Summers escorted Thomas Jones to the garage. She drove him to his home.

"We are here, Agent. Pull into the second driveway. Thank you for driving me home. Will you be my driver tomorrow morning?" Jones asked.

"Yes. Have a good evening. I will be here at eight a.m.," said Agent Summers.

———

Thomas Jones walked into his home and replayed the events of his day. He went over his telephone conversation with the Colonel. He had said nothing to alarm the Surgeon General that he was working with the FBI to incriminate Joseph Bolton in crimes ranging from homicide, to bribery and extortion. Jones wanted Bolton to reveal the identity of the leader of the coalition that developed the suicide drug used by Doctor John Walters against the victims of the gay plague, and was the power behind the euthanasia legislation. This would be difficult, but not impossible. Bolton was a bright man, but very emotional. If Thomas could get Bolton upset, he might reveal his superior's name. With that information the FBI could issue arrest and search warrants for all the members of the diabolical cabal consisting of Doctors Walters, Nelson, and Preston, Nurse Maryanne Logan, Joseph Bolton, and his unknown superior. The FBI started investigating the fifty State Chairmen of the USMA as well. Also contained in the files that Jones provided the FBI were the names of operatives and subcontractors they used to murder, strong arm, bribe, and threaten individuals and companies to comply with their demands. This information alone could bring down the organization that Jones and Bolton had built over the last ten years. The game was heading into the final minutes of play. Thomas felt a sense of peace that he never expected or experienced before in his life.

chapter 48

Jones doorbell rang at 8:00 a.m. the following morning. "Good Morning Agent Summers," he said to the young Agent who arrived dressed as his driver. "I like your uniform this morning," he said complimenting her on the tuxedo and cap she put on to complete her role as his driver.

"Thank you, Mr. Jones," Agent Summers replied cordially. "Are you ready to leave?"

"Yes, let me just adjust my tie," he replied as he looked into a mirror by the door and adjusted his shirt collar and tie. He slipped on the watch Agent Locket gave him the day before. Turning to Agent Summers he said, "How do I look? Is everything straight?"

"Yes, Mr. Jones. You look very nice," Agent Summers said.

"One thing before we leave," Jones said.

"Did we forget something?"

"Would you pray with me?"

"Yes, of course," said Agent Julie Summers.

"Lord, help me today to do your will. Bless me with the strength and courage I need to do what is right. Help Agent Summers and the FBI to succeed in stopping the threat that I helped to create. Give us your grace to do all things in your name. Amen."

Traffic was still bumper-to-bumper so the drive into DC took almost all of the fifty minutes they allotted for the commute. Agent Summers stopped the car in front of the Cabinet Building and opened the car door for Thomas. He picked up his briefcase off the seat of the car and stepped out.

"Thomas," the Surgeon General said as he walked out from behind his desk and offered his hand to him. "It is good to see you again. Let me say how sorry I am about your parents. Please accept my sincere condolences on the untimely deaths of your family. This is a difficult time for you. If there is anything I can do, just ask. I lost my grandparents within a week of each other. It was quite devastating. I understand the pain you must be in," Joseph Bolton said with feigned sincerity.

"Thank you, Colonel," Jones replied.

"Thomas, please call me Joseph. We are in a safe building here," Bolton said smiling.

Jones put a finger to his lips and shook his head. He reached for a piece of paper and quickly scribbled a note to Bolton.

I am wearing a wire. Do not say anything improper. Offer me some water. I am going to spill it on my shirt.

"Can I get you anything Thomas? Would you like coffee, water, or a cola?"

"Water would be fine, thank you Colonel," Jones answered.

The Colonel retrieved a small pitcher of water and two glasses. He poured one for his guest.

A moment later Thomas reached for the glass and clumsily let it slip out of his hand. He immediately stood up and said, "Darn it. I just spilled some water on my shirt. May I use your rest room and dry it off?"

"Of course, Jones. It is the door in the right corner," Bolton replied.

Thomas went into the rest room and took his shirt off and the wire that was attached to his chest. He held it in his hand

and stepped to the door showing it to Joseph Bolton. Using a small hand dryer he quickly blew his shirt dry. He redressed and returned to the meeting with Bolton.

"Well done, Colonel. I was not sure how I was going to ditch that darn thing. The FBI threatened to arrest me on some bogus charge if I did not agree to wear their wire. I could not take the chance to telephone you about this. All they will hear now are muffled sounds."

"Thank you Thomas. That was clever thinking. What can you tell me about the FBI investigation?" asked Bolton.

"I don't think they have a case. This thing with Jeff Johnson is a problem. He was not as careful as we thought. He went over-board on many assignments, and he left a trail that they have been following for some time. They are trying to broaden the investigation into who paid him to commit these crimes. The old man, Joe Johnson, knew how to conceal his business. He was careful. But his son was another story. As you might know, he took it upon himself to kill almost every first class passenger on the flights from San Francisco to Washington that the O'Connell man took with his sister," Jones remarked. "I have to tell you, I am glad he is dead."

"As I am. Is there any way he can tie us to his crimes?"

"I doubt it. The payments to him were made by bogus companies. If they could get their hands on that information it would take them a year to decode the language. I won't say it is impossible, but it is unlikely."

"Good," said Bolton. "I always said you were careful."

"Colonel, isn't it time I knew whom I ultimately work for? After all these years, I am entitled to know, don't you think?"

"Yes, Thomas, I suppose you are entitled to know who I report to, especially in light of the loyalty you demonstrated here this morning with that government wire the FBI had you wear. The Speaker of the House, J. Howard Kennsworth, our esteemed Senator from Texas, set this whole operation up years ago. He is the top dog. His whipping boy is the Vice President, William Lodge. Lodge imagines he is a brilliant manager and decision maker. Without the guidance that Kennsworth gives him Lodge would be impotent. Kennsworth has everyone fooled. He maneuvers through Congress like Santa Claus handing out important jobs to this senator or that senator. He has the final say on the wording on every piece of legislation that runs through the legislative branch of our federal government. He wants this euthanasia bill passed. He has huge amounts of money invested with Amorialse and their new drug, Chlordiazimbatrol. He is already a very rich man thanks to the Lobby Groups who have donated millions to his campaigns and social programs.

"You know, Thomas, when I heard the FBI had you I was concerned at first. Not that I would ever expect you to betray us, but I confess I had some doubts. I prepared my files that would implicate both Kennsworth and Lodge. I thought if I was going down, so were they. Silly thoughts, right?" said the Surgeon General.

"Yes, Colonel, very silly. Yet, we both must be careful with this FBI investigation. I would keep those files accessible, just in case. We have to stick together. In my years of running my division I have exceeded all expectations. I know how things get done. Your instructions over the years dealt with financial matters and security issues coming from Kennsworth or Lodge. You and I have a good working relationship and I am proud to be part of your organization," Jones said with false flattery, recalling all the criminal information he had stored in code now being examined by the FBI.

"Thank you, Thomas. Frankly, much of what Kennsworth and Lodge wanted done came from my recommendations. They claimed to be the people with the vision of where we should be. You and I, Thomas, we make things happen. It will be interesting to see where we go from here after this new euthanasia legislation is passed, and believe me, it will be passed," Bolton said with certainty.

"Why do you say that?" Jones inquired.

"We have purchased so many senators and representatives just for this one issue. The work that Walters has done in San Francisco is quite remarkable. He has created the fear element that will turn the masses over to our side. This gay plague has already begun to frighten the general public. As the disease spreads, people will clamor to be safe. There will be no other sane option than the Ten Day Program Walters created along with his lethal drug. This legislation will result in a huge demand for the euthanasia pill that will be administered to all the sick people in the gay community. With the success of that program, the interest in the pill will skyrocket. If you thought you were a rich man before, Thomas, you have no idea how rich this will make us. The sheer numbers are staggering," said a gleeful Bolton.

"That is exciting, Colonel. The future will be an interesting time for all of us. I am so pleased that we met in person today. We rarely speak face-to-face. I had to let you know what was going on with the FBI. If I learn more about their investigation I will inform you at once. Thank you, sir," Jones concluded.

"Call me if you hear anything, Thomas. Goodbye," Bolton said as he walked Jones to his door.

Outside Bolton's office Jones called his driver to pick him up. Five minutes later Agent Summers pulled up in front of the Cabinet Building and picked Jones up.

"How was your meeting, Mr. Jones?" asked Agent Julie Summers.

"Did you hear everything?" Jones asked.

"Yes, every syllable. You did a great job with the phony wire," the agent said smiling.

"Did the transmission go through to the Bureau?" Thomas inquired.

"They heard everything I heard. Were you surprised by what Bolton told you?" Summers asked.

"I had no idea that Kennsworth was running the show. He is very well insulated," Thomas said.

"Until today, that is," Agent Summers said still smiling.

Agent Summers' telephone rang. She answered it and handed it to Thomas.

"Thomas, this is Jerry Locket. Well done, sir, well done."

"Thank you Jerry," Thomas said. "I have to tell you I almost laughed when I spilled the water on my shirt. He really opened up to me today. The watch you gave me looked genuine. He would never have suspected he was being recorded live."

"That is exactly what we hoped for," said Locket. "I believe the warrants will be executed within hours. Then their plans will be exposed and these people will be seen for just what they are, criminals and murderers. We will get warrants for the bank records for Kennsworth, Lodge, Bolton, and the others. I spoke with the Director a few minutes ago and we have some concerns about bringing you back in to the Bureau right away. We have a plane at Washington National that is heading for California. I want you on that plane. Your mother and father are being buried tomorrow. I thought you might want to attend their funeral."

"I don't know what to say, except thank you," an astounded Thomas replied.

"You won't be alone. I am sending Agent Summers and Agent Joe Andrews along with you for company," Locket said.

"Don't worry, Jerry, I want to testify against Bolton and his pals. I have nowhere to go, no one to run to," Thomas replied.

"Let me put the Director on," said Agent Locket.

"Jones, Morrison here. I listened in to your conversation with Bolton. Good work. Locket told you about California?"

"Yes, he did."

"You will have a few days away from here as the hammer goes down," the FBI Director said. "When you return we will decide your fate. I may hide your identity as a witness. You will be obligated to my service for quite some time. I do not intend to have the Attorney General file charges against you, but you will be sentenced to my service until I deem otherwise. How would that work for you?"

"That would be fine, Director. Thank you," Jones said in amazement.

"One thing Jones," Director Morrison continued. "You are going to have to donate a lot of money to a charity of my choosing. I mean a whole lot. You made money through illegal enterprises. You need to divest yourself of most of it. Is that acceptable?"

"Yes, Director, I would not have it any other way," Jones replied.

"Good. Now get out to your parents and take care of things like a good son should. Please do not corrupt my two young agents," Morrison concluded.

"Director, I think they are converting me," Thomas said, as the Director hung up the telephone.

"We are heading for the airport. We took the liberty to pack some clothing for you. I have never been to California. Is it nice?" Agent Summers asked.

"Yes. And maybe more so on this trip than any other I have ever made," Thomas said.

Thomas spent the next three days in Santa Monica. He buried his father and mother and then spent time with Pastor Michael Powers before completely accepting Jesus Christ as his Lord and Savior.

He returned to his parent's home and decided to donate his parents' things to the American Red Cross. He gave their home to Habitat for Humanity and their car to a Pregnancy Care Center. His dad's antique Chevy he planned to ship east. It was the one way he would remember and honor his father. With the exception of his parents' collection of family photographs, he donated everything he could to charity.

On the morning of the third day in California, Thomas and the two agents went to breakfast and picked up a morning newspaper. Two inch high headlines blared: *Vice President,*

Speaker of the House, and Surgeon General arrested on a number of felony charges including murder, bribery, embezzlement, and theft.

"Well the end has begun, hasn't it?" Thomas Jones remarked peacefully.

chapter 49

In San Francisco Dr. John Walters was meeting with Jim Nelson and Mark Preston. They were reviewing the presentations they would give at the USMA convention in a few days. Outside the conference room, nurse Maryanne Logan was listening to the radio as she went over the charts of her patients in the death ward.

The regular news report was interrupted by a special bulletin announcing that the Vice President, the Speaker of the House, and the Surgeon General were arrested on a variety of felony charges including murder, embezzlement, and other crimes.

Nurse Logan had all of Dr. John Walters files logged in her computer. She quickly scribbled a handwritten note:

Attention: FBI-Complete notes and history of Dr. Walters' Ten Day Plan is in my Word file titled," Walters Program." Maryanne Logan.

Nurse Logan left the note in the center of her desk pad where the police would find it.

Her telephone rang and she picked it up quickly.

"Maryanne, this is Joan at the information desk. There are six FBI agents on the way up to Dr. Walters Office. What is going on?"

"I don't know. I cannot talk right now. Thank you for the

call," Nurse Logan said before hanging up quickly and reaching under her desk for her purse.

Logan walked into the Conference Room, locked the door and removed a large handgun from her purse. She opened fire on Doctor Nelson first, hitting him in the left eye. She hit Doctor Preston in the middle of the forehead. Walters was scrambling for a place to hide. She fired five shots into his upper torso and head.

The conference room door was forced open and the FBI Agents entered with their guns drawn. Maryanne Logan turned at them with the gun in her hand. Slowly she lifted the weapon to the side of her head and squeezed the trigger before the FBI could reach her. Her lifeless body dropped to the floor.

chapter 50

Harry Booth had successful hip surgery early in the morning the day after the assault on the group of family and friends who had sacrificed so much to solve the mystery of Colleen O'Connell's death. Angela went to Georgetown University Hospital and was with Harry when he came out of the recovery room.

―――――

After saying goodbye to Harry and Angela at the hospital, Shaun was placed on board a medical helicopter. He and Kathleen flew to Philadelphia's Jefferson University Hospital where he had spinal surgery later that morning. The seven-hour operation was a complete success and Shaun was expected to make a full recovery. Kathleen called Maura and her friends at the safe house to share the news of her husband's successful surgery.

―――――

Back in Falls Church, Virginia, the group spent time recovering from the trauma of the shooting and the resulting deaths and injuries. Father Chris invited them to pray in the small Chapel and everyone came, including the two babies, who slept like angels through the service.

Around three o'clock in the afternoon the telephone rang. Nick picked it up.

"This is Director Morrison of the FBI calling, to whom am I speaking?"

"Nick O'Connell. How are you sir?"

"I am fine. Let me say first off how sorry I am about your friends, Catherine Harding and Father Frank Murphy," the director said respectfully.

"We are also sorry for the loss of your Agent Eugene Martin. He seemed like a fine man," Nick said quietly.

"He was, and he was a good family man too," Morrison said sadly. "Did the surgery go well for your brother Shaun and for Dr. Booth?"

"The doctors called not long ago with the news that they both did very well. Thank you for asking. Both men are expected to make a full recovery."

"That is very good news," Morrison said, obviously happy to hear the report. "Nick, I have received reports from Agent Locket about your involvement in this matter from the beginning. You suffered loss upon loss, yet you pressed on," Morrison said in admiration.

"It seemed that every time we needed help or protection, the Lord supplied it. Detective John Baker saved our lives at the Police Precinct when our adversaries tried to destroy us. Each person in our family and in our close circle of friends contributed to our survival," Nick explained.

"I understand that you have a child, actually two, I hear," the director remarked.

"Yes, sir, Maura and I have a little girl and we will be raising my sister Colleen's son as our own," Nick said with pride.

"That doesn't surprise me. You are a man of strong character. You are a good, decent man," Morrison said sincerely.

"Thank you, Director," Nick responded gratefully. "Not as strong or as good as my wife, Maura. She was our rock throughout this ordeal. Knowing that Maura and the babies were safe enabled me to focus on the task at hand which was to stay alive and find out who had killed Colleen, and why."

"In that regard I have some good news for you, Nick. We have made arrests in the case. Thanks to Thomas Jones we have gathered enough evidence to make a real case against some powerful people here in Washington. I also wanted to let you know that Dr. Walters, Dr. Nelson, and Dr. Mark Preston are dead. I can assure you they will be unable to bring any harm to you or your families.

"We will continue to make arrests over the next few weeks that will take both major and minor players off the street. Thomas gave us the names of all their operatives and subcontractors. These people are being arrested as we speak. I expect a lot of them to roll over looking for pleas and deals. They will not threaten your family any longer," Director Morrison promised. "We have already heard from Amoralaise Labs and they are turning over all the falsified information on the euthanasia drug. They are coming clean. When the story hits the papers the members of the Senate and House will abandon their support of the Ten Day program of death, and we are looking into the records of every doctor and hospital who signed up for testing the drug."

"The fallout from this will affect every segment of society. We will never know how many lives you saved by exposing the people behind this conspiracy. Your determination to find your sister's killer, along with the information we are getting from Thomas Jones, has exposed and broken a conspiracy of death. In my eyes you are all heroes."

"What happened to Walters, Preston, and Nelson?"

"Nurse Logan shot all three. After the deaths of Jeff and Joe Johnson, Walters pressured Thomas Jones into getting a replacement for them. Jones alerted us to his request. We sent two Agents in undercover and it seems he wanted Maryanne Logan killed because she let you, Detective Baker, and Gretchen Sanders interview his patients. Walters didn't know she had installed a bug in their conference room, and learned of his plan. When our Agents arrived there today to arrest them she decided to exact her own revenge. She took a gun and shot the three doctors. Our agents heard the gunfire and entered the Conference Room. Logan then turned her gun on herself. In some kind of final act of repentance she left a note to the FBI where we could find all of Walter's notes from the beginning of his Ten Day Program. I think justice was served well there today," relayed the Director. "Nick, Nurse Logan also left a message for you. May I read it?"

"Sure, go ahead, Director," Nick replied, wondering what Nurse Logan wanted to tell him, and why she thought of him shortly before her death.

Mr. O'Connell, I wanted you to know that Colleen was not diagnosed with the AIDS disease. She had pneumonia when she was admitted to the hospital. Dr. Walters spoke with someone on the telephone about your sister. Whoever that was wanted her and her unborn child killed. I am sure Joseph Bolton is responsible because his son was treated here for a venereal disease. He said your sister or her friends were responsible. I read Colleen's chart after her admission physical and there was no sign of any venereal disease. I believe he ordered Walters to put her on the Ten Day Program to satisfy Bolton. You showed up before Walters had the chance to complete the treatment. After that they panicked and planned to kill all of you. Please forgive me. Nurse Logan.

"You can go home. You have your life back," said the director.

For a moment Nick could not believe what he had just heard. "That is fantastic news!"

"I thought you might like to hear that. Would you share the news with your team over at the safe house?" asked Director Morrison.

"Yes, I will be happy to, Director," Nick said with delight.

"I also spoke with all your employers and they have agreed to return you to your former positions. I explained to them why you had to fake your own deaths. They understood," Morrison said. "Now look, I want you to call Agent Locket when everyone is ready to return home tomorrow. We will send over some people and some cars to help you get back to your homes. Whatever you need, just ask."

"I will. Thank you, Director. This is good news."

"One more thing, Nick, we will be counting on your testimony at the Grand Jury," Morrison said.

"You could not keep us away, Director. We will testify about everything," Nick answered energetically. "May I ask you for a favor?"

"What is it?"

"Could you find a way to honor Dr. Elizabeth Roberts? She has taken care of our premature babies from day one. She volunteered to come to the safe house to make sure the babies survived. She is the antithesis of Dr. Walters. She fought hard to keep these infants alive. To us she is a hero," said Nick as he described this courageous doctor.

"That is a good idea, Nick. I will make sure that happens. We will be in touch soon. Go home and take care of your family."

Nick hung up the telephone and called everyone together.

"What is it, Nick? Is something wrong?" Gretchen asked.

"I just spoke to FBI Director Peter Morrison. They arrested the top people in the organization that employed Thomas Jones. Dr. Walters and his two pals, Nelson and Preston are dead, along with his nurse Maryanne Logan. The people who plotted against us are dead, under arrest, and incarcerated," Nick said excitedly.

"Does the FBI believe it is now safe for us to return home?" Father Chris asked.

"Yes. The FBI Director believes that as the arrests are made and these people are exposed, their operatives will come out of the woodworks to testify against the top dogs in exchange for plea agreements and shorter sentences. Apparently Thomas Jones' files gave the FBI all the names of the leaders and the operatives in their organization. Some arrests are being made today and will continue until all the participants in these crimes are incarcerated. The plans to introduce the euthanasia drug have fallen apart. The conspiracy has failed. Many lives have been saved. Colleen did not die in vain."

"Is it safe for me to go back to Walter Reed?" Dr. Roberts asked.

"Yes, it is. With Walters, Nelson, and Preston dead the threats from them are gone. They have no other colleagues at the hospital. It will be safe for you to go back to work," Nick responded.

"When can we go home?" Maura asked.

"We will go home tomorrow. Peter told me we should pack up tonight and get ready to leave here. The FBI will send cars for us," he explained.

"Nick, my love, just hearing you say that lifts the fear from my heart. I have prayed each day for your safety and the safety of our family and friends. I had moments of doubt and deep fear for your life. The days when I felt so discouraged, Kathleen and Angela lifted my spirits and helped me to hang on and persevere. You risked everything to do what was right. I am so proud of you. To know now that our home is safe and that our children will be able to live and grow in safety is a precious gift that I will cherish in my heart forever. I thank God for protecting you, and for bringing you home to me. I love you so much," Maura said as she hugged Nick.

"It is finally over," Father Chris said to everyone. "Our long night of trial has at last come to an end. It is a blessing that so many of us survived. The Lord was with us as we traveled this way of fear and sorrow. We lost family and friends who were dear to us, but through it all God's love and grace led the way. My prayer for each of us is that we continue to walk in the light of the Lord. As we awake each day we will treasure it more than the last, for our days are not our own, and our passing is unknown to us. May God guide our every step in love and peace."